"Help me," Madison managed to whisper to the figure backlit from the sun.

Dust stung her eyes, grit caking her mouth. She did not realize it was James who had made entry until his face appeared in the gap under the desk.

"Madison?" He wore an expression of unadulterated surprise and relief. "Thank You, God," he said.

"I was sitting here saying the same thing," she replied, crawling out from under the desk. The trailer had collapsed. Someone had *made* it collapse. Her stomach was flip-flopping madly at the sight of him.

"Are you hurt?" he asked.

She managed a shake of her head before he clutched her to him for just a moment, held tightly against his wide chest, feeling the mad thundering of his heart.

"You're really okay, then?" he repeated.

"I'm okay."

But someone didn't want her to be.

Dana Mentink
and
Lynette Eason

Deadly Pursuit

Previously published as *Seek and Find* and *Honor and Defend*

HARLEQUIN® LOVE INSPIRED® CLASSICS

Recycling programs for this product may not exist in your area.

ISBN-13: 978-1-335-06126-3

Deadly Pursuit

First published as Seek and Find by Harlequin Books in 2016 and Honor and Defend by Harlequin Books in 2016.

Special thanks and acknowledgment are given to Dana Mentink and Lynette Eason for their contributions to the Rookie K-9 Unit miniseries.

This edition published by arrangement with Love Inspired Books.

www.Harlequin.com

Printed in U.S.A.

CONTENTS

Dana Mentink is a national bestselling author. She has been honored to win two Carol Awards, a HOLT Medallion and an RT Reviewers' Choice Best Book Award. She's authored more than thirty novels to date for Love Inspired Suspense and Harlequin Heartwarming. Dana loves feedback from her readers. Contact her at danamentink.com.

Books by Dana Mentink

Love Inspired Suspense

Gold Country Cowboys

Cowboy Christmas Guardian
Treacherous Trails
Cowboy Bodyguard
Lost Christmas Memories

Pacific Coast Private Eyes

Dangerous Tidings
Seaside Secrets
Abducted
Dangerous Testimony

Military K-9 Unit

Top Secret Target

Rookie K-9 Unit

Seek and Find

Visit the Author Profile page
at Harlequin.com for more titles.

SEEK AND FIND

Dana Mentink

Remember ye not the former things,
neither consider the things of old.
Behold, I will do a new thing; now it shall spring forth; shall ye not know it? I will even make a way in the wilderness, and rivers in the desert.

—*Isaiah* 43:18–19

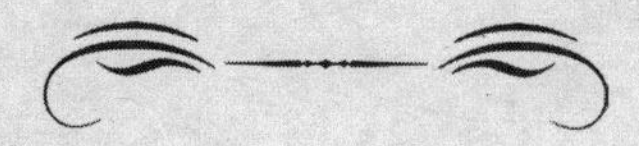

To those faithful K-9 officers and their police handlers, thank you for your dedication and service.

ONE

Murder. The word rattled through Madison's mind along with the outrage. She was driving fast—too fast. Rocks struck the fenders with angry thunks. When the twenty-seven-year-old reporter made the dusty turn that was to take her the final five miles into the hole-in-the-wall town of Desert Valley in northwestern Arizona, her irritation contributed to her lead foot on the gas pedal.

The shooting of a K-9 trainer was just a small piece of the madness in Desert Valley. Homicide, the unsolved attempted murder of a prominent citizen, suspicious cases gone cold. She itched to investigate, but her editor was unmoved by her ambition, sticking her with a story about how the crime spree was hurting business in the area. Other seasoned reporters were working the big cases, and she got stuck with a business story.

Business? When there was a killer roaming loose, or possibly more than one? She felt the familiar hitch in her breathing. Madison knew a thing or two about killers. One might even say it was in her DNA.

Focus, Madison. The most recent slaying, of police-dog master trainer Veronica Earnshaw, had rated a few headlines. On top of that, Marian Foxcroft, wealthy

Desert Valley benefactress, lay in a coma after being attacked in her home. But those big stories had been assigned to the senior reporters who'd already wrapped their pieces and left town.

She flipped on her tape recorder. "And what about the deaths on the night of the police fund-raiser dance? A cop's wife is murdered one year, and then a few years later, rookie Mike Riverton falls down a flight of stairs. And then another rookie, Brian Miller, dies in a fire? All on the night of the dance? Someone should look into that." She flicked the recorder off and tossed it on the seat in disgust. *And that someone should be me.* No one had more motivation to look into the deaths than she. *After all, I am the daughter of a murderer*, she thought with a shiver.

But newly hired reporters with a hundred bucks in their bank accounts and a rent check coming due couldn't afford to lose their jobs. Besides, she was desperate to put down some roots in Tuckerville, her new home some forty-five minutes away from Desert Valley. She wanted to get used to a rural life for a change, and ideally her sister would stay for a good long while. It was the only way they could learn to love their way past the hurt.

Pebbles pinged as she pressed the accelerator. Midday sun blazed onto the windshield, dazzling her. A split second later, everything changed. One moment there was nothing but shrub-lined asphalt ahead and the next, a fawn-colored bloodhound wearing a heavy leather collar shot across the road, followed by a police officer who halted in the bushes, startled, intense sapphire-blue eyes opened wide.

She had only a moment to register that he was very

fit, very tall and more than a little irritated as she slammed on the brakes to avoid the dog. Then the tires squealed, and she skidded off the road and through a screen of shrubbery, bumping to a stop amid a pile of rocks. She sat, heart thumping, panting, nerves jangling from the mad jostling.

The officer ran to the car. “Are you all right?”

She blinked and nodded. He opened the door for her and she got out, noting both her flat front tire and his hair, the color of the desert sand. “I’m okay, but my tire’s another story.”

He called out, and the bloodhound loped from the trees, coming to an ungainly stop next to the officer.

“Your dog?”

“Yes. I’m very sorry, ma’am. Every once in a while, Hawk gets this wild notion, forgets he is a police dog and takes off. I think it has something to do with squirrels. He’s certain they’re mocking him.” He shot an exasperated look at his canine. “Looks like we’re gonna need more training.” Hawk slurped a tongue along the officer’s pant leg.

“Knock it off, dog,” he said.

There was an enticing, familiar scent clinging to the officer.

“I think he tastes garlic,” she said with a smile.

He flushed red. “Oh, man. I smell like garlic? Earlier I was trying to figure out my mom’s recipe for beef stew. I’ve showered and everything, but the scent gets into your pores.”

“Won’t your mom give you the recipe?”

“No. She says once I learn it, I won’t come around as much.”

They both laughed.

The big-bodied bloodhound sat heavily on the ground, staring at her through the fleshy folds of his face. Police dog or not, he was adorable, and his handler was not hard to look at, either. The guy should have been on a police recruitment poster or something.

Hawk gave her a scolding look, as if she had somehow gotten between him and his rodent nemesis.

"Is he a puppy?"

"Two years old, but from what I can see, he's got plenty of puppy left in him. He's managed to destroy two pairs of work boots, a cupboard door and the backseat of my truck. And what is this?" He bent closer, picking a scrap of material from Hawk's lip. "This better not be a piece of the backseat again, dog."

Hawk did not look the least bit contrite. He shook his head, jowls flapping. Madison giggled. "Not your typical police dog?"

"Just a bloodhound. They're not patrol dogs, really more specialized for tracking and trailing. Maybe I should have requested a nice German shepherd. They don't eat backseats." Hawk yawned, and James chuckled. "We didn't become partners until a couple of months ago. Just graduated from the K-9 training center in Desert Valley, and we're assigned here temporarily."

"I heard. You and four other rookies with their K-9s. Marian Foxcroft paid for you all to be assigned to Desert Valley until you solve the murder of Veronica Earnshaw. She was the police-dog master trainer, right?"

"You're well informed."

"I like to keep apprised."

The officer sighed, taking in the flattened front tire. "Anyway, we were doing a search, and he's still learning. He's determined, but he takes off once in a while and breaks the rules. Hawk wins the prize for having to take the most retraining courses."

"I guess I could use some retraining, too. I was going too fast."

"Yes, you were, now that you mention it," he said with a grin. "It's thirty-five along this stretch. You from out of town?"

"Not far out. I live in Tuckerville with my sister." At least, if their disagreement from the night before hadn't driven Kate away. *Things are getting better, Mads. Remember that.* After years of estrangement, desperation had finally driven Kate back. "She got a job in Desert Valley just yesterday."

He arched an eyebrow. "Good for her. Not much work around here to be had."

He was right. Kate had combed Tuckerville and all the nearby towns until she'd finally landed a job, which gave Madison an even greater motivation to help solve the crime spree here in the tiny town. Kate might not want the close relationship that Madison craved, but Madison intended to do what she could for her only sibling, one way or another. At least the town where she worked would be safer if she could help nab a few killers. *You'll thank me later, Kate.*

"So, Officer, are you going to give me a ticket?"

He shot her a rueful grin. "In view of the fact that my dog was misbehaving, I say we call it a draw." He extended a hand. "James Harrison."

"Madison Coles," she said, noting that his eyes were such an intense blue they seemed lit from the inside, like sunlight playing through stained glass. His palms were strong and warm, tough enough to indicate he worked with his hands when he wasn't on duty—or maybe the calluses were from hauling on a leash all day. And the faint scent of garlic was more enticing than any cologne. "That sounds fair to me." She went to the trunk and fished out a lug wrench.

"Let me change that tire for you," he said, taking the tool from her hands and hefting the spare from the trunk.

"I can do it," she said quickly. *Take care of yourself, Mads.*

But he was already crouched over, easily detaching the lug nuts. "I've never let a lady change her own flat, and I'm not about to now."

"Thanks," she said. She hadn't expected to find chivalry in this desert nowhere. It both pleased her and kicked up some anxiety. *He's a cop, Mads. Perfectly okay to let him change your tire.* "What were you searching for, anyway?"

"Just following a hunch."

The trees behind them were thick with tangled branches, the perfect place for someone to hide. A killer, perhaps?

"So, you're following a lead on Veronica Earnshaw's murder? Or maybe the attack on Marian Foxcroft?"

He frowned. "We're all doing our best."

"You must be making progress. You've got a lot of extra rookies assigned to this town, not to mention the dogs."

He knelt to remove the tire. "Yes, that's true. The town is practically crawling with K-9s until we're reassigned elsewhere." There was a touch of cynicism in his voice. "Why are you so interested?"

She shrugged. "Who isn't? Murders and a bludgeoning attack in a small town like this? How is the investigation going?"

He paused in the act of wrestling on the spare. "Slowly."

"In your opinion, is the Earnshaw case linked to what happened to Marian Foxcroft?"

He didn't answer.

She pressed on eagerly. "And those deaths on the night of the police fund-raiser. Officer Ryder Hayes's wife was murdered, and two other deaths were ruled accidental. What's your take on it?"

He kept his eyes on the tire this time, and she drank in his strong profile, noting that his full mouth was now drawn into a tight line. "Why is this beginning to sound like an interview?"

She ignored the question. "Murders, assaults. What is going on in this town?"

They were interrupted by the arrival of another car. This time an older officer got out, late thirties with thinning hair and a gaunt look about him except for his well-padded waist. Hawk greeted him with a flapping of his enormous ears. He scratched the dog's fleshy jowls, earning a lick, which he wiped from his cheek.

"Hey, James. Afternoon, ma'am," the officer said.

"This is Officer Ken Bucks," James said by way of introduction. "Madison Coles."

Bucks eyed her and the car. "Got some trouble? Shall I call for a tow?"

"I'm taking care of it," James said. "Just needs the spare put on."

Bucks quirked an eyebrow. "Madison Coles. I know that name." His eyes shifted in thought, sparking when he'd made some connection. "You might want to let her change her own tire."

James shot him a look. "Why?"

Officer Bucks raised his chin at James. "She's another reporter, *Canyon County Gazette.* Carrie said she's called three times this week."

Great. Now she'd get the cold shoulder from these two cops. Carrie Dunleavy, the Desert Valley Police Department secretary, hadn't given her any information Madison hadn't read herself in her own employer's newspaper. Was the secretary even passing along her messages to the chief and officers? Probably.

"I wouldn't have had to call so much if one of you had bothered to return my messages."

"We're a small town," Bucks said. "We like to respect the privacy of our citizens and play things close to the vest, and we've had our fill of reporters nosing around in police business. Isn't that right, Officer Harrison?"

The change in James's expression from the moment the other cop outed her as a reporter was dramatic. It was as if someone closed the shutters, cutting off all the light from his expression. "You're a reporter?"

She nodded.

He finished the tire and stood. "Should be good to go now. Sorry for the trouble." There was none of the previous warmth in his voice. He handed her a business card. "I'll pay to get you another spare since the accident was my fault."

He summoned the dog, and they walked toward his car, which she now spotted some twenty feet up the road. Bucks remained behind, next to Madison.

"Wait. Can I ask you a few questions?" she called to James.

"No, ma'am," he threw over his shoulder.

"Why not?" she asked his departing back.

"Because he doesn't like reporters," Bucks said, removing a stick of gum from a pack in his pocket and folding it into his mouth. "And he's got a good reason, since a reporter ruined his family."

Ruined his family? Ironic, since a reporter had saved hers, though her sister didn't see it that way. She straightened her shoulders. "Well, how about you, Officer Bucks? I'm actually just here to write a story about how crime has affected local businesses. Would you be willing to answer a few questions? Just for background information?"

"No, ma'am," he said with a grin. "I would not. Enjoy your stay in Desert Valley." With a tip of his hat, he returned to his car, smacking his gum.

"I'm going to be in town writing a story whether you cooperate or not," she called to him.

Bucks gave her a sardonic salute, eased into his driver's seat and pulled away.

She stared after them. Both officers clearly did not want a reporter poking around, but that wasn't anything new. They could throw up all the roadblocks they wanted. There was a story here, bigger than the failing businesses in Desert Valley, and she was going to find out what it was, with or without police cooperation. Sure, she'd write the business piece, but it wouldn't hurt to keep her ears open for something more significant. Instincts prickling, she got back into her car and drove the rest of the way to Desert Valley.

* * *

James turned onto the narrow paved road, allowing his breathing to return to normal. So she was a reporter. So what? He'd met plenty of them recently. Only natural that journalists would start flocking around where there was a potential for a juicy story. Reporters. They were all the same, vultures who reworked the facts to suit their fancy, like the one who'd smeared his brother in the papers, condemning him in the public eye for a rape he didn't commit. He realized his jaw was clenched as usual whenever he thought about his brother. *Take a breath.*

Madison was doing her job, and he was going to do his. Deep down in his gut, he knew the real reason he was upset was that he'd been enjoying her company, chatting easily about cooking and canines, while something had been poking at him. Her red hair and easy smile reminded him of his teen crush, Paige, a girl who had fractured his family, a viper he had let into the nest. *That was a long time ago.*

A movement in the shadows beside the road made him tense. James's pulse ticked up. Was it the dog they'd been searching for? Marco, the police K-9 German shepherd puppy, had gone missing from the training yard the night Veronica Earnshaw was murdered. How in the world could a puppy stay lost for so long? A few weeks ago, a witness had reported seeing someone on a bicycle pick up what looked like a small dog and ride off with it. But it was dark, and the witness couldn't tell if it was a man or a woman on the bike or even if the little dog was definitely the missing puppy—easy to spot with a circular mark on his head. A ground squirrel raced out from behind some bushes and dashed across the street. Not Marco.

He continued up the road, passing a row of small houses on his way into town. He was surprised when Charlie Greer raced down his driveway, arms flailing, white hair mussed.

"Someone's busted into my yard," Charlie said, his plaid shirt stained with axle grease. "Gone now, though."

James got out, Hawk following.

The baying of several dogs caught Hawk's attention, and he lumbered over to the fenced front yard, adding his own noise to the mix, tail wagging. James smiled as Hawk shoved his big nose through the fence to greet the dogs, including a German shepherd puppy named Stormy that Charlie had acquired recently.

"How's your new dog getting along?"

Charlie's face softened, and he looked years younger. "Swimmingly, but that ain't what I wanted to tell you."

James dutifully followed Charlie to his backyard, which was surrounded by a sturdy wooden fence.

"Found it just now when I got home." The bolt on the gate had been cut through, and someone had entered the yard. The back door to the house was still shut up tight. There was no sign the intruder had gone any farther. James tensed. What would induce someone to break into Charlie's backyard? The man lived modestly, fixing cars when he could to supplement his Social Security benefits. There was not much on the premises that could be fenced or sold. "Why didn't the dogs raise a ruckus?"

"Probably did," Charlie said. "I was out buying some spark plugs. Musta just happened because the dogs were milling around, and most of 'em hadn't gotten out yet through the busted gate. I put 'em in the side yard, and then I saw you."

James nodded. "I'll take a look in the woods. Stay here."

He called to Hawk and let the dog sniff around where the person must have been standing to cut the bolt. Hawk nosed eagerly, electrified to be starting off on a possible search. With no scent item to track, it would be up to the dog to catch any odor particles left in the air or soil. Unlikely that he'd find anything, but Hawk was always eager to try.

He clipped Hawk to a fifteen-foot lead, and they took off into the thick canopy of pines. Hawk stuck to a narrow trail that bisected the woods, paralleling a dry creek bed. They hiked for about ten minutes. James was ready to call off the search when suddenly, the dog stiffened, let loose with an ear-splitting howl and plunged ahead. James put a hand on his gun and followed, fending off the slap of low branches. He couldn't imagine that anyone would be hiding in these woods, but he'd learned one thing in the long hours of training with Hawk and the deceased Veronica Earnshaw: trust the dog. With noses that could detect scent a thousand times better than humans, bloodhounds were master trackers. Truly, Hawk was a nose with a dog attached.

Hawk let out another spine-jarring howl.

James saw the heavy branch being swung at his head a second before it hit him. He was able to raise an arm to fend off the blow, but it sent him off balance, and he fell hard on his back. There was a sound of running feet. Hawk darted after the fleeing figure for a few yards, then turned and raced back at his fallen handler's command. James heard a car engine, his hopes for a capture vanishing.

Hawk shoved his wrinkled jowls close and slurped a fat pink tongue over James's forehead.

James sat up. Hawk continued to lick him until he waved him off.

"All right, you big lug. I'm okay. I just fell. That's all." He got to his feet, brushing pine needles from his uniform pants.

As he and Hawk trekked back to Greer's place, he wondered who would be brazen enough to break into his yard in broad daylight.

The striking reporter's words came back to him.

What is going on in this town?

TWO

Madison continued to fume as she squeezed her car into a curbside space along the main street. On her way here she'd stopped at the K-9 training center just to get a visual in her mind of where the grisly Earnshaw shooting had taken place. Twenty minutes was all she allowed herself. The center was larger than she'd pictured, a white stucco building with two outdoor training yards and no dogs in sight. What had she expected to find? She wasn't sure. *Stick to the story you're supposed to be writing, Mads. Get that done first, and then see what else you can unearth.*

In the early hours, the sidewalks were empty, most of the businesses not yet open. It was so different from the bustle of urban life. She was still adjusting to the slow pace of Tuckerville, and Desert Valley was even smaller. Growing up with a father who loved cities, the bigger the better, they'd lived everywhere from San Francisco to Austin until they'd settled in Arizona. It was in sun-bleached Phoenix that her Uncle Ray, a reporter who'd spent fourteen years looking for them, finally tracked them down, delivering the truth in a scorching revelation. Her father was a murderer and a child abductor.

The ever-present tension in her stomach kicked up a notch. Madison Coles had no one now, except Kate. The thought of her sister and the tender closeness they no longer shared cut at her.

Why couldn't Kate understand that the truth had set them free? But Kate had never accepted the loss of their father. His incarceration was the beginning of a very long, troubled path that saw her sister bounce from one disastrous relationship to another until finally she'd hit rock bottom two months ago and called Madison. Two months of ups and downs, but Madison was filled with hope that they might finally be rebuilding some small hope of a relationship. One positive sign? The note from her sister on the kitchen table that morning next to the neatly remade sofa bed where Kate had slept.

Got a waitressing job in DV! Tell you more later.

A job was a start—a great start—and though she wouldn't admit it, she'd kept the scrawled message because of the little heart her sister had drawn there. *Thank you, God*, Madison breathed.

As she cruised downtown Desert Valley, Madison was not sure which restaurant had hired Kate. Not that there were many choices. There was the Cactus Café, a sandwich outfit and a new hot-dog shop that promised to open soon. No sushi place or Korean barbecue, unfortunately.

Stepping from the car, she decided to do some research for the story she'd been assigned while she tried to locate her sister. It was time to start interviewing the local business owners. At the other end of the street, she saw a police car pull to the curb. James Harrison stepped out, long, lean legs, powerful shoulders, a serious expression on his face and Hawk by his side. She might have assumed James always looked serious, but she'd seen his smile and the sparkle in those incredible eyes before he heard what her profession was. *Don't bother dreaming about those eyes*, she chided herself.

He obviously had some megachip on his shoulder about reporters. Fine. When she was occupied in her extracurricular snooping, she'd go around him, find sources other than the handsome Harrison and his sarcastic colleague Ken Bucks. She about-faced and headed in the other direction to keep her distance.

Her stroll took her past the Brides and Belles bridal salon. All that white lace and beadwork on the display dresses made her queasy. Marriage was packaged up in pretty bows and baubles, but her parents' marriage had been a living torment that ended in murder.

He beat her, Uncle Ray had told them. *Your father terrorized your mother until it escalated to murder.* The death of his sister left Ray with a burning need to deliver justice and save his nieces from growing up with a killer.

A killer. The gentle, smiling father who smelled of aftershave and was devoted to his girls. *Daddy* to them, murderer of their mother. The incongruity made her dizzy, and ten years of trying to understand it hadn't made it any more comprehensible.

It was a half hour before opening time, but she spotted two cars in the lot behind the store: a battered pickup and a new black sedan.

Madison swallowed and tapped on the glass front

door of the shop. Inside, a small lady with blond hair pulled into a tight bun jerked her head up from a display case to look at Madison. The blonde shook her head. "Not open," she mouthed.

"I just want to talk to you for a minute," Madison tried.

The lady shook her head firmly. "Not open. Come back later."

"But..."

The woman turned away and disappeared into the back of the shop.

"Could this place be any less welcoming?" she grumbled. "Maybe the Cactus Café will have one kindly soul who will talk to me." Her route took her by the side door of the bridal salon, which was ajar. Angry words floated out.

"No excuses," a low voice rumbled.

She could not hear the reply, but the tone was tense, high-pitched. Madison inched up, poised to knock on the door and offer help if necessary.

"...tell you again." She did not hear the rest except for the name Tony. Careful to step quietly, she edged closer, hand on her phone, ready to call the police.

"Please..." came a woman's voice.

Fear echoed in her tone and rolled through Madison. Fear. How Madison hated the emotion. Hearing it made her wonder what her mother had felt just before she'd been strangled, with the hideous knowledge that she was helpless at the hands of someone she'd trusted, loved.

Madison heard the sound of ripping cloth. It was too much. She could not stand there one more second and allow the woman inside to be harmed.

She darted through the door, emerging into the back room of the salon. Racks of plastic-covered dresses blocked her view. The floor creaked loudly under her feet. Should she call the police? But they already thought she was a trouble-maker, and no one had exactly invited her into the salon. Nonetheless, she kept her hand on her phone keypad.

Heart hammering, she pushed past the dresses, the plastic crinkling under her touch.

The shop owner's eyes were round with fear, hands clasped to her mouth.

"Are you okay?" Madison asked, stepping through the dresses.

The woman didn't answer. Her gaze shifted slightly. Madison saw the shadow of movement in her peripheral vision. She turned and got a glimpse of a man, an impression only of a bald scalp, the swing of an arm, a rush of air.

Then something exploded against the side of her head. Sparks of pain charged through her body. Her vision blurred, narrowed, and she crumpled to the floor.

She heard the woman scream as she slid into darkness.

James was getting into his car to head back to the station. His radio crackled, something about a break-in at the bridal salon. He was about to respond when a black sedan shot past him at a speed approaching fifty miles an hour. Had the car come from the salon parking lot?

James turned on the siren and gunned the engine, taking off in pursuit and praying no pedestrians were in the path of the crazed driver. Hawk sat up, rigid, and bayed so loud James's ears rang.

"Quiet," he called. They took the bend out of town, the sedan shimmying and bucking as if the driver was not fully in control. James tried to catch the license-plate number, but it was covered in mud. As he turned a corner, he rolled past a tiny grocery store. Out in front was a truck half in the road, the deliveryman loading a dolly full of vegetable crates.

With a last-minute correction, the sedan jerked past, barely missing the deliveryman, who fell over, heads of lettuce tumbling everywhere. The sedan plowed into the side of the truck, sending bits of metal and glass flying. James leaped out and drew his revolver.

"Put your hands where I can see them," he shouted.

There was a momentary pause before the driver slammed into Reverse and backed straight toward James. There was no choice except to leap up onto the front of his police car. The sedan smacked the bumper, sending James to his knees and upsetting his aim before the driver put the vehicle into Drive and shot away down the road. James scrambled off of his cruiser, Hawk barking madly in the backseat.

The deliveryman sat on the sidewalk, dazed. James longed to continue the chase, but he could not leave the man there without help. He radioed his position and ran to the victim.

The deliveryman stood on his own, brushing debris from his hair. "What in the world just happened?"

James did a quick medical assessment, and the man assured him he was uninjured. He got back behind the wheel, hastily checked on Hawk and drove a few hundred yards but realized he'd lost the guy. His radio chattered.

Not just a break-in at the salon. Someone had been

attacked. Frances, the quiet single-mom shop owner? He fought the sick feeling in his gut as he wrenched the car around and hurtled to the salon. He was the first officer to arrive on scene. He hastily secured Hawk to a pole outside, shaded by a crooked awning. "Sorry, Hawk, but you're not suited for this type of situation, Gotta secure things first." Hand on his gun, he raced to the back door, which stood ajar.

Listening, he picked up on soft crying. That made him move even faster, pushing through the back hallway and emerging against a rack of hanging dresses. Frances knelt on the floor, tears streaming down her face.

Frances gasped. "I think she's dead."

A woman lay on the floor, facedown, spectacular red hair fanned out around her, in a puddle of blood. His heart thunked as he recognized Madison Coles.

Nerves pounding, he radioed for an ambulance and was alerted that one was already on the way, dispatched from the neighboring county. As gently as he could manage, he lifted the hair away from her cheek and slid his fingers along her neck to check for a pulse. The gentle flicker of a heartbeat sent a wave of relief through him. Not daring to move her, he stayed there, monitoring her pulse, waiting for help to arrive.

"She's alive," he told Frances. "What happened?"

"I don't know. She knocked on the front door, but I told her we were closed. I must have left the back door unlocked. When I went to look for some invoices in the back, she was lying here, like that."

James saw a small but solid plaster bust that must have been used to display bridal headpieces lying on the floor next to Madison. Blood stained the bottom edge. It would make a lousy scent article for Hawk, he thought automatically, since it had no doubt been handled by multiple people.

"So you didn't see the attacker?"

She shook her head.

He put a hand on Madison's back to reassure himself that she was still breathing. Fury boiled in his blood. Who would do this? "Did you hear anything? Voices? Talking? A car outside?"

"No," Frances said. "Nothing."

He pressed for more detail, but she was unable to provide anything. She was probably in shock. "Was there anything stolen?"

"No. The cash register was untouched."

"And you didn't notice anyone come in? What were you doing?"

"Paying some bills in the office."

"What about noise? You must have heard the back door open."

"I was playing music."

He heard no music. Surely she would have seen something. But why would she lie? No, it had to be the shock. He did his best to make Madison comfortable until sirens announced the arrival of more cops.

He heard a soft moan and bent close, mouth to her ear. "It's okay. We're getting you to a hospital." He brushed aside the silky hair that had fallen over her cheek, amazed at the heavy weight of it. Her skin was fair, like porcelain, slightly freckled, her lashes the same rusty hue as her hair. She moved a hand as if to brace herself on the tiled floor. Her slender wrist seemed impossibly fragile.

"Stay still," he said.

"He..." she whispered, then stopped.

"Who was it? Did you see him?"

Her lips moved again, but no sound came out. He did not want to press as her face was deadly pale. *Lord, keep her breathing.* Such a violent blow might easily have caused irreparable damage or death. "Stay with me, Madison. Okay? You're going to make it through this."

The cops barreled in: Bucks and Shane Weston, his friend and roommate in the condo they shared with other K-9 officers.

Shane had left his German shepherd, Bella, outside with Hawk until he could assess the situation. The more bodies nosing around the crime scene, the harder to read the evidence. James brought them up to speed. When, at long last, the county ambulance arrived, James stood back to let the paramedics work. They stabilized Madison's spine and checked her vitals as they loaded her onto a stretcher. Her small frame was swallowed up by the contraption. When they wheeled her to the ambulance, he walked alongside.

She opened her eyes, flicking a frightened glance at him, like the baby owl that had fallen out of the nest years ago on his family ranch. Lost, confused, a fallen creature meant to fly. His gut clenched.

"We're getting you to the hospital. You're going to be okay." He could not resist cupping her hand in his.

Her lips moved as if she wanted to say something. He drew close, noting the glimmer of tears on her lashes. "I'm sorry this happened," he whispered. "We'll find whoever did this. I promise."

He had the mad desire to wipe away the single tear that trickled along her cheek, losing itself in her tangle of hair. Instead he gave her hand a gentle squeeze just before they lifted her into the back. Her long fingers were fragile and cold. Then the doors closed and the ambulance rolled away.

Red-hot anger poured through him. Who had done this? In his town?

The thought surprised him. Desert Valley was a place he'd been temporarily assigned, a town he had no intention of staying in, and he'd met this woman only a few hours before.

"You were running down a black sedan?" Shane asked, interrupting his thoughts.

"Yeah," James tried to snap back into objective cop mode. "The guy who did this, I'm thinking."

Shane nodded, scrubbing a hand through his close-cropped black hair. "Whitney's on it."

James felt a flicker of relief. Officer Whitney Godwin was sharp and determined. He had new admiration for the young mother since she recently cracked a drug ring.

"Did you get a look at him?" Shane asked. Bella was alert, sharp eyes watching the ambulance as it headed with Madison to Canyon County Medical Center twenty miles west of town. A severe head injury would be beyond what the local clinic could handle. James put it out of his mind.

"No, didn't see the guy's face."

Shane thrust his chin toward the bridal-shop owner, who was also being checked by the medics. "Frances give you a description?"

"No help there at all. Said she didn't see or hear anything and didn't even know the assailant was in the shop," James said.

Shane's eyebrow quirked. "Huh."

"Yeah. Gonna get Hawk on it now."

"I'll roll to the hospital after we get pictures here."

"Right behind you as soon as I'm done."

Shane shook his head, eyes shifting in thought. "Bucks told me you had an encounter with her earlier. Lady's been in Desert Valley all of one morning and this happens. This is turning into one dangerous place," Shane muttered. He frowned, and James wondered if he would have any desire to stay in town after his temporary assignment ended, should the opportunity present itself. He pictured the petite dog trainer Gina Perry, Shane's girlfriend. Maybe Shane had truly abandoned his big-city yearnings for the desert, thanks to Gina.

As he went to get Hawk, James couldn't help but agree with Shane about the dangers cropping up in town with growing frequency. Marian Foxcroft was in a coma under guard due to a recent attack. Had she crossed paths with the same guy who tried to rob the salon?

But robbery wasn't the motive in the Foxcroft attack. He thought of the hunted look on Frances's face. Maybe it wasn't here, either. Why would someone hit a bridal salon an hour before it was scheduled to open? It wasn't likely that the till would be full. Something didn't feel right. He hooked Hawk up to the short lead, picturing Madison swaddled up by the thick blankets. She'd looked very small and vulnerable, not the self-assured woman who'd challenged him with that spark of confidence. He blinked. "What is the matter with you?" he muttered to himself. "She's tough as nails."

Still, even though she was the last person he wanted mucking about his town, the sight of her fallen and bleeding softened his ire. He led Hawk toward the salon. First Hawk examined the doorknob which James was grateful he hadn't touched. Then, nose glued to the floor, Hawk made his way into the interior of the salon. The guy had undoubtedly left his trail of sloughed-off skin cells, which were as individualized as a fingerprint to the eager bloodhound. The trouble was, so had everyone else who'd entered the shop. With each human losing some fifty million skin cells per day, the salon was awash in identities for the dog to sort out. With no clear scent article, it was an impossible task.

Hawk sniffed the spot where Madison had lain and the bust, which was being carefully photographed by Ken Bucks. When Hawk whirled and dashed from the building, James followed at a sprint. Trailing Hawk was like holding on to the bumper of a Sherman tank. They nearly knocked over Officer Dennis Marlton in the process.

"Sorry," he called as he ran.

Marlton sighed and shook his head.

Hawk beelined to the back parking lot, then followed a trail out to the street where the car chase had begun. The scent must have gotten lost in the smell of exhaust from the parade of emergency vehicles. Hawk sat down with a huff that ruffled his saggy face. James sighed and patted the dog. "That's what I thought, Hawk. Guy we were chasing clobbered Madison Coles, and we let him get away."

Hawk let out a disgruntled howl that the chase had been cut short.

James felt the same way as they got into the car. He wondered how badly Madison had been injured, and he itched to get to the hospital. He contemplated finding a dog sitter for Hawk. It was approaching midday, and the May temperatures could get uncomfortable. It was best not to work Hawk during the afternoon if possible. His car had air for the dog, but it was a third-hand Crown Victoria, not specially designed for a K-9 like the cars in better-funded departments, which had cooling systems and alarms that went off when the interior temperatures got too high. Plus, the one-hundred-ten-pound bloodhound, trained only to track and trail, tended to get into mischief in medical settings. On their last visit to the local clinic, he'd yanked the leash from James's hand, dashed into the break room and scampered off with a nurse's sandwich. The patients who had witnessed Hawk's escape had been thoroughly amused. The nurse had not. Maybe more retraining would help if he ever had the time to take Hawk.

If he wasn't in such a hurry to get to the hospital to check on Madison Coles, he would have left Hawk with his family, who were staying in the Desert Pines campground for a month. They said they'd made the trip to visit him. He hoped there wasn't a darker reason, like that they'd lost their tiny house, the only possession they'd managed to hold on to since the ranch had been sold.

Hawk whined from the backseat.

"Okay, you can come, but keep your nose to yourself, you hear me?"

Hawk answered with a shake of his massive ears.

James found himself pushing the accelerator a little harder than he ought to as they headed for the hospital. Something was definitely wrong—that was no news flash—but he could not escape the feeling things were about to go from bad to worse.

THREE

Madison woke, awash in pain, feeling as if someone had applied a hammer to her skull. It hurt to breathe, to blink, to turn her head. Where was she and why was it an agony to move? She forced her eyes open, taking in the pearl-gray walls, the blur of white sheets, an antiseptic smell in her nostrils.

I'm in a hospital. She tried to sit up.

A hand pushed her back down. "Stay still. You're at the Canyon County Medical Center. You have a mild concussion, and you're fortunate it wasn't worse than that, from what I hear."

Forcing her eyes open, she became aware that the hand belonged to her sister, Kate. Pale blue eyes, white-blond hair, wearing a denim skirt and a Cactus Café T-shirt.

"What happened?" Madison croaked.

"You would know better than anyone, but the report is that you were struck in the head at the bridal salon." Kate finally smiled, quick and nervous. "If you wanted a good smack upside the head, you could have come to me." She squeezed Madison's fingers, and the pressure did more than any drug to ease Madison's discomfort.

She tried to smile back, but the pain shooting through her temples prevented it. In spite of the agony, she was thrilled to have Kate there, her precious baby sister. "How did you find out?"

"I was halfway through my very first shift with my tray full of burgers and fries when the sirens started up. The whole town heard it. The restaurant emptied out so I ran over. An officer named Harrison was with you. I met his brother Sterling last week when I was here pounding the pavement, looking for work. Sterling was sweet, tried to help me find out where to apply for a job."

Officer Harrison. She recalled a fuzzy image of him leaning over her, holding her hand, saying something low and comforting.

"I can't tell you what I felt like when I saw who they were loading onto the stretcher," Kate said, voice trembling.

"Sorry," Madison mumbled.

Kate's brows furrowed, and she let go of Madison's hands. Their connection ended. "You're digging into some story again, aren't you?"

"I was just going to ask a few questions when I heard a..."

Kate pulled on her ponytail, a nervous gesture from childhood. "I don't want to know. Why can't you get a normal job and quit poking around in other people's business?"

Like Uncle Ray had done in theirs. His actions had ensured their father would go to prison, but Kate steadfastly refused to believe his guilt. Not her daddy, her hero, accused of killing a mother Kate did not even remember. Kate believed her life had been torn apart by

Ray's mission to unmask their father as a killer. Madison felt as if her life had just begun then, as if she was awakening from a long, numbing slumber. Kate had despised Madison for believing Uncle Ray.

"I was just going to ask if the shop owner needed help," Madison said, but she could see her sister did not believe her. "Where's the doctor? I want to get out of here."

Officer Ken Bucks knocked softly on the door. "Ms. Coles? I'm glad to see you're awake." He nodded to Kate and stared at Madison before letting out a sigh. "I feel like I should have kept a better eye on you, and maybe this wouldn't have happened. I should know by now that Desert Valley isn't the sleepy town it pretends to be. I apologize, ma'am."

"It's not your fault," Madison said before introducing her sister. Bucks shook Kate's hand.

"We're all curious to know what happened in the salon," Bucks said. "Are you ready to give a statement?"

Madison peered around him. "I, uh, I thought Officer Harrison would take it, since he was the one who found me."

"He'll be along soon, but he asked me to get the details down now, before they're forgotten."

"Well, I can't really help you identify the man who did this. I just didn't see him that well."

"Can you give me anything? Height? Hair color?"

"Only that he was white, big and bald."

"Excuse me," said the doctor from the doorway. "I've got to do an exam on Ms. Coles now that she's awake." She moved past Bucks and reached for the curtain to pull it around them. "Would you two mind stepping into the hallway?"

Kate and Bucks retreated. While the doctor checked her chart, Madison tried to reconstruct exactly what had happened. She'd been attacked, and she could have been killed. She itched to know what the bridal salon owner had told the police. The doctor's probing awakened new twinges of discomfort, but something else bothered Madison, too.

Why exactly was she disappointed that it wasn't James Harrison there to take her statement?

After getting an initial report from Bucks, James waited in the hallway while the doctor examined Madison. He introduced himself to a young woman who didn't look much like Madison, but turned out to be her sister, Kate.

"I've got to get back to work. My first day."

"Here in Desert Valley, your sister said."

"Yeah. I'm living with Madison in Tuckerville. Not too bad a commute." She sighed and rubbed her eyes. "My dad would hate this little town."

"Did you get word to him about Madison's attack?"

She laughed, a hard bitter sound. "Somehow I don't think the warden will issue him a leave pass."

Their father was incarcerated? James burned to ask her about it, but she had already turned away and stridden down the hallway. He'd find out. Later.

The doctor finished his exam and left the room. James was about to enter when he heard sniffling. Madison. The crying awakened the protective instinct that had gotten James into plenty of trouble in his lifetime. What was it about a woman crying that got right inside him? He remembered his teen crush on sixteen-year-old Paige who'd cried on his chest about some injustice or another. It had awakened such a strong feeling of protectiveness inside James. All these years later and a woman's tears still got to him. Ridiculous…and dangerous.

Madison's tears were perfectly appropriate. She'd done nothing, threatened nobody, yet someone had assaulted her. With the doctor gone, her sister absent, she was likely feeling lonely. And why exactly should he care? She'd been nosing around, trying to rake up some dirt for a story, no doubt. "Aww, just get in there and do your job," he muttered to himself before he knocked on the door.

"Yes?" she said in a small voice.

"It's Officer Harrison. May I come in?"

There was a pause and another sniffle. "Sure," she said after a moment.

She was wiping her face with a tissue, rust-colored hair trailing over the pillow like a spread of fall leaves, freckles showing on her pale cheeks.

"Hi," he said, suddenly awkward at the sight of her.

She flicked a glance around. "Where's Hawk?"

"He's with another officer right now in the lobby. He's not the best behaved in a medical setting. He eats things he shouldn't."

She smiled, but it did not reach her eyes. "If I had any food, he could certainly have mine. I'm not a big meat loaf fan. Don't suppose they serve sushi around here."

His nostrils flared. "Sushi? Raw fish stuff?"

"Not all of it is raw, but yes. You're not a fan."

"Er, no. I prefer eating things that have been up close and personal with the grill."

She chuckled, wincing at the pain.

"How are you feeling?"

"Like someone used my head for a soccer ball."

He had to laugh at that one. "Been there a time or two. Got thrown from a horse more times than I can count, and played in a pickup basketball game last week where I got my bell rung pretty good." He paused. "Can you remember anything about the guy who hit you?"

"Officer Bucks came in a while ago asking the same thing. I told him I can't identify the guy because I only saw him from the corner of my eye before he tried to smash my skull in. Big, white, bald." Her mouth quivered, just for a moment.

James noted that her eyes were the color of coffee with just a hint of cream, or maybe the tint of clover honey fresh from the comb. The image took him back to his ranch, to his father pulling the frame from the beehive, glistening with honey. The wonder of it had overwhelmed him back then. He blinked. "I'm sorry this happened to you."

Her tone went sharp. "Are you? Aren't you thinking I'm a nosy reporter and I got what I had coming to me?"

"No, ma'am, I wasn't."

She stared at him.

He shifted. "Well, I'll admit to thinking the 'nosy reporter' part, but nobody deserves to be attacked, reporter or not."

She shrugged and pulled at the blankets. "Believe it or not, I wasn't bothering anyone."

"Why were you in the store in the first place?"

"I'm working on a story about local businesses, how they've been hurt by the crime spree. The owner didn't want to talk to me, but later I heard some guy harassing her when I went around the side."

"Harassing how?"

"He said something about not telling her again, that someone was going to get hurt."

His stomach muscles tightened. "Frances said she didn't talk to him at all, didn't even see him."

Madison's mouth fell open. "Why would she lie?"

"I don't know that she's lying," he blurted out.

"Well, *I'm* not," Madison said hotly, sitting up against the pillows. "I realize I'm the newcomer here, but I have no reason to make things up."

He shrugged. "I'm sure you don't, except to concoct a juicy story for your paper." Aloud. He'd actually said that aloud.

She stiffened, hands gripping the sheets. "I happen to have integrity."

"I haven't met many reporters with integrity," he muttered, another thing he shouldn't have let slip out of his mouth. *So much for tact, Harrison.*

She blushed. "That was over the line."

He looked away for a minute, let out a breath and remembered what kind of God-fearing man he wanted to be. Slow count to three. "You're right. I apologize. I… I have had some bad experiences with reporters, but I shouldn't take it out on you, especially after what you've been through."

She lifted an eyebrow. "You or the other officers could have returned my calls, you know. Didn't your secretary tell you I phoned?"

"Carrie forwarded the messages like she's supposed to." He toyed with the radio clipped to his belt. "I figured one of the other officers would be better at handling your questions." He tried not to notice her eyes too much. *Keep it professional.* "Anything else you remember from the salon?"

She considered. "The guy said 'Tony,' too."

"Tony?" Now his nerves were good and truly jangled. "Are you sure?"

"Yes, why? Who is Tony?"

He forced himself to answer. "The owner's fourteen-year-old son." Something cold slithered in his belly. Why would a woman lie about being threatened? One really big reason: to protect the person who mattered most…her son. He'd once seen a mother who could not swim leap off a dock to save her drowning toddler. Frances would lie to protect Tony. He was certain of it. He was readying another round of questions when a nurse popped her head in, face grave. "Officer, can I see you out here for a minute?"

He went to her.

"We're going to keep this door closed, okay?" the nurse said to Madison.

"Problem?" he asked when he got to the threshold.

She nodded.

"Be right back," James said to Madison, following the nurse outside.

People were moving quickly outside in the corridor, their shoes squeaking on the floor. He knew the signs. Trouble.

Curiosity burned Madison's insides. Easing herself to her feet one painful movement at a time, she stood, clinging to the bed rail. A moment of dizziness nearly overcame her, but she breathed through it. Forcing her feet to cooperate, she stopped to pull on another hospital gown, using it for a robe. She inched the door open.

Nurses were scurrying along, closing all the doors. She saw James talking to a hospital engineer next to a closed set of metal doors intended to seal off this section of the hospital from the rest. Fire? She'd worked in a hospital gift shop long enough to know that most fire alarms amounted to nothing more than a smoking bag of microwave popcorn, or a patient sneaking a cigarette in the bathroom. Out of the corner of her eye, she caught a movement from behind a cart piled high with towels.

Who would be standing there, hidden between the wall and the towels, when there was clearly an emergency situation brewing? She stepped out, moving quietly toward the cart.

Again a flicker of movement, stealthy, quick.

She caught the faint scent of smoke in the air as she took another step forward. Not a false alarm after all. Hand outstretched, she meant to push the cart, move it backward to flush whoever was behind it out into the open.

Her fingers touched the cold metal bars.

"Hey," James said, startling her. She spun so quickly she became dizzy. As she stood there clutching the gown to her body, she wished he did not have to be so good-looking, with a strong jaw, sapphire eyes and thick blond hair she wanted to touch. He took her firmly by the wrist. "You have to get back into bed and keep the door closed."

"I'm fine."

He frowned. "That wasn't a suggestion."

"But there's someone behind the cart."

James gave her a dubious look, but he let go of her wrist and swiveled the cart away from the wall. There was no one there.

"I saw…"

"You can tell me later. Back into your room."

"I don't need a babysitter," she snapped.

"Apparently you do, and if it's going to be me, I charge nine bucks an hour and all the potato chips I can eat." He led Madison into her room and waited until she climbed back into bed.

Her cheeks burned. "Well, is it a fire? Can you at least tell me that?"

"We're checking it out." James was already heading to the door. "You're going to be perfectly safe. Stay here."

Madison sank down into the blankets, annoyed that even the brief foray out of bed had left her knees shaking and a strident pain in her temples. She wished James would hurry back and fill her in, but he was busy doing his cop thing, and she didn't think he'd tell her much, anyway.

Closing her eyes and trying to breathe away the pounding in her skull, she attempted to relax. The need to know refused to be quieted. *Everything is being handled and no one is going to answer any questions for you, Mads, so just deal with it.*

But maybe she could find out something on social media. Perhaps some patient had heard what was going on and sent out a quick Tweet or Facebook post. She opened her eyes and reached for her cell phone just as a pillow descended over her face, strong hands sealing off her air, cutting off her scream.

FOUR

James didn't pretend to be a fire expert, but the smoke that billowed out of the supply closet seemed to be pouring from one inside corner covered by a pile of blackening paper products. He couldn't see clearly over the shoulder of the hospital maintenance engineer who was spraying chemicals onto the fire with an extinguisher. Sure, there might be flammable cleaning chemicals in the storage room, but on the floor? And the paper products just happened to be dumped there? He knew the hospital was well run and well managed. Piles of debris would not be tolerated.

Now his instincts were prickling. A fire in the supply closet would accomplish what? Create a distraction to allow someone to steal drugs? Unlikely, as the medicines were generally secured. Cause mayhem for some delinquent to enjoy? Possibly, but that didn't happen too often in a place where everybody knew everybody else. Create a diversion for someone to get at one of the patients? A wave of cold swept through him.

"Got it knocked down," the engineer said. "We'll be all clear soon after we clean it up. Fire department is here, too."

James turned quickly and headed back to Madison's room. Cold fear. His nerves were no doubt firing without good reason. She was probably just fine, impatiently ticking off the minutes. Actually, he'd be surprised if she'd stayed put. Not exactly the obedient type. Pushing open the door, he saw a big guy leaning over her, her hands batting weakly at the pillow he held over her face and then falling limp on the sheet.

With a roar, James leaped on the guy. They went down, taking a nearby pitcher of water with them. The man was big, maybe fifty, bald headed and muscular with skin whiter than any desert resident had a right to. The guy surged to his feet, throwing James back a pace.

James tried to get a read on Madison, but the stranger was diving for the door now. James reached for his gun, but before he got it clear of the holster, his opponent tossed a rolling table at him. James threw up a hand to deflect it, sending it crashing into the end of the bed.

There was still no movement from Madison. Had he been too late?

The guy barreled through the door, and James heard a shout as he must have run into someone. Maybe it had slowed him down enough. James got on his radio and alerted Shane with a description as he raced to the doorway. "Heading west toward the stairwell. Stop him."

"Copy that," Shane said. James heard the chatter of radio traffic as he turned his attention to Madison.

What he would have given to be able to run the stranger down, but he didn't dare delay. Fear thickened his throat as he ran back to Madison and shoved the pillow aside. He patted her cheeks. "Madison, wake up."

She did not make a sound; her eyes were closed. Her pale skin might have been carved of pure marble. He yelled for a nurse and tried to find a pulse in her wrist, but there was so much adrenaline firing through his veins, he was not sure whether he was feeling his own hammering pulse or her heartbeat. Was she breathing? "Come on," he said, giving her a shake. "You're gonna wake up, do you hear me?"

Suddenly she gasped for breath and came to, pounding her fists at him.

"Get off me," she screamed in between violent coughs. "Get away."

"It's me," he said, clutching her forearms, thrilled to know she was well enough to take a whack at him. "It's James. Madison, look at me."

Her wide-open eyes were wild for another moment. Slowly she began to focus, coughing hard and sucking in huge lungfuls of air.

"It's me," he repeated. "The guy is gone."

She blinked. "He tried to kill me for the second time today."

He held on, thinking she might burst into hysterical tears. What should he do in that case? Hold her comfortingly? Restrain her? Get a nurse who knew what to do? He figured it might be similar to dealing with a spooked horse: hold on and keep calm. He squeezed her forearms, letting her know he was still there and she was safe.

Instead of hysteria, something that looked a lot like red-hot anger flooded across her face, staining her cheeks pink. She wrenched out of his reach, picked up the pillow and hurled it him. "This is not acceptable," she hollered.

He couldn't help it. He smiled, profound relief pulsing through him. "I completely agree, ma'am."

"Then why don't you do something? This is your town, isn't it? What's the matter with the police here?"

The nurse ran in, looking from Madison to James and back again as Madison continued yelling in between coughs.

"I think she's okay," James said, "but you'd better check her over. She was nearly smothered a few minutes ago."

"And that's completely unacceptable," Madison snapped. "Why don't you arrest the bad guys before they try to smother people? Isn't that what you're supposed to do? Isn't that why you have a badge?"

The nurse raised an amused eyebrow. "Seems as though Ms. Coles is going to be fine."

He smiled, stepping out into the hallway before the pillow hit the door. Shane got him on the radio.

"We lost him. Bucks saw him exit the building and run into the woods."

"I'll get Hawk on it. Send Marlton to watch Madison's room in case this guy's got a partner."

He retrieved the pillow the guy had used to try to smother Madison and raced to the lobby for Hawk. As they headed for the woods, he knew Madison was right. The crimes were popping up in Desert Valley like groundhogs. Now the bridal-salon attacker on the loose was attempting to strangle a woman in a busy hospital? He clipped the leash to Hawk's collar and let him get a good scent from the pillow.

"Find," he said. Hawk took off, jerking James along with him, Shane and Bucks following.

Madison's words echoed back at him.

"Why don't you arrest the bad guys...?"

This time, he thought, he would. They careened

through the underbrush. James slapped branches out of his way. He knew his partners were right behind him, but he was too busy protecting his face to take note of their exact location. Fury rose hot inside his chest along with the adrenaline. The tension on the long leash increased as Hawk surged forward. They were close now. The screen of bushes was so thick, he had to watch his step to avoid tripping. Hawk had no such problem. The dog was a canine bulldozer, plowing his way along, stopping every few moments to redirect. When he quivered in a way that meant, *I've got it*, James's body went rigid, nerves electrified. The guy was close. Very close.

With a jubilant yank, Hawk surged toward a gap between two enormous pine trunks. James used all his strength to pull the dog to a halt. There was no use giving Hawk a verbal command. When he was on a hunt, that was all he could focus on.

James hauled on the leash and stopped the dog, drawing his weapon. Hawk barked and bayed at being thwarted. Shane and Bucks took positions on either side of him.

"Police! Hands up," James shouted.

No answer but Hawk's incessant barking.

He slowly counted to three and rushed into the clearing just past the trees. A motorbike roared to life and their mark made his escape, blazing through the forest. There was no opportunity to get off a shot with so many trees in the way. James ran after the vehicle and was quickly outpaced. Hawk could probably track the motorbike, but there was no use as James heard it roar up to the main road. The scent would be lost quickly because the day was hot with little breeze. He felt like letting out his frustration in a roar louder than Hawk's howling. Biting back the rage, he released Hawk to continue his sniffing, which led the dog to a damp baseball cap lying on the carpet of leaves.

Hawk was about to scoop up his prize when James stopped him. "Leave it, Hawk. That's evidence. Sorry."

Bucks stepped up and took a picture, snared the hat with a pen. He was sweating, red-faced. He told Hawk, "Almost got him, boy. Next time."

James fumed. *Almost* didn't cut it. By this time, Chief Jones had arrived, and they briefed him. At seventy years old, Earl Jones was an imposing man with a large gut and a thick head of gray hair. His expression was fixed in the bland smile he always wore. The chief tended to cultivate that smile while he avoided conflict with his staff, particularly with his stepson, Ken Bucks. He got out an evidence bag and they secured the baseball cap.

"It's the same guy from the bridal salon," James said. "He wants Madison Coles dead."

"Why?" Jones asked. "She's a stranger in town."

"Maybe he thinks she can ID him from the attack at the salon."

"Why attack her in the first place?" Shane mused. At the edge of the clearing, Bella barked, eager to join in. "Place had no cash. Robbery wasn't the motive."

"Someone who doesn't like reporters? Plenty of people got it in for reporters." Jones's tone was light, but James wondered if it was a dig at him.

"Until we investigate," James said, "she's not safe here."

"Can we order her to go home?" Bucks suggested hopefully. "Back to Tuckerville?"

"She doesn't strike me as the type to take orders," Shane said.

The chief chuckled. "Considering my own experience with two ex-wives, I'd say that's more than likely the truth."

James fisted his hands on his hips, wishing they'd all take the situation as something more than a joke. "We need an officer assigned to keep an eye on her as long as she's in Desert Valley."

Jones considered. "I'm inclined to agree. We sure don't want any more deaths in this town. I assume you're volunteering for the assignment?"

"Me?" James said. "No way. I've already got a dog to take care of. Hawk is enough responsibility for two cops."

Shane smiled. "But you're so good at it. Hawk hasn't chewed up your running shoes for, what? Like, a week now? And you still have one basketball he hasn't flattened, right?"

"This isn't funny," James said.

"Absolutely not," Shane said, nodding gravely with a hint of a grin.

Jones did not smile, but something in his expression made James think he was enjoying the situation. They'd had their share of arguments since James found himself assigned to this town with zero say in the matter. He hadn't exactly shown an abundance of tact when he'd complained to the chief about it.

"Excellent, then," Jones said. "Go on back and tell Ms. Coles you'll be her protection detail as soon as she's released from the hospital."

"But I've got other cases to work on, the missing puppy and the police dance next week," James said.

Thanks to his blond hair, he was to be the bait to draw out the police dance killer, if there was one. The two rookies who'd died on the night of the police dance, a year apart, were both blond. And so was Ryder Hayes, who'd been a rookie when his wife, Melanie, was killed five years ago, also on the night of the annual police dance. Coincidence? Maybe. Maybe not.

"Then I guess you'd better help her get her story done so you can go back to work." The chief turned his back to James and went to examine the photographs that Dennis Marlton was taking of the faint motorcycle tracks.

You've been dismissed, James thought. He forced his jaws to unclench. What was he getting so upset about? Was it because Madison was a reporter? Or because he found himself thinking about her red hair and vibrant eyes more than he should? No way was he going down that road. She was a job, an assignment, and he'd do it because he was a professional, not some young kid who wore his heart on his sleeve. "Lord, help me get this job done," he muttered.

He stepped carefully around Hawk, who was sprawled in the shade, drooling. Shane clapped James on the back. "That was quick thinking, rookie. I guess you really got yourself a plum assignment this time."

"Yeah," he grumbled, wondering how in the world he'd managed to snag himself a babysitting detail. For a reporter, no less.

Madison checked herself out of the hospital the next morning against the advice of the doctor in charge. She hadn't slept for more than a few moments all night, even though she'd been told there was a cop stationed outside her door. Who could blame her, really? Two attempts on her life in the space of one day? She'd heard from James that they'd lost the guy in the woods. *Some police work*, she thought. Or maybe they hadn't poured all that much effort into the capture. She was a stranger, after all, a nosy one who was about as welcome as the stomach flu. Something settled heavily inside her.

No time for self-pity, she thought. She had a story to write, even if it was a dull one about local business, and if she wanted to look into other crimes that was her concern.

She found herself in the lobby, heading for the receptionist, who would be able to call her a cab. While she stood at the counter, she felt dampness on her knee.

It was Hawk, happily drooling on her leg.

She could not resist a chuckle as she scratched his enormous ears.

"Sorry about the saliva," James said. "It's just a bloodhound's way of saying hello."

"Better than some of the cheesy pickup lines I've heard." She searched James's face, noting some bottled-up tension. His wide shoulders were taut, as if he'd been given some bad news. "Is there an update you need to tell me about?"

"No. Yes." He shook his head. "I mean, not about the case."

"What, then?"

"We… Desert Valley PD, I mean…the chief, that is…"

The strapping Officer Harrison was nervous? "Well?"

He shook his head and sighed.

"Have you been assigned to drive me to the city limits? Don't bother."

"Oh, were you thinking of leaving?" James asked, eyebrows raised hopefully. "Understandable. Smart, even with everything that's happened."

"No," she said firmly. "The doctor told me I can't drive for a few days, and my sister rides a motorcycle that is not built for two, so I figured I'd stay. Is there really only one hotel in town?"

"Yes, the Desert Rose Inn, but it's only got a few rooms." He cleared his throat.

"I looked online. They're booked. I was thinking of renting a cabin at the Desert Pines campground."

His eyes widened. "My family…uh, well, never mind about that. It's a nice campground, and the cabins are well maintained." He cleared his throat. "But there's something you should know."

She stared at him. "What?"

"The chief has assigned me to your protection detail until we catch the guy who hurt you." His words came out in a flood.

Her mouth fell open. "A protection detail? Are you kidding? How am I going to get my job done with you hanging around all the time?"

His lips twisted into a wry grin. "I was wondering exactly the same thing about my work."

Determined not to be charmed by his little-boy smile, she crossed her arms. "And you were figuring, what? I'd move into the station or something? Into your dorm or barracks or whatever?"

"I live in the condo for K-9 trainees. Believe me, there's not a square inch of room left over there with Hawk lazing around."

"Fine, because I wouldn't stay there, anyway. This is ridiculous. I've got pepper spray in my pocket. I'll be perfectly safe."

James did not appear to be listening. His blue eyes danced in thought. "Now that I think about it, the campground will work great. Plenty of people, lots of eyes and ears. I'll rent a cabin, too. There's a decent basketball court there, and Hawk will love the fresh air." He grimaced. "And the squirrels. You can come with me to the station for briefings. There's a workroom and a coffeemaker."

And then, having seemingly put her life and his in order, he walked off, Hawk bouncing along after him.

She gaped. What had just happened? Had the infuriatingly handsome cop just told her he was going to be her babysitter in Desert Valley?

"That's not going to work," she called across the lobby. Nobody was going to manage her life, especially a man. God hadn't delivered her from her father to make her dependent on anyone else.

But James and Hawk were already passing through the automatic doors to the police car parked out front. James loaded Hawk into the back and opened the passenger-side front door before lazily sprawling against the frame.

Was he waiting for her? He was ready to load her up into the car like some sort of well-trained dog? Did he think he could command her like he did Hawk?

You've got another thing coming, James Harrison. Another thing entirely.

FIVE

It was after lunchtime when James finally got himself settled at the Desert Pines campground. Hawk had to do a complete inspection of the tiny cabin, and James kept a close eye to be sure he did not start to chomp on anything. James meandered outside and allowed himself a moment to drink in the hues of the silver-green saltbush and the massive ironwood trees. He heard the soft burble of water from a creek that would soon be dry. His parents and brother had booked a trailer, purportedly to come visit him the week before, since he had not been able to fly home to Wyoming since the previous Christmas. He knew his brother, Sterling, would be fishing, his only solace since their ranch land had been sold and the horses he'd loved, too. He now rented a room from an elderly couple in Wyoming, ten miles from the beloved ranch that no longer belonged to the Harrisons. James fought down the familiar sting of pain.

They'd had to sell the land and animals to pay his brother's legal fees to defend him against the rape charge ten years before. Sterling Harrison, age eighteen, had become the object of sixteen-year-old Paige Berg's unhealthy obsession, and when he'd spurned her, she'd gotten revenge in the worst way, ruining his brother and the reputation of the ranch. The bad press had finally begun to die away, but not without exacting a terrible cost. James blamed himself. He'd brought Paige to the ranch as his girlfriend. She was *the* one, his teenage heart had insisted. Disastrous judgment, horrific consequences.

Let that go for now, James. You're forgiven. Act like it. Maybe he'd find some time to go fishing with his brother, or at least beat him at hoops.

Madison was safely installed in her cabin, probably still fuming about having landed him as her constant shadow. The feeling was mutual. He decided to take Hawk to the lake to say hello to his parents and burn off some of the dog's energy. Bloodhounds that weren't exercised regularly would find a way to release their great store of energy at the expense of furniture and belongings. Even with a great deal of stimulation, Hawk still did his share of damage. Recently, James had found himself wondering where his hiking boots had gotten to.

They walked up the wooded slope and reached the lake, which sparkled in the sunlight. His parent's trailer was scratched and bulky, and it sprawled like an old hound dog on a shady spot of ground under the pines. How small it looked. How they must miss their acres of ranch land.

He swallowed and saw his brother approach with a rod in his hand. Sterling's head was bowed. He lacked the brash confidence that had marked him in his youth. James missed their carefree days, the hard and fast horseback riding they used to do, tearing up the trails in the evenings when the guests were enjoying their time around the campfire. He could practically smell the wood smoke curling up to the endless expanse of starlit Wyoming sky.

New life now, James. Sterling could start over again with a good woman, if he was ever able to find one, and James was now a canine cop, a profession he loved. Still, there were times he'd trade it all to sit on the back of a horse again, and return to the time before he'd fallen stupendously and blindly in love. His job was satisfying, but he knew at heart he'd always be a ranch kid. Someday he intended to buy the ranch back, even if it took him the rest of his life to do it. Jobs for K-9 officers were scarce in rural Wyoming, and he'd heard through a recruiting program about the Arizona job. He liked Arizona, but his heart had remained in Wyoming.

Hawk's impatient ear flap roused James, and they made their way to the trailer. Hawk lumbered in first through the open door.

His mother flashed a smile at them from the tiny stove in the kitchen. She walked over and gave him a tight squeeze.

"Hey, J.J. You must have smelled my pulled pork."

He inhaled deeply of the concoction and identified the ingredients: garlic, rosemary, bay leaf, chili powder. "No, but Hawk can smell it from five counties away."

She stood on tiptoe to kiss her son. Betty Harrison was all of four feet eleven, a slight woman with enormous energy who never slowed down, except when her eldest son had been overwhelmed by the rape charge and his jail time. Only her faith had gotten their family through it. Barely. Her smile cheered him, but he missed seeing her in the sprawling old ranch kitchen with the checked curtains and her arsenal of pans.

His father rose from the cramped bench seat and

greeted James with a strong hug, stooping to give Hawk an ear rub. Had he lost more weight? The man who'd been strong and robust was now rail thin in spite of his wife's mouthwatering cooking. He had the ever-present notebook and pencil in his pocket, where he used to write a stream of reminders to himself of ranch tasks that needed doing. James wondered what he wrote in it these days.

"Good to see you, son. Gonna join us for lunch?"

Sterling came in and clasped his brother in a hug. "James always turns up when the food's ready." Sterling took an oatmeal-raisin cookie from the platter and earned a poke from their mother. "Did I hear you got yourself a cabin here?"

"Yeah. Gonna stay a while."

"Finally a vacation for my hard-working son?"

"Not really. I'm assigned to keep watch over a woman, and she rented a cabin here."

"The lady who was attacked at the bridal salon?" His mother added salt to her enormous simmering pot. He wasn't surprised at her information. She'd made it a habit to listen to the police radio since James became a cop. "It helps me understand what your job is like," she'd say. She tuned in wherever they happened to be. "That poor girl. Will she be okay?"

"Yes. We're just making sure."

Hawk snaked a tongue up towards the platter of cookies, but James caught him before he snatched one. "Leave it, Hawk."

Hawk's droopy face looked repentant, but James wasn't fooled. The dog never regretted anything where food was concerned. He'd snatched an entire ham off the table at a church picnic they'd attended and never had the decency to look the least bit contrite about it. They'd done some additional training after the ham incident, but James still wasn't completely convinced about Hawk's trustworthiness around pork products.

Sterling folded his arms, staring at James. James waited until Sterling unloaded what was on his mind. It did no good to rush things with his brother. He'd talk when he felt like it. Period.

"Madison Coles, the girl who got hurt—she's a reporter isn't she?" Sterling asked.

"How did you find that out?"

Sterling shrugged. "I was getting coffee this morning at the café. When the ambulance rolled in at the bridal salon, I talked to her sister. She's a waitress at the café. I met her a few days ago when she was job hunting."

"Yes, Madison's a reporter."

His father's mouth tightened, and he looked at the worn tile floor.

"She's doing a story, and then she'll leave town," James said.

"And you're helping her?" Sterling asked. "Seemed like you were offering quite a bit of comfort when she was loaded into the ambulance."

"She is the victim of a crime. I'm investigating. That's called doing my job."

"Your job? What about your family?" Sterling fisted his hand on his hips.

"It's not a choice between the two."

"Isn't it? If you let a reporter into your life, you let her into ours, too." Sterling glared at his brother before turning on his heel and stalking out of the kitchen.

James felt the unsaid. *Like you let Paige in...*

His mother's eyes were round with surprise and

shock. "He doesn't mean it. I'm sure you were doing your best in the circumstances. We just don't want any reporters around us anymore. You understand, don't you?"

His father looped an arm around his mother's shoulders. "Of course he does. He loves his brother, and he knows what we've been through. He's got enough loyalty to stay away from people who dig up headlines for a living. We've been the subject of enough of those to last a lifetime."

James nodded, heart full at the memory of seeing his brother jailed, learning of the hate mail sent to his family's ranch from those who believed Sterling was a rapist. Fed by malicious newspaper reports, many would never believe he was innocent, even after it had finally been proven that Paige's accusation was a lie.

The reporter's actions were bad enough, but what about his? He'd invited Paige into the family, spent every moment with her and loved her with all his soul, or so he'd believed, enough that he'd actually doubted his brother. James Harrison and his flawless taste in women. He kissed his mother and gripped his father's forearm. "I'm going to protect this family," he said, throat thick with emotion.

His mother kissed him again. "We know that, J.J." She looked deep into his eyes. "You didn't intend for anything bad to happen when you started dating Paige. When you realized the truth, you tried to make it right. God's clear on that, and so are we."

His head knew it, but his heart kept tossing up his shame like tumbleweeds tossed up by the desert wind. *Sorry, God. Sorry.*

Hawk was reluctant to leave the simmering pot of

meat, but James insisted. Madison would not waste a moment returning to the story she was sniffing out, and he wouldn't put it past her to sneak away when his back was turned. *That's right*, he decided. He'd treat her like he would a suspect. He would stay wary and play things close to the vest.

He believed God forgave him for his blind devotion to the girl who ruined his family, but he'd never forgive himself if he trusted the wrong woman again.

Just do your job, James.

He'd dig to the bottom of what had happened to Madison Coles and get her safely out of his town and his life.

Case closed.

Madison was just finishing up a list of questions for the local shop owners when she saw James returning along the narrow path with Hawk. She'd meant to call herself a cab or catch a ride into town with one of the locals, because she sure wasn't going to ask James for a lift. He might be her reluctant bodyguard, but she didn't have to let him be her personal chauffeur. A girl had to draw the line somewhere. All well and good, but she was mad at herself for pulling her hair into a smooth ponytail and swiping on a coat of pink lip gloss earlier. Her vanity annoyed her. Why should she care what James thought of her?

Wiping off the lip gloss, she grabbed her bag, shoving in her iPad and camera, and headed out, marching purposefully in the direction of town.

James and Hawk caught up quickly. "Going somewhere?"

"Into town, to do my job."

"Let me drive you."

"Why?"

"So I can do mine," he said, mouth pinched tight. It was obvious he was stewing about something, so she decided not to push the point. She didn't see what right *he* had to be upset. She was the one who'd almost been murdered. Twice. The muscles on his upper arms were well defined as he opened the front door of his police car for her and the back for Hawk, but she tried hard not to notice.

Whatever comfort she'd felt from him at the hospital was obviously a distant memory. Fine. She'd ensure her story was written quickly and get out of Desert Valley and away from James Harrison just as soon as she possibly could. They climbed into the Crown Victoria. "So your story is about how crimes have affected local business, right?"

"Yes, that's why I was in the bridal salon."

He didn't respond.

"You don't believe me?"

"The questions you were asking when I changed your flat weren't about business."

She blushed. "I really wanted to write a bigger story. I tried to get my editor to let me look into the deaths on the night of the police fund-raiser dance, but he wouldn't go for it."

She saw his jaw tighten. "Good for him."

"There's a story there. I've done some research. Mike Riverton and Brian Miller were killed on the night of the fund-raiser. And five years earlier so was Melanie Hayes, a cop's wife. That's a set of whopping coincidences."

"You don't have to tell me the details. The coroner ruled Miller and Riverton as accidental deaths."

"I know. I read the reports. But there's something odd about it—about this whole town, really."

"Enough," James snapped. "I'm a cop. It's our job to solve crimes, not yours."

"Yeah? Well, you're not doing a very speedy work on that, are you?" She regretted her jibe.

His sinewy arms tightened as he gripped the steering wheel. "Just write your business story and leave the crime solving to the police. That's what we get paid to do."

Her cheeks flushed, and her hands balled into fists on her lap. "Reporters get paid to find the truth, also, for your information."

"No." Anger flashed across his face. "They get paid to write stories that are biased and twisted to sell papers."

"Sometimes," she said, voice wobbling unexpectedly, "they save people, too."

James shot her a startled look. "What are you talking about?"

She felt suddenly mortified that her emotions had bubbled to the surface. The head injury had scrambled up her feelings and weakened her self-control. She was not about to tell him her sad life story. "Never mind."

He paused. "Your sister said your father was in jail."

Madison's heart thumped. "She told you that?"

"Yes. What happened?"

Madison felt the same sick sensation that always seized her when she thought about her father. She wanted to tell him to mind his own business, but she knew he could look up the whole sorry mess, and the shadow of softness in his voice somehow changed things. "My father killed my mother."

"I'm sorry." Another pause. "Did a reporter figure in his conviction?"

"I don't want to talk about it."

Mercifully, he did not push, but she knew his mind must be whirling as he mulled it over. How could she put into words what her father's crime had cost her? Her mother, her identity, her trust.

She was relieved when they pulled up on Main Street. She got out of the car without a backward glance and hastened to the door of the bridal salon, ignoring the ripple of fear she experienced at being back there. *No one is going to hurt you, Mads.* James and Hawk trailed into the shop behind her.

Frances looked up from her file over the top of her reading glasses. She stiffened. "Ms. Coles. I'm so glad you're okay."

"Thank you."

"If there's anything I can do, any way I can make it up to you?"

"As a matter of fact, you can tell me about the salon. I'm writing a story for the *Gazette* about how the recent murders have affected business. That's why I was trying to talk to you in the first place."

Frances folded her hands on the counter, looking relieved. Had she expected another line of questioning?

"Business is slow. We struggle. Visitors are not as keen to come here with all the crime, and we weren't a tourist destination in the first place. My sales are down since last year. The florist shop closed, which hurt my business, too. Bridal and floral go together." She sighed, gesturing to the ivory walls. "The place needs painting, the carpets are worn and the light fixture in the sitting room doesn't work, which discourages customers, but there's no money to upgrade. Vicious circle."

Madison couldn't help herself. "Then why would that stranger, the one who hit me, come here? Surely not for robbery? You don't have money to spare, as you've just said. Was there another reason he came to see you?"

Frances opened her mouth, then closed it. "I don't know. He just wandered in. A stranger, like you said."

"But I heard him mention your son, Tony."

Frances took a step back. "You must be mistaken. I told the cops I'd never seen the guy, and my son has nothing to do with this." She gathered up the papers in front of her, clutching them to her chest. "I would like you to leave now. I've got a lot of work to do."

"But…"

"Please," Frances said, voice taut. "Please leave."

James nodded. "All right, Frances. We're sorry to bother you."

Madison allowed herself to be guided from the store. Once they were outside, she said, "She knows more about the man than she's telling."

"Yeah, but you weren't going to get any more information by badgering her. She's scared."

She isn't the only one, Madison wanted to say.

His gaze was riveted a block down the road, where a young boy leaned against a lamppost. Head bent, he was talking to another teen, their bodies close together.

"That's Tony, Frances's son," James said.

Madison started to walk toward him, but James stopped her. "Why don't you let me handle this one? Hawk and Tony have a rapport."

She let James and Hawk lead the way. As they approached, the teens spotted them, and Tony's companion ambled in the other direction, darting guilty glances at James. Tony was a freckle-faced teenager with dark blond hair that fell over his brown eyes. He looked up quickly, hastily tossing his cigarette into the shrubs.

"You're gonna start a fire that way," James said, sticking his hand out. "Hand them over."

"Aww, come on, man," Tony whined.

"Did you turn eighteen overnight?"

Tony shrugged, pulling the pack from his back pocket and slapping it into James's hand.

"Your lungs will thank me. Where'd you get the cigarettes?"

"I found them dropped in our bridal salon. Finders keepers." Tony offered a mischievous smile, dropping to his knees to scratch Hawk behind the ears. Hawk barked in excitement, splatting Tony with a string of drool.

Tony looked curiously at Madison. "You're the woman who got knocked out in the back room, right? The reporter?"

"Yes." Her head throbbed as she said it.

Tony's eyes shifted in thought. "My mom told me not to talk to you."

"Why?" Madison asked. "Is she afraid of the man who was in the salon? Do you know him? Have you seen him before?"

Tony looked past them up the street. "I call him Brick because that's the shape of his head. He dropped the cigarettes in the store a couple of weeks ago, I'm pretty sure."

"So you have seen him before." Madison could not squash the flicker of excitement. Her instincts had been on the mark.

Tony looked away.

"What does he want with your mother?" James asked. "Is he threatening her?"

Still Tony did not make eye contact. "The police can protect you," James said.

"You think so?" Tony asked, voice dripping with sarcasm. "'Cuz my mom isn't so sure."

"Talk to me, Tony," James said. "I can't help if I don't know what's going on."

He shrugged. "Don't know much. Brick's been showing up at the salon for months now. Every time he does, my mom gets super freaked. She..." Suddenly Tony's gaze grew startled, and he sucked in a breath. "I gotta go."

As he sprinted away, Madison caught sight of a sedan idling across the street. The dark tinted windows did not allow her to see more than a shadowy figure inside, but she knew it was him. It had to be. The man who'd tried to kill her.

James was already sprinting to his car as the sedan did a sharp U-turn and raced away.

SIX

James knew the chase was futile, but he called it in and took off in the direction the sedan had sped away from town. The guy had too big a head start. James was not even able to get a glimpse of the license plate.

"That had to be Brick," Madison was saying. "Where did he go?"

The way ahead was blocked by a flagman as a backhoe made slow progress across the road. James banged the steering wheel. "Again." How could Brick possibly best him every time?

Madison sighed. "Tony knows Brick's watching him, threatening his mother. For what?"

James considered. "Not sure, but I've got an idea who I need to talk to next." This was going to take some finesse. He turned to her. "How about I drop you at the Cactus Café? You can get yourself something to eat, and I'll pick you up later. There are plenty of people there, and you'll be perfectly safe."

"No way." Her lips twisted mischievously. "You're supposed to be watching me, remember?"

He did his best not to roll his eyes. "It would be better for you not to come."

"Why?"

"Gotta talk to a guy." There was no way she'd accept that tiny bit of information. He sighed. "His name's Bruce King."

"Who's that?"

"He's a criminal," James said flatly. "A smart and slippery one. He's dangerous."

"You think Brick could be working with him?"

"I don't know, but these make me wonder." He tossed the cigarette pack on her lap.

"Cigarettes?"

"Illicit cigarettes. King smuggles them into the state from overseas and sells them. Makes a fortune, especially since Arizona has one of the highest cigarette tax rates in the nation. Another cop, Ryder, told me they've been trying to nail him for years."

"Ryder Hayes? Is he...?"

"Yes. It was his wife who was murdered five years ago on the night of the police fund-raiser dance."

She nodded and peered at the cigarette package. "How do you know they're illicit?"

"No health warnings on the package and no domestic stamp tax. King gets them cheap and sells them for a whole lot more. Simple setup but real profitable."

"But what would Frances have to do with smuggled cigarettes?"

"I don't know," he said. "That's why I'm going to go ask King some questions. It's called police work."

"You don't say?" she said. "It sounds like reporter work to me."

Her expression was so serious, at odds with the sweetness of her face, that he could not hold back a chuckle. "I guess you've got me there."

She grinned, which made her honey eyes dance. He looked away and focused on the road. It was late afternoon now, and the sun painted the sky with long rays of gold. The sheer beauty of it got to him. He was beginning to develop a liking for this desert, a place of harsh extremes but still brimming with life. A little bird waddled out onto the road, and James slowed.

"Gambel's quail," he said, braking to a stop. "There will be more coming."

He was proved right when a dozen or so more of the birds ambled across the asphalt, heads bobbing comically.

Madison stared at him. "You're a birder?"

"An amateur. Quail remind me of the ruffled grouse we used to see on the ranch in Wyoming. The males would puff out their feathers and tails and do this funky dance sometimes. Hilarious to watch."

"I've never been to Wyoming."

"It's the most beautiful state in the union," he found himself saying without hesitation.

"Does your family still work the ranch?"

His stomach tightened, and he felt the joy of the memory slipping away. "No."

"Why not?"

Because I destroyed our lives there along with the help of an unethical reporter, he wanted to say. He felt like lashing her with the words, punishing her for the wrongs his family had suffered, but the sincerity in her face made him pause.

Not her fault. Mine.

He shrugged. "Bad stuff happened."

"Bucks said your life was ruined by a reporter."

"No," he said slowly. "My family was ruined by me,

but reporters fanned the flames to further their own careers, and that's hard to forget."

"I'm sorry," she said, more gently than he'd expected. "I understand about ruined families."

"I'm gonna fix it, best I can, someday."

She sighed, and there was deep longing in the sound. "I won't ever have that chance, but I hope God will help me save what's left, with my sister," she added hastily. "I want to make things right between us."

Between the two of them, God sure had his hands full, James thought. He hadn't known she was a believer. The knowledge pleased him. They drove the last mile in silence, but James found it to be a comfortable kind of silence, the kind that left space for thinking. Her relationship with her parents was beyond repair. He still had his family, though battered and beaten down. *Thanks for reminding me of the blessing*, he said to God.

He stopped when his phone buzzed. "Shane texted me a photo," he said eagerly. "Someone got a picture of this Brick character on a phone as he ran through the hospital after he tried to smother you."

She leaned in eagerly to see, and her shoulder felt soft against his. A strand of her hair that had escaped the ponytail tickled his face—silky, as he'd imagined it would be, like soft, downy feathers. "His name is Myron Falkner. Been in and out of jail for misdemeanors." Another text buzzed, and James straightened. "I knew it."

"What?"

"Ryder says he's seen him before, when they were working to build the case against Bruce King. Thinks he works for King, though they could never prove it."

"This may be our big break, then."

He nodded. "Might be."

Hawk roused himself as they took the steep drive up a slope thickly blanketed in cottonwood. They reached the top, encountering a wrought-iron security gate. There was no call box that he could see.

"How will they know we're here?" Madison asked, peering through the windshield.

"They'll know," James said, pointing to a small camera mounted high on the gate.

In a matter of moments, a tall man with a long fringe of black hair appeared. Even in the Arizona heat, he wore a jacket, which did not entirely conceal the gun on his hip.

James rolled down the window. "Officer James Harrison here to see Mr. King."

"Do you have an appointment?"

"Do I need one? This is just a friendly visit, for now."

He peered in the window. "Who's that?"

"Madison Coles." James jutted his chin. "Open the gate. I have something to talk over with Mr. King."

The guy tensed, not interested in taking orders. "What makes you think you can barge your way in without an appointment?"

James didn't like the body language, the tightening of the tough's mouth, the belligerent stare. He let his hand drift to rest on the holster of his revolver. The guy didn't miss the gesture. Madison didn't, either. In his peripheral vision, she tensed. "If Mr. King won't see me now, I'll can be back with a warrant and a half dozen cops in thirty minutes."

Maybe. A warrant would take some persuading. He waited, holding his breath. "Open the gate. You're wasting my time."

The man turned away and said something low into

a handheld radio. There was a short response, and he turned back and pressed the button. The bars slid aside with barely a squeal.

"I'll be watching you," he growled at James.

"I'd be disappointed if you weren't," James said, giving him a sarcastic salute as he drove in.

Madison let out a long breath once they'd passed through. "You were bluffing about the warrant, weren't you?"

"Exaggerating," James said, "but it worked."

She laughed. "Smooth, Officer Harrison." He found that it pleased him to have the admiration of this tough lady.

"They're probably running a check on you even as we speak," he said.

They parked on a neat semicircular drive and approached a house that was impressive by any standard, let alone Desert Valley's. Fronted in stone, the house rose in graceful peaks, windows looking out across meticulously tended shrubs. A sprawling elm provided shade to the house.

James rang the bell, and another jacketed man let them in, leading them to a study furnished with a massive bookcase and sleek leather furniture. The floor was gleaming hardwood. Hawk's nails clicked across the wood as he sniffed everything in sight.

Bruce King entered, a cell phone in his hand. He was a short man with clipped gray hair and a neat mustache. His compact torso was muscled, his belly flat under a neat polo shirt. James caught a flicker of movement from upstairs.

"Officer Harrison?" he said. "I can't say it's a pleasure. It's only been a few weeks since you, Officer

Bucks and others harassed me with allegations of smuggling and disrupted my business."

"That long? Then this visit is overdue." He jutted his chin upward. "Tell your guy on the balcony with his hand on his gun if he so much as twitches, I'll drop him." He heard Madison suck in a breath.

"Quite a boast."

"I'm a crack shot. It's not a boast. It's a promise."

King paused for a moment, then waved a hand at his man upstairs, who retreated. James had no doubt there were more men close by, watching.

King turned shining eyes on Madison. "And you must be Madison Coles." He took her hand between both of his. "You look very much like your father."

James heard Madison gasp.

King's expression didn't change, his smile firmly in place. Anger boiled in James's belly at the stricken look on her face. King meant to shock them, shock her. It was his way of getting the upper hand in the situation, putting them in their places. A cruel power play.

If that was the way it was going to go down, so be it. There was no way this crook was going to intimidate Madison. *Game on.*

Madison reeled inside from the shock. She managed to keep her voice in a normal range. "How did you know that? You've met my father?"

King arched an eyebrow. "No, I've only seen a photo, Ms. Coles. Please, sit," he said, taking a seat on one of the leather chairs. Neither James nor Madison joined him. King examined Hawk. "Good-looking bloodhound. My brother used to breed them. That's a handsome specimen. Excellent coloring. Good proportions."

She wondered if that was how he categorized women, too.

"Mr. King," James said, "I believe the lady asked how you know about her father."

"Of course. My apologies. The dog distracted me. What do I know about your father?" He tapped a finger on the ornate wooden arm of the chair. "I know he murdered your mother. Strangled her, I believe."

Madison felt sick to her stomach. *Stop*, she wanted to say. *Don't say those words aloud and give any more power to the past.* But King continued.

"He escaped with you and your sister. He raised you under an assumed name until a reporter—your uncle, I think—revealed the truth ten years ago. Your father is currently incarcerated, serving a life sentence." King smiled. "My facts are accurate, I trust?"

Madison found it hard to breathe, hearing the details of her sordid upbringing unrolled by this stranger as casually as if he was talking about the weather. And in front of James Harrison. She swallowed hard, cheeks fiery, trying to rally an answer.

James saved her from having to reply. "Why do you know all this?"

King kept his gaze on Madison. "I am in need of a nanny for my grandchildren, who are coming to visit me this summer. I placed an ad, and your sister answered it. Naturally, I do a complete background check on anyone who might possibly have contact with my grandchildren." He shrugged. "I'm afraid I do not employ anyone who is a felon, or related to one, so I did not hire her."

The words exploded from Madison's mouth. "That's rich, coming from a smuggler."

King did not exactly frown, but his mouth tightened.

"I see you've been hearing all kinds of unfounded rumors from the local police. I have never been arrested for anything, Ms. Coles, which is more than I can say for your kin."

Madison was mute with humiliation and anger.

King was going to speak further, but James cut him off. "You're a smuggler, and we'll prove it. You'll go to jail sooner or later. It's a matter of time, I promise you."

Hawk cocked his head, reacting to the tension in his master's voice.

King waved a weary hand. "I'm sure you didn't come here just to threaten me. Can we get to the point? I have a session with a personal trainer shortly, and I'm sure you've got crimes to solve, don't you? There are enough of them cropping up in our happy little town."

James threw down the packet of cigarettes on the table. "I know you're peddling smuggled cigarettes, but that's not why I'm here. Myron Falkner. I want him."

"Falkner? I'm afraid that doesn't ring a bell."

"Try ringing harder. Big guy, bald, forty-five and ugly."

King tapped his temple. "Still no ringing."

"Well, listen up, then," James snapped. Hawk let out a whine. "He's tried to kill this lady twice, and he's going to pay for that. I'm going to stick on him like the skin on a pudding until I find him. You know all about bloodhounds, so you'll understand when I tell you that I've got a scent article that is going to lead Hawk right to this guy if he's anywhere in Desert Valley."

King pursed his lips. "I don't doubt that your dog is tenacious."

"Tenacious doesn't even touch it. He won't stop until he has Falkner between his teeth, and neither will I.

We're going to get him, and if he works for you, I'll squeeze him so tight he'll tell me everything about your operation. He'll roll over on you in a heartbeat."

Madison was in awe of the steely promise in James's voice. If she was King, she'd have told him everything. Goose bumps prickled her skin. *He's tried to kill this lady twice, and he's going to pay for that.* The words sent a thrill through her. The only man who'd ever tried to protect her was Uncle Ray. A few guys had attempted to get close over the years, but she'd never let them see the vulnerable places inside. Too risky. Uncle Ray always told her God had someone out there for her if she'd only let him in. She took in James's powerful shoulders, his hands braced on his gun belt, the flat-out determination in his blazing eyes, which were riveted on King.

It's his job, Mads. Don't get all silly about it.

King cleared his throat. "Now that I'm thinking of it, I did employ a man named Myron Falkner six months or so ago, to drive a truck for me." He gave Madison a graceful smile. "I own an import-export business."

I'm sure you do, she thought.

"He became troublesome, irresponsible, late. I found I could not trust him, so I let him go." King smiled. "You'll find he doesn't know much about my business, Officer. He wouldn't be able to tell you much even if you did *squeeze him*, as you say, but I don't want any trouble. I'm happy to let the police have him. He's got nothing to do with me, so our conversation has come to an end." He rose. "It's time for you to leave and take your dog with you. He smells."

Madison saw a ripple of rage spasm across James's face. "Thanks for your time," James said. "If I find out you're lying, I'll be back."

"You won't," King said.

"You'd better hope not."

James led Hawk out the front door, and Madison followed him to the car. They didn't talk until they were back on the main road, the windows rolled down to catch the breeze that had sprung up at dusk.

The ugly words rolled again and again through her mind.

...he murdered your mother.

...strangled her.

...raised you under an assumed name.

...serving a life sentence.

The grief that she kept rolled into a tight ball deep down in her heart swelled up inside. How many times had she prayed for God to take away the pain? And how often had she found herself and her relationships crippled by it?

A life sentence.

Looking down at her clenched fists, Madison tried not to cry, but the tears slipped out, anyway.

SEVEN

James was still reeling inside. He'd known about the murder, but not the fact that Madison's father had abducted his two children. King's facts were correct, he didn't doubt. The shudder that went through her body when King had uttered them was telling. He tried to imagine it. How had she reacted to learning she'd been living a lie? Had she ever suspected the truth about her father, or had she been blindsided when her uncle revealed her father's crime? What did that do to a person, coming to terms with a lie of that magnitude, a lie you'd believed your whole life? He wanted to spend some time in prayer, to ask God how to approach the matter with Madison, but he had to figure out what to do right now. *Gentle*, was all he could think. *Be gentle.*

She had cried quietly on the way back to the campground. When he'd offered to pull over, she'd declined with a violent shake of the head, arms wrapped around herself, taking the box of tissue he offered with a silent nod.

When they finally arrived, she got out without a word. Shoulders slumped, she started back to her cabin, the gathering dusk cloaking her in shadows. She shouldn't be alone, his instincts said. Not now.

"Wait," he called. "I want to check to see if your cabin is secure, but I need to get Hawk some water first. Can you hang out here for a minute?"

She stopped, head cocked, the breeze toying with her hair, which she'd let loose from the ponytail. To hide her face? The shame she didn't deserve? He thought she'd decline his invitation, but slowly, she returned. He handed her Hawk's leash. "Hold tight. If a squirrel runs by, he might just lose his mind and take off."

"And what do I do if that happens?"

"Hunker down and hold on until he stops." It worked. He'd earned a wan smile.

He opened the door of his cabin and went inside. Hawk barreled in, yanking Madison along. *Good dog*, James thought. He filled a bowl with water and put it on a mat for Hawk to slurp down. Without asking, he retrieved two bottles of water from the fridge and handed Madison one. "Sit for a second, okay?" He gestured at one of the two chairs clustered around the tiny kitchen table. "I need to let him cool down before I feed him. Bloodhounds overheat quickly with all that bulk, and he's been out the whole day."

She nodded, taking a small sip. They watched Hawk slopping water everywhere, his long ears dripping by the time he was finished.

"Messy," she said with a faint smile.

"Wait until you see him eat." James took a towel and wiped down Hawk's face, quickly putting in a few eyedrops and rubbing them into the red-rimmed lids. "With all this saggy flesh, you've got to keep things clean. I'll do your ears after dinner, boy," James said to the dog.

The silence grew uncomfortable. "I'm sorry about what happened today, Madison. I shouldn't have brought you to King's place."

She shrugged, tucking a section of hair behind one ear. "You tried to dissuade me. I didn't listen. My sister says I never listen. My father said so, too."

"So you were a teen when you learned the truth?" he asked softly.

She fixed soulful eyes on him that brimmed with heartbreak. "I was a whopping seventeen years old when I started to suspect something was wrong. Can you believe that? How clueless can you be? My dad..." She swallowed. "He was very attentive, doted on my sister and me, but he was very strict. He was an appliance repairman and when he was at work, it was just Kate and me. We had no TV or computer, and we weren't allowed a cell phone. He told us there was a lot of evil in the world and he didn't want us exposed to that. How's that for irony? The worldview according to a murderer."

The acid in her voice cut at him. "I can't imagine living with that."

"I guess the strange thing is that he let us go to church with our neighbors while he was at work. I think he believed it would make us fit in to the community, so people wouldn't become suspicious." She sighed. "Knowing God...it's the only thing that gets me through, so I guess I should thank my father for that, at least."

The dim light stripped away the guardedness, the protective armor she always wore, leaving her looking like the vulnerable teen she must have been. A shadow drifted across her face. "Just after my seventeenth birthday, I was going through a box in the garage, and I found an old photo of a woman and two girls who looked astonishingly like me and Kate. We thought our names were Bethany and Ann, but the back was labeled Madison, Kate and Allison. I asked my father about the photo, and he went ballistic, which wasn't typical for him. He said they were some cousins he didn't speak to anymore. He took the photo and burned it."

Burned it. A memory that must haunt her. "You had no idea until then that he was hiding something?"

"Oh, I was happily oblivious. I would still be, maybe, if Uncle Ray hadn't kept looking for us. The story our father always told us was that our mother's name was Linda and she'd died of cancer just after Kate was born. All lies. Her name was Allison, and she was perfectly healthy until the day he killed her."

"How did your uncle find you?"

She sighed. "Dogged research."

"It must have been."

She nodded. "He knew Dad had previously lived in Arizona, so he figured he might have gone back there. He set to work faithfully calling up every company he thought my dad might possibly work for. He managed to con people at each office into telling him whether or not a man matching my dad's description had been hired. I didn't want to believe him, but he showed up one day at our house when Dad wasn't home. He knew things about my mother and us. He showed a picture of us when we were just toddlers, in my mother's arms. He said to stay put and he would come back with the police, but it took him a while to convince them." There was a little catch in her voice. "I was afraid even to tell Kate, but I did."

"She didn't believe you."

"No, and why would she? He was our father. We had no memories of our mother. This was the man who took us to the park every Wednesday and stayed up late helping us with math homework and taught us to play the piano. She was sure Uncle Ray had made up everything." Madison sighed. "Kate told my dad what I'd done. He was furious, said it was all lies, locked us in our room and immediately began packing."

He thought about how that must have felt to a couple of young teens who were getting the first inkling that their father was not the man he pretended to be.

"Uncle Ray and the police arrived just before we pulled out of the driveway. My father was arrested for murdering my mother. Uncle Ray said she'd tired of my father's abuse, threatened to leave him, and he lost his temper and strangled her. And then, just like that, my life turned completely upside down. It was like being suddenly split open." Her face was bleak.

"I'm sorry," he said.

She shrugged, sitting up a little straighter. "I dealt with it—still am, I guess—better than Kate. That day in the driveway, she screamed at me. I can still hear it clear as anything. 'You wrecked my life. I'll never forgive you.'" Madison's lips twitched. "She was right, in a way. I did wreck her life, and mine, too, when I chose to believe Uncle Ray instead of our father."

There was such a heavy weight of grief in her words. He wanted to hold her then to offer comfort, solace, prayer. "You had no choice."

"Sure I did. I could have trusted my father, the man who raised me, instead of a stranger, a reporter no less, but that nosy reporter instinct was alive in me even then, you see."

"You did the right thing, Madison."

"I think I did, and I hope that Kate will come to see that someday. I can handle losing my father, or the man I thought he was, but not my sister. Not her, too. That would be too cruel, wouldn't it, to lose my father and mother, and my sister?" Moisture sparkled like diamonds on her lashes.

He wanted to say he knew what it was like to have a hand in the destruction of a family, but how could his story comfort her? Her past was a wasteland of distrust and betrayal due in no way to her choices. His could be laid entirely at his own two feet. He reached for her hand. "You're really strong to get through that."

"I didn't get through it. God brought me through it," she said, "and He taught me an important lesson."

"What's that?"

Gently she pulled her hand from his. "You can't trust people, only Him."

It was such an easy thing to believe, especially in his career. Police work could turn your heart to granite. Everywhere, in every circumstance, friends and family let each other down in the worst ways. Snippets of memories circled his brain. The man who beat his wife for burning the pot roast. The mother who left her baby in the hot car to score a hit of drugs. *But there are people to trust in this world,* he wanted to tell her, *people who will stand by you, if you let them.* But who was he to say so? He'd trusted Paige heart and soul and put her above his own family, his God. His struggle rose up afresh. Madison Coles did not trust anyone else.

And tough K-9 cop James Harrison could not trust himself.

* * *

The knock on the door startled Madison. She realized that aside from the soft glow of the overhead light, it was approaching evening. How had the time passed so quickly? James got up to open the door. A man who strongly resembled James stood on the doorstep holding a pot, each of his hands hidden in an oven mitt. A small gray-haired woman stood at his shoulder, smiling.

"We brought you some dinner, J.J.," she said.

Hawk shot to his feet, tail wagging, and bounded over to sniff the new arrivals.

The man who had to be James's brother caught sight of her. "Oh, uh. Sorry. Didn't realize you had company."

James grabbed a towel and took the pot from his brother, sliding it on the stove. "This is my brother, Sterling, and my mom, Betty." James hesitated a moment, she thought, and cleared his throat. "This is Madison Coles. I'm assigned to her protection detail."

I'm assigned...making it clear to his family that this was nothing personal. And it wasn't, she thought angrily, getting to her feet. So why had she just shared the most intimate moments of her life with him? Unloading everything in a moment of carelessness? *You didn't have a choice after King dropped his bombshell.*

"Hello," Madison said, forcing a bright tone. "I didn't realize we were all in the same campground."

"Cozy, isn't it?" Sterling said, brows drawn.

"Uh...hello," Betty said. "How nice to meet you." Her cheer was as forced as Madison's.

"Talk to you later." Sterling whirled around and disappeared into the night.

Betty massaged Hawk's head for a moment. "Well, I didn't mean to interrupt. Since you're staying in the campground, too, I'm sure we'll see you again soon," she said.

James stood helplessly in the doorway as his mother backed away and followed Sterling.

"They hate reporters, don't they?"

"My mother doesn't hate anyone. My brother is… wary."

"I understand. I get that attitude a lot." She went to the door. "I'm going back to my cabin. There's no need to check it over. If there's anyone inside, I'll scream."

"Why don't you stay here and have some of this dinner with me? My mom's a great cook."

"Somehow I don't think your family would want me eating with you."

His expression hardened. "That's not true."

"Isn't it?" She fastened her gaze on those iridescent blue eyes and saw from the flicker there that she was right. As far as the Harrisons went, she was a potential enemy. Fighting down a swell of disappointment she did not understand, she checked her watch. "It's after five. You're off the clock. I'll talk to you tomorrow."

"Madison," he said, stepping out into the night after her. "I meant what I said. You are an incredibly strong person to overcome what you have."

And I meant what I said. You can't trust people…

He was still following her. She offered a vague smile. "I told you I don't need you to check my cabin."

"Guess I'm not going to listen to you on that point," he said. He whistled to Hawk. "Come here, boy."

"Are you expecting him to sniff out Falkner or something?"

"No, but if I leave him alone in the cabin, he'll have that pot licked clean before I get back."

Hawk ambled past her and went ahead to examine the bushes around her cabin.

"Tomorrow's Saturday," James said. "My shift doesn't start until noon, and the church is having a potluck. Would you like to go?"

She felt spark of pleasure until she realized what his motivation must be. Pity. It was the last thing she wanted, especially from him. It was the inevitable consequence of knowing her twisted family story. *Poor Madison.* "Look, I appreciate all you've done, but I don't need you to feel sorry for me, or try to arrange some spiritual mentoring. I know God, and I don't need to go and sing songs with a bunch of strangers."

He gave her a devastating smile that would probably have convinced anyone else. "Once you meet them, they won't be strangers. They put together an amazing dessert table and all the coffee you can drink."

"Thanks, anyway. I've got work to do."

"They won't judge," he said quietly. "They're good people, I've discovered. They wouldn't hold your past against you."

"If you had a past like mine," she snapped, "you wouldn't be so full of advice. Since you insist on keeping an eye on me, pick me up after your potluck tomorrow. Otherwise, I'll go my way and you go yours." She regretted her sharp tone. He'd only invited her to church, for goodness' sake, but it was too late to take it back.

James didn't answer. She stayed in the doorway while he did a quick search.

"Everything's okay," he said.

Far from it, Madison thought, but she didn't say so. "Thank you. Good night, James."

He hesitated on the porch step. The night was clear and spangled with emerging stars. The porch light silhouetted his muscled frame. "You know, you're right. My advice isn't worth much, considering the mess I've made of my own life. Here," he said, taking a chain from around his neck. The metal twinkled in the dim light. "I think you could use this."

"What's this?"

"Something my mom gave me when I hit bottom."

"I can't..."

He waved off her protest and turned to go, Hawk following.

"But..."

"See you in the morning."

She closed the door softly behind him.

Suddenly exhausted by all that had happened, she flopped into a worn padded rocker. Her head throbbed and her eyes ached as she held the chain James had given her up to the lamplight. A small square tag glimmered, still warm from lying against James's chest, and she held it closer to make out the words.

> Behold, I will do a new thing; now it shall spring forth; shall ye not know it? I will even make a way in the wilderness, *and* rivers in the desert.
> —*Isaiah* 43:19

A way in the wilderness? A fresh life welling up, free for the taking? An enticing thought, and she savored it like a mouthful of a rare delicacy. What would it be like to truly cut herself loose from her past? With a man like James? The thought scared her.

Don't dwell in the past? She wasn't. She intended to

march squarely into the future, alone and striding on her own two feet. A successful career, a building relationship with her sister and the knowledge that God had given her the strength to do it on her own was all she needed.

She opened the little drawer on the lamp stand, dropped the necklace inside and slid it closed.

EIGHT

Sunlight blazed through a gap in the curtains the next morning, waking Madison from a deep sleep. Surprised to find it was after ten, she took a shower, noting that her head was not aching as badly as it had been the previous evening. Revived, she pulled on her jeans from the day before and a top the hospital had given her, grateful that her sister had promised to bring her a bag of fresh clothes on her way to work in the afternoon.

Two cups of instant coffee and a quick perusal of her laptop renewed her purpose. She intended to interview the owner of the hardware store, Bill Baxter, and to track down Albert Jennings, who ran a construction business at the edge of town. It was good to be hard at work. It kept other thoughts at bay, at least for a while.

Memories of last night's confession prodded her. Why had she unburdened herself to James Harrison? She recalled the pity in his eyes as he'd listened to her tale of woe. Now he saw her as some kind of damaged goods whom he needed to pack off to church for fixing. Her cheeks burned.

Just get your story. You don't need church, or James, or anyone.

There was a text from her sister. How's your head?

It thrilled her, this little bit of contact.

Hard as ever, she texted back.

On my way to town. Coffee with Sterling before shift. Will drop your clothes. Talk to you soon.

Coffee with Sterling? Tamping down the worry in her stomach, she grabbed her bag and headed out, careful to lock the door behind her, determined not to wait for James to return. She blinked against the morning sunlight, startled to see Officer Ken Bucks leaning against the side of his police car, sipping coffee from a to-go cup and finishing the last bite of a muffin. He nodded and smiled at her.

"What are you doing here?"

He took another sip. "Harrison needed someone to keep an eye on you when he went to church. I volunteered. I'll drive you to the station."

James was farming out her babysitting now? Cheeks burning and unable to figure a way out of the situation, she plopped herself into the passenger seat, crammed next to the radio console, the computer and the shotgun. It was a newer car than James's, without the faint scent of dog.

"So how's the story coming?" Bucks said. "Heard you were writing about local business and crime."

"Yes. I'm going to interview Bill Baxter and Albert Jennings today."

He nodded. "Good men. Bill's gonna be working over at the grange hall today, helping with some repairs before the police dance Thursday night."

The police dance? Her instincts prickled. Her desire

to pursue a meaty story flared to the surface. "Do you believe all the deaths on the night of the fund-raiser are coincidence?"

His eyes widened. "What do you know about that?"

"Three deaths. All on the same night, different years. One murder. One accidental fire. A fall down the stairs."

"Things happen," he said, eyes fixed on the road. "Life's funny that way."

"But you think there's more to it, don't you?"

"Couple of cops think so. James is one of them, and Whitney Godwin's been working that angle. She was close to Brian Miller, the rookie who died in the fire at his house."

"Close to him? Were they in a relationship?"

He kept his eyes on the road. "Not important. Like I said, we've got a plan in place."

A plan? Struck by a sudden thought, she pulled out a manila folder from her bag. It contained pictures she'd taken from the internet of the two officers killed on the night of the ball. Mike Riverton and Brian Miller, handsome in their formal new recruit pictures. What was it? It hit her then, the detail that had been dancing on the periphery of her mind for so long. Both men were big, strapping, blue-eyed blond rookies. Like James. Something cold slithered in her belly. "Officer Bucks, are the cops expecting something to happen this year? Do they think another rookie will be harmed?"

His lips formed a tight line. "I'm not at liberty to tell you that, Ms. Coles, but if there is a killer who gets his jollies by murdering cops on the night of the fund-raiser, we'll get him."

"How?"

He sat back and offered her a genial smile. "Sorry,

but it's not good policy to go around telling reporters about police business."

"Maybe I can help."

"Help?" he scoffed. "Don't even try that line on me. It might be working on James, but I've been around longer than he has."

James? Did Bucks think James was starting to like her? He was sorely mistaken. "It's not a line."

He shook his head. "You don't want to help. You want to sell newspapers."

"Isn't it possible I want to do both?"

"Possible, but not likely. The press was never any kind of friend to law enforcement. You're there to exploit, to place blame and stir up discontent."

"That's stereotyping. Just like saying what cops do all day is swill coffee and eat doughnuts."

A flash of anger hardened his face. Then he laughed. "Okay, well, I guess I deserved that. I like the way you don't back down. Reminds me of my ex-wife. She'd never let me get away with hypocrisy, either. Man. I miss that woman."

"Are you divorced?"

"Yeah. She left me, and I deserved it. I always had to be the top dog, and that doesn't make for a good marriage. I even miss the arguing."

"I'm sorry."

"Me, too." He shrugged. "Anyway, you just stick to your business story, okay?"

And stay away from the real police work. Madison remained quiet, her mind whirling. Again she looked at the photos in her lap. Riverton. Miller. Was there going to be another murder this year? Another handsome, blond, blue-eyed victim?

We've got a plan in place.

Did that mean they were setting up a police sting? Staging the perfect opportunity for the killer to show his hand so they could catch the suspect, if there was one?

She intended to have a conversation with a certain blond rookie as soon as she got to the station.

James pulled Hawk away from the tray of cookies Carrie was arranging on the break room table. The office secretary pushed her glasses up her nose and patted Hawk indulgently.

"Don't worry," she stage-whispered. "I'll slip you a cookie later when James isn't looking."

Hawk licked her hand, making her laugh.

"That's a big pile of cookies," James said. "Did we hire another bunch of rookies you need to feed?"

"We've got some volunteers coming in today to work on decorations for the fund-raiser. I figured it would be nice to treat them, too."

"What would we do without you?" he teased.

She straightened her shoulders. "You'd all fall apart, I'm sure."

He grinned. "Probably true, but we'd all be a couple of pounds lighter. Are you going to the ball, Carrie?"

She sighed. "Stag, if at all."

He felt sorry for the tall, gangly woman. She really was a cornerstone of the department who did her work without many kudos. It wasn't easy fielding all of the calls from concerned citizens and the press in the face of Veronica's recent murder. "You know, if I wasn't supposed to be dateless for this thing as a precaution, we could go together."

Carrie picked up a cookie. "Really? That's a very nice offer, but I don't need a pity date."

It was the second time he'd been accused of pitying a woman. Madison's anguished face flashed through his memory. "Not a pity offer. Just a friendly one."

"You're a nice guy, James," she said.

Too bad everyone doesn't think so. "Anyway, maybe this will be the year we find out for sure."

"So you're the bait?" came a voice from the door.

He turned to see Madison standing there, arms folded across her chest.

"Madison, this is Carrie Dunleavy, DVPD secretary."

Carrie gave her a smile. "Would you like some cookies? They're oatmeal raisin, and the coffee's fresh. Help yourself. I've got to get my laptop for the briefing." She gave Hawk another pat and left.

"Well?" Madison asked. "Is that the plan to find out if there really is a rookie killer at large? You're going to act as bait?"

He tried to read the emotion behind her flat tone. "I'm not going to answer that. It's police business."

Her eyes narrowed the tiniest bit. "So you do think there's a serial murderer in this town, just like I said before?"

And if she thought he would admit that to a reporter, she was mistaken. "I've got a briefing. Make yourself comfortable," he said.

The chief had already started when James took a seat in the back of the briefing room. Carrie was there with her laptop, ready to take notes. Jones didn't have much to add that James didn't already know. Marian Foxcroft was still in a coma, and there had been no progress locating the missing German shepherd puppy that went missing the night of Earnshaw's murder.

Puppy. The word reminded him of his encounter at Charlie Greer's. There had been other break-ins around town, all at houses with puppies. "I think we're on the right track," he said. "Veronica's killer is likely searching for our missing K-9 puppy."

"For what purpose?" Dennis Marlton asked with a belly laugh. "Is he afraid Marco will ID him?"

James ignored his laughter. "It's got to be connected. Earnshaw was a dog trainer. She was microchipping three donated puppies when she was killed. Two were chipped. One puppy is missing. Since the murder, houses with puppies are being broken into. No one has seen the missing puppy anywhere. Too many coincidences."

"Harrison, you've got other dogs to trail, so to speak," Jones said. "Fund-raiser's coming up this week, and now we've got Myron Falkner on the loose, gunning for your reporter."

"She's not my reporter."

More laughter, which he tried his best to ignore. He filled them in on his suspicion that Falkner worked for Bruce King.

"All right. Let's run that idea down and see where it leads us, but there are plenty of cops here to share the load."

"I agree that it's too much to have you act as bait on the night of the dance and work the Falkner case, too," Ryder Hayes said, with his yellow lab, Titus, sitting at his feet. James knew Ryder didn't believe the coroner's ruling of accidental death, either. Two rookie cops dead from suspicious circumstances, both on the night of the police dance. Mike Riverton, an expert climber, dead supposedly from a fall down a flight of stairs. And Brian Miller, a man whose family perished in a house fire when he was a teen, leaving a candle burning that started a deadly fire. It made no sense to James. The only link they had—and it was a shaky one—was that both cops were blond and blue-eyed. He'd volunteered to be the blond-haired, blue-eyed bait to see if they could draw out the killer, if there really was one.

Fellow rookie Ellen Foxcroft helped herself to a cup of coffee. "He's right. We've got to get a handle on things here, to bring this town back to what it used to be." Ellen was the only rookie who had grown up in Desert Valley. He figured that since her mother, Marian, was the one who arranged for them all to stay here and was now in a coma from another unsolved attack, Ellen's opinion carried weight.

"We have to go through with it," James insisted. "It's the only way to know if we're dealing with a serial killer or a set of bizarre accidental deaths." He hesitated, looking at Ryder. "I'm sorry, Ryder. I didn't mean to include Melanie's murder. Of course, she..."

Ryder held up a hand. "I understand what you meant. Melanie's death is the only one of the three that was a clear-cut homicide," he said slowly. "But that doesn't mean the other two weren't related murders dressed up as accidents."

James held his breath. Ryder was the most respected officer on the force, and he had a definite personal interest in the police-dance deaths. His wife's shooting had left him grief stricken, the lone parent to his little girl. The ache of a cop not being able to solve his own wife's murder must have been nearly intolerable.

If Ryder said the sting should be dropped, the chief would make it an order.

Come on, Ryder. Let me act as bait. Let's find out once and for all if there's a serial killer in Desert Valley.

"Do you think you can handle it, rookie?" Ryder asked, skewering James with a look.

"Yes, sir. I know I can."

Ryder nodded. "Then I say we lay a trap and see what falls in, if anything."

Jones agreed, and James felt like pumping a fist in the air. Maybe now they would have the big break they'd been looking for. The chief dismissed his staff, and everyone stood. Veins pulsing with excitement, James went to find Madison.

She was not in the break room.

"I passed her in the hallway a few moments ago," Carrie said. "She was on her way to get into a taxi. I tried to tell her to wait for you, but she rushed out."

Muttering under his breath, he snapped around and headed for the parking lot.

"I know you're supposed to be guarding her, but if it's any help, she does seem like the type who can take care of herself," Carrie called.

If he hadn't seen her almost killed twice, he probably would have agreed.

"Come on, Hawk," he said. "Let's chase her down before she gets into any more trouble."

Madison slid into the backseat of the taxi, thoroughly relieved to be out of the police station. Word had gotten around that she was a vile reporter. Being mistrusted by everyone was fine—she didn't trust them, either—but it was the wasted time that bugged her. If she had to stay in this town for a few more days, she wanted to make the most out of it, have the story wrapped by the time she drove back home.

She had the driver let her out at Albert Jennings's construction company, handed over the fare and told him she'd call for a return ride when she was done. She intended to start at the construction property and work her way back to the hardware store. Her stomach grumbled until she remembered she'd stowed a cookie in her pocket from the police break room. As she munched, she pictured Uncle Ray, who'd shared some sage advice.

"A qualified reporter never passes up a good story or free food."

She would call him, she decided. Tonight. The story would be mostly done by then. It would be good to hear his raspy voice, his country and Western music blaring in the background. And then a visit when she returned to Tuckerville, maybe a barbecue. The thought cheered her. She was not as alone as she felt, not with her sister thawing out and her Uncle Ray nearby. *That's family*, she thought, or what passed for her cobbled-together family. She tucked the remaining half of the cookie into her pocket for later, in typical Uncle Ray fashion.

The construction company was based on a sprawling lot that doubled as a lumberyard, stacked high with planks and bundles of sheetrock. The place was bustling with forklifts moving materials from the yard to waiting trucks, and employees wearing hard hats shouting to one another and talking on radios. She found Jennings in a trailer he used for his office. He was on the phone, his back to the open door. He was nearing sixty, she guessed, with wide shoulders, a well-padded waist and a battered watch on his plump wrist.

"I don't know," he snapped into the phone. "He's

never satisfied. He's draining the well dry and expecting to still drink from it. I told him yesterday that I was finished. I threatened to spill the beans about the whole thing." He grunted. "Let him try. I'm done."

Curiosity burning, Madison tapped on the door frame. "Hello?"

Jennings whirled around, his pale, fleshy face turning pink. "Call you later," he growled into the phone. Rubbing a hand over his thick mustache, he stared at her.

"Who are you?"

"My name is Madison Coles. I called earlier, remember?"

"The reporter?" He licked his lips.

"Yes. I'm writing an article for the *Gazette*. You said you'd answer a few questions for me."

Sweat trickled down his cheeks. She noticed circles of moisture under the armpits of his denim shirt. Odd. It was warm outside, but the air-conditioned trailer kept the temperature cool, almost chilly.

"Uh, well, I can't talk to you after all. I changed my mind. Too busy. Got a big order to fill today. Sorry you didn't get the message I left with your office this morning."

She had neglected to check her work voice mail. "But Mr. Jennings, I promise it will take only a few minutes."

"No, no," he said, putting a hand under her elbow and turning her toward the door. "Really sorry to waste your time."

Madison heard the sound of a motor. Through the window she saw a forklift, heavily loaded with wooden beams, making its arduous way along.

"I don't understand why you wouldn't want to talk to me."

He shrugged and wiped at his forehead. "Nothing personal."

His voice quivered just slightly, and he increased the pressure on her elbow.

She planted her feet and held her ground. "Mr. Jennings, did someone tell you not to talk to me?"

"Tell me? No, of course not. Who would give me orders like that?"

"The person who's shaking you down for money." She watched his pupils contract in fear.

"You don't know what you're talking about."

Her wild toss had hit the mark. "I think I do. That's what you were on the phone about when I came in, wasn't it? Someone is extorting money from you, and you told them you wouldn't pay."

"No, not at all. You were eavesdropping, and you completely misunderstood."

She looked him straight in the eye. "I can see that you're terrified, Mr. Jennings. Tell me what's going on and I can help." She looked him straight in the eye. "I know what it's like to be afraid. The only way out is to expose the truth."

But at what cost? her heart whispered. There was always a price to be paid.

"Please," he said after a moment, his voice low and tense. "I can't talk to you here. It's too risky."

"We can meet somewhere else," she said eagerly. "I won't use your name. Just tell me the truth."

The roar of the forklift grew louder. They both looked outside in time to see it hurtling out of control with its heavy load.

"Get down," Jennings shouted, just before the machine struck with an explosive roar, emptying its massive cargo onto the roof of the trailer.

NINE

James inquired of the one and only taxi driver in Desert Valley and discovered where Madison was heading. As he sped along, he stewed. She couldn't possibly wait another fifteen minutes? Would that have killed her?

He had to admit that if the situation was reversed, he would probably have done the same. No cop wanted a reporter hanging around the station, and she no doubt felt their unwelcoming vibe. Well, what did she expect? Every Desert Valley cop probably had a story about being misquoted or taken to task for letting something slip to an overeager journalist.

Pushing the gas pedal a little too hard, he soon pulled into the parking lot at Jennings Construction. He was opening the back door for Hawk when he heard a dull roar and the ground shook under his feet. Hawk looked at him inquisitively. "I don't know, buddy. Earthquake?"

Then he heard the shouting. Fear detonated inside his gut, propelling him into a dead run, Hawk galloping right behind. As he cleared a tower of sheetrock and rounded a set of metal shelves, his lungs froze up. Jennings's trailer was partially crushed under a massive pile of beams. Half of the metal structure was smashed flat, an overturned forklift lying where it had toppled after it lost its load.

Several men were circling the pile, shouting into their walkie-talkies, attempting to move debris aside.

James called it in immediately, trying to keep from yelling at the dispatcher.

"What happened?" he shouted to the men.

A worker looked up at him, face blank with shock. "Dunno. This forklift just dumped a whole load right onto the top of the office trailer. Someone said they saw the operator take off running. Couple of our guys ran after him."

"Who's inside?"

"Albert Jennings," he said. "And..."

"And?"

"And maybe a girl. A woman. She went inside to talk to him. She might have got out. I dunno. I wasn't watching the whole time."

James scanned the pile of beams, which was still settling, clouds of sawdust lingering in the air. If the two had been in the far end of the trailer, they were dead for sure. He swallowed hard. What if he never saw those intelligent brown eyes glaring at him again? That sassy, determined woman who didn't allow anything to defeat her could not be gone in an instant.

But she could, his brain told him. He'd seen countless cases in which lives were ended just that quickly, without a moment to say "goodbye" or even "I'm sorry." The father who was stricken by a heart attack on the way to his son's high school basketball game. The mother killed in a wreck as she drove to the babysitter's to pick up her two-year-old. Gone. Just like that.

Work the problem, he told himself.

Help was on its way. Already several workers were firing off ideas, attempting to clear the door or at least a window on the intact portion of the trailer. It was like trying to play a deadly game of pickup sticks as the wood shimmied and slid every few seconds.

"Can't use a machine. Pile's unsteady," the foreman shouted. "It could shift at any minute. No one goes up there," he said to his workers, gesturing away from the wreck. "Get back."

The trailer was pinched down on one end like a crushed soda can. James knew their only hope was that Madison and Jennings were in the surviving section, but heavy beams were now tumbled across, blocking their access.

He moved as close as he could get, peering at the jigsaw puzzle of wood, trying to determine which beam to move.

"Stay clear," the foreman snapped.

James ignored him. "Madison?" he yelled.

There was no answer.

"Madison Coles? Albert Jennings?" he shouted. "Can you hear me?"

Had he heard a reply? He strained to listen. He wasn't sure, but Hawk was. The dog barked and leaped around in a clumsy dance that indicated he knew something his master was too thick to sense. Hope warmed James's belly. Was there a chance they were still alive?

Another beam let loose from the pile and slid toward them, sending men jumping out of the way. James grabbed Hawk's collar and pulled him to safety.

In his haste, he'd forgotten to bring Hawk's leash. Rookie mistake. The best he could do was direct a burly guy in a hard hat to hold his collar and give Hawk a firm stay command. He asked one of the other workers to go back to his squad car and bring the leash.

Metal groaned and snapped as the intact portion of the trailer roof began to buckle. They had minutes, maybe less.

"We can't wait for help," James said. "We've got to clear an escape." He gingerly climbed onto the teetering pile, using his hands and knees to crawl along. Someone threw him a hard hat and he put it on, not that it would do much good if the situation went south.

"I'm ordering my guys to stay off," the foreman called. "They've got families to feed, children to go home to."

James nodded. He could not expect any of the men to put their lives on the line to assist. He was going to have to do his best on his own.

The foreman ordered his crew to take positions around the perimeter and keep watch. One ran for the first-aid kit and the portable defibrillator. James had just gripped the end of a beam when the foreman moved in at the bottom of the shifting mass to help. James caught his eye, and they came to a silent understanding. They'd do it together. The foreman would not risk the lives of his workers, but he would offer up his own. For James, it was his job, even though he'd attempt it whether or not he wore a badge. Heroism was expected for cops. For this guy, it was purely a matter of a good man doing the right thing. *Not all heroes wear uniforms*, he thought to himself.

James gave him a grateful nod.

With James at the top and the foreman working down below, they maneuvered the first beam between them. It took all of their combined strength to move it far enough until the other men took over and pulled it clear. Sweat poured down James's face. The sun beat mercilessly, seeming to add weight and increase the amount of muscle needed. When James eased across the trailer roof to grab hold of another beam, his boot punched through the ceiling. Metal cut into his ankle and he lost his balance, going down on one knee.

The foreman's eyes widened in fear as the movement caused the beams to shift.

"Look out," he yelled.

James ripped his foot free, ignoring the sting of pain, and tumbled to one side as a beam rocketed down past him and slid to the ground with a thundering crash. The foreman leaped out of the way so fast his hard hat went flying. His workers scrambled to help him. Hawk bayed at the commotion. There was a collective gasp from the gathered men as the pile settled once again into a tentative stability. Several seconds passed by while James concentrated on getting his lungs to work properly.

The foreman blew out a breath as his men helped him to his feet, and he accepted his hard hat. Then he wiped his forehead and settled his hat firmly on his brow as he fixed James with a look. "Let's not do that again, okay?"

James swallowed hard and nodded, pulse pounding in his throat like a jackhammer. One more of the massive beams to clear and they'd be able to reach the window. He could see red lights in the distance as other officers began to respond along with the volunteer fire department. The trailer roof continued to groan under the massive weight. The tiniest misstep could break loose a flood that would crush the trailer as well as James and the foreman.

Fingers slick with sweat, he gripped the end of the beam and heaved it loose, heart pounding as he listened for any sound of the precarious pile moving. The foreman slowly lifted from his end. Perspiration rolled down both their faces as they wrestled. Inch by inch, they worked it free. All the while, James hoped that his actions wouldn't cause the rest of the trailer to collapse.

Just let us get in there, he prayed.

When the men pulled the beam free, there was a cleared space, no bigger than three feet by three feet, in front of the broken trailer window. He climbed down as carefully as he could and in a moment, he'd yanked out the shattered pane of glass. His throat felt thick with worry at what he might find inside.

Madison, he wanted to call, but his mouth had gone completely dry. Instead he shoved his torso across the window frame and dropped down inside. His weight made the trailer floor vibrate, and he could hear the pile shifting above him, the walls creaking, debris sliding down from a hole somewhere up above and dusting his face. It was dark inside. The accident must have knocked out the lighting. He made out a desk, an upended file cabinet fallen crookedly next to it.

"Madison?" he called. "Jennings? Where are you?"

"Help me," a voice croaked.

Madison would never take an old file cabinet for granted again. This one had saved her life. It had fallen at an angle against the desk, taking the weight of the massive beam that had cut through the metal roof. A God-given reprieve.

"Help me," she said again to the figure backlit by the sun. Dust stung her eyes, grit caking her mouth. She did not realize it was James who had made entry until his face appeared in the gap under the desk.

"Madison?" He wore an expression of unadulterated surprise and relief. "Thank you, God," he said.

"I was sitting here saying the same thing," she replied, crawling out from under the desk. Her stomach was flip-flopping madly at the sight of him.

"Are you hurt?"

She managed a shake of her head before he clutched her to him for just a moment and held her tightly against his wide chest, feeling the mad thundering of his heart.

Palms flat against his shirt front, she pressed them there, trying to make herself believe that she was alive and he was really holding her. She wanted to stay, breathing in the scent of sweat and sawdust, feeling his relief joining with hers. She exhaled, long and slow, and he tucked her head under his chin.

"You're really okay, then?" he repeated. "Jennings?"

Slowly she pulled away. "I'm okay, but he isn't talking. I think he's unconscious. We dove under the desk when the forklift hit, and I didn't see what happened to him." She quickly explained what she heard beforehand.

James nodded. "Let's get you both out of here."

She scooted back under the desk and helped James pull Jennings out by his ankles. When he was clear, James checked for breathing.

"He's alive. I don't see any bleeding. He might have had a heart attack."

"He had a right to," she breathed. "It was like a mountain fell on us without any warning."

They moved him clear. A window on the far side of the trailer exploded, raining bits of glass down on them. James covered them as best he could with his torso. She watched in terror from under his shoulder as the wall sagged, crumpling another foot.

"It's going to pancake," she breathed.

He didn't answer, rolling off her and shoving her toward the window. "Crawl out, quick as you can."

"No, Mr. Jennings first."

He glared at her, eyes sparking. "Madison, get out right now. I'll pull Mr. Jennings clear as soon as you're through."

She didn't answer that time, just grabbed Mr. Jennings under the arms and heaved him toward the opening. She wasn't strong enough, but now James was next to her, lifting the man easily, muttering something about common sense and women who would rather die than follow orders. Officer Bucks's face appeared at the window with Shane Weston.

"Hand him up and get out of there," Bucks yelled. "Trailer can't take the weight much longer."

Bucks and Weston hauled the unconscious man out and away. James knelt on the floor. "Here," he said to Madison. "Step on my knee and climb out."

She followed orders this time. With a foot braced against his strong thigh, she climbed to the threshold. Her fingers gripped the metal, and she felt the pressure of the walls that were on the verge of buckling. All around her came the screeches and howls of metal giving way. "Hurry, James."

Weston and Bucks appeared at the window again. She looked back.

"James?" she yelled.

"Right behind you," he called.

"Come on, Ms. Coles." Bucks gripped her wrist. Shane took one of her forearms, and with a smooth motion, they pulled her free. She was whisked away from the trailer, and she sucked in deep breaths of air. The waiting workers cheered and clapped. Hawk bayed, his ears wobbling with the effort.

Madison's mind spun. *I can't believe I lived through that.*

The ground began to rumble under her feet. She managed to turn, looking for James. He was nowhere to be seen. With a monstrous roar, the trailer collapsed completely.

She screamed. A cloud of dust engulfed them. The roar almost deafened her before it gradually settled, the beams coming to rest on top of the flattened trailer.

"James got out," she found herself saying. "He got out, didn't he?"

Weston and Bucks stood as if they had been frozen, staring at the place where, a moment before, there had been a window. Now it was a compact metal ruin. The dust billowed in a massive wave and then softly ebbed away.

"James?" Madison whispered.

But there was no movement, no reply, only the settling of the debris and one plaintive yowl from Hawk.

TEN

Madison didn't realize her legs had given out until she found herself on the ground. Hawk bumped against her in his desire to get to his master, panting and snorting. A workman did his best to hold back the straining dog. "No, boy," he said in a voice that made her want to cry. "Just stay here, fella." Hawk whined, his sides heaving with concern.

She wanted to reach out and comfort him, tell him that James would be back momentarily, but she could not make herself utter the lie to the animal who loved his master so completely, so unconditionally.

Weston and Bucks ran to the trailer, along with the foreman and all the workers. They'd begun to paw through the rubble, moving beams aside, yelling and then listening for any kind of a response. There was no longer any attempt at caution. Cops joined in as they arrived on scene, heedless of their own safety now as they burrowed to find James.

The minutes ticked on. He could not have survived, her mind told her. There was no way. The trailer was completely crushed, and he had not followed her out. Her eyes stung with tears. He'd insisted she escape first though he knew the trailer was collapsing. A man she'd told herself she didn't trust, didn't want to know. Yet now her heart throbbed so badly she was sure it would stop beating.

More squad cars arrived and the police chattered on their radios, directing two ambulances and a fire truck down to the accident site. They all shared the same stricken look as Bucks and Weston, their mouths drawn into grim lines, voices clipped and businesslike. A cop who introduced herself as Whitney Godwin crouched down and pressed a hand to Madison's shoulder.

Her voice was gentle. "Can I take you to the hospital?"

Madison shook her head. "I'm not hurt."

"It would be good to have a doctor check you out. Sometimes injuries don't show up right away."

"I want to stay."

Godwin spoke slowly. "That isn't a good idea. It could take a while to..." Her voice quivered, just once, before she took a breath and continued. "It's not a great idea for you to stay here. How about if I take you to your cabin? I'll have someone stay with you."

"No." If James was dead, if God had ended his life so abruptly, she wanted to see their friendship through to the end, to finish together a relationship that had changed her in some intangible way. Tears burned but did not fall. She would stay.

Godwin's eyes searched Madison's face and must have read something there, because she sighed and nodded. She was reaching for her radio when a shout drew their attention. Madison couldn't make out exactly what was being said, but the searcher's excitement was unmistakable. Frenzied activity threw puffs of dirt into the air as the men and women scrabbled like wild dogs in the rubble. Madison's nerves caught flame. They hadn't found a body. They'd found someone very much alive.

She leaped to her feet so quickly her head swam.

"Stay here," Godwin said, jogging over to the gathered cops.

Madison wasn't about to stay anywhere until she knew for sure. She raced over in time to see them pull a grime-covered body from the wreck.

"He was in the void below the trailer, under the axles," Shane yelled. "There was a crawl space down there, only about eighteen inches, but it was enough. He's alive."

Alive.

The word echoed through her.

Alive? She was afraid to believe it.

Alive, but would he stay that way?

She could not see past the rescuers' shoulders as they worked on him, two paramedics running forward with a stretcher. Another team was assisting Jennings.

Hawk finally succeeded in breaking free from the man holding him. He bounded forward, barreling past Madison. "No, Hawk," she hollered.

The dog paid no heed.

She raced to catch hold of his leash, but Hawk plowed through the circle of cops, knocking them aside, and dove right on top of James.

There was a scramble and cry as everyone tried to heave the dog off James.

Madison did her part, also, finally succeeding in snatching up the end of the leash. As she did so, she heard a groan. Was it James? She looked at his face, covered with grime, blood oozing on his cheekbone, a trail of dog slobber on his chin. His eyes were still closed.

His lips moved. "We've got to revisit that 'sit, stay' thing," he groaned.

Madison joined in the relieved laughter, and then she stepped back and let the rescuers to do their jobs.

Officer Godwin gave her a ride to the hospital—Madison in the front, Godwin's pointer, who answered to the name of Hunter, in the back. They'd given Hawk over to another cop Madison didn't know. She saw a small photo of a sweet-faced little girl stuck in the driver's sun visor.

"Your daughter?"

Officer Godwin smiled. "Yes, Shelby. Having her picture there reminds me of what my priorities are."

And what were Madison's priorities? Her mind still whirled. A few hours ago they had been to ditch James, get the story and hightail it out of Desert Valley. Now she found her emotions were ricocheting around in such confusion, she could not string a decent thought together. She'd believed James dead. Then, in a blink, he'd been returned to her life and her heart.

Just go see for yourself that he's okay. Then you'll be able to keep moving. That had been her solace since her father was arrested: keep moving, keep doing, run forward without letting any attachments form. No one to trust, no one to let her down.

She pictured the necklace James had given her.

I will even make a way in the wilderness, and *rivers in the desert.*

What would it be like to let go of her past and take a new way into the future? Was that what God wanted from her? A path that included someone to walk by her side into a phase of her life that was not clouded by what her father had done?

She closed her eyes against a sudden throbbing in her head and tried to focus on her breathing for the rest of the trip. It occurred to her that she was grimy, dusty and scratched all over, but she could not put much energy into complaining about it. She was alive and so was James, and those two enormous blessings were enough for now. Add Jennings pulling through, and it would be blessings times three.

They arrived at the hospital, and Madison joined in the throng of people waiting for word on James. Chief Jones was there, Shane Weston, Ken Bucks, Dennis Marlton and others. Part of the time was spent answering questions Shane put to her about the accident.

What had she seen? Only a forklift barreling at them, no clear view of the driver. What did she know? That Albert Jennings was being threatened by someone—possibly Myron Falkner making him pay protection money—and Jennings finally had enough?

Officer Marlton quirked an eyebrow at that.

"Frances is being coerced, too, at the bridal shop, though she won't admit it," Madison insisted.

"And you've got proof of this?"

"Isn't the fact that someone is constantly trying to kill me enough proof for you?"

He looked as though he was trying to tamp down a smile. "You don't think maybe you've collected some enemies along the way?"

"Funny." Madison had only one question for Marlton. "Did you find the forklift driver?"

He shook his head. "Not yet."

"What are you doing to locate him?" She waved a hand. "Never mind. I know you're not at liberty to tell me."

Not yet. Working on it. Official police business. She was getting heartily sick of hearing those words. She wandered down to the end of the hallway to get a drink of water from the fountain. The elevator doors opened, and she was surprised when her sister Kate stepped out with Sterling Harrison.

Kate took one look at Madison and embraced her in tight hug.

Madison hugged her back, clutching her close. Sterling regarded her with outright hostility.

"It's your fault, isn't it?" he snapped. "What happened to my brother?"

She gently pushed Kate away.

"A forklift dumped a load of beams on the trailer I was in. I certainly didn't cause that accident."

Sterling's nostrils flared. "Tell me one thing. Was my brother in that trailer because he was helping you?"

No, she wanted to say. No, no. What happened to James could not be laid on her conscience. She'd not invited him into her life, her heart. *I didn't ask for his help, and I don't want it.* Her silence answered for her.

"That's what I thought," he said. "Do us all a favor and leave Desert Valley."

Kate straightened. "Madison's here doing her job. Your brother was doing his, too."

Madison thrilled at her sister's support.

Kate put her hand on Sterling's arm. "Go see how James is doing," she said more gently. "I'll come in a minute, okay?"

Sterling looked at her, his gaze gentling, too. Then he nodded and strode off.

Was something developing between those two? Madison wondered.

"Thank you for standing up for me," Madison said.

Kate whirled on her. "I don't know why I did. You're my sister and I love you, but he's right. You attract this trouble, and it's almost gotten you killed, and now it almost got Sterling's brother killed."

"I…"

"No, no more excuses. You've got to stop prying into things. I mean it. I can't stand this anymore. I want a normal sister, not an investigative hound."

"I'm not a normal sister," Madison said. "How could I be? After what we lived through, after what Dad did to us?"

Kate's face went flat and cold. "Uncle Ray sent our father to jail."

"He killed our mother, Kate," she snapped. "He's a murderer."

"Maybe you two are wrong about Dad." Madison hated the desperation in Kate's eyes. "He might have made a mistake. I never knew our mom, but I lived with Dad. I loved him. There was no way he would ever have done something like that."

"The evidence…"

"Don't talk to me about evidence or truth or justice," Kate spat. "I didn't want any of that. I wanted a father, and you took that away from me." Tears crowded her eyes. Pink infused her cheeks. She looked so young then, so very young.

Madison reached out a hand, but Kate backed away.

"You know he did it," Madison whispered. "The DNA and fingerprints from the crime scene. It's the truth, and you can't pretend it isn't."

"Why not?" Her voice grew savage. "Wouldn't I have been happier in my life oblivious to those facts? We *were* happy for many years until the truth came out. What if I had never known the truth? Never known what he did?"

Oh, Kate, Madison thought. "Then you'd be living a lie."

"A lie, but I wouldn't be alone," she murmured, sagging suddenly as if all the anger had drained out of her.

Madison seized her hands. "You're not alone. We have each other."

Kate gripped Madison's fingers, her hands icy cold. "Then stop doing this reporter thing. Stop it, right now, before I really am alone. Do you hear me?"

"I have to finish."

"No, you don't." With each word, she crushed Madison's fingers in her own. "Walk away from the story. You don't need to dig up the truth for everyone. You've already done enough of that for a lifetime. Put our relationship first. Walk away, Mads. Please."

Kate pivoted on her heel then and joined Sterling, who stood in front of James's room. He gave her a shy smile.

The doctor came out, and Madison heard his report. James had suffered bruised ribs, a sprained ankle and abrasions, but nothing more. There was a cheer from the cops waiting in the hall. Sterling closed his eyes in relief.

James's parents hustled out of the elevator and rushed by without seeing Madison. They embraced their son and hurried into James's room.

Madison saw the swell of people, the intimate conversations, the shared joy. She felt very much alone, but she was used to that.

Joining in meant there would be hurt, disappointment—betrayal, even.

She'd salved that lonely hole inside with her work, elevating it into some kind of moral imperative. Kate's words struck at her. *"Walk away from the story. You don't need to dig up the truth for everyone... Put our relationship first. Walk away."*

If she did walk away from the story, she'd be turning her back on her job and James, too, and what would be left for her? An empty apartment with mismatched furniture and a view of a parking lot? A town being quietly terrorized because victims were too afraid to speak the truth, much as her mother must have been? Surely those things were not what God wanted for her, for Desert Valley?

God, what do You want? The need to hear from Him throbbed through her.

Why was it so hard to know which way He wanted her to go?

Again she watched the gathering in the hallway, the crush of noise, the music of connection. Longing, fear, duty and past hurt all rolled around inside her until she felt as if she would go to pieces.

Though she desperately craved a moment to see James, to prove to herself that he was all right, she would not intrude on that happy throng. She'd always chosen a different path, a solitary life broken only by the tap of her fingers on the keyboard, a life that did not heal her brokenness but didn't add to her storehouse of hurts, either. After a deep breath, she made her way down the deserted cement stairs and out the clinic doors.

* * *

"Where's Madison?" was James's first question. "And Hawk?" was his second. His mother clasped his hand in a death grip, his father's arm around her waist. Her face was ashen, but there were no tears, and for that he was grateful. He never wanted her to cry because of him, ever again.

"Madison is fine," Sterling said. "A lot better off than you. I talked to her in the hallway."

The throbbing in James's temples increased. "You talked to her, or yelled at her?"

Sterling did not back down. "She's the reason you're in here, brother, or didn't you notice?"

"No she's not."

His dad shook his head. "Not the time for this, boys."

"No better time," Sterling said. "James could have been crushed."

"Sterling," his mother said, "Madison was almost killed, too, along with the lumberyard owner."

"Don't defend her," Sterling snapped. "You know what she is."

She raised her chin. "She's a woman who has just been through a terrible experience, just like your brother, and I thank God that they're both alive. I know she's a reporter, but that doesn't mean she deserves your ill will, and I won't have you talk like that."

James watched his father. How much forgiveness was he willing to extend to a reporter?

"As I said, this isn't the time." He rubbed a hand over the loose flesh of his stubbled cheeks. "Your mother is upset enough already, Sterling. This isn't about you and your past. It's about James. Your mom and I have been talking and praying about it. It's wrong for us to paint all reporters with the same brush, and we've allowed this hard-heartedness to go on too long in our own lives and yours, too."

James felt a stab of surprise. He'd never heard his parents speak in that way about the past.

Sterling fisted his hands on his hips. "That's not how you felt when they were busy cutting me into pieces, accusing me of rape."

"That was a different person," his mom said, "not Madison Coles. Honey, I know the past hurt you a lot, hurt all of us, but we can't let it ruin us now."

"We are ruined," Sterling said bitterly. "We lost the ranch."

His mother bit her lip. "And I miss it every day. So does your father, but that was just a piece of land. Let's make sure we don't lose any more." She took Sterling's hand, too.

Sterling colored, looking down. "I'm sorry, Mom, but Kate tells me Madison finds trouble wherever she goes."

"Kate?" James asked, raising an eyebrow.

He shrugged. "I told you—I met her at the café when she was job hunting. I bought her a cup of coffee. We've gotten together a few times. I didn't know who she was related to until the day of the bridal-salon attack."

James's mind spun. Sterling's gaze softened when he spoke of Kate. He could not seriously be interested in her. From the few facts he'd gleaned, Kate had bounced from one disastrous relationship to the next. For his part, Sterling never dated a woman more than a few times. He needed a good, stable relationship. And his brother, interested in Madison's sister? That had trouble written all over it.

Sterling must have noted the silence. "We're not an item or anything."

Good to know. "Where's Hawk?"

"With Dennis Marlton," Shane said, sticking his head into the room. "He said he'll stay at the condo for a few days with Hawk until you're better."

"Hawk will run him ragged," James said, struggling up on the bed. "That dog will decide he's the boss and ruin the place. I've got to get out of here."

"No," his mother said firmly. "They're going to do a complete exam, and you're staying until they give you the thumbs-up."

Shane shrugged. "Can't argue with a guy's mom. Besides, Chief said the same thing. So I guess I'm gonna have to find someone to sub for you at our basketball game tonight, preferably someone who can make free throws better than you."

Then who was going to watch Madison?

Shane read his thoughts. "We'll take shifts keeping watch on Ms. Coles until you're discharged or she leaves Desert Valley, whichever comes first."

He remembered the overwhelming joy he'd felt at finding her alive in that trailer. She wouldn't leave, walk away with the story unfinished. Somehow he had to get out of that hospital and find out who was behind the protection racket, if there really was one.

Solve the crime.

Keep Madison Coles safe.

He shot a look at Sterling, who was walking to meet a shy Kate, peeping through the door.

And keep my brother away from Kate Coles.

ELEVEN

James badgered and pestered and generally made a nuisance of himself to anyone in the proximity until he was finally released Monday evening.

"It's against my better judgment," said the exasperated doctor while James buttoned up his tattered shirt.

"Duly noted. Thanks for the help. I'll have a follow-up appointment at the clinic, I promise. Appreciate everything you've done for me," he said over his shoulder.

He was burning to talk to Madison. She had not answered his calls or texts, though Shane said she was "quiet and in place" in her cabin and hadn't left. "Quiet and in place" seemed uncharacteristic, and it worried him. Plus, he'd already gotten a string of emails from Marlton about what to do with a cantankerous bloodhound. The last had been ominous: Going to have to replace a few things.

He was in the Crown Victoria and pulling up at the condo within forty-five minutes.

Marlton greeted him on his knees, where he was engaged in a vigorous wrestling match with Hawk over his work boot. They both cut their eyes to him, and Hawk let go of the boot so suddenly, the portly cop went sprawling on his back. James painfully crouched down and accepted a thorough tongue swabbing from the frantic Hawk.

"Hey, boy, it's okay. I'm back."

The bloodhound nearly knocked himself over with his vigorous tail wagging, forgetting his training and batting at James with his big paws. "I missed you, too," James said, wiping his face.

When he'd given Hawk sufficient rubbing, he eyed the condo, noting the ripped cushion and a door that looked to have been chewed through. "You didn't try to lock him in the bedroom, did you?"

"I had to go get some groceries, and he doesn't fit in my truck," Marlton said defensively. "How was I supposed to know he doesn't like to be locked up?"

Didn't like it was an understatement. Hawk went into ballistic missile mode whenever he was shut up anywhere except his crate, and he would tolerate only James stowing him in there.

James shot Hawk a scorching look. "You tried to eat the door?" Hawk stared back with his droopy eyes, completely unabashed. James swallowed his comment to Marlton as he mentally calculated what it would cost him to replace the door and reupholster the sofa. "Thank you," he managed, "for taking care of him."

"No problem." Marlton eyed him. "Feeling okay? We were sure glad to hear you survived with only minor injuries. Forklift operator must have been drugged out or crazy."

Just crazy enough to want to kill Madison to keep her from talking to Albert Jennings. James grabbed some clothes and some kibble for Hawk.

"What do we have from Albert Jennings?" James asked.

Marlton picked up his mauled shoe. "Hawk used it for a chew toy, the furry monster. I don't think he likes me, even after I gave him a hot dog."

"Jennings," James repeated. "Has he regained consciousness? What did he say?"

"Nothing," Marlton said. "He's still in a coma. Docs aren't sure he'll make it."

James's stomach dropped. With Madison taking up so much of his thoughts, he'd put Jennings out of his mind.

"Anyway," Marlton said, "Chief says you're still off duty, so I guess you're out of it for tomorrow night."

"Out of what?"

"Got a tip that Bruce King is moving a shipment of cigarettes through town tomorrow. Gonna intercept it. Ryder's heading up the detail."

While he'd been lying in the hospital, James had been working on a theory. Consummate criminal Bruce King could easily be padding his pockets with protection money. It was also an effective way to make sure no one ratted him out. King moved the stolen product, maybe even temporarily stored it at some of the local businesses, and threatened store owners to keep it quiet. "Where did the tip come from?"

"Guy called the station, wouldn't give his name. He talked to Bucks. Said he's tired of the town becoming a den of thieves."

He wasn't the only one. "Where?"

"Old Mines Road, just before midnight tomorrow."

Not in it? Until he could link Falkner to King and make an arrest, James was in it, all right. There would be an arrest or a confession Tuesday night if he had anything to say about it.

He thanked Marlton again and loaded Hawk up into the car. He rolled down the windows and sucked in the clean desert air, like balm to his soul after the antiseptic hospital environment where he'd had too much time to stew in memories.

He'd woken up in the night, dreaming of being buried alive, gasping for air. It took him back to age sixteen. He'd been so in love with Paige, he'd have done anything to impress her. She'd wanted to explore an old mining shaft on the ranch property, and he'd known every minute of the adventure that it was the wrong thing to do, stupid, forbidden, but he'd caved to her pleadings and taken her down, causing a collapse. He'd gotten loose of the debris and run for his brother.

Sterling had rigged a rope to his truck and climbed down to get Paige. James should have known when Sterling carried her to the truck, the way her arms were looped tight around his neck, her head tucked under his chin. She'd formed an intense attraction to Sterling right then and there that would not be satisfied until one day he refused her so firmly she concocted a story of rape to get back at him.

And the reporter from the city paper had done a thorough job researching Sterling's past, the reckless driving incident, the fight he'd had over a girl in high school, just enough to wordsmith a libelous article that lit a fire of suspicion in the community. Paige was a straight-A student, daughter of a respected banker. Sterling was the rough-around-the-edges, hot-tempered ranch kid who'd barely kept up his grades to get through high school.

Even when Paige recanted her story some six months

later and Sterling was released from jail, the stigma remained. What damage that reporter had caused. *No*, he corrected himself, *what damage I caused.*

He thought about his parents' reaction in the hospital room. They were right. The past was dark enough. God had given them a brighter future, a way in the wilderness thanks to a Savior who forgave.

And James had even forgiven Paige, and started the process of letting go of his anger toward that reporter, too. That left only one person to forgive: himself.

Tall order.

As the car crunched along the gravel drive in front of Madison's cabin, he shook himself loose from his thoughts. Shane, on guard duty, sat on the porch steps and greeted him with a nod.

"I didn't think they could hold you down for long. Doc sprung you, huh?"

"I sort of sprung myself."

"Yeah, well, you're off duty for a couple of days."

"I want in on tomorrow night, to bust King."

Shane frowned. "Marlton wasn't supposed to tell you that. He's a blabbermouth."

James grinned. "He's a better gossip than a dog sitter. Hawk ate through the bedroom door and had a sofa cushion for dessert."

Shane laughed. "Let's hope he's a good people sitter, because he's assigned to watch your girl until you're cleared to come back."

"She's not…"

"Your girl. Yeah, I know." He quirked a smile. "I'm going to call Gina and tell her about Hawk's antics with Marlton. She'll get a kick out of it. And probably want to see him for a few retraining sessions."

James envied the warmth in Shane's voice when he talked about his girlfriend, Gina. The dog trainer dating the K-9 cop. James chuckled to himself. You couldn't write a better headline than that. He left Shane to his phone call, entered his own cabin and quickly put on a clean pair of jeans and a soft T-shirt, then headed back to Madison's. Shane nodded at him, phone to his ear, and walked away a few steps to talk to his girlfriend in private.

Officer Marlton pulled up for surveillance duty just as James knocked. Madison opened the door. A shy smile lit her face, warming her brown eyes with glints of gold. Her hair was loose, a slick of red around her face, and there was a bruise on one cheek and a scratch on her chin.

"I'm glad to see you," he found himself saying. A flush of pink crept along her cheeks.

"Me, too," she said.

Hawk did not wait for an invitation, but pushed his way inside after he licked her hand. "You're supposed to wait until you're invited," he said as the dog shoved on past.

She laughed. After a hesitation, she welcomed James inside.

Uncertainty bubbled inside her as she hovered near the door. What had she done, asking him in? Yet how could she not? Her palms pulsed with the memory of his frantic heartbeat as he held her, grateful that she was alive. Days ago, she'd feared he was dead. Now he looked relaxed, thumbs hooked through the belt loops of his jeans, his face showing scratches and bruises, a bandage taking up six inches of his forearm.

His eyes slid to the laptop on the table next to the half-empty mug of coffee, and her heart skipped a beat. She wanted to leap forward and slam the computer shut, but it was too late now.

"Notes about your father's case?"

She nodded. "I look at them sometimes, to remind myself."

"Of what?"

"That's he's guilty. That Uncle Ray and I did not make a mistake." Her own honesty surprised her. Being close to James seemed to pull things out of her that she would share with no one else.

His gaze was curious, but not condemning. "Your sister was at the hospital. Did you two have a discussion?"

She sighed. "I guess you could call it that. Deep down, Kate knows my dad is guilty, and so do I, but it's easier for her to believe that I was wrong than that our father is a killer. She wants me to give up my work."

He considered. "Tough call. With all that's happened, I can see her viewpoint. At the heart of it, she's scared to lose you."

She pierced him with a look. "Would you give up your job if your family wanted you to?"

"No, because I know it's what God wants me to do. I'm sure of that."

"I envy your certainty." She pushed the laptop closed and gestured for him to sit down. He did with a wince and a groan. "Feeling bad?"

"Like someone used my head for a soccer ball, to quote somebody I know."

She laughed. What should she say next? How did one make conversation with a gorgeous man who had saved her life? A man who made her wonder if her solitary life was missing a piece. "Would you…do you want something to eat? I'm cooking some vegetable soup."

"Is that what smells so good?"

"I taught myself to cook by trying out the recipes on the backs of boxes. I can prepare approximately twenty variations of mac and cheese."

He smiled. "I'm game for soup, as long as there's no sushi on the side."

"I promise."

She walked into the kitchen and looked out the window as she added a pinch of salt and stirred. "I see they've got another cop assigned to me since you're off duty."

"Dennis Marlton. Only for a few days. How is your story coming—if you're still writing it, that is?"

She swallowed. "I know Albert Jennings would have told me everything, if he…"

They were silent for a moment. "Going to visit him at the hospital tomorrow," James said. "It's a sort of prayer vigil. I'd be happy to take you, if you'd like to go."

Tears pricked her eyes as she nodded. She hadn't known Jennings for more than fifteen minutes, but he would not leave her mind. What was happening to her? She blinked furiously.

James was watching her closely. "Maybe your sister is right. Maybe you should let the story go."

She whacked the spoon down on the counter. "Are you going to let the police-dance sting go?"

"No, but that's different. I'm a cop. I don't have a choice."

"Yes, you do." She didn't look at him as she ladled up two bowls full of the fragrant soup. "You could pass, or they could assign it to someone else. It doesn't have to be Officer James Harrison acting as bait."

"Yes, it does," he started, trailing off.

"Why?"

"Never mind."

"Because you're blond and blue-eyed, like the other two rookies who were killed."

He didn't answer as he strode to the table.

"You're hoping someone tries to kill you, aren't you, James?"

"I'm hoping someone makes a move so I can take him down." He stared at her. "Don't worry. I've no intention of letting someone kill me."

She found the blue steel in his eyes both comforting and terrifying. He would offer himself up on a platter. *Here I am. Come and get me.* And what if someone did? What if the outcome she'd feared at the trailer collapse really did come to pass? Then Desert Valley would lose a good officer, the Harrisons a beloved son, and she'd lose… She shook her head. Too much to think about. "Are you always so confident?"

"About most things."

She read the hesitation. "Except for what?"

He shrugged. "Let's eat this soup before it gets cold."

They sat together, Hawk watching mournfully from his spot on the floor. James ate two bowls of soup. "Excellent. My compliments to the chef."

She laughed. "You have low standards, but thank you."

He looked at her for so long she felt her cheeks grow warm. "You don't look like your sister."

"Kate's the pretty one."

"Uh-uh. There are a lot of blue-eyed blonds in the

world. I should know. But your hair…it's the color of fall in the mountains. That's rare. That's special."

She was sure she was blushing madly. "I look like my father," she said, a lance of pain cutting through her pleasure, "but I don't want to. I'd rather not have anything of his."

"Guess we don't get to choose our biology." His brow creased in thought. "I always wanted to look like my brother."

She fought hard not to gape. As handsome as James was…he envied his brother?

James continued. "He has that rebellious air that attracted all the girls."

"Including the one who accused him?" she asked. She'd done a little research on James. As soon as she said it, she wondered if he would shut down, go into cop mode again.

She could see the shimmer of something in his eyes. "Yeah. Paige accused my brother of rape. Got him thrown into jail. We lost our ranch trying to pay the lawyer fees. What bothers me most is that…" He shook his head. "Never mind."

She suddenly realized the awful truth. "For a second, you believed Paige's accusation."

The words fell like boulders onto the table. James stared at his empty bowl. "Yes," he said. "I mistrusted my brother because… I loved her." Slowly he raised his eyes to hers. "The point is, I doubted Sterling, and I think he knows that somewhere deep down. We've never been as close after that, and maybe we never will be."

She reached out and took his hand. "I saw him at the hospital. He loves you, without question."

He pulled her hand to his lips and kissed her knuckles, sending tingles prickling along her arm. For a moment, he pressed his stubbled cheek against her fingers, leaving her breathless. "Thanks for saying that," he said. "Trying to trust myself again has been the hardest thing."

So that was what he was afraid of: giving his heart to the wrong person a second time. *Do what I do, James. Don't trust anyone. Don't let anybody close.* What a painful choice, a lonely one. James let go of her hand and leaned back in his chair. "Sterling's interested in your sister, I think."

Madison nodded, her skin still warm from his kiss. "I suspected it at the hospital."

"He says it's nothing serious at the moment, but my brother falls hard and fast." James toyed with his spoon. "He needs stability."

Her stomach knotted. "And you don't think Kate could give him that?"

"You said she's been lost, wandering from relationship to relationship."

"And now she's straightening things out. She's got a job, staying in one town, working on some online classes." She stood, picking up his bowl before he could do it.

"I'm not judging."

"Oh, yes, you are."

"I don't want to see my brother get hurt."

"And I want the same for my sister." Cheeks hot, she did not try to tamp down the rush of anger. "You know what, James? You're a hypocrite."

He jerked as if she'd slapped him. "How do you figure that?"

"Because you tell me to forget my past, to go ahead and walk out into that future God has in store for me, but *you're* holding on to my past."

"I'm not..."

"Yes, you are. My sister and I are damaged goods. For all your talk about a new path, you are still judging us for our wasteland, our wilderness. Well, you know what? Your brother's spent his time wandering, too, and frankly, I'm not sure he's good enough for my sister." She felt a thrill of victory. She'd been right to keep him away.

"Look..." James started.

"I'm really tired. Going to get my notes together for tomorrow and go to sleep."

"Madison..." he started again.

"Good night, James."

She walked down the hall and shut herself in the bedroom, leaving him to let himself out. Heaving a shaky breath, she pressed her forehead to the door.

You see, Mads? You let him get close enough to hurt you, near enough for you to care about him. Your mistake.

But it wasn't a fatal one—not yet. She would stick around for only a few more days, and then it was goodbye Desert Valley. Maybe Kate would say goodbye to Sterling Harrison, too.

She wondered why it hurt so much to be right.

TWELVE

James awoke in the same foul mood he'd fought against the night before. A hypocrite? Because he wanted to make sure his brother wasn't hurt again? Like Madison wouldn't do anything to keep her sister out of trouble?

The accusation stung like a hornet and that, combined with his aching body, kept him awake. Finally he hauled himself out of bed. Amused as always by Hawk's mealtime dance, he watched the dog inhale a bowl of food. After the morning cleansing of his wrinkly jowls and the dispensing of vitamin supplements, Hawk was ready to roll. The pounding in James's temples and the tension in his gut dissuaded him from breakfast. A bottle of water and a couple of aspirin would do.

"Walk time." He didn't have to ask twice. Hawk was at the door in seconds. Leash clipped in place, they started off. Madison's cabin was quiet, the curtains closed, car still parked outside. Dennis Marlton waved to him from his squad car, where he sat drinking coffee. The poor guy had been there overnight, probably desperately trying to stay awake.

"Help yourself to anything in the trailer," James said.

Marlton nodded his thanks, raising a cup in salute.

* * *

James did as he'd promised and stopped at the hospital to endure a checkup. On the way out, he found fellow rookie K-9 cop Ellen Foxcroft sitting by herself with her golden retriever, Carly, at her feet. She was staring out the reception room window, deep in thought.

"Hey, Ellen," he said.

She started. "Oh, hi, James. How are you doing?"

"I'm banged up, but otherwise fine. Were you visiting your mother?"

She nodded.

"Any change?"

"No. And the guard says there has been nothing happening. He's bored out of his mind."

The bizarre attack on Marian was just one more case they hadn't been able to solve. He knew Ellen desired more than anything to leave Desert Valley and put some distance between herself and her abrasive mother. He might even add *manipulative* as a word to describe Marian. After all, she'd used her money and influence to keep all the new K-9 rookies assigned to Desert Valley for six months, including her daughter.

"We'll get him, whoever did this to her," James assured her.

She nodded, still unsmiling. "Sometimes I wonder if this is God's way of trying to tell me I shouldn't leave."

He was sorry to hear the confusion in her voice, a feeling he understood all too well.

"How are things going with your program?" She was starting a training program for adults and kids to be matched with service dogs, housed at the Desert Valley Canine Assistance Center. Sophie Williams, the trainer who'd taken over for the murdered Veronica Earnshaw, had agreed to share the training space with her.

Ellen shrugged. "Still getting traction, but slow because..." she sighed. "I guess I'm spending a lot of time here with Mom."

"Things will get better," he said, the only lame phrase that came to his mind.

She looked away, showing him she was not inclined to speak more about it. Wishing he could provide some sort of comfort, he settled for giving her shoulder a squeeze on his way out.

It was just after ten when James and Hawk returned to the campground and made their way to his parents' trailer. His mother greeted them, looking up from a jigsaw puzzle and sheltering the pieces from Hawk's madly wagging tail. A few went flying, anyway, and James retrieved them from the floor.

He kissed her and greeted his father. "Would you mind dog sitting for a couple of hours?"

"No problem," she said. "I want to take a good hike today, and Hawk can be our tour guide."

"Hold on tight to him, Mom."

"I'll do it," his father said. "Used to break horses. Think I can manage a dog." James saw the flicker of sadness that his father could not hide. His callused hands flexed on his lap as if remembering the sensation of working a horse, the play of the reins across his palms.

I'm going to get us our ranch back, Dad. Somehow.

His mom brushed back a wispy strand of hair. "Do you know where we can get some flowers, honey? White carnations would be good. The man at the camp store told me the florist shop is out of business."

"The grocery carries some fresh flowers, and there's a florist in Tuckerville if you need an arrangement. Why?"

"Oh." She shrugged. "It's old-fashioned, I know, but I think a man should give flowers to the lady if he's taking her to a fancy dance. Remember when you did that before our high school prom, Ronnie?"

His dad puffed out his chest. "I was the dashing man about town," he said. "And you looked amazing in your blue dress with the beads on the top."

"It was green with ribbons, but thanks, anyway," she said with a laugh. "I wish I could still wear pretty shoes, but these old feet won't stand for that. Otherwise, I'd be at that dance in a moment."

James was trying to catch up. Probably being nearly flattened in a trailer collapse and staying up all night weren't helping his mental faculties. "Mom, I appreciate your idea about the flowers, but I'm not taking anyone to the dance. I'm going solo." He hadn't told them about his participation in the sting. Couldn't exactly say, *"Mom, I'm the bait for a killer."*

"I know you're not taking anyone, honey. I was talking about your brother."

"What?"

"It won't occur to him about the flowers," she said with a sigh. "He doesn't have a mind for those kinds of details."

"Mom, what are you talking about?"

"Sterling and Kate Coles are going to the dance. Didn't you know that?"

The ringing in his head intensified. He was worried about a killer on the loose, and now his brother and

Madison's sister attending the dance? That went beyond a casual friendship, didn't it?

"Your mother is running ahead of the wagon, as usual," his father said. "Sterling said he and Kate had agreed to meet up at the dance. They're not dating, and flowers are way over the top."

"Flowers are never over the top," his mother said firmly. "And what girl doesn't like to be given flowers, even if they aren't technically dating?"

"Hmm," his father said. "What do you think, James?"

He could see them both studying his face carefully, trying to gauge his reaction. Madison's accusation thumped through his memory.

"My sister and I are damaged goods. For all your talk about a new path, you are still judging us for our wasteland." Was she right? Was he being protective or hypocritical? His mother and father waited expectantly.

"I say no flowers," James said, carefully. "Best not to push things."

He walked back to the cabin, shaved as best he could around the bruises and cuts on his face, and dressed in a pair of slacks and a button-up shirt. He stepped outside to find both cars, Marlton's and Madison's, gone.

He dialed Marlton's cell.

"She said she's okay to drive now. Going to the hospital to visit Jennings," he explained. "Don't worry. I'm right behind her."

He hung up. Clearly she was done with James shuttling her around. Probably she was done with him period. It was inevitable.

He drove to the hospital, pulling into the crowded parking lot. Finding his way to Jennings's floor, he saw Mrs. Jennings sitting in a chair in the hallway, her son's arm protectively around her shoulders. He saw Madison off to one side, her hair pulled back into a thick braid, wearing dark slacks and a sage-green blouse. *Beautiful*, his heart said, before he commanded it to kindly hush up. So she was lovely. That didn't make it a good idea to let his heart go crazy around her.

In the chairs next to Mrs. Jennings and her son was the pastor and the bridal-shop owner, Frances Andrews. Elderly hardware-store owner Bill Baxter was seated next to his granddaughter, Phyllis.

James sidled up and sat next to Madison. She cut him a look, detached and aloof.

"Mrs. Jennings is waiting on a doctor's report after the surgery, and the pastor organized a little support group to be with her for the prognosis," she said.

He settled on a nod of acknowledgment and listened to the pastor pray for Albert Jennings, a hardworking man who did his best to support his workers, his family, his church.

Where are you, Falkner? James thought. *Why don't you come on out of hiding, and we'll settle this like men?* He might be out there now, tucked in the shadows, waiting for another chance to get his hands on Madison.

Frances and Bill had their heads together, talking softly. They seemed to be in disagreement about something. Frances turned around suddenly, eyes filled with tears.

"Albert Jennings is a good man," she said softly.

Madison stiffened. "Yes, he is. Are you willing to tell what you know about Falkner now?"

Frances bit her lip.

"Please," Madison said. "Mr. Jennings didn't deserve this. Please tell me what you know before someone else gets hurt."

Frances was silent a moment, and then her chin went up as she came to some decision. "I'll call you later."

"Please tell me now," Madison said.

But Frances was walking hastily toward the elevator.

James was riveted by a newcomer. "I can't believe it," he said.

Madison followed his gaze. "Bruce King?"

King, clad in a neat blazer and expensively tailored trousers, settled into a chair, legs crossed, watching the activity.

James was next to Bruce King in moments. King's bodyguard, the one with the long hair, stood just behind him, moving closer as James approached.

"What are you doing here?" James demanded.

King cocked his head like a cat sizing up a mouse. "I came to offer my support, just like you did." He smiled. "Hello, Ms. Coles. Nice to see you again."

Madison flushed but did not move away.

He scanned the visitors. "Mr. Jennings did some work for me on my house last year. He is a craftsman. I appreciate that. So sad to hear what happened to him." He waved a hand at a fly that buzzed to close to his face. "Have you tracked down the forklift driver?"

"Not yet," James said. "Do you have some information that might help us do that? The location of Myron Falkner, for example?"

King shook his head. "I told you he no longer works for me."

Yeah, right. "I wonder if he'll tell me the same story when I catch him."

"If you catch him," King said. "Ms. Coles, I wanted

to tell you that I do not appreciate you contacting one of my overseas business partners."

James barely kept his mouth from falling open. She'd done what? And how had she gotten the name of his associate?

"I can contact anyone I want," she said smoothly. "Sadly, he wouldn't tell me anything, really. You've got him suitably scared."

"He's loyal, and there's nothing for him to tell. I deal in imports and exports. Legal ones, but…" He waved away the fly again. "I don't like people interfering in my business."

James moved close. "That had better not be a threat."

King laughed. "My sources tell me Ms. Coles has already had three brushes with death here in Desert Valley. I'd have to get in line if I was going to threaten her."

James felt his face go hot.

"Though," King said speculatively, "if I were you, I'd find myself another town." King stood, nodded to Bill Baxter and his granddaughter, who were watching closely, and walked casually back to the elevator.

Madison immediately slid into the empty seat next to Bill Baxter and his granddaughter. James stood close, alternately watching King and keeping Madison's conversation within earshot. She knew he was probably furious that she'd used her contacts to investigate Bruce King. Fine. Let him rage all he wanted to. She had a job to do, and Mrs. Jennings's grief-stricken face renewed her determination to get it done.

"I'm Madison Coles," she said. "I need to talk to you both."

Bill shook his head. “I’m going to speak with Mrs. Jennings.”

“But this is really important, Mr. Baxter.”

He waved her away, turning his back on her.

His granddaughter, Phyllis, offered a bewildered stare. “I’m sorry. He is never rude or dismissive, but I can’t get him to talk lately, either.”

“What do you think is wrong?” James asked. Madison wished he’d stay out of the conversation, but he wouldn’t acknowledge her pointed stare.

“I started helping out with the books at the Tool Corral last year, and every month, we’re off by a couple hundred dollars or so. My grandfather is a stickler—he balances the books down to the penny—but he won’t tell me where the missing money’s gone.” She shrugged helplessly. “He’s started having trouble sleeping, and he insists I go home early sometimes. No explanation, but when I start to argue, he gets upset, manic almost.”

“Have you seen this man?” James showed her the picture of Falkner on his cell phone.

“Maybe,” she said. “I’ve seen a man sitting outside in a black car, but I’ve never seen him close up.”

Bill Baxter returned. “I’m tired. Let’s go, Phyllis.”

“Mr. Baxter, is someone shaking you down for protection money?”

Bill’s mouth clamped down tight. “Don’t be absurd,” he snapped. “Would I let someone shake me down?”

“Good question. Would you?” James asked. “The police can protect you. Tell us, Mr. Baxter.”

Mr. Baxter rubbed a shaking hand over his face. “Albert Jennings almost died. I don’t have anything to say. Come on, Phyllis.”

After a helpless look at James and Madison, she followed her grandfather away.

Madison stared after them. "I don't get it. If Falkner is threatening shop owners and their families, the smart thing would be to tell the cops. Why won't Frances and Bill turn him in?"

"Because Falkner is working for someone with power, someone who can skirt the law and get away with it."

"Bruce King," she said.

"Yeah." He rounded on her. "So it was a bonehead thing for you to do, investigating him. He thinks he's above the law, and he can hurt you."

"Not with my police babysitters around all the time."

"This isn't funny. Don't make a joke out of it." His eyes flamed with intensity, and he gripped her forearm. "You need to stop digging. Your sister is right. Give up your story before you get hurt."

She detached herself from him. "People are in danger in this town, James."

"Don't you think I know that?" He shoved a hand through his hair. "Don't you think it's driving me crazy that people in this town aren't safe? That you aren't safe?"

The softness in his tone eased her anger. Did he really worry so much about her? As one of his cases? Or something more? *Don't even ask it, Mads. He isn't meant to share your life with you. No one is.*

"It's my life, James, and if I'm putting it at risk, it's my decision. I am going to write that story, and I won't stop until the man who almost killed Albert Jennings is exposed."

"You're being stubborn."

She sighed. "Whoever crushed the trailer did it because they were afraid Jennings would talk to me. He's hurt..." Her voice caught. "He's hurt because of me."

The doctor emerged and had a quiet talk with Mrs. Jennings. It must have been good news, because she was smiling through her tears.

James breathed out an enormous sigh, and his hands went to her shoulders. "Don't do that to yourself, Mads. It's not your fault. You didn't cause that accident."

He called her Mads. Why did it soften something inside and make her want to save the memory of it like some kind of treasure?

"My uncle used to say that the truth shines a bright light, but it casts a dark shadow. This is as dark as it gets. I have no choice but to keep going."

He shook his head and straightened his shoulders. "Okay. If that's the way it's going to be, then you'd better get ready for two escorts, and one has dog breath."

He marched off toward the elevator. Madison was too stunned for a moment to follow. Then she trotted after him. Was it joy she felt? Simple relief? "But you're not on duty yet. You can't be my bodyguard."

He didn't even glance in her direction. "Watch me."

THIRTEEN

In spite of James's vigorous arguments, the chief would not allow him back on official duty until Thursday, the day of the annual police fund-raiser dance, though he consented to let him at least participate in the midnight bust of King's truck in an unofficial capacity.

"We could use another set of binoculars on this gig, and maybe Hawk's nose if the guy bolts, but that's it. Watch and report only, or you'll be off duty for a lot more than four days. Got it?"

James nodded. Limited duty was better than none at all. He continued to press the chief about Madison's protection detail until he slapped a file folder down on the desk in defeat.

"Why are you so bound and determined to be a bodyguard for this girl during your recovery time?"

James started to answer and then closed his mouth. Why was he anxious to personally keep eyes on Madison? Fear for her safety, sure, but any cop could provide protection. Why him? After a moment of soul searching, the answer surprised him. Deep down he knew that he was meant to standing with her, though he could not be much more specific as to the why of it. She was maddening, stubborn, illogical sometimes, but he could not deny the feeling that they were connected. "I… I just am," he said. *Lame, Harrison. You must have dented your brain in that trailer.*

"Oh, I get it." Chief Jones offered him a sly smile. "Listen kid, I've been down that road a time or two. You can't fight it. Just try not to get yourself killed over this redhead, okay?"

James felt himself go hot. "It's not like that…"

"Uh-huh," he said. "That's what I said, too, each time a gal turned my head."

"That isn't the case here."

"You just keep telling yourself that." Jones neatened the stack of papers. "Look, if you want to keep watch over your redhead on your own time, go ahead. I could use Marlton for other things. There was another break-in last night, but nothing was taken. The owners recently obtained a dog license for the little dog they adopted. So far, this matches the MO of all the homes that were broken in to but not robbed—all houses with new dogs. Marlton can stake out houses with new dogs in residence and investigate the theory that Earnshaw's murderer is searching for that missing puppy. Why, I have no idea."

She's not my redhead, he wanted to say, but he settled on a weak, "Thank you, sir."

He laughed. "Don't thank me, Harrison. I think you're going to find that your redhead is more of a problem than that couch-eating bloodhound. You know your brothers and sisters in blue have nicknamed her Little Red? Something about her attracting big bad wolves."

Great. He could only imagine what Madison would say when she heard that nickname.

"I think it suits her. Maybe you should get her a red cape so you can spot her more easily when she sneaks away next time." The chief was still laughing when James closed his office door.

Burning with embarrassment, he beat a hasty retreat out of the chief's office, reminding himself of his partial victory and trying to forget the humiliation. His redhead?

You can't fight it.

He didn't have to fight anything. Yes, she was an attractive woman with amazing spirit, but she didn't want a man in her life, and he couldn't blame her, after what her father had done. And he wasn't in the market for a girlfriend, especially one who couldn't stay out of trouble. He'd had a few girlfriends over the years, but not serious, and he intended to remain painfully single until he could be sure, completely sure, that he could trust himself to choose the right one. *And you just might be an old man by the time you get that nailed down.* He had plenty to do in the meantime—killers to be caught, a rascally dog partner to manage, and the need to sock away what little money he could to buy back the family ranch.

His balance restored, he was surprised to find Madison in the lobby with an irate Carrie. Uh-oh. He'd arrived just in time.

Catching sight of James, Carrie shoved her glasses up in frustration. "This lady is thorough, I'll give her that."

Thorough as Hawk on the trail, he thought. "That she is."

Carrie stapled a stack of papers with an emphatic whack of her palm. "But I told her I won't track down

Frances Andrews's cell phone number for her. It's not right."

Madison had the decency to look chagrined. "I wouldn't have asked, except no one is answering at the bridal salon, and I'm sure Frances is ready to talk to me. She was just reluctant at the hospital."

"Thanks, Carrie," James said, giving her a sympathetic look. "We'll let you get your work done, and I owe you a coffee."

"Thank you," she said to James. "You're my new best friend."

The woman now known as Little Red to all Desert Valley cops twirled a paper clip between her fingers. He sighed. "Come with me and we'll pay a visit to Frances at her home," he told her as they left the building.

"I can drive myself. My car's out front."

"No, you're coming with me. I'm your protection detail again."

"Why? You drew the short straw?"

No, it's because you're my *redhead, according to the chief.* He wasn't about to tell her he'd argued for the job. Instead he went to the passenger side and opened the door for her. Hawk was happy to settle into the backseat after he'd given Madison a lick on the back of the neck. She wiped it away with a giggle.

He could only watch her in wonder, this woman who was part giggly girl, part danger magnet and 100 percent fascinating. Little Red. Oh boy.

She felt him watching her. "What?"

He turned on the car. "Nothing."

She checked her phone, eyes opening wide in surprise.

"I can't believe this," she said.

James waited.

She looked from her phone to him. “My sister is meeting up with your brother at the dance?”

“It’s not a date.”

Madison worried her lower lip between her teeth. “I didn’t realize they’d hit it off so quickly.”

“Me neither.”

“My sister is just thinking they’re friends, not anything more. Is that…?” She wriggled on the seat and tried again. “Are you sure that’s how your brother sees it?”

“I haven’t talked to him about it.” It could have been a conversation plucked right from high school, but he wasn’t about to comment further after the turn their conversation had taken the previous night.

“Really?” Her nose crinkled. “I thought you would have warned him away from my sister by now.”

He felt a stab of guilt. At some level, her earlier accusation when she’d labeled him a hypocrite held a grain of truth. How could she be expected to let go of the past and learn to trust when he’d thrown it in her face while trying to look out for Sterling? He let out a breath. “I’m protective of my brother.”

“And I’m protective of Kate.” An awkward silence unrolled between them. “I guess seeing each other at the dance doesn’t really mean anything, right?” she asked.

“Right. I mean, everyone in town is invited. You, too.” He flashed on an image of Madison dressed to the nines, catching the eye of every man in the room, especially his own. He imagined that she’d be enveloped in a delicate scent, something fresh and woodsy, wearing a gown that would enhance the color of her hair. He blinked. What was the matter with him? “Everyone is invited, single or with a date." Had he said *date* aloud? Would she leap to the wrong conclusion? "I'm going stag, of course. I'll be on duty." His words were flopping around like fish out of water. He fixed his eyes on the road and hoped she hadn't noticed.

"You sure it's not going to be dangerous?"

Not for the civilian guests, he thought.

It was as if she read his mind. "Oh, right," she said. "You're hoping for a little danger."

He didn't answer as they pulled up at the bridal-shop owner's residence, a single-level house at the end of a dry gravel road. Relieved to be saved from a conversation that was as uncomfortable as his feelings, he hastened from the car.

Madison was already knocking on Frances's door by the time he'd loosed Hawk. There was no answer, so she tried ringing the bell.

She raised her hand to knock again when she stopped and turned to him, fingers on her lips. "I think I heard something," she whispered.

Now he could hear it, too, raised voices from the backyard area. Angry voices. He put his hand on his gun.

"Stay here," he said without any hope that she would actually do what he told her. Pressing his back to the wall, he skirted the house and headed for the backyard just in time to hear a crash.

Madison stayed as far behind James as she could make herself, but at the sound of the crash, both she and Hawk geared up to a jog. James darted around the corner first.

She skidded to a stop at a tiled patio with a fire pit

in the middle and several worn wooden chairs scattered around. The fire licked softly, puffing a faint scent of smoke into the air.

Odd to use a fire pit at midday, Madison thought, when it was already approaching eighty degrees.

Frances was crouched over a broken flowerpot, gathering up the shards. Her son, Tony, stood with his arms crossed, face red with anger.

After checking out the scene, James took his hand away from his gun. "I'm sorry to intrude, ma'am."

Frances leaped to her feet. "What are you doing here?"

"We knocked on the front door," he said, "and then I heard something break. Is everything okay?"

Hawk trotted over to Tony and began to lick his hands.

Frances eyed James and Madison warily. "We were just...arguing, and I knocked this pot over. We're fine."

"No, we're not," Tony said. Though he continued to rub Hawk behind the ears, his gaze was hostile, fixed upon his mother. "I'm not leaving Desert Valley. My friends are here. That's what we are arguing about. She wants to send me away."

Frances heaved a weary sigh. "To go stay with my sister in Tucson, just until things here are more settled."

"Because you're scared of Myron Falkner?" Madison asked.

"That's the dude that I nicknamed Brick?" Tony asked.

Madison nodded.

Frances looked nervous. "You're going to be better off with Aunt Rhoda," she said. "The reason isn't important."

"Yes it is, Mom," Tony said, turning to James. "If she won't tell you, then I will."

"Anthony William," Frances snapped. "Don't you dare disobey. I want you to go inside and stay there."

"I'm not a child, Mom," he said. "You can't put me in time-out like you did when I was five years old. They already know the guy's been harassing you." Tony looked at James. "He keeps her in line by threatening to hurt me."

"They aren't just threats." Frances gripped one of the pottery shards as if it would somehow protect her. Her glance shifted to the empty lot next to her property. The dry grass was knee-high. The shrubs had grown tall enough to create the perfect screen. "He might be watching right now."

Madison steeled herself against a shiver that crept up her spine. It was as if she could feel his hands pressed to the pillow, sealing off her oxygen, and hear the creaking of the trailer roof as it slowly crept down to crush her. "You have to tell us or he might never be caught."

She shook her head. "No. We can't talk to you. Go away, please."

"At the hospital you were ready," Madison pressed. "What's changed since then?"

She looked away, lips pressed tight together.

"Mom, this can't go on forever." Tony jammed his hands in his pockets. "Falkner, or whatever his name is, comes to the salon once a month to demand money." Francis tried to interrupt, but he ignored his mother's protests. "It used to be fifty dollars, seventy-five, petty stuff, but now it's five hundred a month or bad things start to happen. We tried not paying once, but he made good on his threats."

James frowned. "What happened?"

"Broken windows at the salon, flat tires on the car. Lately, though, when you started nosing around, things changed. Falkner said if we talked to you or the cops, they would up the ante."

"They?" Madison pressed. "Who is Falkner's boss?"

"I don't know." Tony looked at his mother. "Do you, Mom? If you have any idea, you gotta tell them."

Frances shook her head, lines of weariness grooved into her face. "I don't know, but it's someone who has connections, because Falkner's afraid of him."

Madison looked at James. Bruce King.

"And Falkner's hitting up other businesses, too, isn't he?" she asked.

Frances nodded. "Bill Baxter at the Tool Corral, the flower shop until he squeezed them dry and they closed, and..." Her voice broke. "Albert Jennings. We were friends since I moved to town twenty years ago, right after my divorce. He was a huge help to me. He'd fix things for nothing and let me pay when I could. His wife would send over pies and jars of jelly, and we did some quilting together." Her face crumpled. "I can't believe he's hurt. I'm going to do whatever it takes to help them."

James's posture was tight with anger. "Jennings finally said no more?"

Frances sighed. "He'd been getting pressure from Falkner for too long, and he'd had enough. He told me he was going to end it once and for all. I begged him to be careful." She started to weep silently. "I've been so afraid, for such a long time. I came to Desert Valley because I wanted a good life for my son, in a small town where people cared about one another."

Tony put his hand on her shoulder. "Mom, it's okay," he said gently. "Now that it's out in the open, they can arrest him." He looked at James. "Right? You've got enough to arrest him now and put him away?"

"As soon as we find him," James said.

Something was niggling at Madison. "But what made you change your mind about talking to me before? Did he threaten to hurt Tony again?"

"It was more than a threat this time." Frances shot a look at her son.

He nodded. "Tell them, Mom. It's all right. They will believe you."

Frances sucked in a breath. "I was getting ready to take Tony to school—he has one of those late-start days today—and I noticed his backpack was not where he usually dumps it."

Tony shrugged. "I'm not very tidy."

"Anyway, something made me unzip and check."

"She was snooping."

"And there was a packet inside, white powder in a plastic bag."

James let out a whoosh of air.

"Drugs?" Madison could hardly believe what she was hearing. "What kind?"

She raised her hands. "I don't know. Cocaine? Heroin? I'm not an expert on that kind of thing, but I know Falkner planted it in Tony's backpack so when he went to school, there would be some kind of telephone tip and he'd be suspended. He promised it would happen if I talked to you, and now..." Her eyes filled again. "Who knows what he's going to do to us after this?"

"We've got the whole department on the lookout now," James reassured her. "I'll have a patrol car drive by your house and your business every couple of hours. He's not going to come back."

"Yes, he will." Madison could see the glint of fear in Frances's eyes. "He'll do what his boss tells him to. Don't you see? In order to plant those drugs, he was in my house. In…my…house while we were asleep." Her throat convulsed, and Madison shared her horror. "He could have done anything. That's why I want Tony to go stay with his aunt."

"I'm not missing the last few weeks of school. Gonna go to the waterslides with my friends and there's a field day and fun stuff. I like it here, and I'm not going to run away."

"Fine," she said, exasperated. "For one week, then. I'll call the school and tell them and get your work. Please, Tony."

Tony snorted. "That's just caving in. You always told me to stand up to bullies."

Frances put her hands on Tony's skinny shoulders. "Your father walked away from both of us, and I've tried my best to raise you. Please do this for me. I can't keep the salon going and worry every moment about you."

There was a long pause. "Just for a week?" Tony repeated, more to James than his mother.

"I promise you I'll do everything I can to put this guy behind bars," James said. "We have a good lead that might take us somewhere tonight."

Madison's pulse ticked up. He knew something, something that he hadn't shared with her, cagey cop.

"All right." Tony slammed open the back door. "I'll go pack."

Frances let out an enormous sigh of relief. "Thank you for helping convince him."

"What did you do with the drugs?" James asked.

"I burned them in the fire pit."

With a look of horror, James ran to the pit. Madison followed. The flames curled around a blackened mess at the bottom. There was no possible way any of it could be used for evidence. Sighing, he photographed it, anyway.

As they returned to the front, Hawk was snuffling every inch, particularly interested in a spot to the side of the driveway covered in white carpet roses. James looked but spotted nothing unusual.

"Come," James told his dog. Hawk ignored him. Madison got into the car while James went to check on Hawk again.

After what seemed like a long while, James loaded Hawk in the car, an odd expression on his face. He fetched a plastic bag from the trunk, and fiddled with it for a minute before putting it into his pocket.

Frances leaned in to talk through the open passenger window. "Please arrest Falkner and make him tell you who he works for. I'll never be safe until that happens, and neither will my son."

"I'll arrange for you to have some protection."

She shook her head. "No, I can take care of myself. Just catch Falkner."

James assured her he would, and then he started the car.

"Never be safe," Madison echoed. As they drove past the field of long grass, she wondered if Falkner was out there, watching, ready to exact retribution on Frances and her son for talking to her.

Or maybe he'd skip that step and make sure he ended things permanently.

FOURTEEN

James was lost in thought on the way back to the campground. Pain whacked against his temples in a regular rhythm, and he longed to rip the bandage off his arm and yank out the stitches, which itched like crazy. Madison watched him warily as they drove back, and he offered only short responses to her queries. He wanted to get to a place where he could think, to decide what to do about the suspicion that had lodged itself in his mind like a hammered nail.

He pulled up at his cabin just before five, thoughts still zinging madly through his overworked brain.

She was out of the car before he could open the door for her. He let Hawk out.

"Are you going to tell me what's bothering you?" Madison demanded. "Does it have to do with the plastic bag you put into your pocket?'

Was he going to tell her? It was a concern too strange to be broached, yet. "I'm…"

She waited, eyebrows raised, lips quirked into a neat bow.

Seconds ticked by. "…going to cook," he finished, opening the cabin door and climbing inside.

"Cook?" She poked in her head, face lit with astonishment. "We've got to catch a killer and there's something going on tonight you haven't told me about, not to mention this police dance looming in the not-too-distant future, and you're going to go all Betty Crocker?"

He threw a towel over his shoulder and washed his hands. "I think better when I cook."

She gaped. "You're crazy."

He handed her a cutting board. "Are you going to help or call me names?"

She stared from the cutting board to James and back again. He almost laughed at the confusion on her face, which made her look all of eighteen years old.

"Are we making beef stew again?"

"No. I'm giving up on that for now. I've got a freezer full of the stuff back at the condo."

"What do you want me to do?"

He handed her an onion and a zucchini. "Chop and dice."

With a mumbled comment that he did not hear, but which was probably about the state of his sanity, she set to work, peeling and chopping with precision.

He worked on the eggs, cracking them neatly. He greased a heavy iron pan before he mixed in her chopped vegetables. The sizzle when he poured the eggs in comforted him, and it pleased him to have another person to cook for. When the frittata was on the heat, he set her to watching it as he sliced potatoes in another pan and heated oil. While the potatoes were sizzling to a golden brown, he turned the problem over and over in his mind.

He needed someone to talk to, someone whip smart, as interested in the situation as he was, and most importantly, not a cop. No, most importantly, someone he could trust, someone he would trust himself with. But how could that be Madison? A reporter of all things? Yet deep down his gut was telling him to do exactly that. *Lord, don't let me trust the wrong person.*

By the time he'd fed Hawk, slid two plates of frittata and fried potatoes on the table and poured glasses of iced tea for them both, Madison was nearly wriggling out of her seat.

"Okay," she said. "Point one, you're a great cook. This smells incredible."

"Thank you. You should come when I'm making gumbo."

"Point two, you have much better restraint than I do."

"True."

"Point three? If you don't tell me what's up, I think I'm going to explode."

He laughed. "After we pray." He caught her fingers in his and said a simple prayer for the blessing of food and company. The blessing of Madison Coles sitting in his kitchen, he added silently, because he could never hide anything from God, anyway. Her soft amber gaze made his stomach tighten when he opened his eyes.

"That was nice," she said quietly. "I haven't shared a meal and a prayer with a…friend in a long time."

He could not hold back from stroking her hand, the skin satiny soft, the long fingers strong but so much more delicate than his own. It was nice—more than nice. *Dangerous territory*, he thought as he let go and picked up his fork and took a bite.

She was right. He was a good cook, he thought immodestly.

She nibbled on the frittata. "Excellent, but I can't

wait any longer. What's got you utilizing cooking therapy?"

The point of no return. He pulled a plastic bag out of his pocket and held it up it so she could see. "It was stuck to Hawk's ear. I think he picked it up nosing around the bushes by Frances's driveway."

"What is it?" she said, peering close to what was inside. "Looks like red plastic."

It was no more than a scrap, a half inch across. If Hawk hadn't shown such an interest in Frances's rosebushes, he never would have noticed it. "Yeah. If you look close, you can see a tiny black line from a printed letter, I think."

"I know I should be picking something up here, but I'm drawing a blank. What are you thinking?"

The moment had come. "Madison, this is something I can't tell a person who is going to use it in any way. I might be totally wrong."

Her mouth quirked. "Are you trying to decide whether or not to confide in me?"

"If I tell you, it can't be cop to reporter."

"What will it be, then?"

What would it be? His mouth felt dry, his pulse heavy. "Friend," he said finally. "A friend who will help me think it through."

"Friend?" She was a little bit surprised and pleased that the friendship feeling wasn't just one-sided. "After all the trouble I've caused you? And your past relationships with reporters? Why would you consider me a friend?" Again that direct gaze that both disarmed and excited him.

He let God pick out the words from the million phrases muddling about in his mind. "You love God.

You love your family. Same as me. The other stuff isn't important anymore."

"But I've made enemies in this town. Your brother counts himself on that list."

"I was remembering when we were back in the trailer, with Jennings."

Her face twisted.

"You held his hand. You comforted him, a man you didn't even know. After what you'd been through just then and in your life, your instinct was to care for a stranger."

Her eyes grew misty. "And so was yours."

"Like I said, if you take away the badge and the notepad, we're the same."

She gazed at him for a long time. Then a slow smile illuminated her face, erasing all the shadows from the room, it seemed to him, and tracing a path through the air and into someplace deep inside his heart.

"Okay, then," she said. "Friend to friend." With a final squeeze of his hand, she let go. "What's on your mind?"

"I may be completely wrong." He blew out a breath. "I want to be wrong."

She was surprisingly patient, waiting for him to say it.

He fingered the plastic bag, peering at the red bit inside. "This looks an awful lot like the kind of tape we use to secure drugs in our evidence room."

Her eyebrows arched, but still she did not speak.

"It wasn't stuck on Hawk's fur until we got to Frances's place. I'm sure of it. So what if..." he tapped the fork on the table. "What if Falkner took the drugs out of a sealed evidence bag before he planted them in Tony's backpack?"

"But how would he..." Her shoulders went stiff and straight. "Are you saying he got it from a cop?"

"No. Absolutely not." His tone was harder than he'd meant. "It's not a cop. It couldn't be."

"And how do you know that for sure?"

"Because they're all good men and women doing a job that could get them killed at any minute. It wasn't a cop. I'm saying the thought occurred to me that someone might have taken it from our evidence room for Falkner to use. We've had people working on the fundraiser, helpers in and out a lot."

They both sat stock still for a long moment. "So it might be that Myron Falkner is working for Bruce King, who's got a mole in the police department. Who could get that kind of access?"

"Pretty much anyone around the department—volunteers, technicians. Let's face it—we're a small-town police department, and protocols aren't that strict. Even visiting reporters might be able to get in unnoticed if they were good at lock picking."

She held up her hands. "Don't look at me. I can't even work my bicycle lock without help. Have you smelled any whiff of impropriety? Heard any rumors?"

"No, but I'm new. I wouldn't be the one to hear it. I could talk to Ryder and Shane, but..."

She nodded. "But once you've dropped that bomb, it's hard to undo the damage if you're wrong."

"Exactly. I know and trust my fellow cops, but as far as the others go, I don't want to impugn anybody's reputation unless I'm one hundred percent sure. Maybe this isn't evidence tape after all. Could be I'm just making things up in my mind."

She toyed with the rim of her glass. "Hear me out on something without getting defensive, okay?"

He grinned. "No promises, but I'll do my best."

"Okay. I did some digging when I was trying to convince my editor to let me do a bigger story. A couple of years back, Veronica Earnshaw's brother, Lee, was arrested for participating in a gas-station robbery. He's never stopped claiming to anyone who would listen that he was framed by someone working for the police department."

He sat back. "His claims don't hold much weight with me or anyone in the DVPD. Criminals lie. Jails are full of innocent characters who were framed. Just ask them." Had that been defensive? Probably, but it was the truth, and she needed to hear it.

"So Lee Earnshaw is in prison…"

"Where he belongs per his conviction," James said.

"All right. How do we prove that Bruce King is the big boss and he has a mole in the police department?"

"One thing at a time. We got a tip that King is moving a shipment tonight through Sunset Gorge, and we're going to bust him. Best case is that Falkner's driving the truck. Worst case, it's some other lackey we can squeeze until he rolls over on King. Once we've got Falkner or King, it's a matter of time until we get the mole."

"All right. So where do we go from here?" She checked her watch. "It's only six thirty."

He yawned. "Feels like midnight already. Anyway, I assume you want to ride along tonight?"

"You assumed correctly, and while we're waiting, I'll

see if I can find out anything else about Myron Falkner that might lead to a connection to someone in the PD."

James was about to interject when she held up a hand. "Don't worry. I am going to be careful about it." Her voice went soft.

He was grateful that she seemed to understand. "When I'm back on duty, I'll find a reason to poke around the evidence room and see what I can turn up." He picked up his plate and carried it to the sink. "You know, I could be completely wrong about this tape."

"And you could be completely right."

In this case, he thought to himself, *I hope I'm not.*

Madison helped with the dishes, and they took Hawk for his evening walk. Bats scuttled through the sky, chirping and diving for mosquitos. The air was crisp and full of evening scents, which Hawk could not get enough of. She knew James was hurting physically, as his movements were slow and he sucked in a breath when Hawk pulled sharply on the leash. She marveled at his strength. It was not long ago the guy was nearly crushed to death, and he'd been going full tilt since he'd bullied his way out of the hospital. Here he was, hauling a hundred-pound dog around. She knew that it would take more than a trailer collapsing on him to keep James from tending to his four-legged partner. The dog-human bond was something of a marvel.

They returned to the cabin, and James knelt on the floor and began to brush Hawk, grimacing as the movement pained him.

She went to him. "Let me give it a try." He handed over the brush, and she set to work. James sat on the couch, watching.

"Not bad for an amateur."

"I've got some experience. My dad let us take care of the neighbor's dog once when they went on vacation. It was a little schnauzer, and she was convinced the brush was her evil nemesis." She felt the familiar tension of happiness and grief at the memory. Moments of joy with her sister, viewed through the lens of a later time, when she'd realized her life was a lie. But as she began to stroke the brush along the Hawk's flanks, she felt the pain of the past dissolve into a strange haze of contentment. Right here, right now, she was in a place of safety with a friend, a man who had trusted her. Strangest of all, she'd decided that she trusted him, too.

As a friend, she chided herself. *Friends.*

"Thank you for making me dinner," she said, still stroking the brush over Hank's thick body. "And for letting me in on your thoughts." *Letting me in and trusting me. I won't betray you.*

Receiving no response, she turned to find him asleep on the couch, breathing softly. She continued to brush Hawk and gaze at James, the planes of his face, strong chin, thick lashes, the scratch that ran across his forehead. In sleep he looked younger. Perhaps in his unconscious state he could let go of the burden of bringing King and Falkner to justice, juggling his suspicions and protecting her. She offered a prayer that he'd sleep deeply and well. When Hawk was sufficiently groomed, she put the brush away and found a blanket. It was old and handmade, squares of different colored fabrics stitched together by some patient hand. She draped it over James, intending to wake him if he was still sleeping when they needed to leave.

On impulse, she leaned down and pressed her lips

to his temple. He sighed in his sleep, and for a fraction of a second, she wondered how it would feel be kissed properly by James Harrison, to accept love and give it to a God-fearing man.

Friendship, not love, she scolded herself silently before she let herself out, shutting the door behind her.

FIFTEEN

"How's the story coming along, Mads?" Uncle Ray asked. She heard him breathing hard into the phone, pictured his heavy frame slouched in the worn recliner that he refused to replace. He did not do anything quickly, and he hadn't returned her call until after ten o'clock.

"It's coming. I think things are about to break wide-open here," she said, gazing out the window into the night. There was no sign of movement from James's cabin.

"I looked into that past case you asked about."

"You did? Oh, that's right." Madison felt a swipe of guilt that she'd commissioned her uncle to pry into James's family history when she'd first arrived in town, curiosity about the blue-eyed cop needling her. *But that was before we were friends*, she told herself, and it didn't hurt to know things. He'd probably researched her life, too, and that had given him plenty to chew on. "What did you find out?"

"Not much more than you already knew. Paige Berg, good kid, honor student, accuses Sterling Harrison, local bad boy, of raping her. He's eighteen. He goes to jail to await trial. She waits too long before making the accusation to present any physical evidence, but she produces a witness who said he heard her calling for help the night of the alleged rape. Later we find out it's a friend who lied for her, and she made the whole thing up in the first place. Sterling is released. Some folks continue to believe that Sterling intimidated her into recanting and are still convinced he's guilty. The Harrison family spends a bundle on legal fees, and the ranch is sold a couple of months after Sterling is released."

She groaned. Innocent until the public decides you're guilty. "Thanks for looking into it, Uncle Ray. I guess it doesn't much matter anymore."

"Never hurts to know." It was another of Uncle Ray's mantras.

"I'll be back in Tuckerville soon. We'll have dinner."

He paused. "With Kate?"

"I hope so."

"She sent me a birthday card," he said.

Another good sign. "I'm glad."

"Me, too. I'll make one of the lasagnas with extra cheese my doc says I shouldn't eat."

"That sounds great." She was about to tell him goodnight when he interrupted.

"This Paige girl—did you know she was James's girlfriend? Wonder how that makes a guy feel? To introduce your brother to the girl who's going to ruin his life?"

Madison's heart squeezed. "Yes, I knew." How did that make James feel? Guilt-ridden, crippled with agony. It could take him a lifetime to learn to trust a woman again.

Yet he'd trusted her.

She thanked her uncle and hung up. Her fingers

found the little drawer and she opened it, pulling out the necklace and tracing the words engraved on the metal.

> Behold, I will do a new thing; now it shall spring forth; shall ye not know it?

God was teaching James how to trust himself again, to let go of the past and walk a new path. Could He… was it possible for Madison to learn such a thing about trust? Clutching the necklace, she fought back the thrill of hope and fear. A light turned on in the window of James's cabin, and she saw his silhouette as he passed by the glass. She felt drawn to him like a moth seeking out the golden glow in the darkness. *I won't betray you, James.*

What was she doing? What were these strange, unaccustomed notions that banged around in her heart? She remembered her father watching her feeble school performances, the proud dad smiling from ear to ear. Hadn't she trusted him completely? Believed with all the rest of the world that he was what he appeared to be? He was her dad, a criminal, the supporter of his girls and the man who murdered their mother. How could he be all those things? How could she ever trust someone with her future again?

The fear grew too strong and, with shaking fingers, she slowly returned the necklace to the drawer. It was time to focus on other things.

She pulled on a Windbreaker, then stowed her phone in one pocket and her notebook in the other. Hawk was already prancing around the car, eager to greet Madison.

"Hey, I'm sorry I fell asleep," James said. If the lighting had been better, she probably would have seen him blush.

"You needed the rest."

"Yeah, but it's really bad manners to nod off in front of your company. My mother would be horrified."

"I don't hold it against you. My Uncle Ray can sleep standing up. I've actually seen him lean against the wall and doze. It defies the laws of nature."

They drove out of camp, and James took a steeply sloped road she hadn't known was there.

"Why Sunset Gorge?" she asked. "Seems an out-of-the-way route for King's truck."

"It eventually connects to the freeway, where a truck wouldn't be noticed. In a small town like Desert Valley, people might pay attention to a big vehicle rumbling through the streets at midnight."

"What do you think King is planning?"

"Tipster said he's moving a truck full of stolen cigarettes through town on his way to bigger cities, probably, where they can be quietly distributed and sold at a hefty profit." His fingers drummed on the steering wheel.

"What's our role?"

He shot up an eyebrow. "Ours? Hawk and I are on strict watch-and-report since I'm not officially back on duty. That means you aren't to get out of this car, okay? Since you're even less official than I am?"

"Don't stray into the woods," she said in a dramatic sotto voce. "Got it."

He threw back his head and laughed, looking more like a little boy than a cop.

"Am I that funny?"

"No." He shook his head, the smile still on his face.

"You just reminded me of Little Red Riding Hood for a minute."

"I always thought she could have taken care of that wolf by herself if she'd had a mind to."

The smile vanished, and he shot her a warning look. "Let's not try any heroics, okay? This isn't a fairy tale."

She smiled. "Copy that, Officer Harrison, but you should be telling yourself the same thing."

James drove to the top of the slope, where they would have a clear view of anyone traveling the winding road below. He parked the car near the cover of some monstrous shrubs and listened to the radio chatter, chiming in with his location. She was only half listening, thinking about what King's reaction would be when the cops arrested his driver. Maybe that would finally crack his smug exterior.

"Little Red secure?" a voice she recognized as Dennis Marlton's asked.

"What?" she demanded, snapping to attention as the pieces fell into place. "Little Red? That's my cop nickname?"

James looked away. "Uh…well…um…yes, ma'am," he finally admitted, still not meeting her eye.

"You tell Officer Marlton that Little Red is here and ready to catch herself a big bad wolf."

James laughed so loud she could not resist joining in. How lovely, how precious just to share a hearty laugh with another person. She basked in the rare warmth of the moment. When he'd gotten control of himself and wiped his eyes, he radioed back. "Affirmative. Little Red secure."

She was about to ask what else the cops saw fit to say about her when they heard the distant rumble of an engine. James was instantly alert, night-vision binoculars to his eyes.

"White truck, Washington plates," Ryder said quietly into the radio. "Heading north toward you, Bucks."

"Copy that. On him," Bucks said.

James peered through the binoculars before he handed them to Madison. "Too far away to see clearly. Ryder, can you ID the driver?"

"Negative."

Her nerves tightened into a ball. "Where will you make the arrest?"

"Bucks and Marlton will stop him after he goes about a mile, when he gets to the clearing right before the final climb to our position. We'll alert if he takes off down a side road. Ryder will bring up the rear."

It seemed so straightforward. She could not help but compose an article in her mind.

> Desert Valley Police seized a truck carrying a load of illicit cigarettes being transported through town. The truck is owned by Desert Valley resident Bruce King. The driver, Myron Falkner, was arrested for outstanding warrants and suspected involvement in a protection racket that victimized local businesses.

It would be the ultimate satisfaction for Madison when Frances and Bill found out they were finally free of the abuse. The plan seemed cut-and-dried, but a detail still niggled at her. "Who was the tipster?" she asked.

"Anonymous. Called in from a pay phone in town."

She knew he could tell what she was thinking. His expression was troubled—that much was clear even in the darkness. If there was somebody inside the department working for King, then the whole bust might be a diversion or some kind or a trap. But for whom? Though she turned it over every which way in her brain, she could make no sense of it as she watched the slow and steady progress of the truck grinding up the grade toward them.

James rolled the front window down partway, and the thin night air carried the sound of the approaching truck. Hawk stood on the backseat, so James rolled down his window a couple of inches, too. The dog shoved his fleshy face into the gap and happily slobbered all over the glass as he snuffled in millions more scents that Madison could dream of.

"He's slowing," Ryder said via the radio.

James was tracking the progress. "What's he doing? He can't possibly have spotted Bucks and Marlton. He's not close enough." Yet the truck eased to a stop a hundred yards or so before it reached the plateau where the two cops were poised to make the arrest.

"Maybe he's figured out the cops are waiting for him," she murmured. *Maybe he's got some inside information.* Abruptly the truck turned off down a path that Madison hadn't seen at first.

"He's heading east," James yelled into his radio. "Taking a cut through."

"Copy that," Ryder said. "I'll stop him at the bottom. Bucks and Marlton, stay in position in case he changes his mind and reverses."

Bucks and Marlton both radioed to confirm.

James spoke into the radio. "Following him down, Ryder, toward your twenty."

"I thought you were supposed to watch and report only."

"I'm not leaving Ryder without backup." He gripped the wheel tightly, easing the vehicle slowly down the slope, gravel and twigs crunching under the tires. "I'll stay back far enough that he won't spot us."

Madison strained against the seat belt, trying to keep the white truck in sight. It disappeared for a while as the swell of land and trees obstructed her view. Hawk whined from the backseat.

"There," James said. Their vehicle had just topped a sharply peaked section of road, and the truck was barreling down the slope below them.

"He's seen us. No need for stealth anymore." James started up the lights and siren and took off in pursuit, alerting Ryder, whom they could barely make out at the bottom, his vehicle blocking the road.

Madison thought with a squeeze of panic that the truck was going to ram right into Ryder's car. Her breath froze in her lungs.

Ryder was out of the vehicle, aiming his weapon at the truck. She heard the crack of a gun being fired, which made her jump. Glass shattered. James did not even flinch. He pressed the accelerator and they flew on, careening over the ground.

The truck was between Ryder and James when it suddenly took a sharp turn to the left.

"The bridge," James shouted, pulling his reluctant vehicle into a tight turn. Hawk skidded to one side of the car, barking.

"What bridge?" she managed over the violent jostling.

"There used to be an old wooden bridge that spanned

the deepest part of the gorge but it's ruined, rotted away," he called.

Madison felt her heart thudding in her throat. "Then what's he doing driving in that direction? Does he not know the bridge is out?"

James didn't answer. Ryder joined them now, lights flashing, the siren adding to the noise.

"Hold on," James shouted as they raced toward the rotting bridge. "I'm going to try to get in front of him."

Flooring the gas pedal, he inched closer to the passenger side. "Can you see who it is?"

A glimpse of bald head under a cockeyed black hat, the flat nose and cruel mouth. How well she remembered the face of the man who had repeatedly attacked her. "It's Myron Falkner," she yelled back.

Just then Falkner cranked the wheel, and the truck swiped to the side and clipped James on the front fender, causing the car to buck and shimmy.

James fought to keep control. The car veered dangerously toward a bank of massive trees before he pulled it back again. James tried a second time to move past the truck. Once more Falkner yanked the truck to the side, smashing it into their cruiser. There was a pop, and the car wobbled and shied.

"Took out the front tire," he shouted. "Hold on."

He hit the brakes, trying to keep the car from skidding on the loose rock. Only a hundred yards from the trees. Madison clung to the door handle so tightly her fingernails bit into her palm. Still fighting against the wild spinning of the tires, James managed to slow the car just as they slid into the shadow of the trees.

"Stay here," he said, ripping off his seat belt. "I'm going on foot."

"No," she said. "James, wait for Marlton and Bucks."

"Ryder needs backup, now." He fixed her with an intense look that made her realize just how much dedication and self-sacrifice it took to pin on a badge every single day. For his police family, he would face any danger, any threat. No wonder he would not believe, even for a moment, that there was a cop behind the protection ring. "Keep Hawk here. He's not trained for this."

"I'm not going to say 'be careful.'" She took a breath. "You know there are wolves in the woods."

"Copy that, Red."

Then he tore away into the darkness.

Madison's own pulse was so loud in her ears that it almost drowned out the sound of Hawk's panting.

SIXTEEN

James ran over the uneven ground, ignoring the stab of pain in his ribs. He shouted into the radio as he went. Marlton and Bucks responded, and he could hear the wail of sirens as they hurtled down the mountain.

Ryder's vehicle had just reached the top when it stopped abruptly. He was close enough to hear Ryder's door being thrown open and the bark from Titus, his dog in the backseat. James forced his legs to move faster, sweat pouring down his face as he covered the last few yards. Gunshots ripped through the air.

Electrified, he pulled his gun and sprinted for all he was worth, head ducked low, toward Ryder's car.

He crashed to a halt on the ground next to Ryder, behind the cover of his open driver's door.

"You okay?" James panted.

"Yeah. He's a bad shot."

James breathed a silent prayer of thanks that he had not found his friend and Titus wounded or worse.

Ryder's front headlight exploded as Falkner shot at them again. Titus barked crazily.

"Down," Ryder commanded. James was grateful Madison and Hawk were safely away.

"I'll lay down some fire and see if we can't convince this guy he's outgunned." Ryder took aim with his Glock and squeezed off a couple of rounds, which punched holes into the driver's side door and shattered the side mirror.

They waited for a moment, tucked behind cover. Ryder nodded.

"Hands up and step out of the vehicle," James roared. "Right now, Falkner. You've got nowhere to go."

The silence seemed to last for an eternity, but it was probably no more than ten seconds. A vibration shook the ground, the squeal of car tires complaining against a sudden acceleration.

"What?" James said. Ryder's expression was blank with disbelief.

They peered through the window in time to see the white truck surge forward, bumping and shuddering.

"He's going for the bridge," Ryder said in utter astonishment.

The truck crashed through the danger signs warning that the bridge was closed. Surely Falkner would slow as the situation became clear, but the truck did not lose speed. Ryder and James scrambled from their shelter and raced after the careening vehicle.

"He's crazy," James said. "The guy's crazy. Where does he think he's going to go?"

With a roar, the truck shot over the worn wooden planking, which ripped to pieces under the weight.

They watched in open-mouthed shock as the truck tumbled through the air and down into the deep canyon, rolling and smashing against the rocks. With a final deafening bang, it hit the bottom, exploding into an orange ball of fire. An echo from the impact billowed back up from the depths. Ryder and James stared into the void.

Marlton and Bucks joined them, both panting, peering off into the gorge at the wreckage below.

"He drove off the bridge," Marlton said. "The guy just drove right off the end of a busted-up bridge. Why would he do that?"

Bucks shook his head, holstering his gun and wiping his forehead. "Don't know, but it saves us the trouble of booking him, I guess."

James's stomach convulsed as he looked down into the ruins. He felt sickened at the death, angry that justice would not be served, confused that what was to be an easy arrest had gone so horribly wrong. "We're going to have to get down there," he said. "Falkner might have survived."

"No." Ryder returned to his car to quiet Titus. "That's a job for the fire department guys. Falkner couldn't have survived the crash or the explosion. And no one is going down there. Am I understood?"

His tone brooked no disagreement.

"Copy that."

James turned away from the mess to see Madison standing in the moonlight with Hawk at the end of his leash. He went to her.

"Don't tell me I should have stayed in the car. I did my best, but Hawk was about ready to break a window." She searched his face. "He drove over the cliff? On purpose?"

"Looks that way." He sucked in a deep breath and groaned as the effort pulled on his ribs. He pressed a hand to his side.

"Are you okay?"

"Physically, yeah, I guess."

"But…"

"I wanted to get him. I didn't want him to kill himself."

She traced a hand over his forearm. "There was no way for you to guess he was going to do that."

The moon darkened her eyes to deep black pools, and he found himself wanting to fall deep into them, to forget what had just happened and slip into the comfort of her understanding. Her touch was gentle on his arm, tracing her way to his hand. He had no words, but he laced his fingers through hers, and they mourned together for a moment, grieved a life lost to evil.

"At least…at least it's over," she said. "He won't be able to hurt Frances or Tony or Bill Baxter anymore. You got your man."

"Yeah." Got him, but not in the way James or any of them had wanted. He watched additional police cars roll up, the bustle of activity as the scene was secured. His body ached, and he felt light-headed from the effort and adrenaline. As much as he wanted to go add his observations to those of the other officers as they pieced their statements together for the chief, he could not shake a feeling of unease deep down. He sat on the front fender of his car and tried to get the echo of the crash out of his mind.

Madison was deep in thought. Why had Falkner stopped and changed directions instead of heading up to Marlton and Bucks? What if he'd been tipped off that he was heading toward an arrest? Why not leave the truck and try to lose them on foot? He had no way of knowing there was a bloodhound there to assist, unless someone had informed him of that fact. But an informant with that much knowledge about the police sting? It wasn't something a volunteer or technician would be privy to. A fiery discomfort traced its way through her body. James did not want to find out there was a bad cop working with Falkner. Loyalty could blind a person to the truth. She knew that for certain.

She was pacing now, Hawk following back and forth. James stared toward the edge of the canyon. "I wouldn't have thought Falkner was the kind of guy who would take his own life rather than go to jail again. Was he that scared of going to prison?"

"He didn't strike me as a man who was afraid of much."

What if things were not what they seemed to be? Maybe it was time for James to think like a reporter instead of a cop. She gazed at the ruts in the dirt left by the truck as it took Myron Falkner to his death.

James got up abruptly and went to his trunk.

She followed him. "What are you doing?"

"Just following a hunch," he said, calling for Hawk. "Let's go, boy. Time to earn your kibble."

Madison didn't have a clue what James was doing. His actions were even more incomprehensible when he took a plastic bag from his trunk and opened it, offering it to Hawk to sniff.

"What is that?" she asked, jogging along behind as Hawk took off, passing by the cluster of police cars.

"Scent article. The hat we picked up in the woods after Falkner tried to smother you in the hospital. The lab returned it when they were finished testing. The scent is still plenty strong enough for Hawk."

"Wait a minute," she said, stopping dead in her

tracks. "Are you implying...?" Since he didn't wait, she started trotting again and caught up.

"James?"

"I'm not implying, or suggesting, or hinting. I'm investigating," he said over his shoulder.

"But you think..."

He held up a hand, intent on his dog. "Hold that question. I'm about to go for a ride."

Hawk shivered as if he'd been doused in a bucket of cold water, let out a deafening bark and took off through a narrow slice of dried grass. Madison tried to process and follow at the same time. Did James think Falkner had faked his death? Perhaps leaped from the truck before it tumbled into the canyon?

It was more important what was running through Hawk's mind just then. The hound beelined through the grass, and James struggled to keep his footing as he was tugged along. She knew from James that the cool night air would help hold any scent in place, making it easier for the dog to track.

His nose was glued to the ground as he made his way along. Though the shrubs were clinging to her socks and imbedding burrs into her clothing, Hawk's droopy folds would protect him from such irritants.

Hawk stopped when he got to the edge of the trees. Down below, Madison heard the burble of water. James talked into his radio as Hawk strained ahead, baying. When James let him forward again, the dog raced down to the water and barked when James stopped him.

"Can Hawk follow the scent even in the water?"

"Yes," he said, voice low, "but he's probably picking it up from the other side, too."

Hawk lunged at the leash, letting loose a frustrated howl.

"What's wrong?" she whispered. "Why aren't you letting him follow?"

He tried to soothe the dog, who was not the least bit placated. "Hang on, Hawk. Slight delay."

"Why?" she asked again.

Then Ryder and Bucks arrived, and she understood. He was making sure that she was safely removed from the situation before he freed the dog. She gave James the same look she imagined Hawk gave him from time to time. "You're not going to let me go with you any farther, are you?"

"Can't. I'm sorry." He looked as if he really meant it. "Bucks will take you back home and stay with you until I get there."

She wanted to be angry that the chase had been interrupted. Even now, Falkner might be getting away if James's hunch was correct, yet James had brought it all to a grinding halt because it was not safe for her.

Hating to be put aside like a vulnerable child, she could hear in his voice that it was not a decision she could argue her way out of. The thought struck her like a thunderbolt. Above all things—the chase, a possible fugitive—he wanted her to be safe.

Warmth flooded through her. This man, determined as he was, cared about her deeply. She filed away the feeling and nodded. "Okay."

Ryder and his dog stayed with James, and Bucks stepped aside to allow her to return. She started back, wondering if James was still looking at her, silhouetted perfectly in the moonlight. Or would he be turned away now, focused on his mission? She risked a look and found him still with his face turned toward her, fully committed to his work, but with something else there, something more tender, reserved just for her.

Imagination, she told herself, but the uptick in her pulse continued. Other, darker thoughts crowded into her mind as she and Bucks hiked back. What if Falkner was out there waiting? He was armed, fully hidden perhaps, waiting in ambush for anyone daring enough to follow.

"Lord, please watch over James, Ryder, Titus and Hawk," she murmured.

"What did you say?" Bucks asked.

"Nothing." *A prayer*, she added to herself.

He kept up a good pace on their way back and didn't stop until they'd reached the cars. Marlton hastened up to them.

"How can James think anybody escaped from that wreck?" he demanded.

Bucks opened the passenger door for Madison. Marlton shot a look at her. "None of this is going in a story, right?"

Her face flushed. She had been forcing herself to resist texting her editor to tell him there was another story developing. She still wasn't sure why she hadn't sent the text, except that she knew James was in a delicate position. "No story. For now."

Marlton glared at her. "Keep it that way."

Bucks said something to Marlton that she couldn't make out before he took the wheel and they were driving back to her cabin.

"Gotta excuse Marlton. He doesn't like it that we didn't make a proper arrest. Afraid it makes him look bad."

"So, what do you think?" she asked him.

"About what?"

"About James's idea that Falkner escaped the crash."

He frowned, eyes on the road. "Would be quite a feat to pull off and require some smarts. Most criminals aren't that smart. They're too greedy."

"But Hawk's alerting on something."

Bucks laughed. "And he's got a nose, all right. He's a good dog, and a good cop, so if he says Falkner's out there, maybe we should pay attention. Still..." Bucks fingered the steering wheel. "Doesn't seem like a good idea to go out searching the woods at night."

"Are you worried?"

He shrugged, but she saw a kernel of something deep down that made her warm to him. "Harrison and Hayes can take care of themselves, but..."

"But what?"

He cocked an eyebrow at her. "The woods are full of wolves, Ms. Coles. You should know that by now."

And who would know better than Little Red herself? She looked out into the darkness, imagining James and Hawk pushing through the night as Falkner tracked their every move.

Be careful, James. A completely unexpected thought rose up to follow the first.

I don't want to lose you.

SEVENTEEN

Though Ryder was probably questioning James's wild theory, he nonetheless stayed with the trail, keeping behind James and Hawk, Titus at his partner's side.

Thanks for watching my back, James would have said if he wasn't so focused on Hawk. He knew Falkner's scent was drifting on the air currents, attaching to the ground and nearby vegetation. He tried to imagine what it would be like to be aware of those infinitesimal nuances, and he could only shake his head at Hawk's skill in fixing on one scent out of the millions floating on the desert breeze. *God knew what He was doing when He made a bloodhound*, James thought, not for the first time.

Hawk plowed along, splashing through the creek, which was fortunately only six inches deep at its widest section, his powerful body moving easily. The cold water jarred James, soaking him up to the knees. The dog reached the other side, took a moment to reconnoiter and charged up the opposing slope, James and Ryder and Titus following. Hawk barreled on for a couple hundred yards until he came to the edge of a gravel road.

"Old fire road. Loops around to the highway," Ryder said.

James made a move to follow, but Ryder stopped him, shining a flashlight on the ground. "Motorbike tracks. Hard to say if they're fresh or not."

James groaned. "Falkner had it parked here." He turned to Ryder. "He staged the whole crash."

Ryder raised an eyebrow. "Why?"

"I'm not sure."

"Pretty elaborate."

"You don't believe me?"

Ryder didn't answer at first. "Going to wait on a verdict until we can get down to the crash site."

"It might take months to collect all the evidence, if there's any left after the fire."

"If there's a body, we'll find it quick."

"Falkner's out of control, and if he's on the loose, I can't allow for a delay. I'm going to follow the road."

Ryder put a hand on his shoulder. "James, we're going to have to call this one, at least for now."

Hawk continued to tug on the leash. "Hawk's got him. We'll trail him."

"Even if Hawk has a scent and you're right about everything, the guy's jumped on a motorbike. He could be in a different city by now."

James gritted his teeth. "We'll track him, Hawk and me, for however long it takes."

"We don't have the time or resources to allow you to do that, and you know it. You're not on duty, anyway." Ryder thumbed his radio. "I'll tell them we're coming in."

"But…"

Ryder's jaw tightened just enough to remind James of his own rookie status. "That's the way it's going to be."

"Ryder…" James said, keeping his voice low. "What if there's a leak in our department?"

Ryder raised an eyebrow. "What are you talking about?"

After a breath, James told him about the red tape he'd found at Frances's house. "And Falkner knew we had units at the clearing, waiting for him. How would he know that unless…"

"You need to be careful here," Ryder said, tone stern. "You're close to making an accusation that can't be taken back."

"I know. I don't believe it's a cop, but…"

Ryder's eyes shifted in thought, hard to read in the moonlight. James wondered if he had just crossed a line with Ryder.

"I'll see what I can find out, discreetly, but let's not ruin any reputations unless we've got something solid. Do you understand me?"

James nodded. He felt relieved to have confided in Ryder, a man he trusted with his life. But didn't he trust any of his fellow cops to have his back at any moment? Marlton, Bucks, Weston, Godwin, Foxcroft, McKeller, all of them depended on each other. The blue brotherhood was real. It was what cops relied on to keep them alive and sane. He had to be wrong, and now he'd dragged Ryder in, planting the seed of suspicion in his mind, too.

What are you doing, James? Had the need to protect Madison from Falkner made him desperate enough to see a conspiracy where there was none? A picture of Paige flashed across his mind. His intense love and devotion to her had blinded him to a lot of things, even created a wedge between them when he'd imagined Sterling was interested in her. But God had helped him to trust himself again. This was not a case of James Harrison being blinded by his feelings for a woman.

Was it?

Ryder was already splashing back through the creek.

"Good boy," James said, rubbing Hawk along his wide back.

The dog barked, irritated at being kept from his quarry.

"If he's out there, we'll get him," James whispered.

As he stood, there was a sharp sound of a branch cracking. He jerked to his feet. The noise did not repeat itself. Maybe he was paranoid. Hawk had not seemed to notice, though he was still doing his best to persuade James to continue the chase.

James stood silent, listening, one hand restraining Hawk, the other on his gun. The silent seconds ticked away. Finally James hauled Hawk along to return to the crash site, but the skin on the back of his neck prickled the whole way.

Chief Jones was on scene along with a volunteer fire crew who were fixing ropes, readying themselves to rappel down to the crash area.

"It's still burning pretty bad," Jones said. "It's gonna be a while."

James looked out into the darkness. Was Falkner lying dead in the bottom of the gorge? Or was he out there laughing, knowing once again he'd bested the cops?

He realized the chief was staring at him. "Take your

dog home, Harrison. You've done enough for an off-duty cop."

Was there a tone of hostility in Jones's voice? He did not think Ryder had shared his suspicions with Jones, since he knew Ryder did not have a great respect for their boss, but Ryder was a loyal cop and Jones was the chief.

"When are we going to interview King?"

"We'll bring him in tomorrow and see if we have enough evidence to charge him with anything. We'll let you know how it goes."

Jones turned his back on James. He loaded Hawk into the car, grateful that one of the cops had changed the tire for him, and left.

He knew Madison would be up, and he was right. As soon as his car pulled into the lot, she opened the door.

Bucks waved a hand at him as he drove off.

James let Hawk inside his cabin, where he heard the sound of him slopping up water. Madison approached, tentative at first. Then, to his enormous surprise, she threw her arms around him.

Pleasure at the softness of her embrace trickled through him. She smelled of shampoo, and he gathered her to his chest, fighting the urge to bury his face in her hair, the sweet curve of her neck. It was as if she was made to fit perfectly into his embrace. Her lips brushed his chin before she put space between them.

"I was worried about you."

His heart hammered against his ribs, and he found it difficult to speak. More than anything he wanted to hold her close again, but he forced his feet to stay planted where they were. "Didn't find him. I think he had a motorbike stashed."

"Can't Hawk follow?"

"Yeah, unless we're ordered not to."

"Oh," she said. "So that's where things stand?"

"For now. We'll interrogate King tomorrow."

Her expression was crestfallen. "I was hoping… I mean, I guess I was counting on it all being over tonight."

"Me, too."

She brushed her hair back from her eyes. "James, I called my editor. He wants me to write up an article about the possible smuggling connection with King and the protection racket."

His chin went up. "Not now. We haven't got enough to make a case. You can't write that story. Did you tell him no?"

"It's a big career break for me." She paused. "But I told him I couldn't write it yet."

He blew out a breath. "That's good. We have to nail King and Falkner before anything goes to print."

"That will be too late for my editor."

"I don't care about your editor," he snapped, the rigors of the day fraying what was left of his patience. "You can't write that story."

She squared her shoulders. "Are you ordering me not to write that story? Because you don't have that kind of power over my life."

He looked at the floor for a moment. "I'm not ordering," he said in a softer tone. "I'm asking."

Slowly her posture relaxed, and in a quiet voice she replied, "Okay."

And then she turned and walked away, leaving him to muse over the meaning.

Okay? Did that mean she would forgo the story? Or

write it, anyway, knowing that it would complicate matters immeasurably for him?

"You don't have that kind of power over my life."

He didn't want power, he realized with a lurch of uncertainty. He wanted a partnership. With her.

He swatted at a mosquito that buzzed around his ears. Partner? Enemy? Friend? Rival? What was he to Madison Coles? What were they to each other?

Madison found it hard to concentrate as she and James drove to the station Wednesday morning. Her own emotions had become indecipherable to her. She'd fallen into a nervous morass while she'd paced the cabin floor, praying for James and Hawk to return safely. Then came the flash of the old Madison, distrustful, guarded, when he had warned her off writing the article. If he'd ordered her to stop, she'd have had her proof that he was what she'd suspected—an opponent, nothing more—and her feelings were purely one-sided.

But he hadn't ordered. He'd asked. The impact of that still ricocheted through her like a rock skipping off the surface of a lake. It was what had restrained her from dashing off an article for her editor. Instead she settled for recording her observations in the form of notes. A simple outline for now. The thoughts kept her silent for the rest of the trip to the station.

When they arrived, the tantalizing smell of coffee made her mouth water.

She expected to be directed to the lobby while James attended the morning briefing. If only the department secretary, Carrie Dunleavy, was more of a chatty type, Madison might make use of the time to glean some information.

James was headed for the back when the door slammed open and Bruce King strode into the room, wiry frame stiff with rage. A smaller man followed him, dressed in a neat suit and tie.

"Just what do you think you're doing?" King raged at James. "This is a frame-up from the beginning."

Madison saw Carrie quietly pick up the phone.

James's eyes went flat in that expressionless cop way she'd seen before.

"Can I help you with something, Mr. King?"

"Help me? My truck was stolen last night, and now I find out it's at the bottom of a gorge and the cargo's all burned up."

"How did you hear about that?" James asked.

"Who cares? My truck was stolen and destroyed in some cop sting last night. I understand there were cops at my house this morning, too."

"And you were conveniently out."

"I'm here now, and I'm telling you that truck was stolen from the lot where I pay to park it."

"Is that right?" Ryder asked, joining James. Madison almost smiled at their identical "cop" postures, feet firmly planted, hands resting on their gun belts, faces stern, implacable. "And what about the cargo?"

King's nostrils flared. "I heard it was cigarettes. They're not mine," he hastened to add.

"The truck was filled to the brim with cigarettes," Ryder confirmed. "Most were burned up, but we managed to save a few that were tossed clear when the truck went over the cliff. They're not legal cigarettes."

King's mouth tightened. "Well, whoever stole the truck picked up a shipment somewhere. The cigarettes weren't mine."

"Right." James did not hide the sarcasm. "Your truck was stolen, and the thief used it to pick up a load of illicit cigarettes and then drove it off a cliff."

"You cops forced him over the cliff, from what I hear."

"That's not accurate," James said, voice still flat and hard.

King waved an impatient hand. "The driver. My sources tell me it was Myron Falkner."

"You have good sources," said the chief as he joined them. "Who told you that, exactly?"

King's hands clenched into fists. "Doesn't matter. Did you find the body?"

"We are not going to disclose that information at this time," Jones said.

"I hope for Falkner's sake he died in that fire, because if I ever get my hands on him, he's going to wish he'd burned up."

Madison recoiled at the hatred in King's tone.

"You're tough on your employees," James said.

"He's doesn't work for me anymore," King spat, "just like I told you. You cops are working hard to set me up."

"We're not doing anything but investigating," the chief said. "But while you're here, come on back and have a seat. We have some more questions for you."

The smaller man stepped forward and cleared his throat. "I'm Jeff Barnes, Mr. King's lawyer, and unless you're going to charge him with something, he's not going to answer any questions."

"We aren't going to charge him…yet," Jones said. "We've got some facts to fill in first. I'm sure since Mr. King is a businessman, he appreciates our thoroughness."

James and Ryder didn't react, but she knew adding a lawyer to the mix would hamper their investigation.

"You're not going to touch me, and if you won't do anything to punish whoever stole my truck, then I will." King whirled on his heel and hammered the door open as he and his lawyer left.

Bucks joined them. "No body yet, but the truck's wedged in there pretty deep. Going to need some heavy equipment to uncork it. Messaged Flagstaff and they're sending a team, but it's gonna be tomorrow late, best case. Terrain's too unstable to send the dogs or search-and-rescue personnel at the moment."

"Great," James said.

"And here's a news flash. Marlton found a stash of illicit cigarettes at Jennings's lumberyard when he was helping with the cleanup. It links King to the protection racket, circumstantially, anyway. I..." When he noticed Madison standing there, he nodded at her and about-faced. "We'll talk more in the briefing room."

Ryder jutted his chin at James. "Call you later to set up the details."

For what? she wondered, and then it occurred to her. Tomorrow night was the police fund-raiser dance. How had she forgotten? Falkner might be on the loose, but there was another case to put to rest. Was there or wasn't there a serial killer at large in Desert Valley? James Harrison was going to offer himself up on a platter in order to find out.

EIGHTEEN

Madison felt as if her feet would wear a path in the floor for all the pacing she did in the hours before the dance. She tried to force her mind back to other matters. King and his dirty cigarettes were now firmly linked to Albert Jennings's accident. It made sense with what she knew. Falkner was threatening Jennings to pay protection money and store the smuggled cigarettes on his property. When he refused… She shivered, recalling the shrieks and groans of the collapsing trailer and the few terrifying moments when she'd believed James dead. It almost made her forget about their tiff over her story. Almost. The clock approached six thirty.

How was Ryder feeling, she wondered, on this anniversary of his wife's shooting? Another death on what was supposed to be a happy evening. She knew rookies Miller and Riverton had been killed in the hours leading up to the event, and she was glad her cabin was only a few hundred yards from James's cabin, where he'd been getting ready. There were police around with eyes on James's every move, though she hadn't seen any sign of them concealed in the woods.

Madison went over what the police knew: last year

and the year before, rookies Riverton and Miller, both blond, had been killed at their homes on the night of the dance. Five years ago, then-rookie Ryder Hayes's wife had been killed on a dark path leading to her house, the same night. Ryder: also blond.

As was James. Someone had it out for blond rookies? Why? Or was the hair color a coincidence? Was Ryder's wife's death connected? So many questions and no answers.

Madison wasn't sure she hoped there would be answers tonight. She didn't like James being used as bait.

James had gone out about an hour before to deliver Hawk to his parents' trailer for safekeeping, and she'd watched from her kitchen window. He'd lingered on his way back, eyes raking the tree line, scanning the porches of the trailers parked all around, resting for a moment on her cabin. She found herself desperately wanting to talk to him, but he was on duty, and she would not do anything to cause a distraction.

But now, a half hour later, she saw him walking to her cabin door, so handsome in his formal uniform that her breath stilled for a moment. If she hadn't known him, she probably never would have had the nerve to look in those startling blue eyes and talk to him. Stomach jumping, she answered his knock.

"There's protection here at the campground," he said. "I'm going to have to leave for a while."

"Why?"

"I'm supposed to be living in the police condo."

Her chest tightened. "So you're going there and giving the killer the best chance to find you."

He didn't answer, just gazed at her with eyes like troubled oceans.

It was almost impossible not to tell him to be careful. Instead, she forced a light tone. “Don’t let anyone mess up that sharp uniform.”

He smiled, looking down at his formal jacket and creased pants as if he’d forgotten that’s what he was wearing. “Anyway, I’ll check in with you later. I…” he paused and she waited, something about his tone setting her pulse humming. He took a breath. “If things were different, a police dance would have been fun.”

“Yes.” *If you weren’t trying to attract a killer, and I wasn’t a reporter who was in your way. If I trusted you completely and you trusted yourself. If, if, if.*

“Okay, well, good night, then.”

“Good night, James.” She watched him walk to his car, strangely alone without Hawk galloping beside him.

Just as the cabin settled into darkness again, her sister called.

“You should come to the dance,” Kate said. “The whole town is going to be there.”

“Along with you and Sterling?”

“Don’t use that tone. We’re not on a serious date. I’m attending to enjoy some music and nice conversation, okay? So don’t make a big deal out of it. He’s a good guy and we’re starting off a friendship, that’s all. Just a dance and a glass of punch.”

“Okay,” Madison said. “I can’t go, anyway. I don’t have a dress.”

“Yes, you do. I brought it along with your other things yesterday, just in case. It’s hanging in your front closet. You should go to the dance and write a nice, normal story about people having a good time.”

How odd to be getting life advice from her baby sister, but Kate seemed charged with a new confidence.

A by-product of her relationship with Sterling? If so, Madison might need to rethink her feelings about that.

And so as James made his way along to tempt a killer at his condo, she put on the green dress, piled her hair loosely on her head and pulled on a pair of pumps that her sister had thoughtfully included along with the dress.

An hour later, as she entered the grange hall, the soft satin gown swished around her legs. Flickering hurricane lamps twined with flowers cast a golden glow over the old space. Her nervousness swelled as she searched, hoping she'd spot James quickly. There had been no sirens, no sign of police activity to indicate any attempt had been made on his life. Only silence—the long, painful kind.

Hurry up, James. I won't rest easy until I see you with my own eyes.

James could not make himself sit for another moment on the partially chewed chair in the condo. There had been nothing out of the ordinary, not so much as a car backfiring, let alone any stranger sightings or someone trying to break into the condo and kill him. Again he checked in with Ryder via the radio.

"All clear," Ryder said. "Let's pack it in."

"It's almost eight. Give it a few more minutes."

Ryder's tone was heavy. "We're not going to get any action, James. Pull the plug and get over to the hall."

Was it disappointment he heard in Ryder's voice? How could it not be? Another year gone by searching for the perpetrator who'd murdered Melanie. Another chance to prove there was a serial killer at large, a chance that slipped further away with each passing moment.

Had they been wrong the whole time? Riverton and Miller were accidental deaths, and Melanie an unrelated murder? He wanted to rip off his jacket, get Hawk and go follow the trail to find Falkner. At least that was something he could take action on, if he hadn't been wrong about that, too. Instead he drove to the hall.

The wind set the pine branches rattling in the area behind the hall. He knew his fellow cops had done a sweep of the grounds and the wooded shortcut between the center of town and the Ryder home—where Melanie Hayes had been shot. How badly had that hurt Ryder? Revisiting the spot where he'd lost the lady who had been his whole world? James was startled when a picture of a certain redheaded reporter swam into his brain.

Focus, Harrison.

He was able to do so until he walked in through the double doors and immediately set eyes on the most beautiful woman he had ever seen.

Madison Coles.

He stood there dumbly, until Carrie Dunleavy jostled his arm.

"Hey, James. Glad you made it."

He tried to gather himself and gave Carrie a smile. The police department secretary had put some curls into her straight hair and wore a skirt and blouse. "Glad to see you, too."

Carrie was called away to help with the refreshment table, and James found himself drawn to Madison. She was magnificent, the emerald of her dress making her hair come alive with copper fire. Long lashes framed her brown eyes, and when she looked at him, he felt as if he'd been touched by a live wire.

"I didn't know you were coming," James said finally.

"I didn't know I was, either. My sister talked me into it. I'm on duty."

"Duty?" he asked, still trying to make his senses work properly.

"Writing a story for the lifestyle page of the *Gazette*." She held up a hand. "Don't worry. It's just a fluff piece. I won't mention the past." Something changed in her eyes, and she lowered her voice and stepped closer. He got a whiff of some delicate perfume, heard the rustle of her skirt as she moved. "I take it nothing happened?"

"Not so far."

She sighed. "That's both good and bad news."

Her hair, her eyes, her dress. It was too much. "Beautiful."

"What?"

His cheeks went hot and his body went cold. "You're...you look beautiful."

She was still for a moment. "Thank you."

Beautiful? What was he doing? He searched for some topic to return them to safe conversational ground as his brother approached and clapped him on the back.

"James," Sterling said. He stood with Kate, who wore a soft pink gown and a jeweled clip in her hair. His eyes went to Madison, narrowing slightly. "You two here together?"

"No..." James and Madison said in unison.

Madison finished up. "No, Sterling. Don't worry. We're not on a date." She gave him an elaborate wink. "Your brother is safe from the big, bad reporter."

Sterling's mouth quirked. "Yeah, well, Kate's been

telling me I shouldn't be so hard on you, but I'm still not convinced."

"Me neither," Madison said. "I'm not sure you're good enough for my sister."

James wondered what in the world he was supposed to say to intervene between the two when to his great relief, Sterling laughed. "I'm sure I'm not, but she's certainly a woman who can cause a guy to try to improve himself."

Kate blushed.

Sterling stood tall and straight, his demeanor calmer and more peaceful than James had seen since the days long ago when they were two teens riding horses and hauling hay.

His brother arched a brow at Madison. "And what about you two?"

"You don't have to worry about that," Madison said. "There is no 'us two.' I'm just here to write a story about the dance." She caught her sister's look. "A nice, normal story about people having fun with no murder and mayhem mixed in."

Though James forced a smile, her words cut into him, burrowing down inside. *"There is no 'us'..."* But of course he'd known that. It was no surprise.

No "us."

"We're going to get some punch." Kate tucked her arm through Sterling's. "Do you two want to come?"

James was saved from replying when Chief Jones caught his attention.

"You go ahead," James said. He turned to Madison and lifted his chin toward the chief. Madison nodded and followed her sister toward the punch table.

"Okay. Come join us when you can," Sterling said.

The thought echoed dully in his mind, resonating there as he watched Madison walk away, hair like flame. *There is no "us."*

Madison secured some suitably festive quotes from the partygoers, including ones from Carrie Dunleavy and Dennis Marlton. She took pictures with her phone. *A happy story for a change*, she thought as she scanned the crowd. Kate had been smart to suggest it.

Her sister stood close to Sterling, holding his hand, her head barely reaching the height of his shoulders. At some remark he made, she threw her head back and laughed, the sound silvery and precious. Madison felt a tickle of something that was close to envy, but mostly happiness. Who was she to say Sterling's past should preclude him from enjoying time with Kate if that was where things were headed? *New path, new life*, she thought, and she thanked God that her sister was happy, at least for now.

James had slipped off somewhere. The event was well underway at almost nine o'clock, and it seemed the danger was over. Time of death for both rookies and Melanie Hayes had been before the start of the dance, so it looked as if James was in the clear. She'd gotten her story and pictures. It was time to go back to the cabin and write up the article. Her deadline for the protection-racket piece loomed large, and she still hadn't decided how to complete her assignment in the next two days without making things harder for James and the Desert Valley PD. Maybe the fluff piece would buy her more time with her editor. She had to do a bang-up job on the bigger story. It was her chance—maybe her only chance—to show her editor she was ready for the big time.

She headed for the back of the hall, intending to leave without attracting attention, when Dennis Marlton stopped her.

"No one out this door, ma'am." He smiled, but there was little warmth in it.

"Is there something going on?"

"No."

"Would you tell me if there was?"

"No." His smile was wolfish, and for a moment she did feel a bit like a little girl in a red cape who had wandered off the path.

"But there isn't anything going on," Marlton said. "I'm happy to escort you to your car if you'd like."

"No need. I'll go out the front, okay?"

He nodded. "Thank you, ma'am. Have a nice evening."

She headed to the entrance, stopping for a few moments to peruse the silent auction table, which held everything from baskets of homemade jams to sets of embroidered table linens, helping a woman who stumbled as she passed the loaded table. Madison fished out her keys from her purse, scanning the hall one more time as she did so. Chatting couples dotted the room, their heads pressed close in intimate conversation. One older cop whose name she didn't know reached out to caress his wife's cheek, and the gesture brought unexpected tears to Madison's eyes.

At one time, very long ago, had her father loved her mother like that, before their lives had spun out of control? Their marriage must have been flush with promise, full of bright expectations, shiny and untarnished like a new penny. How could married people trust that love would last and endure and thrive as the years went by and youth fled away? How did they continue to trust each other as things went wrong and promises faded?

The trust had to come from higher up, she realized. When things seemed wrecked and ruined, the enduring love was rooted in something much bigger that two people.

"I am making a way in the wilderness and streams in the wasteland."

That was the secret of marriage, she thought with a start. Two people trusting each other because they trusted their Father in Heaven first. The thought released a dam in her heart, and a warm stream flowed through a place that had felt like a wasteland for a very long time. Maybe she was on her way to that new place where her father's betrayal was left with God, buried in that past where it belonged.

Deep in thought, Madison reached out a hand to push open the front doors. As she did so, she noticed that Dennis Marlton was no longer standing sentry in the back. Odd. Where had he gone?

She stepped outside, allowing her eyes to adjust to the darkness. There was a moon, but it was playing hide-and-seek with a bank of clouds. Strains of music floated out of the hall. She gripped her keys, intending to scoot into her car without delay, until she heard the low murmur of voices coming from the edge of the parking lot where crowded trees hemmed in the asphalt. Probably just a couple discussing the evening's events before they, too, left early. There was a slight creaking that sounded familiar, and she thought she caught the outline of a figure wearing a hat.

She put her key in the lock.

One startling phrase drifted across the parking lot.

"…another murder."

Madison's heart slammed into her ribs. She'd misheard. Or maybe it was the cops discussing the case.

"You're taking too many wild chances. Get out of town while you can."

The tone was menacing, hard. Her pulse began to race. She would get into her car and call James. Heart dropping, she realized she'd left her phone inside near the auction table when she assisted the lady who'd tripped. *Dumb, Mads. Real dumb.* She tried to ease the key in slowly, but the key ring slipped from her fingers and felt to the pavement with a clink. The talking stopped.

She frantically patted the asphalt, searching for her keys, which must have bounced under the car.

"Who is that?" one of the men snapped to the other. Her blood turned to ice. One of the men was Falkner.

She did not pick up on the response, only the sound of running feet.

NINETEEN

The choices raced through Madison's mind as her nerves went rigid. Run back inside the hall. It was a much better idea to get where people were than to keep searching for her keys in a deserted parking lot. But with the keys she could hit the panic button, which would surely dissuade whoever was following her. She reached one more time under the car, but when she heard a man's heavy tread she withdrew her hand, ducking down as small as possible.

He was two car lengths away now, unsure of her exact location. Her own breathing sounded so loud she was sure he could hear it. Slowly she eased around the far side of the car. He was waiting for her to unlock the door, perhaps. She thought about screaming to attract the attention of someone inside, but the music and conversation would drown her out.

Back pressed to the cold metal, she crouched there, slipping off her pumps in case she had to run. Toward the hall? The best option. The man had a heavy hand on the hood of her car now, a flashlight pricking the darkness as he located her keys underneath. They jingled as he poked them with his foot. She remembered with a jolt that she had a photo key ring. Now he knew exactly who had been eavesdropping on their conversation.

"The reporter," he snapped. "What did she hear?"

Was the other man still there at the edge of the lot? Had he circled around to come at her from the other side? She gathered the edges of her skirt in her hands as she heard the squeak of boots. He was moving around the headlights now. *Run now, Mads. You can do it. You have to.* The edge of the flashlight beam was worming its way closer. In a matter of inches he would shine it right in her face.

She exploded from her hiding place, sprinting toward the grange hall. Though the long skirt hampered her, she was moving well away from the parking lot. The hum of party noises grew louder, and she was opening her mouth to scream when something hit her in the ankles. She fell hard.

A fist connected with her temple, and she felt her body go numb. Then she was hauled over a big shoulder. The ground moved dizzily in her vision as he carried her to the woods.

James scoured the hall again for Madison. "Where is she?"

"Looking for Little Red?" Marlton asked, working his way through a plate piled high with cheese and cookies.

"Yeah. Have you seen her?"

"Talked to her about fifteen minutes ago. She was trying to exit out the back, probably going to do some snooping, but I redirected her out the front door, since you and Ryder were doing another security sweep out there."

"Did she leave?"

"Guess so."

"And you didn't walk her to her car?" James snapped.

"I'm off protection duty. I'm on personal time," he said with a shrug. "She's somebody else's problem."

Biting back a retort, James whirled on his heel and hastened toward the front door. He'd probably missed her and she was on her way home. He'd try her cell. As he reached for his phone, Ryder met him at the front door. "Godwin reports that they've got a crane in place to haul up the truck. Going to finish up here and head over to relieve her." Ryder looked near exhaustion.

"Ryder..." James started. He wanted to express to his friend how sorry he was that the sting had come to nothing. No sign of a rookie-cop serial killer, and still not the slightest hint that there was any connection to the slaying of his wife.

Ryder shook his head. "I know. Gonna go brief Chief Jones." He gave James a slap on the back and walked away, shoulders bowed.

James dialed Madison's cell. No answer. Probably driving. He went out the front door and made his way to the parking lot. Her vehicle was still there. He puzzled over it for a moment. "Must have missed her inside." Something caught his eye in the moonlight. Lying just under the front tire, a set of keys, a silver heart attached, with a picture of Kate and Madison. Next to it was one of her shoes. He swallowed hard.

Skin prickled all over, he was on the radio in an instant, with Ryder promising to get help on the way without alarming the guests. Ryder was the first one to join James as he frantically scoured the ground in the beam of his flashlight. Nothing unusual, no sign of anything amiss except her key ring.

Okay. Play it through in your mind. She's getting into the car. Maybe she hears something and bolts. Or maybe someone takes her. Breath coming fast now, he went to the browned grass at the edge of the lot.

"I got something here," he barked, training his light over the crushed dry stalks. "Broken grass, maybe from a scuffle." What he wouldn't give right then to have Hawk by his side. The dog would find her in an instant. He didn't wait for any discussion with his fellow cops before he headed to the woods behind the grange hall.

Plunging into the deep shadows, he stopped to listen. Nothing. Suddenly he had the irrational fear that he was going to find her dead, lying in the woods like Melanie Hayes all those years ago. He'd been so focused on himself, certain that another blond-haired rookie was the target. Had his mistake caused Madison her life? Fear thickened in his throat. *No, it's not going to be like that.* The long, arcing beams from the cops' MagLites began sweeping through the trees.

Weapon in hand, he tried to be like Hawk, reading the signs on the ground that would take him to Madison.

Madison felt her senses gradually beginning to return. She realized she was being carried into the woods behind the grange hall, her head bumping against a muscled back. She flailed, trying to slide off the man's shoulder, but his arm around her waist was like an iron band. Wild panic surged through her body before she forced herself to think. What had she learned in self-defense class? Go for the eyes.

Curving her fingers, she tried to reach out and claw

where she thought his eyes must be. Her plan worked. With a grunt, he dumped her on the ground, the impact driving the breath out of her. Immediately she flipped over and scrambled on hands and knees toward the grange hall.

With a muttered oath, he grabbed her ankle and tugged. She kicked and bucked, one foot connecting with his face. She heard a soft crunch. He jerked back, freeing her. In that precious moment, she moved faster than she'd ever imagined, long enough to scramble along, hands shoving at the branches that slapped at her, stumbling over the uneven ground.

Get away, her brain screamed. *Get away and hide.*

She plunged deeper into the foliage, heedless of direction now, blindly moving like a drowning person searching for air. A branch cut at her face, and another snagged on her skirt until she yanked it free and kept running. When she hoped she'd put some distance between her and her attacker, she stopped to get her bearings. Tucked under a thorny shrub, she fought against her rasping breath and thundering heart. Any second she expected to feel him reach out of the darkness and grab her again.

Think, Mads. Where was she? She saw only trees distorted by the moonlight, painted with eerie shadows. *Listen and use your head.*

Forcing her body to obey her mind, she strained to make out the tiniest welcoming noise from the ball. The seconds ticked by endlessly. There, she had it. The sound of laughter floated out from the grange, which must be away and to the right of her location. Peering from under the shrubs, she tried to see some indication of where her attacker was hiding.

Wherever it was, he could not possibly be prepared for a record-breaking sprint, which was exactly what she meant to attempt. Slowly she gathered up her dress, now soiled and torn. Her fingers balled up in the satin, rigid.

On the count of three…

When her mind had ticked off the seconds, she bolted with all the strength and speed she possessed. Branches cracked under her feet. Arms pumping and legs churning, she shot through the trees as best she could. In a matter of moments, the lights of the grange hall shone tantalizingly close.

She pressed even harder and then, in a gap between the trees, she saw him there, figure large against the moonlight. Screeching to a halt, she screamed. He did not move.

Fear froze her body as he lurched for her. She pivoted. One hand fell heavily on her back, enough to send her off balance. She rolled over to scream again when she felt his body collapse across her legs. Wriggling and squirming, she sought to free herself. He made no move to grab her.

Pinwheeling, she wrenched her body free and scuttled backward until her back hit a tree trunk. He lay on the ground, facedown, still.

The moonlight cleared the clouds just enough that she could see the edge of the hunting knife sticking out of her attacker's back.

James heard Madison scream. He charged through the undergrowth. "Madison?" he roared. His voice echoed through the woods, thrown back at him. She did not respond, or he could not hear her, anyway. The shifting shadows from the clouded moonlight made the woods come alive with movement.

He yelled for her again. Was she hiding? Or unable to answer? He forced away the thought and called out again. Still no response. She was smart, savvy. She would have run toward the grange hall if she could, toward the people who would help her, toward him. Smashing the branches aside, he plowed on until he reached a gap in the trees. He heard gulps and sobs. Madison.

Gun drawn, he emerged on the path, trees looming on either side. Scanning quickly, he realized that she sat with her back against a tree, hands pressed to her mouth. His relief almost took his breath clean away until he noticed the second figure.

There was a guy lying facedown on the ground, not moving.

"Police," James shouted. No reaction, except a startled yelp from Madison.

"Stay still, Madison," he said quietly.

She didn't respond, crouched in a ball against the tree.

He approached, warily, looking for any signs of movement, the sign of a discarded weapon. His flashlight beam found the hilt of a knife protruding from the guy's back. His mind reeled. Madison was trying to say something, but her words were garbled by fear, no more than a whisper.

"It's okay," James said in as soothing a voice as he could rustle up. "Just stay right there for a minute." Inching to the prostrate form, he reached tentatively down with one hand to check for a pulse on the guy's wrist.

Ryder and Bucks raced up, guns drawn, covering the downed man. James holstered his. "He's dead." They all stared at the fallen man.

Bucks let out an amazed whistled. "Well, Harrison. Looks like you finally got Myron Falkner this time, for sure."

The moonlight shone on the dead man's bald head. "No," James said. "But someone else did."

TWENTY

He left Ryder and Bucks with the body and approached Madison, kneeling at her feet. She was staring at the front of her dress, eyes wide with horror at the stains splashed across the ruined satin.

"There's blood all over," she whispered. "Falkner's blood."

He let out a slow breath. "Madison, are you injured?"

When she didn't answer, he bent lower to force her to focus on him. "Hurt?"

A small shake of the head. He silently thanked the Lord. "I want you to tell me what happened."

"I'm not sure."

"Take all the time you need."

She breathed hard for a minute, trying to wipe away the blood with her palm. "It's all over. So much blood."

He reached out and gently stopped her, taking his hands in hers and pressing. "Tell me," he repeated, voice low and steady.

"I overheard him, Falkner, talking to someone in the parking lot. They were talking about murder and someone leaving town. I dropped my keys and he heard me. Chased me. Then someone…stabbed him."

"Who?"

"The man he was talking to, I guess."

"Who was it? Did you see his face?"

Her eyes widened, dark pools. She pulled her hands away and laced the fingers together, squeezing. "No, but it was a cop." Her whisper carried perfectly on the night air, and Ryder and Bucks moved closer. Marlton joined them.

"What did she just say?" Marlton asked.

James ignored the question, still focused completely on Madison. "How do you know it was a cop? Tell me what you saw."

"When they were talking, I got a glimpse of a hat, a uniform hat like yours."

"Are you sure? It was dark," Ryder said. "Could you have been mistaken?"

"No," she said, eyes snapping to his. "I'm sure. There was a cop working with Falkner, and he stabbed him. I didn't see it, but that must be what happened."

James could feel the confusion and defensiveness in his two colleagues, sensing their disbelieving body language as they processed the accusation.

"You're saying a cop did this." Marlton said, voice tight. "So when we dust the knife for prints, it's gonna point to one of our own?"

"Yes," Madison repeated.

Marlton stood straighter, his tone derisive. "You sure we aren't going to find your prints on it, ma'am?"

He heard Madison gasp. "What? You think I killed him?"

He gestured around the woods. "Well, you're here with a dead body and blood all over you, accusing cops of murder," Marlton said. "I'd pick a reporter over a cop for a murderer any day of the week."

"I didn't kill him." Her voice shook.

"You're the one out here alone with a dead guy, missy," Marlton fired off.

"That's enough," James warned.

"You can't possibly think that I killed this man," she said.

"Oh no?" Marlton stared at her, arms folded across his chest. "Well, guess what? That's exactly what I think."

James moved to insert himself between Madison and Marlton, but Ryder put a hand on Marlton's shoulder. "We need photos and help to secure the scene. Get people out here to cordon off the area. Keep the guests from seeing. Call the coroner. Get him en route."

Marlton looked as though he was not going to follow orders, but he reluctantly moved away, jogging toward the back door of the grange hall, talking into his radio.

Ryder stood for a moment. "Miss Coles, we'll have the medics check you out and get a formal statement." He gave her another calculating glance and returned to organize his people as cops began to pour out of the grange hall.

The wind blew through the trees, making the pine needles quiver above them. James's gut tightened as the facts thundered through his mind. A knife. Another body in the wooded shortcut to a residential area, a man who'd faked his death the night before. Who was the other man? King. A crooked cop? And Madison Coles at the center of it all, like she had been from the moment he'd met her.

"James," Madison said. "I didn't kill Falkner. You know that, right?"

Madison Coles, a woman he could not get out of his heart, a woman who clouded his thoughts and made him question everything. He chose his words carefully and the cop in him came out. "I know people can have a dramatic reaction when their lives are being threatened."

Her mouth dropped open. "You think I killed him?"

Did he? His heart, gut, mind and soul said no. "No, I don't. I'm saying I would understand how it could have happened if you were afraid for your life."

Wrong thing to say. His diplomacy did nothing but make her draw away further, until her back was scraping against the tree. "That's cop talk. You don't believe me about the stabbing or the fact that it's a cop behind all this, do you? Why not be a man and say it?"

"You're putting words in my mouth."

"Then tell me you believe me right now." She fixed on his face, hers a tender expression of longing and deep need. "James, look me in the eye and tell me you trust me enough to believe what I'm saying."

He wanted to, desperately desired to tell her he believed her 100 percent. But the cop part of him, and the hardened part of his heart that had calloused over when he'd believed Paige, stopped him from answering. Betrayal flickered across her face, dulling the fire in her eyes and dousing whatever there had been between them. What had he just done? He wanted to touch her, hold her, erase the grievous injury he'd just inflicted, but she was stepping gingerly away, avoiding the rocks that cut at her bare feet. He reached out a hand to steady her. She jerked away.

"You need to stay here, wait for the medics."

"I'm going."

"Madison..."

"I'm going," she repeated, and there was a terrible finality to the words. "If you want me to stay here," she said low and hard, "you're going to have to arrest me."

"I'm not going to do that," he said quietly. "I'm asking you to stay."

"Yeah?" The moonlight sparkled in her eyes, or perhaps it was the fury. "Well, here's my answer."

She turned her back and walked away toward the grange hall.

It was a long night before Kate drove her back to the cabin. She'd been able to retrieve her purse, phone, and keys, but somehow, she'd forgotten her sweater inside the grange hall and she had not found her pumps, so she curled her feet up under her on the sofa, trying not to look at the bloodstains on her dress.

"I'm going to stay with you tonight," Kate said. "I've got a shift tomorrow morning, and it's too late to drive back to Tuckerville. Go take a shower."

Madison should have been thrilled. Instead she was numb and cold and dead inside as she headed to the bathroom. James did not trust her. When it came to the place where the rubber met the road, he'd not believed her.

Even when she had stripped off the ruined dress and stood under the shower until the hot water ran out, she could not rid herself of the iciness inside. A man had died right at her feet, and it felt as if something had died inside her, too.

Wrapped in a robe, she padded into the kitchen, where she found her sister texting.

"James was checking on you. I told him you were okay." She peered at her sister. "Are you okay?"

"Yes," Madison said.

Kate tapped the phone against her palm. "You don't look okay. There's something hopeless in your eyes."

"That's a determined look, not a hopeless one." She took a breath. "Falkner's dead. There's a police connection to the crime and the protection racket. I've got a story to write."

She paled. "Mads..."

"I'm sorry, Kate. I love you and I'm happy you've got Sterling in your life, but you know what I've got? My job. That's it. That's all I've got, my job, and I need to do it."

"But James...?"

"I said, that's all." Her voice was so bitter she didn't even recognize it. "I'm going to nail down one more detail tomorrow, and then I'll be finished with the piece and I'm leaving Desert Valley."

Kate stared at her. "I think you're hurt because James isn't jumping on your police theory. Well, he's a cop, Mads. What do you expect him to do? He's loyal to his colleagues, and you wouldn't respect him if he wasn't."

"That's not it."

"Then what is it?"

I love him, and he doesn't love me back. Not enough. Not nearly enough. She cleared her throat. "I've got some writing to do. You take the bedroom and I'll sleep on the couch."

"Mads..."

"It's all right. I'm going be working late, anyway."

She got up from the table, but Kate stopped her with a touch on her arm. "James was hurt badly in the past,

Mads, just like you…" She stopped and swallowed hard. "Just like we were. It's hard to let go of the past, isn't it?"

Her sister's touch was warm and gentle and full of a strong surety Madison had never known in her before. "Yeah," Madison said, throat going thick with tears. "It sure is."

Without a word, Kate got up and embraced Madison. They clung together, and Madison felt the twin pangs of anguish and joy. She cried, and so did Kate. They mingled their grief about a father who had fallen into deepest sin, and a mother they would never know. Madison added tears of gratitude that God had returned her sister. When their tears were depleted, she kissed Kate and pushed her away.

"I've got a job to do."

"Just promise me you'll talk to James one more time before you hit the send button and leave town."

"I'll think about it," she said, turning to her laptop. Let James into her life one more time? Could she? Her heart supplied the answer. No way. No more. Lesson learned.

James didn't arrive back at the campground until after two o'clock in the morning. His eyes were bleary with fatigue, and his shoulder ached. Someone had given him Madison's sweater, which she'd forgotten inside the grange hall. He left it in his car, lying on the front seat, faintly scented by her perfume. Since Hawk was still at his parents', the trailer was silent, lifeless. He'd stayed on scene long enough to know that the only fingerprints lifted from the knife were Falkner's, indicating whoever had stabbed him wore gloves. He'd known in his core that Madison's prints wouldn't be there, but part of him had been hoping King's would be. In his perfect scenario, King had killed Falkner after he'd botched the truck job. The evidence tape at Frances's house had no doubt been a false lead. There was no evidence to suggest that police were involved in any part of the protection racket, and that whole mess could be put away with no reputations ruined and no dirty cops exposed. Neat. Tidy. Easy.

Madison had been so sure the guy talking to Falkner was a cop. But she was scared, and it was dark. Fear. Poor visibility. Easy to make a mistake. Could have been King or one of his guys. He threw off his jacket and unfastened the top buttons of his shirt, staring out the window at Madison's cabin. Everything was dark and quiet, as it should have been at 2:00 a.m. He continued to stare, anyway. What was he hoping for?

To see her walk by the window so he'd have an excuse to go talk to her, he realized. The look in her eyes haunted him, the expression that revealed how much he'd meant to her and how massively he'd blown it. He'd shown that his first loyalty was not to her, but to his brothers in blue. *You didn't believe her. You broke her heart.* He dropped down onto the couch and folded his hands to pray.

What should he ask? How could he fashion the pain into a plea? He prayed for Madison Coles, that she would be delivered from the past that still imprisoned her, that she would find a partner to trust completely, though it burned inside to think of her with someone else.

Something poked at him. The reason he'd not supported her wasn't loyalty. There were cops in the department—Marlton, Bucks and others—whom he did not respect much. That was not the entire reason he'd let her down. He had stepped as close as he'd ever come to giving his whole soul to a woman, and it scared him. Could he trust his heart, the ridiculous organ that had beat feverishly for Paige? There was still doubt, a pervasive shadow, that made him question himself.

"Let go of the past." Were they just divine words to comfort others? The quiet seeped into him along with the current of emotion he'd buried deep for so long.

He got down on his knees then.

Lord, help me to trust myself again. To believe that the past is forgiven and You're making a new path for me, if only I would have the courage to follow it.

To trust, to believe, to forgive.

Overcome with his burdens, he lay on the couch and tried to sleep.

TWENTY-ONE

King's guard peered at Madison through the iron gate. "Lady, it's barely eight o'clock in the morning, and Mr. King had a late night."

"I need to see him."

"Got an…?"

"No, I don't have an appointment. Tell him I believe he's being set up by the Desert Valley PD."

His eyes widened, and he made a call. In a few moments she was standing in Mr. King's lush front room. King sauntered in, dressed in workout clothes and holding a bottle of water.

"Fortunately I'm an early riser. What do you want?" He made no move to sit, and neither did she.

"Information. I know there is a protection racket going on in this town, and the police suspect you're the ringleader, especially since they found a stash of your cigarettes at Jennings's lumberyard."

"Those were planted. I have nothing to do with muscling local business."

"I believe you."

He cocked his head. "Why?"

"Because someone killed Myron Falkner last night. You wouldn't have stabbed him in the back."

"And why are you so sure of that?"

She stared him right in the face. "Because you're the kind that would have wanted him to see what was coming, to know who took him out before he died."

King smiled. "You're very perceptive. I have an alibi for last night, anyway. Cops already came here. I'm clear, so why do I need you?"

"Because they still suspect you. They will stick to you and watch your every move, and you don't want that because it messes with your smuggling business."

He started to protest.

"I'm not interested in the smuggling," she said. "I just want the cop who's behind the protection racket exposed. I'm sure you do, too. It will take some of the pressure off you."

He eyed her warily. "So what do you want from me?"

"Tell me what you know about the Desert Valley cops. Rumors. Innuendo. I'm sure you hear things with your connections. This cop, whoever he is, arranged for Falkner to steal your truck and wreck it, to focus the attention on you."

"Why assume it's a cop?"

"Falkner knew where you parked your truck because he used to work for you, but someone also knew how the cops would set up the sting, exactly where the cops would intercept the truck, and passed that on to Falkner. That's how he made his plan to send the truck off the bridge and escape before the cops closed in. Who could have known that kind of information unless they were on the inside?"

He regarded her, unreadable. "All right. I'll play

along. I'll tell you who I think it is, but there's a little something you need to understand first."

"What's that?"

He put the water bottle down on the table and moved one step closer to her, mouth in a tight line. "If I find out you betrayed me, or you're trying to get info on me to pass along to the cops, you will die. Do we have an understanding, Miss Coles?"

She forced a nod. "Yes. Tell me who you suspect."

She left King's house an hour later, facts and worry swirling around in her mind. One more bit of research and a talk with Frances and she'd have enough to write the story. It was not easy to get an appointment at the prison to see Veronica Earnshaw's brother, Lee Earnshaw, but after an interminable wait, she was granted a visit. The prison was an hour outside Desert Valley, and the drive gave her time to put some order to the questions swirling around in her mind.

When Lee Earnshaw was escorted in, her stomach tightened into knots. He sat, facing her across the table, hands cuffed. His dark brown eyes and hair stood out against his pale face. He was tall, muscular, twenty-eight years old and a rancher before he went to prison, she knew.

"Why did you want to see me?"

"You claimed you didn't have anything to do with the gas-station robbery you were convicted of."

His face was wary. "That's right."

"You further claim that evidence against you was falsified."

"Also correct."

"I want to know by whom. Which cops handled your arrest?"

He frowned. "You can get all this from the files. Why come here to ask me?"

"I've only seen the public records that name Bucks and Marlton as the arresting officers. The cops aren't interested in letting me see their detailed files."

He laughed. "You're a reporter, right? Working on some sort of police-corruption story, I gather? I can see why you're persona non grata."

"Which cops handled your case, Mr. Earnshaw? Who do you think framed you?"

"I'm not sure I want to talk to you."

"Why? It can't make your situation any worse, can it? If I can expose a crooked cop, maybe you can get your conviction overturned."

He considered for such a long time that she was afraid he was going to decline to speak with her. "The three cops who handled it were Ryder Hayes, Ken Bucks and Dennis Marlton."

Hayes, Bucks and Marlton. "Which would have reason to want you to go to jail?"

He didn't need to think about that question. "Bucks. He blames me for stealing away the girl he loved." His eyes clouded over. "Her name was Shelley Graves and she was a few years older than me. The short version is she had a rough time because Bucks was obsessed with her, followed her around, stalked her basically. I offered sympathy which she mistook for love. Bucks went nuts. Made my life miserable in every way he could."

"Did he hate you enough to fabricate evidence?"

"No doubt, but I didn't get any warm fuzzies from Hayes or Marlton, either. Both could have framed me to get an arrest credited to them, or deflect blame from someone else. Now they're supposedly out there solving my sister Veronica's murder. I know she was a hard woman in some ways, and she made a lot of enemies, but she deserves justice. I don't see the cops making much progress." He rubbed a hand over his eyes. "I'm not a real believer in the justice system at the moment."

"Sometimes justice is a long time coming, Mr. Earnshaw."

"You say that like you've got some experience."

"I do."

He considered for a moment. "I am innocent. I know you probably don't believe that because everyone in here would claim the same thing, but you're looking at a guy who doesn't deserve to be here." His eyes were intense.

What if he was telling the truth? What if Lee Earnshaw had been set up? Incarcerated and stripped of his freedom by the people who were supposed to protect him?

She thanked him, and the guard let her out of the room.

Hayes, Bucks and Marlton. She reviewed her plan as she walked out. She'd check with Frances and Tony again. They might have seen one of the cops lingering around the bridal shop or her house, heard Falkner drop a name. Something. She'd compare their answers to King's. Then she'd write up what she had and hope it was enough to please her editor, and put enough pressure on the bad cop to force him to make a mistake.

As she hurried to her car, her heart thudded to a stop. James was there in uniform, leaning against his Crown Victoria. Hawk sniffed and slobbered his way over to her, and she scratched his wrinkly head.

James frowned. "What are you doing here, Madison?"

She kept scratching the dog. "Researching."

"By interviewing Lee Earnshaw?"

"He says he was framed."

"They all do."

"Maybe he is the one who really is telling the truth."

He let out a long sigh, and she flicked a glance at him, noting that he looked exhausted. She knew he hadn't returned to the campground until early morning. He'd probably gotten no more than a few hours of sleep. Worry squeezed at her. If he was working with a crooked cop, how safe was he?

He can take care of himself, Mads.

"I heard you went to see King this morning, too."

"You don't have to keep tabs on me anymore, James. Falkner is dead, so he's not coming after me."

"But the guy who killed him might, if you keep nosing around in things."

She stood as tall as her frame would allow. "I'm going to find out the truth, whether you like it or not." She expected anger, belligerence. But she saw only sadness, and it puzzled her.

"Madison, I am sorry I hurt you."

She blinked, confused. "You were doing your job. I'm doing mine. It's business."

"No it's not, not all of it. Fact of the matter is, I think you're right. You're onto something, and I believe you. I'm sorry that I hurt you, because I couldn't say that earlier."

She was thunderstruck. "Thank you for that."

He moved closer. "And I'm worried—beyond worried, more like terrified out of my mind—that you're going to get hurt following this trail. I want you to stop."

"Stop?"

He put his hands on her shoulders and moved her closer to him, close enough that she could see herself reflected in his eyes. "Let the story go for now, Madison. Please. And before you say it, I'm not ordering. I'm asking."

Her soul stirred at the entreaty in his voice. How she longed to have someone care about her as much as he appeared to. She found herself leaning into him as he pressed a kiss to her temple, her cheek, tracing his lips down her face toward her mouth. She felt so safe, so cherished there in the circle of his arms.

Through the heady sensations, she felt the seed of doubt take hold again. He wanted her to stop writing because it would embarrass his police force. He wasn't what he seemed to be. He wasn't someone she could trust with her heart. With a wrenching ache, she pulled out of his grasp.

"I'm writing the story, and you're not going to talk me out of it by faking concern."

He jerked as if she'd slapped him. "I wasn't faking."

"I'm going to meet with Frances and write the story, and then I'm out of here. No more Little Red Riding Hood in your way."

"Madison, you were never in my way." The words were so quiet, so tender, that she wanted to cry.

"I've got to go, James."

"I want you to stay," he said.

One long moment of staring at the sweet emotion on his face nearly made her change her mind. Would she trust him? Could she take the new path that her heart tugged her toward?

She shook her head, got into her car, and drove away as fast as she dared.

James pulled up at the police station, her words still ringing in his ears.

"...in your way."

"...faking concern."

Was that really how he'd made her feel? How had he managed to send those messages when she filled his every moment and thought? Was it his past or hers that was keeping them apart? He no longer knew or cared. He was filled with a profound sense of dread that if he didn't get to the bottom of who was behind the protection-racket scheme, Madison's life was in danger. If there was no future for the two of them, then the only thing left was to ensure her safety.

The station was quiet. Carrie sat at the reception desk, working away on her computer. She waved at him. "I can't believe we had another death on the night of the dance."

James nodded. "But not in the way we'd anticipated."

"I'm just glad it wasn't you."

"Thanks, Carrie. That makes two of us. I'm going to work at my desk for a while."

He pulled up Lee Earnshaw's file on his computer. The arrest had been made before his time began in Desert Valley, but he knew the particulars. The primary cop involvement had been from Hayes, Bucks and Marlton. He mentally crossed out Ryder. There was no way he was a crooked cop. James didn't know either Bucks or Marlton well. Which one? If either? It was possible they were wrong, all wrong about everything. He gripped the file and scanned every line, every detail.

When his eyes began to burn, he left Hawk snoozing under his desk and went to follow another lead. He checked in with the supervising clerk who had a desk opposite the evidence room, a sandy-haired lady of some fifty-five years named Alice. She greeted him warmly and swiveled a binder toward him so he could sign in. Then she handed him a key.

He unlocked the door and stepped inside. The shelves were neatly stacked with plastic bags, labeled and sealed with red evidence tape. The air was stale, the only movement from a spider busily tending a web in a far corner of the ceiling. Nothing stirred his instincts. What had he been expecting? A neon sign pointing to a clue?

Feeling more than a little foolish, he closed and locked the door again and checked out with Alice. "Removing anything today, James?"

"No, ma'am."

After he signed out in the log, he flipped back a page to the week before he'd scrounged around in Frances's bushes. There was no signature for that period or the entire week before. Theoretically, no one had visited the evidence room anytime recently.

His eyes wandered to Alice's desk, where there was a little plastic vase full of pink carnations. "Nice," James said.

"A birthday present from Ken Bucks. I was sure surprised he actually remembered my birthday was Monday."

"So, Bucks was here on Monday?"

She nodded, still smiling.

"He's not logged in to the book."

"No, he didn't go in the evidence room. He just dropped off the flowers."

James mulled it over. He'd never figured on Ken Bucks to be the thoughtful type, but he didn't know the guy well. He began to walk away. Then a thought struck him.

"Hey, Alice. Did the flowers come in that vase?"

"That's an odd question." She gave him a sly look. "Are you planning on some flowers for your girlfriend? I understand that reporter is quite a looker."

"Just wondering," he said, ignoring the stab of embarrassment. "Did they? Come in the vase?"

"No. Ken watched the desk for me while I ran to the kitchen and found the vase and arranged them. That was real sweet, wasn't it?"

Real sweet. Though there was no proof that the tape Hawk found was actually from the Desert Valley evidence room, the other facts were beginning to come together. When Bucks arrived with his flowers, Alice had run to the kitchen, giving Bucks plenty of time to duck into the evidence room and take a packet of drugs to give to Falkner And Bucks knew every detail of the truck sting operation, which he could easily relay. *All guesses, James. You don't have any proof.* He thought of Lee Earnshaw.

What if he is telling the truth?

He ran to Bucks's cubicle. Hawk heard him rush by and woke with a startled bark. Bucks wasn't at his desk. Racing to the front desk, he asked Carrie, "Where is Ken Bucks right now?"

"Taking an early lunch, I think. Why?"

He didn't answer.

"James, where are you going?" Carrie asked.

"Tell you later," he called over his shoulder as he and Hawk ran to the car.

TWENTY-TWO

Madison stopped her car a block from Frances's bridal salon and dashed off a couple of paragraphs on her iPad. The piece would need refining and editing, and the finishing touch would be a quote from Frances about how she'd been shaken down. Now that Falkner was dead and both Frances and Tony had revealed everything they knew, she hoped Frances would not be too scared to make a statement. Her hand was on the door when she saw Ken Bucks exit the back door of the salon and get into his car. Frances peeked through the window, face pale, before she quickly pulled the curtains back into place.

Ken Bucks was the cop King believed was guilty of framing him. Madison had found it hard to believe until that moment. What would Bucks be doing calling on Frances? Police business? But something in the way he slammed the salon door and drove out of the back lot made her question that conclusion. He looked irate, the customary "good old boy" smile missing.

She reached automatically for the ignition, heart thudding. Follow? Stay put and keep to her plan?

Ryder Hayes, Doug Marlton, Ken Bucks. She knew

deep down that one of them was the boss in charge of Falkner, the brains behind the intimidation. King said Bucks was the smart one. Good old boy Bucks? She'd follow, staying safe, watch and listen. If she was wrong, no harm done.

When Bucks pulled out along the main street, she let him drive nearly two blocks before she started along behind him. He was meandering, seemingly with no specific destination in mind, until he idled near the little storefront on the end of the street where the Hot Dog Spot was set to open the following month, if the sign was to be believed. She thought he would pass by, but then he pulled around the back to park in the rear. Madison stopped at the curb a few blocks away, got out her handheld recorder, and crept along the sidewalk.

She could not accept what she was witnessing. The whole thing was crazy. There was no way Ken Bucks would march into a closed restaurant to shake down the owner in broad daylight. It was too brazen, even for a guy like Bucks. Still, she kept on, easing her way past some piled-up pallets to the back entrance. Bucks's vehicle was parked next to a dusty pickup truck.

She noticed the back door was partially open. Easing close, she tried to peer through the gap.

Bucks stood next to some newly installed shelving. The owner, an older man with a prominent nose and wide-set eyes, stood across from Bucks, clutching a stack of foam trays.

"We're not even open yet. There's no money coming in," the man said.

"I understand your problems, Joe," Bucks said with a smile. "I got some of my own. The guy that works for me got a knife in his back. Imagine that? That's what a lack of cooperation will get you."

Madison's breath froze in her lungs. *You're taking too many wild chances.* Bucks killed Falkner.

Joe's face went milk white.

"So you see, I had to make this call on you myself. One grand. That's the price for opening a business in Desert Valley. Then five hundred a month thereafter."

"I don't have that kind of money to spare," Joe choked out.

"Now you see," Ken said, taking out his nightstick, "that's the kind of attitude that will only end in defeat." He smashed the nightstick into a tray filled with glasses, sending them crashing down in shards onto the floor.

Madison nearly screamed aloud. She clutched a hand to her mouth, the other recording every word.

"Please..." Joe said. "I've sunk everything I have into this business. I'm sixty years old. I can't start over."

"You'll pay up, Joe, because you don't have a choice."

A glint of defiance showed in Joe's face, and his chin went up. "I'll... I'll go to the cops."

Bucks laughed. "You know what, Joe? You remind me of Albert Jennings. Do you know Albert? He ran the lumberyard. He threatened to go to the cops, too. Know what happened to Albert? I had my associate pay him a visit." He leaned closer and rapped his nightstick on the counter. "Now you can visit Albert in the hospital—if he hasn't died, that is."

Madison gasped.

Joe closed his mouth and tightened his grip on the stack of trays.

"Why don't you give me a little tour, Joe?" Bucks said. "Show me the dining area. Since we'll be in business together, I'll be dining here often. Nothing better than a hot dog with all the fixings."

Bucks and Joe moved away into the front of the shop.

Madison's hands trembled so badly she could hardly manage to hold on to her phone as she crouched down. *Steady, Mads.* She forced herself to breathe in and out a few times. Ken Bucks was behind it all. A cop, responsible for intimidation, the near death of Albert Jennings, planting drugs in Tony's backpack. He'd tried to throw the police off the trail by having Falkner fake his death while incriminating King. When she got control of her hands again, she started to text James. Bucks is dirty. I'm here at...

Then a hand came across her mouth, and she was jerked to her feet. Bucks pulled her against him, ripped the tape recorder and phone from her hands.

"Who've we got here?" he breathed into her ear. "Why, I do believe it's Little Red. I thought I heard you sneaking around outside Granny's house."

She struggled, trying to peel away his fingers, but he was strong.

"Didn't you learn anything yet, Little Red? I told you the woods were full of wolves."

Though she thrashed as hard as she could, she was not able to rip his hand away so she could scream. His other arm crooked around her neck and he squeezed, choking off her oxygen. She clawed at his arm, but he only tightened his grip. Head swimming, she kicked out a foot to try and knock him off balance. Her ears began to ring, and she felt her arms go numb and drop uselessly at her sides.

Vaguely she was aware of him opening the trunk of his cruiser, and he dumped her inside.

Her vision blurred. Darkness descended as he slammed the trunk closed.

Since Madison had mentioned she was going to meet with Frances, James went to the bridal salon first, but the doors were locked and the curtains drawn across the windows. It was almost one o'clock. Perhaps Frances had taken a lunch break? He'd decided to try the Cactus Café, to see if Madison had gone there to check in with Kate, when he saw her car parked on the street.

The door was unlocked. He scanned the street. Where had she gone? He ran into the hardware store.

"She didn't come in here," Bill said.

James's gut tightened in frustration.

"But I saw her walking that way." He jabbed his finger. "Toward the new place."

The new place, James thought as he and Hawk took off. A closed-up restaurant?

Inside the Hot Dog Spot, he found Joe sweeping up the broken remnants of a tray full of broken glass.

"What happened?"

Joe glared at him. "Nothing."

"Did you see a woman? A redhead?"

"Ain't seen nobody."

"How about an officer named Ken Bucks?"

The jerk of surprise on Joe's face confirmed it for James, even though the man remained stubbornly silent.

"Which way did he leave?" James demanded.

Joe pointed toward the parking lot.

"I'll be back to talk to you later," James said. He took off through the restaurant and out the door. The lot was empty except for the owner's pickup truck.

There was no sign of a struggle. Where was she?

Then he noticed the faint puff of dust from the dirt trail that led up to the woods. Stomach clenched, he sprinted back to his car, Hawk at his heels. He rounded the corner of the building, tires screeching, and took the path he knew Bucks had traveled.

Hold on, Madison. Just stay alive. I'm on my way.

Madison floated back to consciousness. She was tossed from one side of the trunk to the other as Bucks took what must be a rough trail. Her throat was dry with terror, head still fuzzy from the choking. She tried to calm herself. *Father God, help me.* Her phone was gone. Of course he'd taken it, along with her recorder. She squirmed her way around, fighting the movement of the car, feeling with numb fingers for a trunk release that she could not locate.

A hard jolt banged her head against the trunk lid, and she cried out in pain. Tracing her hands along the edges of her prison, she felt the gap that led to the tail-light. Pushing with all her strength, she popped it out. A spark of hope lit inside her. She felt the sweet rush of fresh air on her face and immediately thrust her hand out, waving frantically to attract attention.

"Help me," she yelled. Swirls of dust obscured her vision, but she kept on, waving and yelling, until she realized the road under the tires was dirt. She caught glimpses of thick brush, and the trees overhead were dense and dark. Her stomach fell. Bucks was taking her deep into the woods to a remote spot where no one would overhear his bloody business.

She could hardly breathe through the panic. *Think, Mads.* She had to get free of the trunk and run. She was certain she could outpace Bucks with enough of a head start. Frantically, she fumbled in the darkness, trying to find something to use as a weapon. Boxes of plastic bags, a first-aid kit, bottled water. Another bounce tossed her on her side, and her legs banged against a jack. She grabbed it. When he opened the trunk, she could swing it at him and ideally drive him back a step, but her angle would be poor, and he was very strong. Her chances weren't good.

Had the car begun to slow? Cold with terror now, she continued to search, scrabbling around until her knee banged against something metallic and cylindrical. A fire extinguisher.

She grabbed it and pulled the pin. Her hands shook as she gripped the lever, ready to squeeze, and aimed the hose. The car was definitely slowing now. Ken Bucks was closing in on the place he intended to kill her.

Shaking all over, she gritted her teeth.

"Go ahead and give it your best shot, Bucks," she hissed aloud. "God didn't make me a survivor so I could be taken down by the likes of you."

The movement stopped. The brakes creaked. She felt the car lurch as Bucks stepped out. Her hands were trembling so badly she thought she might drop the extinguisher. Would he open the trunk and fire his weapon point blank? She didn't think so. It would make too much of a mess. He would order her out and kill her.

Three steps and then the trunk opened. A crack of light dazzled her eyes.

As the lid rose, she squeezed the lever, and yellow powder exploded right in Bucks's face. With a grunt he leaped backward. She scrambled from the trunk. Feet pounding, arms pumping, she raced for the trees, running for her life.

* * *

James radioed for help.

"Wait for backup," Ryder commanded. "You're not taking him on yourself."

"He's got Madison. I'm not waiting."

"You—"

James threw down the radio as he jerked to a stop and leaped from the driver's seat. Buck's car was there, the rear taillight punched out. A fire extinguisher lay on the ground, powder everywhere. Madison's handiwork, he was sure of it. She was alive. His spirit soared. Bucks must have gone after her. The trees closed around him on every side. Which direction had they taken?

Hawk circled, ears flapping. He thanked God that his canine partner was a bloodhound.

James grabbed Madison's sweater from his front seat and lowered it to Hawk, who sniffed diligently.

"Find her," he said, clipping on Hawk's long leash. "Find Madison."

Please, God.

Madison lunged through the trees, fighting at the foliage that clung to her. She had no idea where she was or in which direction she'd find Desert Valley. A tall ridge of rocks stood sentinel to her left. She could hide there, climb up and get her bearings, hunker down in some dark cleft until Bucks left. He was on duty, so he couldn't stay there too long without causing suspicion. Sooner or later he'd have to give up if she could just hide long enough.

Straining to hear any sound that might alert her to Bucks's location, she could not make out a thing.

Slowly, keeping down behind any and every bush, she crept toward the pile of rocks.

Twisting and squirming through low lying boulders and slapping at the bugs that flew in her face, she kept on. Rock bit at her hands, leaving them bloody and raw. Reaching the bottom of the ridge, she crept around the periphery of a jagged piece of granite.

Where Bucks was waiting for her, smiling.

Hawk strained at the leash, dragging James along through the heavy vegetation. It was hot, and the dog was panting. Sweat dampened James's forehead as he followed Hawk, praying every moment he would not be too late.

Hawk plowed on with a steady certainty that heartened him. Hawk would lead James right to Madison. He had no doubt of it.

The wagging of Hawk's tail indicated the dog was closing in. Up ahead, a ridge of rock punched high into the blue sky. James pulled his gun.

Hawk yowled and barked, surging forward before James could secure him. Half stumbling, they stopped short of the rock pile. Hawk let out a bark as Bucks stepped in view, his arm tight around Madison's shoulder, his gun pointed at her head.

James gripped the Glock. "Let her go, Bucks."

Bucks shook his head. "No, James. I don't think so."

Madison grimaced as Bucks's hold around her neck tightened.

James saw the glint of desperate determination in Bucks's eyes. "It's all over. Ryder knows, and the chief. There's no reason to hurt her, because everything's out in the open now."

Bucks smiled. "You watch too much TV. I'm not just going to throw in the towel and surrender. Not to you, some wet-behind-the-ears cop."

"So why'd you do it?" James asked, mind whirling. If he fired, there was a chance he'd hit Madison, or Bucks would squeeze off a shot and get her. *Keep him talking.* "Did you need the money that badly?"

"I've been a cop for years, doing the job, collecting my two-bit paychecks while people like Bruce King rake in the bounty. How's that fair? Follow the rules, put it all on the line every day, silently take the disrespect from every Tom, Dick and Harry who feels he was mistreated, and keep your mouth shut. It's too much. I'm tired of bowing and scraping. It's not fair."

Madison was stiff with fear, her hands clenched around Bucks's forearm.

"It's not fair to victimize people who were just trying to run a business in this town," James said.

Bucks grunted. "Save it for someone who cares. I got no one to go home to, no one in this whole town who will shed a tear for me, either, so listen up. Here's how it's going to go down. I'm walking out of here, back to my car, and you're not going to stop me, because if you do, I will kill her. Got that, tough guy?"

Madison squirmed, and he gripped her more tightly.

If Bucks left with Madison, she was as good as dead. He held the gun steady, praying he could get off the shot of his life.

Hawk yowled, jerking the leash from James's hand. Hawk bounded toward Madison, and instinctively Bucks aimed for the heavy body barreling toward them. Bucks's finger tightened on the trigger. James fired.

And then it was all over.

Ryder and Marlton burst from the trees and raced up to them. Bucks was on the ground, gripping his bleeding shoulder as Hawk slobbered his pleasure all over Madison, his reward for finding his quarry. Ryder secured Bucks's gun.

"Medics en route." He looked from James to Madison. "Okay?"

James nodded.

Madison was standing stone still as if she was carved from marble, oblivious to the dog dancing around her feet.

He holstered his weapon and walked to her. "Madison," he said softly. "We'll get you to a hospital."

She shook her head. "No. I'm not going to a hospital." Her brown eyes were clear, calm, in spite of what she'd been through. She held her chin up. "We got him, didn't we?"

"Yes, Mads, we sure did."

A tear leaked down her cheek, and she swiped at it with her tattered sleeve. "Lee Earnshaw...will he be released now?"

"We will reopen his case, and he'll get a fair hearing. I'll see to it." He held out his hand, and she took it. He walked her away, where she could no longer see Bucks on the ground or the officers milling around.

They moved into a distant pocket of trees. The sunlight filtered softly down on them. It was quiet and fragrant with pine.

"Madison," he said. He stopped, voice breaking, overcome with gratitude that she was alive, unharmed, delivered from a killer who would no longer terrorize her or the town.

"Madison," he started again. Then he gave up and kissed her.

He felt her arms circle up around his neck, fingers twining in his hair, as she kissed him back. Relief spiraled together with a pure, golden happiness. It seemed as if he'd been waiting all his life to find her, to kiss her, to love her.

"I love you," he whispered. "I love you so much. I'm so sorry, for everything, for doubting you, for doubting myself. I know now isn't the right time to tell you, but for a few moments there I thought…"

She put a trembling hand to his cheek, fingers soft as satin.

He cleared his throat. "I thought I might not see you again. I didn't want to wait one more second to tell you the truth."

She looked at him with eyes full of wonder, lips parted, and she stepped away a pace. For a moment, she didn't answer. "It seems like I've spent my whole life looking for the truth, James. It always comes with a price tag."

"What's that?"

"Giving up independence, making yourself vulnerable. That's hard."

"Yes," he agreed. "It is."

"I've never trusted anyone, not really, since I found out about my father."

His heart clenched into a painful fist. She was going to push him away, and he deserved it. She'd nearly been killed, partially because he hadn't trusted her. He deserved to have Madison Coles ripped out of his life forever. He looked at his boots, searching for the control he'd need to let her walk away.

"Until now," she finished.

His head shot up. "What did you say?"

Her hair caught the sunlight, copper fire. "I'm a stubborn student," she said. "Guess it took being nearly killed a few times, but I'm ready for a new path now, James. God's convinced me, and so have you." She went to him then, those magnificent eyes filled with love, and hugged him close. "Thank you for saving my life. I love you, James."

Thank you for rescuing my heart, he wanted to say, but he couldn't. His voice was silenced by a fierce joy, awed by her incredible courage, and the honor she'd bestowed on him by offering her heart. He'd spend the rest of his life making sure she was not hurt again. Adoring, protecting, partnering with Madison Coles. All he could do was cling to her, hold close the woman who'd brought him back to life again, restored his trust in himself.

"My brother and your sister are going to be surprised."

"Oh, I'm not so sure about that," she said with a chuckle.

"And someday," he said, tightening his arms around her, "I want to show you the Harrison ranch. I'm going to buy it back."

She traced a finger along his cheek. "I know you will. I can't wait."

He was leaning in for another kiss when Hawk trotted up and bonked Madison in the leg with his boney head.

James laughed. "Are you going to be able to handle loving a stubborn, slobbery dog, too?"

She laughed, a pure, silvery sound. "Of course. Little Red Riding Hood has to have a wolf around."

Hawk shook his massive ears and flopped over on his side, tired out from his mission.

"I love you, Madison," James whispered, pulling her to him.

She kissed him again, and Hawk added his yowl of assent.

* * * * *

Lynette Eason is a bestselling, award-winning author who makes her home in South Carolina with her husband and two teenage children. She enjoys traveling, spending time with her family and teaching at various writing conferences around the country. She is a member of Romance Writers of America and American Christian Fiction Writers. Lynette can often be found online interacting with her readers. You can find her at Facebook.com/lynette.eason and on Twitter, @lynetteeason.

Books by Lynette Eason

Love Inspired Suspense

Wrangler's Corner

The Lawman Returns
Rodeo Rescuer
Protecting Her Daughter
Classified Christmas Mission
Christmas Ranch Rescue
Vanished in the Night
Holiday Amnesia

Military K-9 Unit

Explosive Force

Family Reunions

Hide and Seek
Christmas Cover-Up
Her Stolen Past

Visit the Author Profile page at Harlequin.com for more titles.

HONOR AND DEFEND

Lynette Eason

The Lord is good, a strong hold in the day of trouble; and he knoweth them that trust in him.

—*Nahum* 1:7

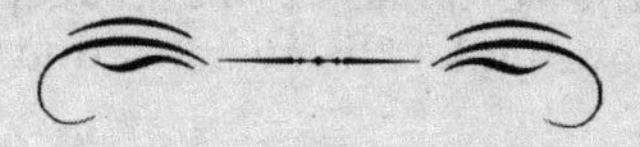

This book is dedicated to all of the heroes
in law enforcement—two-legged and four!
Thank you for your bravery, your service and,
most of all, your dedication to justice.
May the Lord bless you and keep you;
may the Lord make His face to shine upon you.

Acknowledgments

Thank you to my fellow authors Terri Reed, Lenora Worth, Dana Mentink, Valerie Hansen and Shirlee McCoy for your tireless willingness to answer my questions day and night! It's always a pleasure to work with such professionals!

Thank you to Emily Rodmell for letting me do one more. I appreciate you! :)

ONE

K-9 police officer Ellen Foxcroft shot a sideways glance at the man who drove in silent concentration. Just ten minutes ago, they'd picked up three puppies from Sophie Williams. Not only was Sophie a trainer for the Canyon County K-9 Training Center, she also worked with the Prison Pups program. A program Lee Earnshaw, the man behind the wheel, was intimately familiar with, since he'd been part of it up until two weeks ago when he'd been released from prison. Framed. Set up by a dirty cop, he'd lost two years of his life. He'd developed a new hardness and more lines around his eyes than when she'd last seen him.

Two of the dogs they'd just picked up from the prison program were ready to start training to be assistance animals for Ellen's clients—adults and children with disabilities. In addition to being a K-9 officer with the Desert Valley Police Department, she also ran the Desert Valley Canine Assistance program she'd started a few weeks before Lee was released. Already she and her four employees were making a difference in the lives of the people in their community, training the dogs to be service animals for the disabled.

Thanks to Sophie's generosity, Ellen hoped to have the two older puppies ready for the summer camp she planned to offer next month. The younger puppy needed more work—a job Lee would take on as soon as they got back to the facility. "You're awfully deep in thought," she said. "Are you all right?"

Lee blinked and sighed. "I'm fine. I just wish we had some better leads on who might have killed Veronica." Veronica Earnshaw, Lee's sister, had been murdered a little over three months ago. Her killer still walked the streets, and Ellen could tell Lee's frustration level was about to boil over.

"I know. We're working on it, Lee—we really are."

He scowled at her, then turned his attention back to the road. "That's what everyone says, I wish I could see evidence of that."

Ellen grimaced. She wished she could, too, frankly. "An investigation like this takes time. It's unfortunate, but it just does. At least you're out of prison now, and that happened as a result of this investigation. Look at the positive side."

His lips quirked. "You would look at it that way." The puppies in the travel carriers in the back barked and yipped. "I appreciate your giving me this chance to work with you and the pups. Not everyone believes I'm innocent, in spite of the press conference and Ken Bucks's arrest."

"You're welcome."

Former Desert Valley sheriff's deputy, Ken Bucks had been arrested and, in order to secure a deal and a lighter sentence for himself, had confessed to framing Lee and sending him to prison two years ago for a robbery he didn't commit. "I just really want to put it all behind me."

"I'm sure you do." Probably easier said than done. This was Lee's second day on the job. Two days ago, after much self-examination and encouragement from Sophie, she'd approached Lee about working for her, and he'd been reluctant. With their history, she couldn't say she blamed him. They'd dated in high school. Until she'd allowed her mother to chase him away. Her jaw tightened. She didn't want to go there.

Instead, she remembered the flare of attraction she'd felt just from being in his presence again. Just from talking to him and looking into his eyes. Eyes she'd never been able to forget.

Eyes that looked years older and much harder than she remembered. But she'd shoved aside her attraction—and her pride. After some fancy talking, he'd agreed to give working with her a trial run. She figured his love of animals and training had convinced him. She didn't care what it was, she was just glad he'd conceded. He'd started yesterday with a tour of Ellen's assistance facility, which connected to the Canyon County K-9 Training Center. "You know, I was thrilled when Veronica said she was fine with me leasing the unused portion of the K-9 training center."

"Veronica never was one to turn down money."

"Well, whatever her reasons, I'm just glad she let me."

Coming from a wealthy background, Ellen knew people looked at her differently, had various expectations of her, some good, some bad, most wrong. But at least she'd done something good with some of that wealth.

She'd started the program with money from her trust fund. And then listened when Sophie Williams insisted that Lee Earnshaw would be the perfect person to hire to help train the dogs.

Today she could see his eagerness to get started working with the new animals. "Sophie said when it came to working with the dogs at the Prison Pups program, you were the best she'd ever seen. She called you a dog whisperer." After Veronica had been killed, Sophie had taken over the program that trained dogs and rookie K-9 officers. She often used inmates at the prison to help with the training of the puppies until they were old enough for the center. Lee had been one of those inmates.

He gave a low laugh then frowned. "A dog whisperer?" He shrugged. "You know me. I've worked with animals all my life. I like them and they like me. The Prison Pups program was the only thing that kept me sane these past two years."

"I know. And I'm sorry."

"Yeah. I am, too, but it is what it is. I'm trying to move on."

"You're not bitter?"

He glanced at her from the corner of his eye. "I'm bitter. I just fight it on a daily basis, hoping I'll eventually win the battle."

"You will," she said. "Whatever happened to your plans to become a vet?"

He sighed and shrugged. "Life happened."

"But you graduated from college."

"Yes, with a degree in biology. I even started on graduate school, then everything kind of went south with Dad and I had to help him pay bills. Breeding and training dogs was the way to do that."

"Do you have plans to finish school?"

"Yes. One day. Ken Bucks kind of messed that up pretty good. And then Veronica was murdered..."

Ellen heard the unspoken end of the sentence—*and her killer is still out there.*

She couldn't help studying his features. Brown hair with a brand-new cut, brown eyes that at times looked hard and cold but were always alive and warm when he worked with the animals His strong jaw held a five-o'clock shadow. She used to kiss that jaw on a regular basis. She cleared her throat and tried to shake her memories, but they just wouldn't leave her alone. Memories of being his girlfriend, the vicious conflict with her mother. And then Lee had walked away from it all.

Now she was back in town and he was out of prison and she was working in Desert Valley. For the time being. Thanks to her mother's stipulation that she and the other rookies had to stay in Desert Valley until Veronica's murder was solved or she would withdraw the funding she'd given the department. Funding the department couldn't afford to lose. Ellen planned to have a few words about that with her mother when she woke from the coma she'd been in for the past three months. Someone had broken in to her home and attacked her, almost killing her. "I can understand your frustrations, Lee. I feel the same way about my mother's attacker." Ellen desperately wanted to find out who did it.

"I know, it's just—"

The back windshield shattered and Ellen gave a low scream of surprise. Lee jerked the wheel to the right.

"Get down!" Outside sounds rushed through the missing window. Someone was shooting at them!

Ellen ignored his order and turned in her seat to look out the back. "He's coming up on your five o'clock. Coming in for another shot." It was the perfect place for an ambush. On a back road that didn't see much traffic just outside a small town.

Ellen's tension mounted and she was extremely glad she'd left Carly, her golden retriever K-9 partner, at the training center for this trip. It was supposed to take no more than two hours all in. An hour to the prison and an hour back. And while Lee had been as tense as she'd ever seen him at returning to the prison, he hadn't said a word. She released her weapon from its holster and gripped it in her right hand, readying herself for the next attack.

Four months, she thought.

Less than four months ago, she'd finished the twelve-week training session at the Canyon County K-9 Training Center. The state of Arizona had started the program years ago and found it quite successful. They trained new police academy recruits to be K-9 officers. She was a newbie, a rookie officer with the Desert Valley Police Department.

And now she might have to shoot someone.

The thought wanted to paralyze her, but her training kicked in and she knew she could do what she had to in order to protect herself and Lee.

The car roared up beside them and she got a brief glance at the driver and the gun he had pointed at her. Lee stomped the brakes, throwing her against the seat belt. She jerked forward then back, her head slamming into the headrest, her hand against the door. She lost her grip on the weapon and it clattered to the floor. The next shot took off the passenger-side mirror of the truck. Another hit a tire. Lee fought with the wheel and the truck listed to the side, but that didn't stop him.

He spun the wheel to the right and they roared onto a side road. The other vehicle swept past. Lee hit the brakes again and backed up, the truck lurching, the rim of the flattened tire grinding. But he managed to complete his three-point turn so that the front of his truck now faced the road. She watched the disappearing taillights of the other car.

As soon as Lee put the truck in Park, Ellen rolled out of the passenger door, grabbed her weapon from the floor and aimed in the direction the other car had gone. "Lee, are you okay? Come out the passenger door."

"I'm fine." He landed on the ground beside her, kneeling behind the protection of the open door. He radiated tension. "I'm going to check on the dogs."

Ellen registered the barking. "I'm calling for backup." She grabbed the radio from her hip and put in the call. When Dispatch answered, she rattled off the information. She glanced at Lee who was also watching the road. "Anything?"

"No, not yet."

"Help is on the way."

She maintained her vigilance even as her mind searched for answers. Who would want to attack her and Lee? Probably the same people behind the other trouble the police department and her fellow K-9 officers had faced since being assigned to solve Veronica Earnshaw's murder. Then again, Lee had just been released from prison. Could it be someone after him?

The drone of an engine caught her attention and all

speculation fled. She heard it coming closer as Lee pulled the two crates from the backseat of the king cab one after the other and set them on the ground by the blown tire. He handled the heavy cargo as though it weighed nothing, but she knew the two six-month-old pups weighed about fifty pounds each. "I hear something. Are they coming back?"

"Sounds like it." She raised her gun and aimed it. When the car crested the hill, she knew they were in for a second attack. "That's them." The dark gray Buick slowed; the barrel of a rifle appeared in the window. She figured it was now or never and tightened her finger, heard her weapon bark, felt the kick against her hand.

The sedan's front windshield exploded. The driver hit the gas and the vehicle blew past in a drunken weave. Ellen spun from her position and moved to the back of the truck near the crated, yapping puppies. This time the car didn't turn around—and she got a partial plate. "Oh-four," she whispered. "I didn't get the rest of it. But I got 04."

She turned to find Lee hovering over the puppies, his features tense, face pale. "Are you all right?" he asked.

"Yeah. You?"

He nodded. "The puppies are fine, too."

Ellen pulled her phone from the clip on her belt. "I'm going to find out where backup is. Keep an eye out for them to come back while I'm on the phone, will you?" Not only did they need a tow truck for Lee's vehicle, they needed a ride back to town and a Be On the Lookout—a BOLO—put out for the gray sedan.

"Of course." He looked distracted. Thoughtful. His brows pulled together over the bridge of his nose as if he knew something and was pondering it.

"What is it?" she asked.

His eyes flicked to hers then he shook his head. "Nothing."

The dispatcher came on the line. "Where's my backup?"

"On the way, Ellen. They should be there within minutes."

"Tell them to be looking for a dark gray sedan—a Buick—with 04 in the license plate."

"Copy that."

Ellen hung up and paced behind the protection of Lee's truck while she watched the road and thought about what had just happened. "Did you tell anyone about us going to pick up the puppies?" she asked.

Lee frowned. "No. But it's not because I thought it was some top secret mission—it's just that I don't talk to too many people."

Ellen heard the bitterness behind the words. Being imprisoned for two years for a crime one didn't commit could do that to a person. She also knew that people in Desert Valley, Arizona, had long memories and weren't very forgiving. Never mind that the man before her had been set up by a corrupt cop.

When she'd heard Lee had been arrested for robbery, she'd been stunned. Then disbelief had set in. But the evidence had been overwhelming. Now she knew why. It was easy to frame someone when the investigating officer planted evidence. Disgust curled inside her. She had nothing but contempt for those who used their power to hurt others, to fulfill some kind of personal agenda.

Sirens broke the silence and she straightened, her eyes once again going to the place where the gray sedan had disappeared. Some of her adrenaline eased now that she felt sure they weren't coming back.

Chief of police Earl Jones stepped from his cruiser. Seventy years old, he topped six feet two inches and carried himself well in spite of his large gut. His gray hair looked mussed, as though he'd run his hands through it several times. His gaze landed on Ellen then slid over to Lee. "Not out of prison two weeks and you're already causing trouble? Not a good way to start your new life."

Lee nearly bit through his tongue to keep the words he'd like to fling at the man from making their way past his teeth. He simply stared at the chief. He wouldn't defend himself. He didn't have to. The fact that he stood here a free man was defense enough as far as he was concerned. Chief Jones raised a brow, a glint of respect lighting his eyes before he hitched his britches and held out a hand to Lee. "You got a raw deal. I'm glad it all worked out for you."

Lee blinked and swallowed his anger. He shook the man's hand. "Thanks. I am, too."

The chief looked at Ellen. "What's going on here, Foxcroft?"

Ellen's gaze darted between the two them. Lee maintained his cool stance. Deputy Louise Donaldson exited her cruiser and joined them on the side of the road. The woman was in her early sixties and, if Lee remembered correctly, had been widowed at a rather young age.

She was tall and solid, her hair cut in a no-nonsense brown bob. Her dark eyes were serious and concerned. He also knew she planned to retire soon. In fact he wondered who would retire first, the chief or Louise. And why he was even thinking about that confused him.

He attributed it to some kind of coping mechanism. If he thought about the mundane, he didn't have to think about the fact that he and Ellen could have been killed a short few moments ago.

"We were shot at," Ellen was saying. "I think there were two of them in the vehicle. They drove a dark gray Buick and I got a partial plate." She gave it to him. "They've also got a busted windshield."

"I'll call for a tow truck," Louise said. She got on her phone and Earl rubbed a hand over his craggy face.

"All right, let's get you two back to town and get this figured out. Donaldson!"

"Yes, Chief?" She slid her phone back into the clip.

"Get Marlton and Harmon out here to take care of the evidence collection before the sun goes down. We've only got a couple hours before dark." Dennis Marlton and Eddie Harmon, two more of Desert Valley's finest—only Lee had come to figure out they weren't quite so fine. Between ready-for-retirement cops and simple ineffectiveness, Lee decided it was a wonder enforcement of the law even happened in Desert Valley.

Chief Jones was a good man, but his upcoming retirement had him slacking off. The chief continued, "I'll stay here while you chauffeur these two back to town. Officer Foxcroft's got some paperwork to fill out on the shooting. Make sure her gun is turned in and all is done according to procedure."

Louise's jaw tightened as though she didn't like being told how to do her job, but she simply nodded. "Of course. Come on."

Lee put the crated puppies in the back of the DVPD SUV cruiser then he climbed in the back while Ellen took the front passenger seat. Louise started the vehicle and pulled away from the edge of the road. Lee reached over and settled his hand on Ellen's shoulder. She started and turned to look at him, confusion clouding her eyes. But at least she didn't pull away. "I'm glad you're all right," he said. "That was some quick thinking and good shooting out there."

She shot him a tight smile. "Thanks. I just wanted to stop them."

"You did that, all right."

She fell silent and Lee removed his hand from her shoulder to look out the window and watch the scenery pass by. He didn't take for granted the fact that he could do this now. He'd missed riding in a car for the past two years. Missed driving his truck. He'd missed a lot of things. The anger wanted to bubble up, but he took a deep breath and forced it down. Anger at what he couldn't change wouldn't help anything. It would just cause the bitterness to grow, and he didn't want to go through life that way. Had made a vow he wouldn't let it consume him. Not like it had his father. He forced the thought away.

Within minutes they were at the police station. Lee climbed out of the cruiser, grabbed the puppies from the back and waited for Ellen to climb out. He let her go in front of him, watching her enter the station, her steps light, movements graceful. He realized his feelings for her hadn't diminished one bit from their high school days. No matter how hard he tried to deny it, he was still attracted to her. And her mother still hated him. No doubt even more so at this point. He wasn't just a kid from the wrong side of the tracks anymore—he'd been incarcerated. Oh, yes, that would go over well with Marian Foxcroft. Assuming she ever woke up from her coma to find out he was now out and working with her daughter. As much as he disliked the woman, he realized he could feel compassion for her. She was in the hospital in a coma, a victim of a home invasion and a vicious attack. No one deserved that. He swallowed hard and pulled the rolling crates behind him. He trailed Ellen as she led the way through the Desert Valley Police Department lobby.

"Ellen?"

Ellen paused and turned to the woman who'd called her name. "Yes, Carrie?"

Lee racked his brain trying to place what he'd learned about the secretary and couldn't come up with much. In her thirties, she wore thick horn-rimmed glasses and her brown hair was always in the same style every time he'd seen her around town. Up in one of those messy-bun things some women managed to twist their hair into. She was quiet and kind and did her job well if the rumors were true.

She handed Ellen a piece of paper. "The hospital called just to say there's been no change in your mother. Dr. North said to let you know he had a family emergency and wouldn't be able to meet with you this afternoon, but if you'll call his secretary to reschedule, she'll fit you in as soon as possible."

"That's fine. Thanks." She frowned. "I wonder why he didn't call my cell."

"He said he did but you didn't answer."

"She was kind of busy," Lee said.

Ellen nodded. "Thanks, Carrie."

"Of course." She turned back to her computer and Louise continued the trek to a conference room.

Officer Donaldson shut the door behind them and

Lee saw Ellen check her phone. "Yep. Missed call." She glanced at Lee. "Right in the middle of our little incident. I never heard it ring."

He hadn't, either.

Ellen removed her weapon and placed it in the bag the officer held out for her. "You know the drill," Officer Donaldson said. "There'll be an investigation. You're off duty for the moment."

Ellen sighed. "I know."

"The good news is since there are no wounded or dead bodies, you could be cleared for return to duty as early as tomorrow or the next day. We'll let you know."

"Thanks, Louise."

The woman's brown eyes softened a fraction. "You're welcome. You did good, rookie."

Ellen gave a faint smile. "Thanks."

"How's your mother?"

Her smile slipped. "She's still alive. We're just praying she wakes up soon and can tell us who did this to her. Until then, she's under twenty-four-hour guard to make sure no one can get to her and finish what they started. Chief Jones was willing to have you all take shifts guarding her, but I know Mom wouldn't have wanted to take you away from your duties here. I've hired a private agency to make sure there's a guard on her door. So far, that's worked out well."

"We're all praying for her." Louise set the weapon aside and motioned for them to sit at the table. Once seated Lee wanted to fidget. He wasn't interested in being in this building ever again. Louise pulled a laptop in front of her. "All right, let's go through it all again."

Lee started to say something when Carrie entered the room. Louise raised a brow. "Yes?"

"Sorry to interrupt, but someone found a glove behind a Dumpster near veterinarian Tanya Fowler's office and brought it in." She held up the bagged glove while he pictured Tanya, the veterinarian he'd seen occasionally when she'd come to the prison to vaccinate the dogs with the Prison Pups program. A sweet lady whose nonjudgmental eyes never failed to raise his spirits. He tuned back into what Carrie was saying. "Two kids were waiting with their mother while she had their dog in with Dr. Fowler and they ran around the side of the building playing hide and seek. Little Justin Daniels found it and gave it to his mother."

"Okay. And it's important because...?"

"It matches the set worn by one of the robbers who robbed that bank in Flagstaff six months ago."

Louise frowned. "How would she have known that?"

"She wouldn't. She turned it in to us because it had five one-hundred-dollar bills in it and thought someone may have reported it missing."

"Has someone?"

"No." Carrie pushed her glasses up on the bridge of her nose with her forefinger. "But when the robbery first happened, we got all those wanted notices faxed to us, remember? The chief also got the video footage of the robbery." She walked farther into the room and placed the glove on the desk. "He and I watched it together just in case I spotted anyone hanging around town. Turns out I recognized the gloves in the surveillance video. They're a pretty popular brand and I sent this exact pair to a cousin for Christmas last year." She wrinkled her nose. "Well, not *this* one, but a pair just like them. So I just checked the bank footage again to be sure, and this sure looks like one of the gloves."

Louise nodded. “Okay, that’s good news. I wouldn’t have thought there would be any chance of picking up that trail again. Send the glove off to the lab. Take Justin Daniels’s fingerprints as well as his mother’s and send them for comparison.” Carrie nodded. “Also, get the serial numbers from the bills and send them to the Flagstaff PD. I don’t know that they’ll need them, but it can’t hurt to have them just in case.”

“Got it.” Carrie turned and walked out, carrying the evidence.

Louise looked up at Ellen. “You heard about that bank robbery, right?”

“Vaguely. It happened shortly after we started our training with Veronica and that’s where my focus was. I think I remember that they never found the money, right?”

“No, it happened just as the bank was closing on a Friday afternoon. Two men in masks and semiautomatics in broad daylight. Shook the whole city up.”

“They were obviously professionals and they had it well planned.”

“True,” she sighed. “They got away that day, but the FBI was called in and arrested one of the robbers—a Nolan Little. The second robber got away, but the FBI tracked him down right here in Desert Valley two days later, hiding in an abandoned mobile home. He got into a shootout with them and was killed. They searched and found his weapon and a few bills, but he didn’t have the bank money on him.”

“Let me guess, the one they caught isn’t talking.”

“He couldn’t if he wanted to. He was killed about two months into serving his sentence.”

"So anyone who might have known where the money is can't talk because they're dead."

"Yes. At least the ones we know about."

"You think there's someone else involved?"

"The FBI was convinced there was a third person—a driver—but they've never been able to prove it. He wasn't in the video and there wasn't a car at the scene."

"How did they get away?" Ellen asked.

"On foot. Ran right out the back door through a back alley and disappeared. That's why we think there was a third person involved. Someone with a car that was never seen. Someone who knew where the security cameras were and made sure to park out of view. The robbers climbed in and they drove away." She sighed. "The FBI sends the chief an update every so often, but I think they've probably given up on ever recovering the money—or the third person if there ever was one." She shrugged. "Who knows? Maybe with the glove, they'll get a fresh trail to follow." She drew in a deep breath. "Now, Lee, what can you tell me about the shootout that just occurred?"

Lee shifted. "I think I have something that will help."

"What's that?"

"I have a dash cam on my truck. We just need to watch the video." He held up his phone and pressed the screen to pull up the app.

He shook his head at the irony. After everything this department had put him through, he had something that could possibly help them. And he was going to push aside his initial reaction of "let them fend for themselves" and do it.

This time they'd better not mess up.

TWO

An hour later, Ellen and Lee walked out of the building with Lee rolling the puppies behind in their carriers. "A dash cam?" Ellen asked him.

He shrugged. "I don't know. Call me paranoid. But after everything that happened with the crooked cop and..." He shook his head. "I'm not going to be in that position again. So I mounted a dash cam on my rearview mirror as some sort of protection, I guess. Maybe it was stupid."

"And maybe you're brilliant. I can't say I blame you a bit. And it allowed us to see one of the men in the car."

"Yes." He frowned.

"Everything all right?"

"Yes. I'm just thinking."

"About?" She spotted the SUV in the road, getting ready to turn in to the lot. "Hold that thought."

Whitney Godwin, also a rookie K-9 officer, pulled in and parked. She climbed out of the truck, her shoulder-length light blond hair blowing around her face. She shoved it back and waved at Ellen. "Hey, there. Are you okay?"

"We survived. That's the good news. Thanks for

bringing the car," Ellen said. "Lee picked me up at my home this morning so we're a bit stranded." She took the keys from Whitney's outstretched hand. Looking into her friend's eyes, she could see contentment. Happiness. All due to the new man in her life. A doctor named David Evans. They'd had some hard times but had made it through to the other side. Now they were planning a wedding.

It made Ellen happy for Whitney…and sad for herself. Would she ever have that look? She glanced at Lee. She'd actually had it years ago. Back when she and Lee were together. When they weren't fighting about her mother, they'd had some great times, been happy. She sighed. Whitney's features clouded in concern. "Why the heavy sigh? You okay?"

Ellen forced her lips into an upward curve. "Yes, just…reminiscing, sorry. Do you need a ride anywhere?"

"No." Whitney's smile came back. "David's on his way to get me. We're taking Shelby for a picnic." Shelby was Whitney's baby daughter.

Lee found a spot of grass, clipped leashes to the three pups and let them loose to take care of business. When they were finished, he got them back into the carriers and rolled them over to the vehicle where she and Whitney stood.

"Lee, do you know Whitney?"

He set the puppies in the back area of the vehicle where Carly usually rode, then held out a hand to Whitney. "I don't think we've met. It's a pleasure."

"Same here." She eyed the building and grimaced. "I hate to go in on my day off, but I have some leftover paperwork I need to finish up before David and I can enjoy the rest of the day. I'll see you later."

She disappeared through the glass doors. Lee turned to Ellen. "I'm starving," he said.

"Want to hit a drive-through and take the food to the training facility? We can eat and talk business if you're up to it."

"I am if you are."

He still looked a bit distracted. What was on his mind? The shooting probably. "You okay?"

He blinked and climbed into the passenger seat. "Yeah."

"Something's bothering you."

"How do you figure?"

She gave a low chuckle. "Come on, Lee, we used to be best friends." Actually, they'd been more than that, but that sentence was much safer than saying they'd one time been in love. The flare in his eyes said he was thinking it. She cleared her throat. "I can read you pretty well even after all these years. You have that little tic in your forehead that gives you away every time."

He pressed his fingers to it and his brow furrowed. "Let's get back to the facility so we can talk without distractions."

Ellen wasn't crazy about the fact that he wanted to wait to talk, but she could be patient. When she had to. But... "Why don't you just tell me what it is that's bothering you?"

He sighed. "Fine. When we were attacked, I thought I recognized one of the men in the car. The dash cam confirmed it."

Ellen stared at him even while she cranked the vehicle's ignition. "What? And you're just now saying something?"

"I wanted to know for sure before I said anything."

"And you're sure now?"

"No, but I figured you could help me find out if I'm right or not."

"So who do think it is?"

He sighed and rubbed his eyes. "I'm not sure so maybe I shouldn't say anything, but if it's him—"

Her ringing phone cut him off. She glanced at the dashboard. Chief Jones's number flashed. "Hello?"

Her Bluetooth kicked in and his voice came over the speakers. "Foxcroft. Where are you?"

"Just leaving the station. Do you need me to come back in?"

"No, just wanted to let you know we got a hit on that partial plate." While the chief talked, she drove.

"And?"

"There was a vehicle stolen last night. When we ran the partial against all of the ones in the system, we managed to narrow it down to the one that was used in the attack. Who knew you were going to pick up those puppies today?"

Ellen thought. "I don't know. It wasn't a secret. I've already checked with Lee and he didn't mention it to anyone. I told my staff at the assistance center so they could get an area prepared, but other than that, no one that I recall. Sophie could have mentioned it to someone, I suppose."

He grunted. "And it's possible the attack had nothing to do with that anyway. All right, rookie, be careful. Hopefully we'll get all this cleared up in the next day or so and you'll be back on duty. Tell Earnshaw the dash cam thing is paranoia at its finest. Glad he had it installed. Sorry he felt the need for it."

"He heard you."

"Thanks, Chief," Lee said before falling silent.

She hung up and within minutes, she was pulling into the parking lot of the Desert Valley Canine Assistance Center attached to the K-9 Unit Training Center.

Ellen threw the vehicle in Park and climbed out. Lee followed, rolling the puppies with him. He took them into a fenced area that had been specifically set up for them and let the three pups out of the carriers. They bolted into the warm grass, tumbling over one another, nipping and yapping, clearly glad to be able to run off some energy. "What are their names?" she asked. "They should be on their tags."

He pointed to the one running laps around the space. "That one is Dash."

"Appropriate." She looked at the other two. One sat on his haunches, tongue lolling as his gaze bounced between his friends. She walked over and snagged his tag. "This is King. I see why they named him that. He looks like a king ruling over his subjects."

"You're right, he does," Lee said with a nod. He grabbed the last dog by the collar as she wandered past and checked her tag. "And this is Lady."

She licked his hand and Ellen laughed. "Dainty and sweet."

He smiled. "All right. Dash, King and Lady. Poor girl is outnumbered, isn't she?"

"It'll make her stronger."

He nodded and locked the gate and walked toward her.

She waited for him, hands on her hips, mind only partially on naming the pups. She wanted to focus on what he'd revealed before the chief's call. "So you think you know one of the guys who attacked us?"

"Yes. A guy from the prison who was released around the same time I was."

She studied him. "What were you mixed up in at the prison, Lee, that would inspire someone to come after you like that?"

His jaw went rigid and Ellen blinked at the flare of rage—and hurt—that flashed in his eyes. "Really? That's the first thing that comes to you mind? That's what you think?" His fingers curled into fists. "You're just like her, aren't you?" he said, his voice low and strained.

"What?"

He jabbed a finger at her. "You're just like your mother."

"That's not fair."

"No, it's not. It's not fair that she didn't like me just because of who my family was. It's not fair that she interfered in our relationship. A lot of things aren't fair. And you're following right in her footsteps. You're judging me without all the facts. Well, that's fine. You're entitled to think and say what you want, but I don't have to stand here and listen to it." He started to walk off.

"Where are you going?"

"Home."

"How are you going to get there? You don't have a car, remember?"

He held up a cell phone, his eyes narrowed. She shivered at the coldness there. "All too well. However, while there aren't many, I do have a few friends left in this town. I can get a ride. Or I'll just walk. It's not that far." He spun on his heel and kept going.

Ellen sighed and dropped her chin to her chest. Was he right? Was she being judgmental? The fact that he compared her to her mother made her shudder. "Wait, Lee. Stop. You haven't even eaten your food."

"It's still in the bag, I'll take it with me."

He stopped his march at the car, opened the door and pulled out one of the fast-food bags. Then he turned his back on her once more and headed for the edge of her property, which would lead him to the main road. "Who was it, Lee? Who did you recognize?" He didn't answer, just kept walking. "Lee!"

"I'll talk to you tomorrow, Ellen." And then he disappeared around the edge of the house.

She gave a low groan and took off after him. "Stop, will you?"

She rounded the corner and slammed into his hard chest. "Oof."

He caught her biceps, the white food bag dangling from one hand. She looked up. The chill in his eyes hadn't thawed one degree. His features resembled granite. She drew in his scent and swallowed, the past rushing in to blindside her. She remembered clearly being held in his arms. Sitting in the hammock, her ear pressed against his chest, listening to his heart thud a steady beat. She remembered his sweet kisses and whispered promises. She remembered it all. And yearned to go back to recapture each and every moment.

He gently set her away from him and reality intruded. She straightened. There was no going back. There was only now and what the future might bring. And that didn't include Lee. Once the murders were solved and her mother woke from the coma—and she refused to believe she wouldn't—Ellen was going to request a transfer. There was no way she was staying Desert Valley forever. She was simply marking time until everything was wrapped up.

No matter what her mother thought—or wanted.

She was still leaving once the murders were solved. Ryder Hayes' wife's case was still open after five years, and the two deputies whose deaths originally looked like accidents now appeared to be possible murder victims. And so she and the other deputies were in Desert Valley until these cases were solved. But until then…

"Don't go," she blurted. Then bit her lip.

His eyes didn't soften—but he did hesitate. Hope flared. "I need to think about some things," he said, "and I need to do that at home. We'll talk later."

She sighed. When he was in this kind of mood there was no talking him out of it. "Fine. I'll give you a ride home. Let me get Carly."

He studied her a moment, then gave a terse nod. She walked up the steps to the front door, unlocked it and whistled for Carly. The sleek golden retriever with the soft brown eyes bounded over to her and expressed her delight in Ellen's presence. Ellen scratched the dog's silky ears then led the way to the truck. She opened Carly's door and the dog hopped in, sniffing the area. The pups had left their scent and Carly definitely noticed. She finally seemed to accept the smell and settled down. Ellen shut the door and climbed into the driver's seat. Lee was already in the truck with his seat belt fastened. "Will you at least tell me who you recognized? I need to know."

She started the truck and backed out of the spot. Lee considered keeping the information to himself, but couldn't do it. When she hit the main road, he finally answered her.

"A former inmate," he said. "And while he served at the same I did, I knew him before I went to prison." He winced. "Even after everything it still galls me to say that sentence." He tightened his jaw against the anger then breathed deeply before exhaling slowly. He could tell her this. He used to tell her everything. And even though he wasn't exactly happy with her jump to judgment, if he had information that could lead to Veronica's killer, he'd swallow his pride. "I used to hang out with him before I met you."

"So who is he?"

He sighed. "A troublemaker. Like I said, he was released about the same time I was. Not because he was innocent, but because he'd served his time."

"A name, Lee."

He sighed. "Freddie Parrish."

She lifted a brow. "Freddie Parrish? Wait a minute. I know him. We went to high school with him."

"Yep. He and I graduated together. I kind of lost track of him after high school, though. We went our separate ways."

"Yeah. You went to college."

"Yes."

"And so did Freddie, for a while. He had options. He could have finished school. He could have just gone to work if he didn't want to do school. I wonder what made him turn to a life of crime."

He shook his head. "Some people just make bad decisions, get mixed up with the wrong people. I don't know." He rubbed his chin. "You know, they offered a lot of college courses at the prison."

"Sure, I know that. Including the vet tech program through one of the local colleges in Flagstaff."

He nodded. "A lot of the inmates take advantage of it to get their education. It gives them hope that when they get out, they can stay straight and get a good job."

"I think it's a great idea."

"I know Freddie took a couple of the courses, and was even real close to finishing the program before he was recruited to work with the program's veterinarian, who took care of the puppies."

"What was he in prison for?" she asked.

"He had several DUIs and had gotten off with fines the first couple of times. Then he got into a bar fight with a guy who was supposed to be a friend and cut him with broken bottle. The judge gave him three years. He served all three."

She tapped the wheel. "We'll check him out, see if he has an alibi for the shooting." She handed him her phone. "Send a text to the chief with the information, will you? Tell him I want Freddie brought in for questioning."

Lee did as she'd asked.

She drove with confidence, and then he caught her looking at him from the corner of her eye. "What?" he asked.

"Don't take this the wrong way, but did you renew your friendship with Freddie in prison?"

Her question rocked him and he shot her a black look. "No, we didn't renew our friendship. The only reason I was ever around him was because he was a vet tech for the Prison Pups program. We worked together and that was it. I liked the program. Sophie Williams is a good woman and amazing with the dogs. I kept my mouth shut and my head down because I didn't want to lose out on the only thing that allowed me to forget—if just for a brief moment—what my life had become."

She swallowed and looked down. "I understand."

"No. You don't. And I hope you never do. Anyway, I caught Freddie mistreating the animals and told Sophie. She was furious and kicked him out of the program."

She pursed her lips and raised a brow. "I would think that might cause him to hold a grudge."

"Yes, but he doesn't strike me as the type to work alone."

"What do you mean?"

"He's a bully only when he feels like his victims won't—or can't—fight back or when he knows someone's got his back. In prison, during the time in the yard, he only hung around with those he'd earned favor with."

"Earned favor with?"

Lee sighed. "You've been in law enforcement long enough to know that prison has its own culture. There are rules and regulations just like on the outside, but they're tailored for prison life. It *looked* like Freddie was behaving himself. It *looked* like he was a model prisoner, but mostly that was because he was so sneaky. He never got caught doing anything wrong—until I caught him being rough with the pups. But he had access to areas of the prison that others didn't have. As a result, he was able to gather information that he could either use to gain favor with those who had more clout than himself or sell to the highest bidder."

"I see. He had friends who would watch his back so he could continue his sneaky activities. Friends that would do his dirty work if he needed them to."

"Exactly."

Ellen frowned. "Okay. Hopefully the chief will have someone bring him—and whoever was with him—in for questioning soon."

"Hopefully." He rubbed a hand through his hair. "And now, if you don't mind, I'd like to change the subject," he said.

"All right. What is it?"

"I don't want *you* to take this the wrong way, but you cops are looking at the wrong people for suspects in Veronica's murder."

"What do you mean?"

"You're looking at the troublemakers, the people with grudges—and that's a list a mile long and is going to take forever to cover. You need to be looking at the not so obvious."

"We're running the investigation exactly as it's supposed to be run."

"I know that's what you think, but I'm not sure I agree." He held up a hand. "No, I'm not a cop and, no, I haven't been trained in criminal investigation, but I can't help thinking that you need to be looking at Veronica's last day. Who did she come into contact with? Who did she speak with? Interact with? Fight with?"

Ellen pulled up at his house and simply sat while she digested his words. He watched her mull them over and knew she was formulating a response to appease him. He let her think while he looked at his home trying to see it through her eyes.

He loved what he'd managed to do with it. Now it had an outbuilding attached to a kennel. The exercise areas were fenced in and ready to see action. He'd built a good business before he'd been incarcerated.

His gaze wandered to the small three-bedroom ranch

house that he'd grown up in. One her mother considered to be on the wrong side of town, but one where he knew Ellen had found acceptance and many hours of happiness—as long as Veronica wasn't home. They'd all been happier when his sister hadn't been home. Guilt hit him at the thought and he grimaced.

"I hear what you're saying, Lee, I do," Ellen said. "And we're looking into all of that. I promise we're doing our job."

"I'm not saying you're not. I'm simply saying your focus is in the wrong place. Ordinary people can snap when pushed too far, not just the troublemakers." He'd learned that in prison.

She sighed. "I don't know what else to tell you. We're aware of this. We're working on it. Investigations take time." She tapped her fingers on the wheel. "Okay, I'll tell you this." She paused.

"Tell me what?"

"One thing that's really got our attention is the break-ins that are happening all around town. I'm sure you've heard of them."

"Yes, of course." Everyone in town was on edge due to the break-ins.

"There's been a rash of them," she said. "Residents are worried and so are the cops. We understand their need to protect their property and their families, but we also don't need a trigger-happy home owner accidentally shooting his neighbor."

He grunted and climbed from the truck. "A valid concern. On both sides. But what do the break-ins have to do with the investigation into my sister's murder?"

"They're not your average, run-of-the-mill break-ins. The people doing them don't steal anything. Yes, if there's some cash lying around, they take it, but they don't steal expensive electronics that could be easily fenced or even things like jewelry. One woman had a thousand-dollar diamond necklace hanging on her mirror and they left it."

"Maybe they just didn't notice it."

"That's possible. But it's not just that. This just *feels* different. It's like they're looking for something and when they don't find it, they just leave."

"So what are they looking for?" He'd forgotten his anger with her for the moment, simply glad she was sharing the information with him.

"When we found your sister, we also found her with two German shepherd pups. We know she was planning on microchipping three."

"Yes, I know all that." He'd been told this when he'd gone to the station after his release from prison demanding answers about the progress in his sister's investigation. "Hold that thought. Grab your food and let's eat inside."

She snagged the bag and released Carly. The dog sniffed the ground as she followed the humans toward the house. Ellen stepped inside his childhood home. She looked around. "I heard about your dad dying. I'm so sorry."

Lee closed his eyes. "I am, too. Even sorrier that he drank himself to death and there wasn't anything I could do to stop him." He cleared his throat and moved aside a stack of magazines from the kitchen table. "Veronica kept the house up for me while I was incarcerated. As much as I hated this place growing up—with the exception of the times that you were here—I sure was glad to have it to come back to when I got out a couple of weeks ago."

"I'm sure." She looked at the dog. "Carly, sit." Carly's hind end hit the floor. "Good girl." She scratched her ears.

He pulled the food out of the bag and set it on the table. "Water okay? I don't have much to drink around here."

"Water sounds great." He filled the glasses and a bowl for Carly. The dog lapped it and Lee joined her at the table. "So enough about that. You said you found Veronica with two puppies, but she was supposed to be microchipping three."

"Right. We still haven't found the missing puppy, Marco."

He lifted a brow. "I've seen the signs around town, the posters asking for information. Is he really that important to the case?"

"We believe so. And we believe the person who killed your sister is the one breaking in to the houses. We think they're looking for that missing German shepherd puppy, as well."

He frowned. "But…why?" He took a bite out of his hamburger and shook a few fries onto the wrapper.

"We don't know," Ellen said. "Unless the people who broke in to the K-9 training center were after the puppies in the first place. Maybe they wanted them to sell." She shrugged. "Veronica was there microchipping those puppies as a last-minute thing. Maybe the people who broke in to the training center thought she would be gone. We don't know. We haven't put it all together yet, but the missing puppy is definitely a connection in your sister's murder."

He rubbed his eyes. "Thanks for telling me that. It helps to know there's at least one lead you're following."

"So..." She cleared her throat. "I'm sorry."

"For?"

"Judging you. I shouldn't have reacted like that. I'm sure while you were in prison you came across a lot of troublemakers. Troublemakers you'd recognize once they were back on the street." She shook her head. "I jumped to conclusions. I was wrong and I'm sorry for hurting you. Again."

A lump formed in his throat and he looked away for a moment to get his emotions under control. He took a sip of water. "It's hard not to get defensive sometimes. I'm working on it. I worked on it for the entire two years I was locked up for something I didn't do. I watched my father become a bitter, hateful man after my mother walked out. Veronica changed, too. She went from being a loving sister to a nasty person I didn't want to be around for very long. I determined at a young age that I wouldn't let life do that to me." He gave a low laugh. "I never thought life would throw an undeserved prison sentence at me, though, so it's been a struggle to keep that promise to myself, but my grandmother's influence, her unwavering support, visits—and prayers—have helped."

"I'm sure. Your grandmother was a sweetheart."

He nodded. "Still is." He glanced at his plate. "She's living in a retirement home now in Flagstaff and is loving it. I'm happy for her. I wish I could get down there more often to visit, though." Flagstaff was about four hours south of Desert Valley. Lee took another sip of his drink and set the glass on the table. "You have some big plans for the assistance center. I like the way you think."

She raised a brow. “Well, thanks.” Her eyes started to glow. “You know, coming from a wealthy background was often a pain when I was growing up. Everyone thought my life should be perfect because I was a Foxcroft. Didn’t matter that my parents fought all the time or that, when my father finally left, my mother started micromanaging my life.”

“I know your life wasn’t perfect.”

“Yes, you understood more than the average person. At first when I graduated from the K-9 training center and was given this assignment, I was furious.” She twisted the napkin between her fingers. “To be honest, I actually thought about quitting.”

“What?” He stared. “Why?”

She shrugged. “Well, it was only a brief thought. But I didn’t want to be back under my mother’s heavy thumb. I was afraid if I came back to Desert Valley, I would…ah…revert to my wimpy high school self, I suppose.”

He tilted his head. “But you haven’t.”

“No.” Her jaw tightened.

“So why did you move back in with her?”

Ellen sighed and pinched the bridge of her nose. “I didn’t really want to, but…she played on my guilt.”

“How so?”

“Oh, you know. She was so glad I was staying in town, she went on and on about how worried she’d been about me going off and being a cop in a strange place and how she was so lonely.” Ellen sighed. “It was just supposed to be a temporary thing. I told her I’d move back until I found a place to stay.”

“Why didn’t you stay with the other officers? In the apartment for the rookies?” The apartment had been part of the program, set up to house all the trainees during their sessions. Now that the town was in the midst of a crime wave and the latest group of rookies were staying in town, the apartment had been opened up for them to continue living there should they choose to do so. Some had, but not Ellen.

She grimaced. "I felt like it would be a slap in my mother's face, so I sucked it up and moved in with her." Her eyes narrowed. "However, when I learned I was coming back here for an extended period of time, I was determined I would do something good with all that money sitting in the bank."

"Hence the assistance program."

"Yes."

"It's an awesome use of the money, Ellen. The assistance program is very much needed and not just in Desert Valley—you'll be touching lives all over the country. There are never enough trained animals to go out to those in need."

"I know. I've been thinking about that. If this thing gets up and running like I hope it will, the center could always expand as needed."

"I agree. Expanding would be great. And I have an idea of what we'll need in order to consider that at some point in the future."

"What do you have in mind?"

"I've been meaning to discuss this with you and just haven't had the chance. We had talked about ways to get the community involved in the center and, like we discussed, I have several tours of the space lined up. Some politicians, some families and some school groups. In spite of the money you've put into it, I think we should let the public give to it, as well. When people give money to a cause, they tend to pay attention to it and hold it close to their heart. We need that from the good folks in Desert Valley. Once we have that, we can think about other areas."

She nodded. "That's a great idea." She smiled and his heart warmed. "You've done all of that in such a short time. That's impressive." She reached across and grasped his fingers. "I'm so thankful you said yes to working with me, Lee. You're an amazing addition to the team."

He felt the heat rise in his cheeks but focused on the feel of her warm hand on his. Her touch reminded him of the past, of the days they'd laughed and held hands as though their time together was as long as eternity. "Thanks." His voice came out husky and he cleared his throat. "And I think your summer camp idea is a fabulous one, too." She'd gone into detail about that when she'd hired him. "We won't be able to do many weeks this summer, maybe the first two weeks of August before school starts back, but next year we should be able to get off to an immediate start when the school year is over."

Ellen stilled and went quiet. Then gave a slow nod. "Yes, next year."

"What is it?"

She blew out a low breath and shook her head. "Nothing, nothing. Your ideas are wonderful. Your long-term planning is amazing and a real benefit to the program."

"But?"

She sighed. "But I don't know where I'll be in a year."

His heart dropped and he cleared his throat. "I… ah… I see. So what does that mean?"

"Lee, I'm not hanging around here. I'm doing my best to get away from Desert Valley." *And my mother.* He heard the words even though she didn't say them out loud. Which meant she'd be leaving him, too. Again. "And as soon as we solve Veronica's murder," she continued, oblivious to his aching heart, "my assignment is complete and I'm free to move on to another city. Or state."

He gave a slow nod. "Okay then. Thanks for the heads up." And the warning to guard his heart. The one that was beating a sad rhythm as he tried to reign in his emotions. He fell silent for a moment then sighed. "At least when—if—you decide to go somewhere else, you'll be leaving behind a legacy that will continue to help people for a very long time." Because while he intended to finish vet school, he could see himself returning to Desert Valley to continue working with the program. Maybe even as the program's full-time vet.

Maybe.

The thought of doing all of that without Ellen by his side left a bitter taste in his mouth. He pulled his hand from under hers and returned to his food. For the next few minutes an uncomfortable silence hovered between them.

Ellen finished her dinner and stood. "I should get going. I need to go by the hospital and check on my mother." She tossed the wrappers into the trash can, then glanced at her phone. "I know if there was any change in her condition, they would call me, but sometimes I hope that just by my being there, she'll know it. That it might trigger something in her brain and she'll wake up. Even if it's the desire to tell me I'm ruining my life." She gave him a rueful smile.

"You're a good daughter."

The smile slipped off and her jaw tightened. "Too good sometimes, I'm afraid. And not good enough at other times." She looked into his eyes and Lee's heart beat a little faster at what he saw there. "I have regrets, Lee, I just want you to know that. I really do."

He reached out a hand and dragged a finger down her soft cheek. He knew what she was referring to. "I do, too. Unfortunately, I don't think it's possible to go through life and not acquire a few regrets." He sighed and pulled her into a hug. She stiffened then relaxed and let him hold her. It hit home how much he'd missed her. "I'm sorry you're having to go through this."

"Thanks, me too." She sucked in a deep breath and pulled back. His arms immediately felt empty but he didn't protest. "Do you need me to come get you in the morning?" she asked.

"I suppose. I'll need to get a rental car, I guess."

"You can use one of my mother's cars. She has a Jeep and a BMW. I recommend the Jeep."

"Um, no way, thanks. If Marian Foxcroft wakes up and finds that you've let me drive one of her vehicles, she'll have both of us arrested for grand theft auto. I'll pass on that one."

"Ha-ha. She will not." *She might try, though.* "I have some pull with the police around here should she try anything. Seriously, I should have thought of it before I brought you home, but we'll take care of it tomorrow."

He was touched by her offer. Mostly because he hadn't been expecting it. Still… "I really don't think it's a good idea."

"Well, I do. End of discussion."

Lee drew in a deep breath. "Okay, if you're sure."

"I am."

"Then… I'd appreciate it. I'll call George at the body shop first thing in the morning and see when he thinks he'll have my truck ready. Might be a while, though."

"That's fine. I'll come get you in the morning."

He nodded and stood to walk her out the door. A low thud made him pause. He looked at Ellen. "Did you hear that?"

Carly rose to her feet, ears cocked, attention on the front door. "I did and so did she." Ellen lifted a finger to her lips and pulled her weapon. "Stay here. Someone's out there."

THREE

Ellen motioned for Lee to step back into the protection of the kitchen area. He frowned but followed her silent order. “Carly, heel.” Carly was at her side in a split second. She would stay right there until commanded to do otherwise. Ellen moved to the side window, staying away from the front of the door, and gently moved the curtain so she could see out.

Nothing. She flipped the porch light off, then let her eyes adjust. When nothing happened, her nerves tightening with each second, she eased the deadbolt to the right and slowly opened the door. Darkness greeted her. Stillness. At least no one shot at her.

Yet. Carly nudged her leg, her ears perked forward, attention on the outside.

“Who’s there?” Ellen called.

Again, nothing.

And yet Carly nearly vibrated.

She caught Lee’s eye. His frown deepened and he shook his head when he realized she meant to step outside. She frowned right back, moved out the door and slipped to the side, pressing her back against the wall of the house. She waited for Carly to pad out, then used her left hand to slowly shut the door. It was the best she could do to make herself as small a target as possible. She stood there, listening. Silence. No sound. Nothing that alarmed her.

She moved toward the steps, then froze when she heard a rustle to her left. She spun, lifting her weapon, wishing she had on her vest. But she could see nothing.

But her senses told her someone was out there. Watching. The hair spiked on the back of her neck. "Police! Who's there? Show yourself," she called. Then moved quickly in case someone decided to shoot in the direction of her voice.

But no bullets came her way.

Carly stayed right at her side, waiting for the command that would send her after whoever was hiding. But Ellen wasn't ready to do that yet. As long as her own life wasn't in danger, she wouldn't let the dog go in blind. Ellen moved down the steps and out into the yard, taking cover behind the nearest tree. Her heart thundered in her ears.

Should she call for backup?

But no one had done anything yet. A flash of light in the direction of the kennel pulled her attention. She hesitated only for a moment. "Carly, seek," she said and pointed.

Carly took off like a shot. Ellen moved quickly, following behind the animal. Sweat trickled down her back. She drew in shallow breaths and reached for her phone.

The sound of running footsteps just ahead of her reached her ears. She stayed behind Carly and whoever she was chasing only to stop when she heard an engine turn over and then a slight squeal of tires as the vehicle sped off into the night. At the edge of the road, Ellen bent and placed her hands on her knees. She took a long breath. Carly barked twice then settled at Ellen's side. "Got away, didn't he, girl?" Ellen slipped the dog a treat and Carly wolfed it down, proud of herself. Ellen scratched her ears and straightened when she heard footsteps.

"Ellen?"

She spun to find Lee behind her, only slightly winded. "What are you doing? Trying to get yourself killed?"

"Sorry, I had to make sure you were all right."

"I can take care of myself. That's what I'm trained for, remember?"

Again her words caused a flash of hurt to darken his features. She sighed. She was tired. It had been a long day. But that was no excuse to snap at the man and hurt his feelings. "Again, I'm sorry. I can't seem to get the filters to line up with my tongue." She paused. "I appreciate the concern. Next time it might best if you stay back, though."

The mask fell away and he barked a short laugh. "You don't have to pretty it up for me, Ellen. You've always been blunt. No sense in trying to change now."

She felt the heat rush into her cheeks. "Well, when you put it that way…fine. Do you have a flashlight?"

"You want me to turn the floodlights on? Or would that put us in the spotlight?"

She hesitated. "I think whoever was snooping out here is gone, but we probably don't want to make it any easier to spot us should the person double back. I'm nervous enough standing here in the moonlight."

"Gotcha."

Because while she'd heard the person drive away and Carly no longer seemed concerned, Ellen felt the need to take all kinds of precautions.

Still worried that the intruder might return, Lee entered the kennel where he used to keep the dogs he'd loved to work with. That was before he'd had to make other arrangements for them when he was sentenced to prison. Veronica had helped him out with that. He even knew that a couple of them were now working dogs, trained by his sister's skilled hand and rehomed to help those who needed it. Anger at all he'd lost surged through him and he had to squelch it before it grew.

That was in the past, he reminded himself. He had a future now. A future that included this home, this kennel that he'd built with his own two hands in his backyard. Thankfully, Veronica had hired someone to keep the outside area cut and trimmed while she took care of the house herself. He supposed the house hadn't been much work since no one was living there. Simply dust and vacuum once a week. His backyard had been another matter, though. And while this area might be empty at the moment, he hoped to fill it up soon with more puppies to train for people who needed them. After all, he still had the rest of his schooling to pay for.

One step at a time.

They'd left the puppies at the training center, so tomorrow he'd get the one golden retriever pup from Ellen. Dash. That little one seemed to need a bit more of his expertise than the other two. He grabbed the flashlight he'd come for and hurried back outside to find Ellen making notes on her phone. "You're going to report this?"

"Yes. We need to keep everything documented. I don't want whoever is doing this to slip through our fingers on a technicality. I've got the date, time and description of what I heard and saw—and Carly's reaction, as well."

He handed her the flashlight and she clipped the phone to her belt then flipped the light on. She aimed the beam toward the ground. "Follow me and let's use both sets of eyes. You may spot something that shouldn't be there before I would. Carly will let us know if anyone comes back."

He moved closer to her. Drew in her familiar scent. He used to dream about that smell while he was in prison—and even before. A combination of vanilla and strawberries. He was glad some things hadn't changed.

Even while his mind remembered, his eyes scoured the ground. They worked in a grid pattern. Up toward the road, then back. Finally, he pointed. "There. Near the gate." She moved closer and aimed the light where he indicated. "The grass is pressed down. I've been meaning to get out here and cut it, but haven't had a chance. With the rain a couple of days ago, it seems like it grew about a foot overnight."

She pulled her phone off the clip and snapped pictures. "I don't know what good the pictures will do. There aren't any footprints to cast or anything like that, but I see what you mean about the grass."

Her light flashed across something shiny in the grass and he bent down to pick it up then stopped. "Do you have a tissue or gloves or anything?"

"Not on me." She moved closer and looked over his shoulder. Her nearness made him long for things he shouldn't. She wasn't going to be around any longer than it took to solve his sister's murder. He needed to remember that. "I wasn't planning on working a crime scene," she said, oblivious to his inner turmoil. Good, he planned to keep it that way. "What is it?"

He drew in a breath and forced his thoughts to the object on the ground. "It's the clip that keeps the gate closed. Some of the dogs can figure out how to lift the latch so I just use the clip. Someone undid it and gave it a toss." He stood. "Be right back. I've got some paper towels and paper bags in the room I used to use as an office."

He left her once again to retrieve the items. When he returned, he handed her a paper towel and she scooped up the clip and slid it in the bag. "We'll send this off to Flagstaff and have them try to find any prints," she said. "If the person wore gloves, it'll be a lost cause."

"Thanks. It's worth a try."

"If I were to go inside the gate, where could I get to?"

"Just inside the building I used as a kennel. It's got some cages and dog runs out the back. I would put the dogs inside when the weather was too cold or too hot for them to be outside. But I keep the door leading into the actual building locked. There's nothing worth stealing in there—just pet food, a few tools, water buckets, training toys..." He shrugged. "It's really just a storage area."

"This makes me nervous," Ellen said. "Someone shot at us today and now someone is snooping around your home tonight. I don't like it."

"I can't say it's been the highlight of my week, either."

She sighed. "All right. Let's go back to the house. I want to make some phone calls."

He led the way back into his kitchen. She settled into a chair with Carly at her feet and dialed a number.

"Who are you calling?"

"Two other K-9 officers in my unit. Tristan McKeller and Shane Weston. I'm going to ask them to take turns watching your house tonight." She bit her lip. "I suppose I should call Chief Jones, too."

While she made the calls, he rubbed his eyes and considered the past few hours. He had to admit he hadn't realized what he was signing up for when he'd agreed to work with Ellen. He hadn't realized how much the past would come back to haunt him. How much he would wish for what could never be. He watched her talk, examining her face, her expressions, her intensity. Beautiful, ambitious, smart… He sighed. And what was he?

Before he'd been arrested and imprisoned, he'd had big dreams. He'd been building his dog-training business and even had two college students who'd worked for him on a part-time basis. He'd also been attending graduate classes that would get him started on the path to becoming a veterinarian. And then he'd walked into a convenience store in the middle of a robbery. The clerk had been shot and he'd tried to save her. The robber had fled, and Officer Ken Bucks had arrived on the scene. Just in time to set him up. He'd held a grudge against Lee ever since a woman Ken loved had chosen Lee over him. Ken had never forgotten it—nor cared that Lee hadn't returned the woman's affection.

The anger bubbled, threatening to come to the surface once again. He blew out a sigh.

Why was he going down that path again? It was in the past. He couldn't change what happened. He'd been in the wrong place at the wrong time with the wrong cop—and while the woman had lived, she hadn't seen who'd shot her. The jury hadn't believed Lee's defense in the face of all of the evidence Bucks had managed to gather. False evidence. Manipulated evidence. Like altering the video footage.

"Lee? You okay?"

He jerked at Ellen's question, then followed her gaze to see his fingers curled into tight fists. He relaxed them. "Yes, thanks. What did you find out?"

While he could still see the concern in her eyes, she didn't question him further. "Both officers can help out. Tristan has a fourteen-year-old sister he's raising, but she's spending the night with a friend so he's free for the first six-hour shift. Then Shane will take over."

"Not having had the best experience when it comes to dealing with cops, I have to say I appreciate their help."

"You got a raw deal with Ken Bucks. It's time you realize we're not all cut from the same cloth." She smiled.

"I realize it. If you trust them, then I do, too."

"I trust them. With my life."

"That's good enough for me, then."

When Tristan arrived, Ellen introduced them and Lee sized up the rookie who was not just a member of the unit, but a good friend to Ellen. Lee felt a twinge of jealousy, but mostly he was glad she'd done well with her life and had people she could count on when she needed to. He wasn't sure he could say the same.

She grabbed her keys. "I'll be leaving now. Tristan, would you mind asking Shane to drop Lee at the training center in the morning? His truck is out of commission. I was going to come get him, but Shane'll be heading that way."

It didn't escape his attention that she'd just gotten out of picking him up. And that his feelings were hurt by it.

"Happy to ask," Tristan said, "but you and I both know it won't be an issue."

"Thanks."

Lee pushed aside the hurt. Maybe she had her reasons for not wanting to swing by and get him. He nodded to his Keurig coffeemaker and the K-Cup tree next to it. The tree held about five different flavored coffees. The Keurig and the coffee had been one of the first things he purchased after he was released from prison. A splurge he hadn't regretted for a moment.

"Help yourself."

Tristan didn't hesitate and Ellen smiled. "You just made a friend for life."

Lee walked to the door but stayed away from the windows. Ellen followed him. "Be careful. You were with me when everything happened. If Freddie thinks we can ID him, he'll be looking for you, too."

"I'll keep that in mind."

He turned to look at her. "Why did you choose to become a cop? You were determined to be a doctor from what I remember," he said. "What changed?"

She sighed. "It's a long story. The short version is that a friend of mine and I were almost mugged. She was a karate instructor. She defended us, took down the guy and held him until the cops got there. As soon as we were safe and I had a chance to process everything, I knew that if she hadn't been there, or if she hadn't had the training she'd had, the night would have ended a lot differently. And plus, I was mad. I decided I wanted to be the one to protect others, to catch the bad guys, to defend those who can't defend themselves."

"I can imagine how your mother reacted to that one. From medical school to the police academy would be quite the step down in her eyes."

"Yes, you're right about that. I didn't tell her at first." She shrugged. "Finally, I had no choice and after a rant or two, she…adjusted."

"I can't see that."

"Okay, so…she's still adjusting. I have hopes. Now I've got to go." She glanced at her phone's screen. "I'm not going to make the hospital tonight. Give me some time to make a morning visit. See you around ten at the center?"

"I'll go ahead and get there whenever Shane's ready. That way I can start working with the pups."

She rubbed her eyes and stifled a yawn. "That's settled, then. I'll see you in the morning." She started toward her SUV, Carly at her side. Then she stopped and spun. "Actually, do you mind answering one more question? It's been on my mind for a while now."

Wary, he shrugged. "What?"

"Why did Ken Bucks hate you so much?"

He flinched. "You sure you want to hear that tonight?"

"The short version."

"That's all there is anyway." He raked a hand through his already mussed hair. "Do you remember Shelley Graves?"

"Yes. She was a little older than you, wasn't she?"

"Yes. Three years older. Anyway, Ken decided he was in love with her and followed her around like a love-sick puppy, wrote her notes, parked outside her house to watch her come and go. All kinds of crazy stuff."

She blinked. "Okay. So what does that have to do with you?"

He sighed and looked away. He really didn't want to remember that time but he'd tell her the story and be done with it. "About four years ago, Ken was still after her. He'd never given up on her even after all those years."

"She never married?"

"No. And she and her boyfriend had called it quits after someone left threatening messages at his house."

"Ken was stalking her."

"Yeah. One afternoon, I ran into Shelley at the Cactus Café and she invited me to sit at her table. She was nervous and looked upset. I felt sorry for her so I sat with her. She started telling me what was going on and asked me what she should do. I told her she needed to go to the chief and tell him what Ken was doing." He blew out a breath. "But she was afraid to. After all, Ken was the chief's stepson, right?"

"Yes, I knew that."

"Anyway, Ken came in about the time we finished eating and came to the table. He tried to pick a fight with me, but there was no way I was going there. I could see the headlines: Local Dog Trainer and Vet Wannabe Assaults Deputy Sheriff."

She grimaced. "Ouch."

"Anyway, I simply told Ken to leave her alone."

"How did he take that?"

"I thought he was going to spontaneously combust." He grimaced. "Anyway, after that, Shelley started to look at me like I was some kind of hero or something.

One evening, she came over to my house. She told me she was in love with me and had come to convince me that I felt the same way about her. When I told her that I didn't return her affection, she kissed me. I immediately stepped away from her, but the damage was done."

"Oh, my."

"Apparently Ken had followed her to my place and…uh…he saw the whole thing."

"Oh, no."

"Oh, yes." His lips tightened. "He's hated me ever since."

"But you moved away from her."

"I did, but he didn't stay to see that part. From then on, he became more snide and rude. He even stopped me one night and harassed me. Made me take a breathalyzer test and all that. Gave me a ticket for going five miles over the speed limit." He shook his head. "I filed a formal complaint with Chief Jones, but I don't know that he ever did anything. The harassment stopped so that was good. I managed to steer pretty clear of him until the night of the robbery."

"And he held on to that grudge all that time," she whispered.

"Yep. All that time. And when the robbery went down and I was there—" Lee shrugged, fighting the emotions the memories brought to the surface "—he finally found a way to get me back."

"Unbelievable."

"You would think so."

"What happened to Shelley?"

"She wound up moving to New Mexico with a friend. She's a nurse and is working at one of the hospitals there."

Ellen walked back to him and wrapped her arms

around his waist to hug him. "I'm so sorry, Lee. You didn't deserve that."

He almost couldn't speak through the tightness in his throat, but managed a husky "Thanks. And I guess that was more the long version than short. Sorry."

"No apologies necessary. See you tomorrow."

And then she was walking away again. Carly trotted at her heels then jumped into her space in the truck. Ellen shut the door then climbed in the driver's seat. He heard her truck rumble to life and then the tires crunch on the gravel after the concrete ran out. He sighed and went back inside, making his way into the kitchen.

"Women, huh?"

Lee schooled his features and looked at Tristan, who'd made himself at home at the kitchen table. "What?"

Tristan shook his head. "I'm right there with you, man. Trying to understand them is like trying to understand a foreign language with no training. I've got custody of my fourteen-year-old sister and I can't seem to do or say anything right. Just yesterday I told her what a pretty young woman she was turning into and she started crying. Big old sobs that threatened to rip the heart right out of me." He shook his head. "I don't understand her, that's for sure."

"Sounds like you're on the right path, then."

Tristan grunted and Lee ran a hand down the side of his face. "I'm exhausted. I'm going to get a shower and head to bed. You need anything?"

Tristan lifted the coffee mug. "I've got all I need."

Lee nodded. "Well, there's more where that came from. Help yourself. I probably won't see you before you leave, so thank you for doing this."

"Absolutely."

Lee headed for his bedroom at the back of the house. His footsteps echoed on the wood floors. He checked each window, and when he was satisfied his home was as secure as possible, he finally allowed himself to relax and dream about returning to school one day. He was financially set whenever he decided to go back. While he'd been in prison, Veronica had handled his money and had done a good job with what little he'd had. She'd invested it and when he'd gotten his statements, he'd been impressed with her ingenuity. He'd also been surprised and grateful. Somewhere under that sarcastic, nasty personality she'd shown to the world, Lee wanted to believe there'd still been a part of the sweet older sister who'd looked out for him.

And he'd learned soon after her death that Veronica had left everything to him in her will. He had enough money to live on whenever he was able to return to school, which was nice. But going to school would require him to leave Desert Valley, and he wasn't ready to do that yet. Not with Veronica's murderer still running free. He'd return to school when the time was right. Which reminded him that it wasn't right. Not with the shooting that had happened. And the person on his property. And the fact that his heart was once again leaning toward Ellen's.

All of that combined to make the tension come roaring back, and he knew he wouldn't be sleeping much at all.

Ellen stepped into the home she'd grown up in, kicked off her boots and released her belt with her weapon, setting it on the coffee table. The mansion echoed around her and she wished someone else were here. Like her mother. Because it would mean she was whole and healthy.

Carly nudged her as though reading her mind, and she scratched the dog's ears, suddenly not feeling quite so lonely. But the big house felt weird without her mother's commanding presence. Her father hadn't been around for years. She missed him and wished she could pick up the phone and call him, but her mother had chased him off, too, with her dictatorial personality. And then he'd died a broken, lonely man. First her father, then her relationship with Lee had crashed and burned because her mother had had the audacity to publicly call Lee out and tell him he wasn't good enough for her daughter…

The anger burned deep inside her. Ellen cleared her throat and refused to go that route.

She called the hospital and checked on her mother.

"There's no change, Ms. Foxcroft," the nurse said. "She's still sleeping and healing. She's not in pain. She'll wake up when her body is ready."

Her shoulders sagged at the answer that never seemed to vary. It definitely was not what she wanted to hear, but it was better than her mother taking a turn for the worse. With everything in her, she didn't want her mother to die. Especially not with all of the unresolved issues between them. She bit back the rush of tears and headed for the shower.

And for the first time in days had a real chance to think about the one person whose footprint had never faded from her heart. Lee Earnshaw. He made her head spin and her heart long for things better left forgotten. He also made the guilt sweep in. She should have had more faith in him. She should have gone to see him in prison. But she hadn't. She'd thought about it. One time, she'd even made it to the parking lot of the prison before turning around and going home.

Why?

Because it had felt like a betrayal. She'd loved him and he'd turned to a life of crime. What had hurt the most was having to admit her mother had been right about him. *He's a loser, Ellen. He'll never amount to anything. You're too good for him.* Her mother's words rang in her ears and once Lee had been arrested, she'd finally had to admit that while the evidence was solid, she'd had a very hard time accepting Lee could be guilty of such a thing.

Self-loathing assaulted her. He hadn't been guilty. He'd been framed, and she'd just…gone about her life.

And thought about him every day. She should have visited him, believed in him, supported him.

But the evidence had just been overwhelming…

Her mother had wasted no time in letting Ellen know about the arrest: *I told you so.*

It had been depressing. So Ellen had moved out and moved on in spite of her mother's vociferous protests. Ellen had made a life for herself apart from her mother, apart from Desert Valley. And she'd had no intention of coming back. Only it looked as though God had other plans. She sighed.

She had a murder to solve. Well, more than one, really. K-9 officer Ryder Hayes's wife, Melanie, had been killed five years ago and her murderer had never been caught. Then Brian Miller and Mike Riverton, two rookie officers with the Desert Valley Police Department had been killed a year apart. Their deaths had been ruled accidents, but Tristan had been friends with Mike, served in the army with him and said he didn't believe for a minute that Mike had fallen down his steps to his death. And then exactly one year later, to the day, Brian had died in his home when it caught fire due to an unattended candle. That in itself was enough to raise the suspicions of those who knew him. His entire family had died in a fire when he was just a teen, and he never used candles or his fireplace. So the consensus was that the deaths had been made to look like accidents. But why? And who wanted them dead?

Ellen slipped between her sheets and Carly settled herself at the foot of her bed. So much death, Ellen thought. She just prayed neither she nor Lee would be next.

FOUR

Lee opened the passenger door and climbed out of Shane Weston's vehicle. "Thanks for the ride."

Shane nodded. "Not a problem."

Lee turned to find Ellen standing at the entrance to the training center. She'd arrived before him after all. A large boxer with a gray muzzle sat at her side. "Good morning," she said. "Did you get any rest last night?"

"A bit. You?"

"A bit." She motioned him inside, and he followed her into the lobby area where she had the three pups running free. The puppies chose that moment to playfully attack the boxer, who flopped onto the floor. He patiently let them climb all over him.

Then the smallest pup made a beeline for the area behind the front desk. Ellen snagged him and lifted him.

"Dash," Lee said.

"Yep."

The puppy licked her chin. Lee smiled and scratched its silky head. "He's living up to his name." She handed him the wriggling pup. "Who's your friend?" he asked.

"This is Kipper. He was waiting for me when I got

here this morning. A family pet no one had time for anymore."

He scowled. "Some people shouldn't have pets."

"I agree, but at least they brought him to me and didn't leave him abandoned on the side of the road somewhere."

"True." He looked around. "I can't get over how great this place is. I remember it being an empty building just sitting here waiting for someone to come along and give it life again."

"Thanks. I couldn't believe Veronica agreed to let me move my center in here. I don't think she ever really liked me that much."

"Veronica didn't like anyone very much."

"She loved you."

"Yes, I guess she did. In her own way. When we could talk about animals and training, we were on the same wavelength. If I tried to confront her about her immoral activities or vicious treatment of people, she froze me out." He shook his head. "The only reason I even believed we could possibly be related was because of the animals and her rapport with them." He sighed. "It's too bad she didn't use some of that talent with the humans in her life."

"I agree." She gave him a small smile. "I've got to make a call to see what my status is and if I'm cleared to go back to work. Why don't you take the puppies into the training area outside? I'll catch up to you after I finish my call and then we can go pick up the Jeep for you to use until your truck is ready."

He nodded. "That still makes me nervous, but as long as you're willing to take the fall, I'm willing to go along."

She laughed. "I'm willing."

"All right, then." He headed for the back area and placed the puppies in the yard. He then walked over to where Ellen kept the treats for rewards. After shoving a handful into his front pocket, he got to work with Dash.

"Come on, boy. Sit." He tapped the puppy's hind end and pressed until he sat. The he slipped him a treat. "Good job, boy. Good job."

When Ellen emerged from the building an hour later, he realized he was sweltering and thirsty. He'd been giving the puppy water at regular intervals but had forgotten to bring himself something. He motioned to the air-conditioned building. She held out a water bottle, which he gladly took. "Thanks." They walked inside and he downed half of it. He gave the other half to the puppy, who eagerly finished it off.

"How's it going?" she asked when he came up for air.

Lee swiped his mouth and chin with the edge of his T-shirt and grinned when she wrinkled her nose. "We have towels inside, you know."

"It's a guy thing."

She gave a light snort. "Oh, I know."

"And in answer to your question, they're doing great. Especially King. He sure likes food."

"Good, should make him pretty easy to train."

"I think so. Dash might be another story. I got him to follow through a couple of times, and other times he acted like I was speaking Greek."

"He'll get it."

"Yes, he will." He went to the sink attached to the building and washed his hands. When he turned he found Ellen with Lady cradled against her. "So I never asked. How was your mother this morning?"

Sadness pulled her lips into a frown. "The same."

"I'm sorry. Are the doctors still offering hope that she'll wake up?"

"Yes, they seem to think she will. They just say that her brain needs time to heal."

"Do you think she saw who attacked her?"

"I don't know. That's why there's a guard on her 24/7. Just in case the person is afraid she did and comes back to finish the job." Her lips tightened. "I really want to find who did this."

"So you think there's any connection to all of the other stuff going on in town?"

"Like?"

"Like the murder of Ryder Hayes's wife five years ago. Like the supposedly accidental deaths of two other rookies exactly one year apart. Like the death of my sister." He pinched the bridge of his nose. "She was only thirty-two, Ellen."

She reached out and laid a hand on his shoulder. He felt the warmth of her hand and knew she felt the hard muscle beneath her palm. But more, he read the sympathy in her eyes and knew she felt the pain coming from his heart. A pain he hadn't realized he needed to share. Most people hadn't liked his sister. Respected her way with the animals, yes. But as far as liking her as a person? No way. And he couldn't say he didn't understand it, but...she was his *sister*. "I know, Lee," she said softly. "And I know you're grieving her every day." She dropped her hand and cleared her throat. "And yes, I'm convinced there's a connection. We all think so, we just can't prove it. Yet."

He nodded to the cell phone she still held in her hand.

"Are you back on duty so you can get back to working on making that happen?"

"You're full of questions, aren't you?" She nodded. "I am."

He breathed in and finally managed to ask the question he'd been working up to. "Then, are you up for dinner tonight?"

She blinked at him. "Dinner?"

"Why not? How about the Cactus Café?" She bit her lip and he sighed. "Not like a date, Ellen, just dinner."

A hint of red crept into her cheeks. "Sure, that sounds good."

"Great. Now let's get busy with these dogs. Want to play a game of fetch?"

Ellen had enjoyed spending the time with Lee and watching him work with the dogs. The training session had gone extremely well. Even the puppies were charmed by him and wanted to please him. She glanced at her watch. Now she had a meeting with an extra-special client. She smiled. When she'd decided to put together the assistance program, she hadn't realized it would grow so big so quickly. Which was why she'd needed Lee and the other workers. She wondered if she'd really be able to leave when it came time. And she knew that time would come. She would have to make a choice. Stay or leave? The thought made her sad and antsy all at the same time. One things was certain, though. She was meant to be a cop. She just wasn't sure she could be one in the same town where mother lived. And ruled. She stepped into the lobby area of the training center and spotted her client at the same time the little girl saw her.

"Ms. Ellen! Ms. Ellen!"

Ellen grinned as Gabby Crenshaw rolled toward her in her motorized wheelchair. Gabby's mother, Patty, hurried behind her, trying to keep up. The child had cerebral palsy so her words were slurred, but the smile on her face had Ellen's heart singing. She waited for Gabby to roll to a stop, then squatted next to the nine-year-old. "Hello, Mrs. Crenshaw and little miss Gabby, how are you two today?"

"I'm good." She waved her hand, then tried to clap as she bounced in her seat. Her body might be twisted and bent from the disorder and her movements awkward, but her love of life was infectious. "I came to see Popcorn."

Ellen smoothed a hand down the child's messy ponytail and smiled up at Mrs. Crenshaw. The woman looked harried and tired, but when she looked at her child, love shone in her eyes. Ellen looked back at Gabby. "Then, let's go find him. Do you remember where to go?"

"Yes ma'am!" Ellen stood, took Gabby's right hand and let the child lead the way. She walked alongside the humming chair and together they entered the kennel area. The training center was designed to be wheelchair accessible, but she'd paid special attention to this area. Those clients who came to be trained to work with their dogs had to learn to let them out of their temporary homes and how to put them back in.

Gabby let out a low squeal of delight when she spotted her companion in his kennel. She looked up at Ellen. "I missed him."

"I'm sure he missed you, too." Gabby wheeled over to Popcorn's cage and released the lock. The black Lab stepped out, his tail wagging. Popcorn was a gentle soul who seemed to understand he had to contain some of his energy when around the little girl. Gabby leaned forward to wrap her arms around the Lab's neck and bury her face against his fur. Popcorn simply stood there and let her. Ellen smiled. "Are you ready?"

"Ready." Gabby leaned back. "Come, Popcorn. Want a treat?"

The Lab's ears perked up and he followed Gabby to the treat jar. Gabby lifted the lid with slow, measured movements, used her other hand to scoop out some treats, then carefully replaced the lid. She dropped the treats into her lap, then turned to look at her mother and Ellen. "I did it!"

"You sure did," Ellen said. "Great job." She thought she caught a glint of tears in Patty's eyes. Her own throat tightened and she cleared it.

Gabby let out a chuckle and spun her chair around to face the door. Popcorn walked with her, his gaze on her, tongue lolling out of the side of his mouth.

Once in the training room, Ellen let Gabby take over while she looked around at the other children, service animals and adults.

When they noticed her, they waved and she stopped to speak to each one. By the time she was ready to go, Ellen knew Gabby and her mother and Popcorn were in good hands.

And she realized her own were sweating. She rubbed them together and pondered what she'd agreed to.

A date with Lee. No, not a date with Lee.

Dinner with Lee.

Which was probably a date.

She drew in a deep breath and hoped her heart would survive it.

* * *

Ellen looked in the mirror and sighed. Why was she so nervous? She'd eaten many dinners with Lee and he hadn't had this crazy effect on her before. At least not in the sense that she was so tense she practically had the shakes. She'd brought him home after work to get the Jeep, and he'd left with promises to clean up fast and get back to pick her up. She'd offered to just meet him at the café as it was only four blocks away from her, but he'd insisted on driving. For some reason, Ellen had given in and agreed. Now she wondered what in the world she'd been thinking.

Carly perched on the edge of the bed, watching. "What do you think, girl?" Ellen asked.

Carly tilted her head then lowered it to her paws.

Ellen scowled. "That's not an answer. That's just staying neutral." Carly's eyes closed and Ellen smiled. She really appreciated the animal's company. She walked over to scratch the dog's ears. "You get the night off, girl. Enjoy it."

Carly licked her hand.

Ellen picked her cell phone up from the bed where she'd tossed it and punched in the number for the hospital. After getting the same message about her mother's condition, she breathed a prayer that God would let her mother wake up. *Please, God, don't let her die with all of the issues we still have to resolve. As crazy as she can make me, I still love her.*

She inhaled slowly and walked down the steps into the foyer. She heard a car pull into the drive. *Lee.* Her heart thudded and her hands were instantly sweaty. She swiped them down her black pencil skirt and wished she'd worn the slacks instead. She straightened the collar of her royal blue shirt and fingered the gold earrings dangling from her lobes. She was too dressed up. Yep, she should have worn the slacks. Or jeans. Maybe she could just run upstairs and change.

Then it was too late. He knocked on the door and she had no more time to think about it. She twisted the knob and opened the door. Lee stood there dressed in khakis and a dark T-shirt layered under an open short-sleeved collared shirt along with loafers and a gentle smile on his handsome face. Memories invaded her, a longing for what they'd had in the past swamped her. No, she didn't want the teenage love they'd shared. She wanted something more, something richer, deeper. Just…more.

Oh, no. No, no, no. She wasn't going to go there. She wasn't. She couldn't. "Hi," she said before giving an inward wince at the breathless quality of that one word.

"Hi." He blinked. "Wow, you look amazing."

She swallowed. "Thanks. So do you."

"Are you ready?"

Was she? "Sure." Ellen stepped outside and gave a relieved sigh that the heat of the day had dissipated, leaving the night air cool and refreshing. She pulled the door shut behind her and let him lead her to the Jeep he'd left running. She climbed in. The Cactus Café was one of her favorite places to eat and she looked forward to visiting it tonight.

Ten minutes later, they walked inside and she followed Lee to a private booth in the back. Once they'd gotten their drinks and place their orders, he clasped his hands in front of him on the table. "So," she said. "I'd ask you how your day went, but I think I already know that." Her phone rang and she glanced at the screen with a sigh. "Do you mind? It's the chief."

"Of course not."

"Hi, Chief."

"I don't have anything earth shattering—just wanted to let you know that spot on the news about Freddie Parrish is working. Someone spotted him at a gas station just outside town. They called it in, but by the time a cruiser got there, he'd disappeared."

"Oh. Okay."

"We're having them run the segment again. Be ready for some action if we get some leads."

"Of course."

"Talk to you later."

She hung up and relayed the message to Lee.

"Everyone always said Freddie was headed for trouble," he said.

"They said that about you, too."

He gave her a small smile. "I know—and they were right. But then I met you."

She bit her lip as her heart thudded. "And that made a difference?"

"A big one." He cleared his throat. "Do you mind if we talk about something else for a few minutes?"

Slightly disappointed that he obviously wanted to change the subject, she took a sip of her tea. She wanted to explore what he meant by the difference she'd made in his life. Instead, she nodded. "All right, but if it's about Veronica's death, I don't know any more than what we've already talked about."

"No, it's not that."

She arched a brow. "Then, what?"

"I was curious as to how the Desert Valley Police Department was suddenly able to hire five rookies when they'd been talking about making cutbacks."

Ellen frowned and shrugged. "What about it?"

"I was getting groceries the other day and Chief Jones was talking to Louise Donaldson."

"Okay."

"I didn't mean to listen in, but I walked past as Louise said something about wanting to know if the mayor planned to use Marian's money to hire her replacement when she retires—or use it to keep the rookies she'd paid for."

Her lips tightened, then she blew out a slow breath. "Yes, and?"

"What that tells me is that it was your mother who funded the hiring of the five new rookies—you included—and their dogs."

She went still. "Yes. She did." It wasn't like it was a secret. She supposed it would be news to Lee, who'd only been back in town for two weeks.

"And you're all right with that?" he asked.

She paused before replying. "I didn't say that I was all right with it. I just said she did. She means well and has the money to do some good. Just like I have the money to run the assistance center and do some good while I'm here."

"Come on, Ellen. You know your mother has *always* had a hard time letting you go. What if she did this to keep you close to home?"

The waiter chose that moment to deliver the food. He placed it on the table. "Anything else you need?" he asked.

"No, thanks," Ellen said, and Lee shook his head.

For the next few minutes, they focused on the food. She finally looked up. "You really believe she would do that?"

He sighed. "We both know how your mother works."

She went silent for a brief moment then looked up and met his gaze. "Yes, the evidence of my mother's manipulative actions can be a bit overwhelming when you consider the past, but there's no way she'd use her money to buy me a position here in town." The very thought made her stomach turn. Or was it turning because she wasn't 100 percent sure her mother wouldn't do exactly that?

"She would do exactly that and you know it."

Lee's echo of her own thoughts disturbed her. Ellen tossed her napkin to the table next to her half-eaten dinner. "I'm not hungry anymore. I can see myself home, thanks."

He groaned and dropped his head. "Ellen—"

"This was a mistake. We can work together, but given your feelings about my mother—and the fact that you think I'm just like her—I don't see how we can… socialize. I'll see you tomorrow, Lee."

"So you're just going to walk out?"

She sighed. "No, I'm not just going to walk out. I'm finished. With the food and this conversation."

His eyes flashed. "Fine. I'll take you home."

"It's not necessary. It's four blocks up the street. I can walk." She tossed enough money on the table to cover her food and his. For the first time in her life, she was thankful her mother's house sat in the middle of town on Main Street. "I'll see you tomorrow."

"Ellen—"

"Tomorrow, Lee." She ignored the look of frustration on his face and headed for the door. Her mind spun. She was so tired of debating this with herself—and others who obviously thought the same thing. It wasn't the first time she'd been aware of the speculation regarding her mother's true motives in putting up the money, but it still got under her skin. Yes, there was the possibility that her mother had once again interfered in her life. In a huge way. Sure, she knew her mother had offered to pay the salaries of the rookies so they could get some answers and find Veronica's killer, but she hadn't done it specifically to keep Ellen in town.

Or had she? And that was the million-dollar question, wasn't it? Too bad her mother had been attacked before she had a chance to bring up the subject. She shouldn't have hesitated in asking. Then again, why did she even care? It wasn't as though it was a permanent assignment. The job would end and she would move on. Regardless of what her mother had or hadn't done. But it still irritated her.

Ellen walked home, the cool of the night a welcome respite from the heat that burned when the sun was up. She walked up the drive and glanced around. Her parents had been blessed with family money, and the large yellow house Ellen had grown up in was now on the historic register. Yes, blessed. So her mother had done something good with her money. That was fine, right? Great, even. But now, thanks to Lee, Ellen couldn't help wondering about the motivation behind the goodness.

She opened the front door and whistled to Carly. The dog bounded into the foyer and Ellen shut the front door behind her. "Come on, girl, you need to go out?"

Carly padded to the back door and Ellen opened it for her. While Carly sniffed bushes and took care of business, Ellen's brain whirled. She pulled her phone from her pocket and let her finger hover over Chief Jones's number. He was friends with her mother. He could answer the question once and for all about the woman's motives. No, she didn't want to bother him. She dialed Louise Donaldson's number. It's possible the deputy would know. She and the chief were friendly. The call went to voice mail. "Louise, when you get this message, will you give me a call? I have a question for you. Thanks." She hung up and called for Carly. "Come on, girl. Let's go check on our new friends. I'm restless and need something to do besides think." What she needed to do was apologize to Lee. She shouldn't have left that way. The way he'd left when he'd been mad at her for questioning his involvement with Freddie Parrish in prison. The same way her father had left her mother when he couldn't take it anymore.

The same way she'd left town so she wouldn't have to deal with her mother.

If everyone kept leaving, nothing would get resolved.

So she owed Lee an apology and the consideration of hearing him out. He was entitled to his opinion.

Carly trotted over and Ellen led the way to her SUV and opened the back door. Carly hopped in and made herself comfortable while Ellen slid into the driver's seat.

As she drove, her mother stayed at the forefront of her spinning thoughts. Would she have truly handed over that much money, been so manipulative, just to make sure Ellen returned—and stayed in—Desert Valley? Now that Lee had brought it up again, she couldn't stop the question from looping through her mind. She had to know. One way or another. Then again, would knowing for sure make any difference? Maybe. Maybe not. She wouldn't know until she *knew*. She glanced at her phone, hoping Louise would call her back tonight.

She arrived at the training center and let Carly out of the car. The dog trotted to the front door of the assistance center and Ellen went to unlock it but found the door cracked open. "What?"

She pulled her weapon and gave the door a gentle push. It swung in on silent hinges. She stepped inside, Carly at her side. The dog was tense and alert. "Hello?" Where was the night security guard? After all the recent trouble at the training center, she'd hired two men to rotate watching the place at night. They'd started two weeks ago and, thankfully, had reported no problems. So where was he?

"Benny? Frank?" She wasn't sure who was on duty tonight but she saw no sign of either of them. Carly nosed her way to the back where the kennels were and Ellen gasped. The kennel doors had been opened. The pups were trapped in the larger open area and were playing with one another. But it wasn't the pups that had captured her attention, it was the body sprawled in front of the cages that swept the breath from her lungs. "Benny!"

She started forward, heard the footsteps behind her and Carly's low growl. She turned to see a figure dressed in black lifting a gun to aim it in her direction. Ellen's training rose to the surface and she lashed out with her right foot and slammed her heel into his arm. The gun spun from his hand and skidded across the floor and under a chair. He cursed and dived at her. Carly barked and lunged, throwing herself against the intruder's back. He landed hard on the floor then scrambled to his feet. But Ellen was already moving, and she threw a solid punch into his face. He screamed and reared back against the reception desk. Ellen's fist throbbed, but she went for her weapon just as something crashed into the side of her head. More pain flashed, Carly barked and Ellen tumbled to the floor.

FIVE

Lee sighed and pushed a hand through his hair. Why hadn't he just kept his mouth shut? He sat in the borrowed Jeep across the street from Ellen's home and wondered where she'd gone. Not fifteen minutes after she'd walked out of the café, he'd driven over to apologize, and now she wasn't answering her door. He frowned and glanced at the clock on the dash. He'd give her a few more minutes. Maybe she'd stopped in at one of the stores along Main Street. An idea hit him. He climbed from the Jeep and walked to the garage. A quick glance in the window revealed her car was gone. So. She'd come home, gotten her car and left again.

He got back in the Jeep and pondered what to do. He really didn't want to go home with the tension still between them. Could she have gotten a call from the hospital about her mother?

Possibly. He dialed the number to the hospital. "Hi, I'd like to check on Marian Foxcroft. Has there been any change in her condition?"

"Are you a family member?"

"No, a family friend." Sort of.

"Then, I can't give out that information."

He sighed. "Okay, could you at least tell me if her daughter, Ellen, is there with her?"

"Hold just a moment, please." He held. In seconds she came back on the line. "She's not here."

"All right. Thanks."

He hung up. So where would she go? She could have gotten a call about the case she was working, but most likely, workaholic that he knew her to be, she'd gone to the kennels. She'd been mad when she'd left the restaurant. Even in high school when she'd been upset she'd gone to find an animal to love on.

The puppies would make her feel better. He aimed his car in the direction of the kennel and again considered the fact that Marian had paid for the rookies to be assigned to Desert Valley. He knew Ellen didn't want to believe Marian had done it to force Ellen to stay in town after graduating from the K-9 center, but Lee knew he was right.

He also knew Ellen would want to find out immediately if that was true, and he hoped she got her answers before the question drove her nuts.

Ellen lay on the floor, her head pounding. She hadn't blacked out, but the hit had stunned her. She rolled to see the figure grabbing at the puppies. He snagged one. She reached for her weapon and found it wedged under her right hip. Relief swept through her. She wrapped her fingers around it and brought it up. Now he was going after the one of the other pups.

She brought the gun up. "Police! Freeze or I'll shoot!"

He spun, the one puppy he had a hold on wriggled from his grasp and fell to the floor. His weapon followed. Her vision blurred and she hoped she'd be able to hit him if she had to pull the trigger. A curse slipped from his lips and he started toward the gun.

"Touch it and I'll shoot you!" she shouted.

He froze and backed toward the door.

She tracked him with her weapon. "Don't move." The words echoed in her skull as did the pain that came with shouting them.

He cast one more glance at the gun on the floor. "I'll be back," he whispered as he slipped out the door. She tried to scramble to her feet, but the room swam. She gritted her teeth and shut her eyes. She had to let him go.

Something wet swiped her face and she gasped. Then blinked against the assault of the puppy's tongue on her cheek. She lifted a hand to her head with a groan and swallowed a wave of nausea as she squinted through still-blurry eyes.

Wait a minute. She slowly turned her head. And there was Benny, quiet and still on the floor next to her. "Benny," she whispered. She moved toward him, ignoring the pain racing through her head. She slipped her fingers over his wrist and bit her lip on a cry of relief. A pulse. A strong one.

Her phone. Where was it?

She slapped a hand against her waist and found the device still in the clip. With a grimace and a groan, fighting dizziness and the desire to black out, she unclipped it and hit the second speed-dial button on the screen. She knew Ryder was on duty tonight, so she tried his personal number first. And he answered.

"Ryder?"

"Yeah? Ellen? You okay?"

"I need backup at the training center. And an ambulance."

"Are you hurt?"

She could hear him scrambling in the background. "I'm all right, but Benny, the security guard, was attacked, too. He's still unconscious."

"Tristan and I were having a late dinner, discussing Veronica's murder. He and I are about three minutes away. We're moving now."

"Okay."

"Is the attacker still in the building?"

"No. He left. Unfortunately, I couldn't stop him." At least the one she had seen had left. What if he'd had a partner? Partner… Carly. Where was Carly? Fear for the animal hit her. "Carly?"

Through the phone she heard a car door slam and knew her fellow officers were on the way. "Where's Carly?" Tristan demanded. She must be on speakerphone.

"I don't know. I remember hearing her bark and then I was hit on the head."

"Hit on the head!" Ryder yelled. "I thought you said you weren't hurt."

"I said I was all right. And I am."

"You still have your weapon?"

"Yes. I fell on it when I was knocked out. I have a feeling Carly and I surprised the intruder and the only thing on his mind was getting away." But what if there was someone else there? There'd been two people in the vehicle when she and Lee had been attacked on the way back from the prison. And only one had left the center. She got to her feet and swayed. She held her weapon in her right hand and braced herself against the nearest kennel fence. Where was Carly? She didn't want to call out again. Not yet. Not until she knew if anyone else was in the building.

When her head quit spinning, she listened to the puppies yapping and playing, but she tried to hear beyond them. She heard nothing, but that didn't mean anything. What did they want? He'd gone after the dogs. But why? Her head still throbbed but her mind was clearing along with her eyes.

She heard Ryder calling to her and realized when she'd braced herself against the chain-link fence, she'd lowered the phone from her ear. She pressed it back to her ear. "Hey, I'm still here. I think whoever broke in left, and I don't think anyone else was with him."

"Stay put. Don't go looking for anyone else."

She realized she didn't have the strength to go after anyone. She leaned her back against the cage and let her legs fold her back to the floor. "I'm not looking. Trust me. I'm just going to be sitting here." But she wanted to find Carly. Sirens sounded and drew closer quickly. "I think I hear the ambulance."

"We're pulling in, too."

Just one of the perks of living in a small town. Help was never too far away. Ellen took a deep breath and moved back to the fallen security officer. That was when she noticed the glass bowl on the tile floor. Strands of long light brown hair were stuck to the drying blood. Her hair. So that was what he'd hit her with.

She checked Benny's pulse once more and squeezed his hand. "Help is on the way, Benny, hang on."

Lee pulled into the parking lot of the training center and leaped out of his car. Flashing blue-and-red lights shouted trouble. "Ellen!" He spotted her SUV in the first parking spot next to the door and rushed toward the entrance.

"Hey, you can't go in there."

Lee realized it was Chief Jones himself who had the iron grip on his forearm. "I have to see if Ellen's all right."

"She's fine. She's giving a statement right now."

Lee felt his pulse slow slightly. The chief released him. "Good. What happened?"

"Someone broke in."

Lee resisted rolling his eyes. "I figured that. And the alarm didn't go off?"

"Benny, the night security guard Ellen hired when she started the training center, was caught by surprise."

"Is he all right?"

"Yes. He was out cold for a while but was waking up by the time the ambulance arrived. I was able to talk to him a bit before they pushed me away to check on him."

"So what did he say?"

"Someone knocked on the door. Benny said when he looked out, he saw a person standing there with his back to him. He had a large dog in his arms. Thinking it was someone who wanted to drop off a stray animal, Benny immediately disabled the alarm and opened the door. When he did, the masked person dropped the dog, spun and jammed a gun into Benny's stomach. Benny backpedaled and the attacker shoved him off balance then cracked the gun on his head. Twice."

"Ouch."

"Exactly. And he got Ellen with a heavy bowl that had dog treats in it."

"I thought you said she was all right." He started toward the door and once again the chief stopped him.

"She'll probably have a headache, but she's fine."

Lee ran a hand through his hair. What was going on in this town? Would it never end? "Did you get a description from Benny?"

"No, the mask kind of prevented that."

Lee refused to grit his teeth with the frustration running rampant through him. "Of course. I meant like height, weight, details like that."

"Not yet. We'll ask those questions soon. He's off to the hospital for now to get a head X-ray."

"Lee?"

Lee turned at the sound of Ellen's voice. "Hey." He noticed her gloved hand holding something against the side of her head. An ice pack. The other gloved hand held a crystal bowl he remembered seeing the treats in. "How bad are you hurt?"

"He stunned me for a few seconds." She grimaced. "Long enough to get away."

"You should be in the hospital."

"No way." She looked back. "Carly, heel." Carly appeared at her side. "We're going to see what we can find." She handed Lee the ice pack and held the bowl in a gloved hand to let Carly sniff it. "Track, Carly." Carly immediately went to work, her nose to the ground. Ellen set the bowl on the ground and motioned to an officer. "Bag that, will you?"

Without waiting for an answer, Ellen followed behind Carly. Lee stayed with them. Carly bypassed the law enforcement and went in almost a straight line all the way to the edge of the road where she sat with a whine. Ellen knelt beside the dog and scratched her ears. "This is where the getaway car was, I guess. She's lost the scent." Ellen stood and winced, her hand pressing to her head for a brief moment. Then she slipped Carly a chew toy and the dog latched on to it. Her reward for doing a good job.

"Ellen, you need to get that looked at."

"I've got a pretty hard head. Want to come help me get the puppies put away for the remainder of the night?"

"Well, if you're not going to take care of yourself..."

"I'm taking care of myself. It wasn't that hard of a hit."

"Fine." Lee followed her and Carly away from the road and back into the building, where he noticed the deputies gathering evidence and going over what was now a crime scene. He hoped they knew what they were doing. As far as he could tell, Ryder Hayes and Chief Jones were the only really competent officers on the force—discounting the other rookies. He shook his head and gathered the pups. And Chief Jones was counting his days.

"I had the new puppies in the back area of the kennel," Ellen said. "I wanted them away from the other dogs so they wouldn't pick up any bad habits." Carly came to her side and sat. She placed a hand on the dog's head. "Whoever did this managed to get Carly in one of the kennels and lock her in. I found her just before I took her out to track."

"She didn't fight back?"

"No. Once the person wasn't attacking me anymore, she stood down. And that worries me."

He nodded. "Because it means it's someone she knows and likely trusts."

"Possibly—or it could simply mean the person who did this is comfortable around dogs and knows how to be the alpha."

"That's just awesome." He glanced around and noticed something that interested him. "Tristan and Ryder seem to be leading this. Chief Jones is just kind of standing back."

Ellen sighed. "Chief Jones is ready to retire. He's good at his job, but he's already made it known that he has one foot out the door and he's not worried about letting the up-and-coming officers take over a bit."

"Yes, that's what I'm hearing. I have a feeling he'll retire before much longer."

Ellen rubbed her eyes. "Okay, so I'm going to get this place cleaned up, see if the video footage got anything and then head home for some sleep."

"All right, let's get it done."

"Thanks." She started to turn and he gently clasped her upper arm. She looked at him.

"I'm sorry," he said.

She bit her lip and gave a short nod. "Thank you, but I've been thinking about what you said and you're right. I do know how my mother operates. I can't say I haven't thought about it, but I want to know for sure if she had ulterior motives behind her more than generous offer. I've got a call in to Louise Donaldson to ask her about it, but—" Her eyes locked on Chief Jones who was standing by his cruiser. "I guess I can find out right now."

"Ellen, it doesn't matter."

"Yes. Yes, it does."

SIX

Ellen stepped up next to Chief Jones, who was talking to Ryder and Tristan, whose dogs sat at their sides, alert and ready for action should they be called to it. Tristan's yellow Lab, Jesse, looked over at Ellen's approach. Ryder's dog, Titus, simply tilted his head.

"...called about the glove. They didn't find any prints, but they got some DNA off it."

"They're running it through CODIS?" Ryder asked.

"They are."

The men looked at her, as well. "How are you feeling?" Chief Jones asked.

"I had some ibuprofen and took a couple. I'll be okay. It was a hard knock, but I don't have a concussion, according to the paramedic."

"Good to hear," Chief Jones said. "You need some time off?"

"No." He lifted a brow and she shrugged. "If something changes between now and tomorrow I'll let you know. I've had worse headaches than this. Really, it was just a glancing blow." She cleared her throat. "Are you talking about the bank robbery?"

"Yes."

"So they found DNA on the glove. That's great."

"Yes, I'd love to have this case solved and soon."

"There are a lot of cases that need solving and soon," Lee muttered.

The chief looked at him. "Yes, we're concentrating on that one, too, Lee."

Tristan nodded to Ellen. "You need to take care of yourself," he said. "Head injuries aren't anything to play around with."

"And I will. But for now, Chief, I want to ask you a question and I want a straight answer."

The chief frowned at her. "Of course."

"I've heard a lot of speculation about my mother's motives in putting up the money to pay for the rookies' salaries and I'm tired of wondering about it. You're friends with her. Did she have an ulterior motive?"

"Like?"

"Like forcing me to come home so she could have me under her thumb again."

His deer-in-headlights look gave her the answer she didn't want. Her shoulders slumped and she felt Lee's hand at the small of her back. Her head throbbed harder and she swallowed. Well, she'd wanted to know and now she did.

"Come here." He took her arm and pulled her aside. She felt Ryder's, Lee's and Tristan's gazes follow them. "Ellen, it doesn't matter how we got you here. You're here to do a job that needs to be done and that's all that matters."

Her fingers curled into fists at her side. "But she once again has interfered in my life. Lee was right. She did it because she wanted me home."

He sighed and shifted his heavy belt. "I'm not going

to say that your staying in Desert Valley had nothing to do with her offer. Your mother loves you. But mostly she wanted the murders of Melanie Hayes, Mike Riverton and Brian Miller solved. She said their deaths were a pall over the town and she wanted it gone. She started ranting about how Desert Valley was losing residents and tourist dollars and how her ancestors who founded the town would be so disappointed."

Ellen refrained from rolling her eyes. Barely. "Ah, yes, the ancestors." Hadn't she heard enough about them and living up to their expectations her entire life?

The chief cleared his throat and continued. "She was also mad because the county fair last year only brought in about half of its normal visitors. Said something had to be done and it looked like it was up to her to do it."

"Unbelievable," Ellen muttered.

"I know it sounds manipulative and maybe part of it had to do with getting you home, but truly, I think she was more concerned about the town losing revenue than keeping you here."

She didn't believe it for a moment. "Nice try, Chief, but you can't cover for her, and I can't ask her myself. If you know her motives, come clean, will you, please?"

He sighed. "Ellen, come on. I'm not covering for her. The morning after Veronica was killed, Marian showed up with her offer. She said if we would hire you five rookies who had just graduated Veronica's class, then she would bestow the training center with a half-million-dollar endowment and pay the rookies' salaries for as long as it took to solve the murders. Since you all hadn't been assigned anywhere at the time she made the offer, the governor thought it sounded like a win-

win situation." He cleared his throat. "And honestly, I can't say I wasn't relieved to have the help."

"I see."

"Would she have done it if you hadn't been one of the rookies hired?" He shrugged. "I don't know. I don't really care to be honest. I'm just glad y'all are here."

Ellen's throat worked. She didn't know whether she wanted to scream or stomp her feet.

Or both.

Both.

Definitely both.

She drew in a calming breath. "All right, then. Let's focus on solving this case as fast as possible." Because only then would she be free to leave Desert Valley—and her mother—for good. Assuming her mother ever woke up. The twinge of grief that pierced her at the thought of her mother never waking didn't catch her by surprise this time. She loved her mother, she just didn't want to live in the same town with her. And she sure didn't want to be around so the woman could hone her manipulation skills on her.

Ellen pushed the grief away and told herself not to go there. She waved Lee over. Tristan and Ryder followed. "Have you found anything that might lead us to the person responsible for this latest incident?" Ellen asked.

"Well, the only thing left behind that might tell us anything was the bowl that was used to hit you. We'll check for prints."

"Don't bother. He wore gloves." She remembered turning, the flash of the gloved hand, the crashing pain against her head.

"And it's likely someone who's familiar enough with

the program to know that the door would be opened to anyone with a pet in his arms," Lee said.

Ellen nodded, then grimaced. "And that."

"Come on, I'm taking you to the hospital to get your head looked at," Lee said.

She waved a dismissing hand. "The paramedic already checked me out."

"Yeah, well, I want a doctor giving you the green light."

"I'd feel better about that, too," Chief Jones said. "Go with him."

"Come on, Chief, it's a twenty-minute drive out there and back."

"Go see your mother while you're there. Give her my best."

Ellen stilled. She knew when she was outnumbered—and knew an order when she heard one. And the mention of seeing her mother again was compelling. "Fine."

Lee pulled the keys to her mother's Jeep from his pocket. "Chief, can you lock up here?"

"Of course. Tristan, why don't you follow them? Watch their backs. After the shooting and now this, I'm afraid we're all going to need to have each others' backs."

Tristan nodded. "I can do that."

Lee shot Ellen a smug look. "There you go. No more excuses. Everything's taken care of."

She groaned, not really upset about going, but not wanting to be bossed around, either. A smile played at the corner of Lee's mouth. He knew exactly what she was thinking. She commanded Carly to heel and followed him to the vehicle. Carly took the backseat and

Ellen climbed into the passenger seat. Once Lee was settled behind the wheel and they were pulling away from the parking lot of the training center, she looked at him. And kept her mouth shut. She let him drive while she thought. The minutes passed quickly and the silence stretched.

"I don't think you're like her," he finally said.

"What?"

"I don't really think you're like your mother. I shouldn't have said that you were."

"Oh. Thanks. I'm glad."

He sighed.

"What are you thinking?" he asked.

She touched the wound on her head and winced. "About this break-in."

"Of course. What about it?"

She glanced at him. "I keep circling back to the fact that it's similar to the others."

"The others?"

"The ones I was telling you about. Where someone breaks in to a house or whatever, but doesn't take anything."

"Right, you mentioned that. So they're looking for something."

"Yes."

"The German shepherd puppy that's missing?"

"Yeah. Marco. All of the break-ins are the same, including this one. It's the only thing that makes sense. There's a lot of equipment in that building that's worth a lot of money, and yet nothing was taken." She sighed and closed her eyes, wishing she could just put all the pieces together and get this thing solved.

"Maybe they didn't have time? Maybe you got there before they had a chance."

"Maybe, but I'm guessing the training center was just next on the list of places to hit to look for Marco."

"Where do you think they'll go next?" he asked.

"I don't know." She sat up, her mind spinning as much as it could with the pounding in her skull. "But that's a really good question."

"What do you mean?"

"We can get a map, make a list of all the places already hit and narrow it down to a few possibilities that could be next." She had her phone out and was punching in a group text to Ryder, Shane, Whitney James and Tristan.

When she finished, her phone pinged several times. Great idea. We're on it, Ryder texted back.

She gave him a half smile. "Nice job."

"Glad I can be helpful." He paused and turned right.

"Why do they want that puppy, Marco, so bad?" she whispered. "What is so special about that dog that someone would go to such lengths to find him?"

"All of the puppies are worth a lot of money," Lee said. "They're purebred."

"I know that. But I just have a feeling there's something more going on with that puppy than we're seeing."

He parked and turned the Jeep off. "Well, we'll have to discuss it later. We're here."

At Canyon County Medical Center, the doctor reiterated the paramedic's diagnosis of no concussion but said that she needed rest.

Tristan had come in to wait, as well. Even Shane had shown up. The two officers and Lee had discussed the case while Ellen had her head examined. When she came out of the room, Lee took in her pinched features and tired eyes. "Take the day off tomorrow and take it easy," he said. Then wondered why he bothered. He was probably just wasting his breath.

"I may try to sleep in, but no promises after that."

Shane raised a brow. Tristan met Lee's gaze and Lee sighed. "Well, one thing worked in your favor tonight," he said.

"What's that?"

"Your hard head."

Tristan and Shane snickered, and Ellen wrinkled her nose at Lee. "Funny."

"Hey, you took a hard knock and didn't get a concussion. The evidence speaks for itself."

She gave him a light punch on the arm.

"Okay, heads up," Tristan said. "I've got news."

Ellen turned serious. "What?"

"Ryder's mapped all the break-ins and pinpointed two other homes that are possible targets. They're families that recently got German shepherd puppies but haven't been broken into yet. We thought we'd set a trap and see if we can catch whoever's doing this."

"What kind of trap?"

"It'll take some coordination, but I think we can pull it off. We'll have two teams. We'll ask one of the families to leave for the evening and not come home until we give them the okay. We'll have them make it well-known that they won't be at home and hopefully word will filter down to the person we're after."

Ellen nodded. "I see where you're going with this."

"Have the break-ins happened on a specific night of the week?" Lee asked.

Tristan shook his head. "Not that we can see. A couple of Mondays, a weekend, several Thursdays."

"But none of the owners were home," Shane said, looking at his phone. "I've got the reports here. All of the break-ins were when the home owners were gone."

Tristan scratched his chin. "Yes, that's one of the common denominators."

"Tell me about the two remaining families who have German shepherd puppies and no break-in," Ellen said.

"One is an elderly homebound resident."

"And the other?"

"Works here at the hospital third shift, but her husband and kids are home at night while she's working."

"And she'd be sleeping during the day while the husband works and the kids are at school," Ellen said.

"But it's only a matter of time before one of the houses is empty. The weekend is coming up. The multishift family will spend the day at the lake or the elderly resident will have a doctor's appointment. Something."

"And that's when our would-be puppy snatcher will strike."

"Exactly. That's why we're going to give this person the perfect opportunity. An empty house and a German shepherd puppy," Tristan said.

Shane nodded. "Let's get it set up." He stifled a yawn.

Ellen did the same. "I know we're all tired, but before we leave I need to check on my mother. I can't come here and not go see her. Do you three mind?"

"I don't mind," Shane said. "If Tristan has this, I'm going to head into the office for a bit and work on this plan of ours."

Tristan nodded. "I got it."

Ellen looked at Lee. "Are you sure you don't mind?"

"Of course you have to see her," Lee said. "Lead the way."

Shane took off for the sliding glass doors while Ellen headed for the elevators with Carly at her side. Lee, Tristan and his Lab, Jesse, stepped in beside her. They made their way to the fourth floor and Ellen led them to the nurse's station. Lee noted the looks Tristan and Jesse got as well as Ellen and Carly. People wanted to pet the dogs, but the official working-dog vests they wore were sufficient to keep most people at bay. "You can wait here," Ellen said. "I'll be right back. Her room is the second one on the left." She told Carly to stay with Lee and headed in that direction.

Lee scratched the dog's ears and watched Ellen speak to the guard sitting outside the door. She nodded then slipped into the room. The floor was quiet, the atmosphere subdued. Tristan pulled his phone from his pocket. "Excuse me while I make a call? I need to check on my sister." Jesse stayed right at his side watching Tristan's every move.

"Sure."

Tristan walked a few paces away and pressed the phone to his ear. Lee checked his own phone, but no one had called or texted. Sadness invaded him. He and Veronica hadn't been close. Not like some siblings, but at least he'd known she was there if he needed her. Only someone had taken that away from him, and it angered him. The injustice of it, the personal loss, everything.

Ellen appeared in the doorway. She stopped, spoke to the guard again, then swiped at her eyes and took a deep breath. She looked up and caught his gaze on her and offered him a shaky smile as she walked toward him. "Thanks for waiting."

"No problem. Are you okay?"

"I am. It just hurts to see her so incapacitated. I mean, we've had our moments, arguments and disagreements, for sure. Definitely plenty of those. But I always knew she was there for me if I truly needed her to be, you know what I mean?"

Exactly what he'd just been thinking about Veronica. Lee's throat clogged with a sudden tightness. He cleared it. "I'm sorry," he said.

"I am, too."

"No, I mean I'm sorry about…before."

Her brow knit. "Before?"

"In high school." He sighed and ran a hand through his hair. "We were so young and I was…stupid. I thought if you truly loved me you should choose me over your mother. That… I don't know…that we'd run away together and live happily ever after."

She bit her lip and looked away. "I know."

"I was wrong and I'm sorry. I shouldn't have put that burden on you. Given you that ultimatum."

"No. But like you said, we were young. And stupid. I have to take some of the credit, too."

He gave her a small smile and rested a hand on her upper arm. "I've missed you, Ellen."

She nodded. "I've missed you, too, Lee, and I just want you—"

"Are you two ready?"

Lee turned to see Tristan and Jesse standing behind him. Frustration bit at him. What had she been about to say? He smoothed his features. "We're ready. Ellen?"

She shot him a quiet look full of regret then shrugged.

"I'm ready. Take me to get my car, so I can go home and get that rest you keep harping about."

"I have the right to harp," Lee said. "A doctor backed me up."

She gave a low chuckle. "I'm not going to win tonight, am I?"

"No."

"Fine." She and Carly followed him out of the hospital and to the Jeep while Tristan and Jesse jogged to Tristan's vehicle and climbed in. Once she had the door shut and her seat belt on, she laid her head back and closed her eyes.

Lee smiled and pulled out of the hospital parking lot. He'd take her to get her car and then get some rest himself. He had a feeling tomorrow was going to be a long day. As he drove, he watched the road behind him. Every time he passed a side road, he tensed, almost expecting someone to dart out in front of him.

The fact that he knew Tristan was on guard behind him offered him a large measure of comfort. Apparently it worked for Ellen, too, as within seconds her breathing turned deep and even. Good. She needed to sleep. He drove slower than he needed to, stretching out the minutes to give her as much rest as he could before pulling into the parking lot of the training center. With regret that he couldn't give her more time to sleep, he nudged her. "We're here."

She opened her eyes and blinked at him. "Did I fall asleep?"

"Naw, you were just resting your eyes while you thought about the case."

She laughed and yawned. "Right. We'll go with that

one." She studied him for a moment then leaned over and placed a kiss on his cheek. "Thanks, Lee."

Surprise held him still. Surprise and emotions he'd thought—hoped—he'd buried long ago. He lifted a hand, slid it under her loose ponytail and gently grasped the back of her neck. Her eyes widened and she opened her mouth as though to say something, then closed it and swallowed hard. He leaned in, never taking his eyes from hers. Closer. His gaze dropped to her lips and she tensed. He paused. Then dropped his hand and leaned back. "Good night, Ellen."

She let out a little puff of breath that whispered across his cheek. Tristan's headlight flashed through the interior of the Jeep. Ellen stared at him a moment longer, and he would have given anything to know what she was thinking behind the intense gaze. "Good night, Lee. Drive safe."

She climbed out and shut the door, then opened the back so Carly could jump out. He watched her and Carly walk to her car. Ellen looked back. This time there was no problem reading the expression on her face. Longing with a hint of fear. Not a fear for her physical safety but for her emotional well-being. He let his lips curve. Good. He wanted her off balance. Because he planned to finish what they'd started in high school. He planned to make it his mission to convince her that they belonged together. The timing had been wrong when they were teens. Their time was now.

As soon as Veronica's murderer was caught.

Or before, if it came down to it.

He wanted justice for his sister. He craved it, wanted to demand it and have it happen. But he knew there was the distinct possibility that whoever had killed Veronica might actually get away with it. The thought made him want to shout out a huge denial, but he stayed silent and watched Ellen drive away. He knew she and the team were working on the case—cases, if one included the other deaths—and he also knew that they didn't have a whole lot to work with. *God, don't let whoever did this get away with it. Please.*

Tristan waited patiently in his vehicle with Jesse in the backseat. Lee walked over. "I'm just going to check on the puppies." He noticed the police cruiser in the parking lot. "Who's that?"

"The chief asked Eddie Harmon to stay the rest of the night to keep an eye on the center."

Eddie? Lee kept his groan to himself. Eddie wouldn't notice if a crook came up and slapped him in the face with a handwritten confession. He was a good man but a lousy cop. "Ah…okay. I'm sure his wife is going to love that. I'll be right back." Everyone knew Eddie was more of a family man than a cop. He'd rather be carrying a baby on his hip than a gun.

"I'll wait," Tristan said. "I'll escort you home when you're ready. Ellen and the chief have arranged for an officer to keep an eye on your place tonight, too."

"Who?"

"Dennis Marlton."

"Okay." Dennis was in his early sixties and retiring this year. Having him watching his home didn't inspire much confidence. So Eddie was on the center and Dennis was on Lee's home. Great. He'd be sure to sleep with one eye open.

As though his thoughts had transmitted to Tristan, the man smiled. "Dennis is older, I know, but hopefully having him sitting in his official vehicle will deter anyone who might come snooping around."

What choice did he have? "That's fine. Sit tight, I won't be long."

He made his way into the building and to the puppies in their kennel at the front. They yipped when they saw him, and he gave them each a scratch and a treat. They were fine. He could go home and rest easy. If he could shut his mind off, that was. He slipped back out the door and made sure it was locked tight with the alarm set. He started the engine and waved to Tristan, who followed at a safe distance.

The training center was only about a five-minute drive from his home, and when he pulled into the long drive he saw the cruiser sitting off to the side. The officer waved and Lee kept going. He was glad to be home, glad that Ellen was safe. And doubly glad Ellen had turned at the last moment so he got a glimpse of her inner feelings.

Because there were two things he knew with rock-solid certainty. He wanted to finish veterinarian school and open his own practice. And number two, he wanted to be in Ellen's life on a permanent basis. He just had to convince her that she wanted that, too. He could do that.

"Right?" he whispered. He nodded. "Right. Maybe."

SEVEN

Ellen tossed and turned and finally threw the covers off and slid out of her bed. Carly lifted her head, and with the moon filtering through her blinds, Ellen could see the animal's annoyance with her. "Glad one of us can sleep."

Carly huffed and lowered her head back to her paws and shut her eyes. Ellen rubbed the dog's silky ears and then made her way down the hall and into the kitchen. She had to work tomorrow. She glanced at the clock. Today.

And she had to stop by the training center and leave some notes for those who would be working with the special-needs children and their dogs. Working on training and pairing animals to the appropriate child was a delicate dance but it was also one of her favorite things about working with the children. Seeing their eyes light up and watching them learn right along with their dog.

She yawned and hoped she wouldn't be worthless with her less-than-stellar night's sleep. She sighed and finally realized she needed to face the real reason she was restless. She could try to blame it on the unsolved murders. She could try to blame it on her still-throbbing head. The truth of the matter was that she was still re-playing the almost kiss.

Lee had come so close to kissing her, and she'd had a moment of indecision that he'd read as though it had been stamped on her forehead. And like the gentleman that he was—and had always been—he'd backed off.

Much to her regret now. No, she wouldn't regret it. There was no sense in getting her heart tangled up in his once again. She was his boss. She was leaving Desert Valley as soon as the opportunity presented itself. Kissing Lee would just make things much more complicated than they needed to be.

She groaned. "God, I don't know what's going on or where all this is leading, but I need Your guidance on it." She whispered the prayer aloud and it did seem to help calm her racing thoughts. "What's the right thing to do, God? You've brought me back to Desert Valley for a reason. Maybe my mother's sole purpose in giving the money to the police was to get me back here for an extended period time, so she'd have the opportunity to dictate my life again. I don't know. I don't know much of anything right now, since You've also brought Lee back into my life. Show me what I'm supposed to do with my feelings for him, okay?"

She paced back and forth, waiting to see if she had a sudden burst of inspiration. Nothing.

She sighed. Okay, so she didn't have a clear answer but she felt better taking the matter to the one who was in control. "Well, I'll just wait on Your timing, then. Okay, Lord?"

She went back into the bedroom and thought about Veronica's murder.

She'd been sprawled at the gate of the puppy yard

of the Canyon County Training Center and she'd been shot in the chest twice. The plan had been for her to microchip the puppies, then go over to James Harrison's home to give him a training refresher for his dog. Only she'd never made it over there. Who was responsible for her death and why was it taking so long to figure it out?

Ellen sighed and rubbed her eyes. Carly moved beside her and laid her head in Ellen's lap. Ellen scratched the dog's ears and let her eyes droop shut.

Lee gave up on sleep and sat on the edge of his bed while he thought. He was hot and it was stuffy in his room. He hated to turn the air on when the nights were cool. He walked to the window and lifted it a fraction, then padded down the hall to the kitchen. He grabbed a bottle of water from the refrigerator, then returned to his room and flopped on the bed again.

So. Ellen. He sighed. He'd almost kissed her. But then he'd come to his senses. She was his boss and he had to respect that. For now.

A sound from outside caught his attention and he sat up listening. Voices?

"...not in the house," the voice whispered.

Lee slid from the bed once again and moved on silent feet to the window while his heart pounded out a faster beat. Who wasn't in the house? Did they think he wasn't there? But the Jeep was right outside in plain sight.

"Keep looking." A lower voice. Deeper than the first. A voice he thought he recognized, but couldn't place. His adrenaline pumped. They were looking for something. What?

Lee moved to his end table and grabbed his phone from the charger. He hesitated only a fraction of a second before shooting a text to Ellen. A text she might not get. His backup plan had him punching in Officer Marlton's number. No answer. Where was the man? He dialed 911.

"Nine-one-one. Where is your emergency?"

He stepped into the hall, away from the open window, and gave her his address. "This is Lee Earnshaw. I have two people outside who are trespassing. I have an officer watching my home, but can't reach him."

"Who's the officer?"

"Dennis Marlton."

"Are the two men armed?"

"I don't know, but I'd assume they are."

"Stay hidden. Don't confront them. I have a unit on the way."

"Good."

"And stay on the line with me."

"Okay." He moved back into his bedroom and looked around for something he could use as a weapon. He didn't own a gun. Veronica had sold them all after he'd gone to prison. Might be time to buy another. There wasn't anything in his room he could see that would be a good defense against a gun. So he just wouldn't let them see him. But he'd try to figure out who they were and why there were there. He stood as close to the side of the window as he dared and looked out. The two men were still there, heads tilted toward one another and still talking in hushed tones. Lee leaned closer, but could only make out a few words.

"…the message…"

"…the backyard…"

"…boss is going to go ballistic if he doesn't get the information."

Information? About what? And why would he think Lee had it?

The two men headed for his backyard and he caught one more partial sentence. "...can't get the info without the dogs."

"Lee? Are you there?" The 911 dispatcher.

"Yes," he whispered when he figured it was safe. The two men had moved far enough away that they wouldn't hear him.

Something nagged at him. He hadn't gotten a good look at either of the two men, but there was something familiar about one of the voices.

"...they're not here, I'm telling you."

He sucked in a breath. They were back beneath the window. "Then, let's break in and beat the information out of him."

Lee heard that clear enough.

Where were the cops? He huddled near the window, listening to the sound of their footsteps heading toward his front door.

He grabbed a lamp from the end table next to his bed and carried it down the hall and into his foyer. He stood off to the side of the front door, his heart pounding. He'd had to defend himself enough times in prison that he knew he could handle himself if he had to. He'd learned how to move fast and fight dirty. Skills he hadn't planned on needing once he was out, but he might be glad he had them tonight.

The doorknob gave a light rattle, but he knew that unless they had a battering ram, they weren't getting in this way. The dead bolt was engaged; the knob lock was twisted into the locked position. Double protection that would keep them out. Would they dare break a window? He didn't have an elaborate alarm system here. No neighbors to hear the crash of broken glass. If the trespassers came in a window…

He grimaced. Two against one wasn't great odds, especially with him armed only with a lamp. He might have time to take out one, but if the other one had a gun…

He finally heard the sirens.

And so did the men on his porch.

They bolted down the wooden steps and seconds later the police cruiser was in his drive. Dennis Marlton pulled in behind them. Lee opened the door and stepped out. "They went that way!"

"Get back inside, Lee!" Ellen called to him. He stepped back and shut the door. Ellen and Carly bounded up the front porch and he let them in.

Marlton and the other officer went in the direction he'd pointed.

"Are you all right?" she asked.

"Yes, I'm fine." He raked a hand through his already mussed hair. "Getting real tired of losing sleep over all this, but I'm fine."

"Join the club on the losing-sleep part."

She paced to the window and peered out, then spun to face him. She winced and held a hand to her head. "Still hurting?"

"Yes. I expect it will for a while. I'm doing my best to ignore it."

"You got my text?"

"I did. I texted you right back. Then called and got no answer so I hopped in my car and headed your way."

"I heard you beep in. I was on the phone with the 911 dispatcher."

"As I was driving over here, I heard the call go out over the radio." She touched his cheek. "It scared me to death, Lee."

The touch of her soft hand on his skin nearly undid him. How many times had he dreamed of it in prison? Deliberately remembered her smile, her lilting laugh and even her mulish frown when things weren't going her way? He swallowed and held her gaze. She drew in a deep breath and dropped her hand.

"Tell me what happened," she said.

He opened his mouth but was interrupted by a knock on the door. Ellen peeked out then opened it. Dennis Marlton and Louise Donaldson stepped inside. "Did you catch them?" Lee asked.

"No." Louise planted her hands on her hips and drew in one quick breath after the other. She panted and Ellen waited until the woman finally got her breath back. "Now I understand why the chief wanted me on patrol tonight—and why I'm retiring soon."

"What happened to you, Dennis? I thought you were watching the house?"

"I was!"

"And why didn't you answer the phone when I called earlier?" Lee asked.

"What are you talking about? You never called."

"Yes. I did."

Dennis frowned and pulled the device off the clip on his belt and looked at it. He sighed and rubbed his forehead. "I didn't answer the phone because I didn't hear it ring. It's on silent," he said softly. "Sorry."

"And you didn't see the intruders come onto the property?" Ellen asked.

His already flushed cheeks deepened to dark ruddy

red. "I...ah...well...they must have come in from across the yard because I didn't see 'em drive in the driveway."

"But you were supposed to do foot patrols, right?" Louise said.

"Now, look," Dennis blustered, "I was doing my job and I didn't see anything. They came across the backyard. When we chased them, they hopped in a vehicle and took off.

Lee wondered how much chasing actually occurred. What chance did two officers in their sixties have of catching up to the two would-be intruders? Or anyone for that matter? Lee bit his tongue on the words he was tempted to hurl at the man. Instead, he took a calming breath. "Did you get a description?" he asked.

"No," Louise said. "We didn't actually see the car. We just heard it. It was parked on the other side of a house a street over. We made it in time to see the taillights disappear. I called it in and told officers to be watching for it."

"Who else is on duty tonight?" Ellen asked.

"Well. No one, I guess. Eddie Harmon is on the training center that was broken into."

"Right."

Ellen gestured to the living area. "Well, now that we're all here, why don't you tell us what happened, Lee?"

Lee waited until everyone was seated. He stood in front of the mantel and shoved his hands into the front pockets of his sweats. "I had the window open," he said. "I couldn't sleep and voices outside caught my attention. I only heard a few words, it was hard to catch everything, but apparently whoever was out there was looking for something."

"What?" Louise asked.

"I don't know. Not for sure." He looked at Ellen. "But the more I think about it, I think they were looking for the golden retriever puppies."

Ellen straightened. "What? Why?"

"I don't know. But there's a connection. I recognized one of the voices. At first I couldn't place it, but I just realized it was Freddie."

"The vet tech from the Prison Pups program," Ellen said, "the one who shot at us the other day."

"Yes. I told you I got him kicked out of the program for not treating the animals well."

"I remember."

Lee shook his head. "He was mean, but a coward. He would only take a chance like that if there was something big in it for him—like a lot of money."

"Okay."

"I've been thinking about all the people who had access to the German shepherd puppy someone seems to want so bad and also to the three goldens we have. Freddie's the common denominator."

She nodded. "What have you come up with?"

"So you have the veterinarians and the vet techs who initially worked with the dogs. Veronica chipped the German shepherd puppies, right?"

"Right."

"Veronica was killed approximately four months ago," Lee said and held up four fingers as though they needed a visual, "and Sophie took over the facility. The golden retriever puppies had come in just the day before so Sophie inherited them when she took over the program. She then had the pups in the Prison Pups program for some training before she passed the puppies on to Ellen, right?"

Louise shrugged. "That sounds right."

"I'm guessing that Veronica didn't have time to microchip the goldens so maybe the veterinarian working with Sophie did. Who took over Freddie's spot as a vet tech after he was kicked out of the prison program?"

Ellen got on her phone and made a call to find out. "His name is Gerald Nees," she said when she hung up. Her eyes were wide and glittering. "He's also close to getting out of prison."

Lee pursed his lips and let his brain whirl. "The golden retriever puppies were microchipped at the prison. The two vet techs that worked with the dogs were both inmates at the same prison and likely know each other."

"Yes," she said slowly. She lifted a brow. "You think someone put something on the chip while they had access to the puppies."

"Yes. And in order to get the information off that chip, they need to have the dogs."

"I think you may be on to something." Ellen stared at him, admiration gleaming in her eyes. It hit him how badly he wanted her respect. And there it was. It nearly took his breath away.

Ellen's phone rang and the moment was broken. Lee waited for her to check the number. She looked up. "It's the chief. Excuse me a minute." She nodded for Lee to follow, and they walked into his kitchen. "Hello?"

Lee followed and listened to her side of the conversation. "Yes," she said. "That's right." Pause. "Uh-huh. Yes, sir." Another pause. "All right, we'll do that. See you in the morning."

She hung up and turned to Lee. He raised a brow. "Well?"

"The chief wants us to call it a night and come in first thing in the morning to discuss everything."

"Fine."

They walked back into his den and Ellen looked at Dennis Marlton. "Do you mind staying here to finish the shift and then following Lee into the station in the morning?"

"No, I don't mind." He crossed his arms across his belly and his chin jutted. Lee knew the man's pride had been trampled tonight.

"Thanks, Dennis, I appreciate it," Ellen said.

He shrugged and dropped his defensive stance at her soft tones. "Yeah."

Dennis left and Louise followed him, leaving Ellen and Lee alone. She took his hand. "You have to be careful tonight."

"Not much tonight left."

"I was worried when I heard the call come over the radio."

"So you said." He pulled her closer. When she didn't resist, he kept tugging until her lips were a mere centimeter from his. "I'll be careful."

"Good," she whispered.

He covered her lips with his. When she let him deepen the kiss, he slid one hand up her back and under the sloppy ponytail she seemed to love so much. When he lifted his head a fraction she made a sound in her throat. A protest that did wonders for his heart.

He opened his eyes and stared down at her. "We have a lot to talk about when all of this is over."

He heard the husky roughness in his voice and didn't

care. His feelings for her had never died. Instead, they'd smoldered, just waiting for her to come back into his life so they could spark into flames once again.

She blinked and stepped back. "Lee—"

He held up a hand. "No, don't say it. I know. I'm sorry. You're my boss."

"Yes, ah…yes. I am."

"I respect that, I promise."

"Good." She nodded. Then seemed to gather her thoughts. "Good. Because we can't let that happen again. This is just a temporary stop for me, Lee. I'm not staying in Desert Valley. Hopefully I'm here long enough to solve your sister's murder and the others and see my mother wake up. Then I'm gone." Her eyes shuttered and he could no longer see her feelings.

Sadness gripped him. She was right and he knew it. Didn't like it, but knew it. "Fine."

"Fine," she echoed.

He grasped her fingers. "I lied."

She blinked up at him. "About what?"

"I'm not sorry about that kiss."

She flushed, pulled her hand from his and walked to the door with Carly at her heels. She gripped the knob and turned back to face him. "I texted Shane. He's going to sit out here the rest of the night."

Shane Weston. Another rookie who'd graduated with Ellen. Lee frowned. "What about Marlton?"

"What about him?"

"I thought he was going to be outside watching."

"He is."

"So?"

"So that's why I asked Shane to be…um…backup." She turned the knob. "See you at the station, Lee."

"See you." He shut the door behind her and leaned his forehead against the wood. What was he *thinking*? What was he *doing*?

Ellen had done it again. She had his brain scrambled. Was he really going to let himself be hurt again? He let the memories flood over him. Of the hurt Ellen had caused him when she'd chosen her mother over him. Of when she'd left Desert Valley to go to the academy. And now she was back and her presence was threatening to break his heart once again. He sighed and revised his earlier vow. He'd back off. Protect his heart. Because if he didn't, the hurt would be the end of him this time around.

EIGHT

Ellen looked up from her seat in Chief Jones's office and her heart stuttered to see Lee in the doorway. Truly, it had to quit doing that. Carly nudged her hand and she scratched the dog's ears. She always seemed to know when there was a change in Ellen's emotions, and Lee could certainly send them into a tailspin.

In fact, Lee was the one person who could tempt her to revise her plans and stay in this town that her mother ruled. Especially after that kiss last night. Oh, yeah, staying was becoming more and more tempting.

Her heart was wavering. *No!* her mind shouted. Lee had walked away from her once. It would only be a matter of time before he did it again. She really needed to focus on that fact. "Hi."

His eyes landed hers, cool and distant. "Hi."

Confusion flickered through her. What was that about? Was he mad because she'd tensed up and he thought she hadn't wanted him to kiss her? No, that didn't sound like Lee.

She didn't have time to wonder further. The chief slipped into the chair behind his desk and steepled his fingers in front of him. "All right, I spoke with Tristan and Shane earlier. They've worked it out so that the house will be empty tonight."

"That's the woman who works third shift at the hospital?" Ellen asked.

"Yes. We're going to be there tonight when they leave. Tonight's her night off and they're all going out for a family dinner, compliments of the department. They keep their puppy in the laundry room in his kennel when they're not home so we'll be watching to see if anyone goes after him." He looked at Ellen. "You'll be there, too."

"Of course."

Lee shifted as if he wanted to say something. To object or insist on coming along, she couldn't tell.

The chief turned, nodded. "All right, then. Tell me everything about last night."

Ellen blinked. "I think you know most of it."

"Humor me." Ellen nodded and started to speak but before she could, a young woman entered the office. Chief Jones raised a brow. "Yes, Missy?"

Missy had her blond hair pulled up in a loose bun that allowed a few strands to curl around her cheeks. Her green eyes sparkled behind fashionable glasses. "Um. Oh, I need you to sign this form. Carrie said to give it to you."

"Not that one, Missy, this one." Ellen's gaze bounced back to the door where Carrie stood.

"Oh," Missy said. "I'm sorry." She crossed the room and traded papers with Carrie, then walked back to hand it to the chief.

"And," Carrie said, "I told you it could wait until he was finished with his meeting."

"I know." She blinked. "I thought you meant the meeting he just got out of."

"No, Missy, I meant this one." Carrie sighed, a long-suffering sound that had Ellen feeling sorry for Missy and biting her lip against a smile of sympathy for Carrie.

"Right." Missy crossed the room with the signed paper and handed it to Carrie. "I'm sorry."

"Why don't you go answer the phones for a while? I'll handle the rest of the paperwork."

"Of course." Missy slipped away and Carrie shifted then tugged at her dowdy flower-print dress. "I'm sorry, Chief."

"No apologies necessary. She's new. She'll catch on."

"But I hired her."

"And there must have been something about her that told you she could do the job. Give her some time."

Carrie used the tip of her index finger to shove her glasses to the bridge of her nose. "Yes, on paper, she looked great. All right, Chief, thanks." She took a deep breath as though bracing herself then turned and walked out.

"Missy?" Ellen asked, her question directed at Chief Jones.

He nodded. "The new temp. With all of the added workload five new people coming into the department creates, not to mention Veronica's murder, reopening the murder of Ryder Hayes's wife and so on, poor Carrie was really struggling to keep up. It wasn't fair to put that much on her, so I told her to hire someone."

"Missy."

He pursed his lips. "Yeah, Missy." He gave a slight smile. "She's one of the improvements around here made possible by your mother's money."

"Oh."

"Like I said, she'll catch on." He waved a hand. "Moving on."

"All right." Ellen shot a glance at Lee. "I think you're the best one to tell him. After all, I was only there for the tail end of it."

Lee nodded. "It's very simple. I heard voices outside my window, called the cops, they arrived and the two people planning to break in to beat information out of me ran."

"What information were they looking for?"

Lee rubbed his chin. "I have no idea what the information is, but Ellen and I came up with a theory last night that we think is probable."

"What's that?"

Ellen explained.

The chief blew out a breath and leaned back. "Good thoughts, check it out. Take the dogs in and see what's on the chips."

"Great. Thanks." She shot a text to Sophie, asking if she could check the chips later this afternoon, then set aside her phone to focus on her boss.

Chief Jones rubbed his ever-expanding belly. "Look, I know I'm on the fast track to retirement. The whole town knows it." His jaw tightened and his eyes narrowed. "But I want to solve these murders, deaths, whatever, before I go. I need you and the rest of the team to step it up, Ellen. Whatever you need is at your disposal."

Ellen nodded. "I'm glad you said that, Chief."

He lifted a brow. "What do you need?"

"I want to see Veronica's evidence box." She heard Lee pull in a sharp breath.

The chief studied her for a moment. "Okay, sure. You want to tell me why?"

She shrugged. "I don't know. Has anyone looked at it since she died?"

"Of course. Quite a few times."

"Well, I haven't. If you want me to step this up, then humor me."

"All right." He nodded and hefted his bulk from the chair. "Follow me." Lee looked at Ellen and hesitated.

Come on, she mouthed.

Chief Jones led the way to the back of the station and came to a stop before a gray metal door. The supervising clerk wasn't at the desk.

"Where's Alice?" Ellen asked. Alice, a sandy-haired lady in her midfifties, usually sat opposite the door.

"She called in sick today, but it's nothing I can't take care of myself."

"Seems like she's been sick a lot lately."

"Seems like." He signed the log that lay open on the desk, then pulled a set of keys from his front pocket. He unlocked the door and waved them in. "Have a seat at the table."

She did so. Lee sat opposite her and the chief still didn't say anything about Lee being in the room. Was he going to let Lee sit in, as well? Should she insist that he wait outside? Carly shifted at her feet and she let the dog find a comfortable spot. She looked back up, and before she could decide whether or not to bring up the breach of protocol, the chief returned with the evidence box. *Earnshaw, Veronica*, had been written on the end with a black marker. Her case number was in the right-hand corner. The chief set the box on the table in front of her.

Lee bowed his head, and she heard him draw in a

deep breath. She looked at him. Saw the grief in his eyes and wanted to offer words of comfort. But she knew that nothing she could say would lessen the pain of his loss. His hands rested on the table. She leaned over, grasped his fingers and gave them a squeeze, silently asking if he wanted to wait outside.

He met her gaze with reddened eyes. No tears, but she thought he might be on the verge. Then his expression hardened. "Let's take a look."

Ellen nodded, reached over and lifted the lid.

She gasped.

"What is it?" the chief asked.

"It's empty!"

Lee bolted upright in his seat. He'd held back, not sure he could handle seeing what had been left behind at his sister's murder. Ellen's touch had strengthened him, reminded him of his purpose in being there. Now he gazed down into the box, staring at the empty space. "How is this possible?" His head pounded. He glared at the chief, who had paled to an alarming shade of white.

Ellen must have noticed. She jumped to her feet, grabbed his arm and shoved him into her chair. "Chief?"

He swiped an arm across his forehead. "Give me a minute."

"Chief, are you okay? Does your left arm or chest hurt?"

"No, no." He waved a hand. "I'm just in shock. Feel like someone punched me in the gut." He blew out a breath and took another look in the box as though he had to see it again to believe it.

"What happened?" Lee demanded. "Who has access to this area?"

"I do," the chief said. "And so do half a dozen other people. Cops, Alice, Carrie, Missy now. We all have access."

"Unbelievable," Lee muttered, sinking back into his chair.

Ellen's gaze bounced between his and the chief's. "When was the last time someone looked at the evidence?"

Chief Jones sighed. "I looked at it day before yesterday. Let me take a look at the log." He stepped out of the room, grabbed the log then walked back to her and Lee. "Like I thought, I was the last person to look at it. My name is on there two days ago and then again just now."

Ellen glanced at Lee then back at the chief. "I have to ask, Chief. I'm sorry. Did you kill her?" she said, her voice soft, tentative.

Chief Jones blanched. "Ellen? You really have to ask that?"

"You loved her like a daughter. We all know you did." She bit her lip and glanced at Lee before looking back at her boss. "But we all know how Veronica was, too. She could incite a person to do things he'd never believe himself capable of doing. And she was in rare form right before she died."

The chief closed his eyes and breathed a heavy sigh. Lee's muscles tightened even further. Was the man going to confess? Was he sitting across from his sister's killer?

"No," the chief said, opening his eyes. "I didn't kill her. I don't know what was going on with her before she died. I don't know why she was like she was period. Probably had something to do with the way you grew up." He shot an apologetic look at Lee. "No offense, but your parents' history isn't exactly confidential."

"No offense taken," Lee murmured. "You were there for her, a male role model who was able to reel her in sometimes when she was going too far overboard with her snarkiness and wild ways. She loved you, even said if she could have handpicked a father, she would have chosen you."

The chief swallowed and his eyes reddened. "But unfortunately, she didn't confide in me about a lot of things, so I don't know who she antagonized enough to kill her." He met Lee's gaze. "But it wasn't me."

Lee looked at Ellen and she nodded. He could see her mind spinning. "So," she said, "only police and employees of the station have access." She cleared her throat. "You know, your new hire isn't the brightest bulb on the strand. Is it possible someone could have slipped past her and gained access to the evidence room? Maybe when you and Carrie were out?"

"But the person would need a key to get in."

"Where are the keys kept?"

"I have a set on me at all times and…in a drawer." He held up a hand. "And before you ask, no, the drawer isn't always locked."

Lee held on to his temper. How had this place not been shut down? Or at least cleaned out by now?

Ellen paced in front of the table, "I'm not going to address that one. Let's talk about what we know. It's common knowledge that Veronica was microchipping the puppies the night she died. She told James that she'd be over to his house to help with a training issue when she was finished."

The chief nodded. "Right."

"The two German shepherd puppies found the night of her murder had already been scanned and they show the station address. Nothing odd there. It's what we expected to find. However, since we've come up with our theory that the goal of the attempted break-in at Lee's was to get the three golden puppies that were microchipped at the prison, I don't think it's a stretch to believe that Veronica was interrupted by the killer and might have managed to chip the third German shepherd puppy with some information about her killer."

"Which would be why she fought so hard to make sure the puppy got out of the fence," Lee said. "I think she was trying to send a message—that she put some information on Marco's chip."

Ellen nodded. "So Veronica dragged herself from the clinic to the gate and let the third puppy, Marco, escape just in case the killer figured out what she was doing and got rid of the puppies."

"I think Veronica was hoping the puppy she'd chipped with the killer's information would be found and her killer brought to justice," Lee said. Chief Jones's head swiveled back and forth between them. "And I think it's reasonable to deduce that the killer might have come to this conclusion, as well."

"Which would explain all the break-ins around town," Ellen said. "The killer is looking for the puppy to get rid of it and any evidence Veronica might have planted on it."

"So where's the puppy?" Lee asked. "It's got that distinct marking on its head, it should be easy enough to spot. How do you hide an eight-month-old puppy? And why would you do it anyway?"

"For several possible reasons. One," Ellen said,

"whoever took the puppy has come to love it. And if the person knows that the police are looking for it—and with the flyers all over town, how could this person *not* know—he or she may not want to give it up now."

"Or, two," Lee said, "the person has sold it to someone who lives out of town and we'll never find it."

"Or that. But I don't know. There was a witness who saw a person on a bicycle pick the puppy up and ride off with it. A bicycle would indicate someone in town has that puppy."

"And, not to be the voice of doom, but it could have run off and gotten hit by a car or just not have survived."

Ellen grimaced. "I was trying not to think of that one."

Lee rubbed a hand across his eyes. He was so ready for this craziness to be over. "Let's keep going on the assumption that the puppy is still alive and out there somewhere. I think we need to get a plea out for this person to return the puppy, that it's needed in an ongoing investigation and could be the only key to solving a murder."

The chief nodded. "We can do that."

Ellen placed the top back on the empty box. "I'll put this back. Let's not let on that we know the evidence is missing."

"All right." The chief was eager to agree to that one, Lee noticed sourly. "What are you thinking?"

"Just that I want to keep this under our hats for now."

"Fine." Chief Jones swiped his forehead again with his sleeve.

"Are you sure you're all right, sir?" Ellen asked him.

"Just reeling right now. I've been in this business a long time and this case just beats all I've ever seen."

"I know, but we'll figure it out. It might not happen as fast as we'd like, but we will." Ellen picked up the box. "I'll be right back."

She walked down the aisle and Lee could see her looking for the right spot.

"I'm sorry about your sister, son."

Lee looked into the chief's eyes. "I know."

"You've had it pretty rough in this town."

"Yes." He really didn't feel like small talk.

"I also want to apologize for Ken's involvement in sending you to prison. If I'd known anything about that, I would have intervened."

Lee sighed. "I believe you." And he found he did. Out of the corner of his eye, he saw Ellen stoop down and reach for something. "What is it?" he called.

She slid a hand in between two of the metal shelves. "This."

NINE

Ellen pulled her hand back and stared at the shiny object that had caught her eye.

Lee and the chief walked up beside her. "What is it?" Lee asked.

"An earring." Ellen studied the pretty pearl with the simple gold clip.

"What's that doing there?"

"I don't know. That's a really good question. There's no dust on it so I wouldn't think it's been here long." She looked up. "Chief, look at these cases here and tell me which ones are open and currently being investigated."

He stepped forward and studied the names on the boxes. "Huh. On this rack, it holds cases with last names starting with *A* to *E* so that would just be Veronica's."

"What about this rack?"

"This is *F* to *J*, so Melanie Hayes is the only case anyone would be actively investigating."

"And her box is on the other end of the shelves."

"What are you thinking?"

"Just trying to put this together, figure out where the person would be standing for the earring to drop off and land here." Ellen raked a hand down her ponytail. "Well, it's a given that whoever came in with the intention of stealing the evidence didn't sign the log. But at least we have a time line. The stuff was stolen either yesterday or early this morning. Can we check the security cameras?"

Chief Jones nodded. "Yes, I'll pull up the footage and we can start going through it."

She looked at the earring again. "I know I touched this, Chief, but do you think the lab could try to get some DNA off the part that hooks to the ear?"

"I think it's a long shot, but bag it and note that you handled it." He walked to a drawer and pulled out an evidence bag. She dropped the earring into it and snagged a marker from the cup on the shelf. She noted she'd handled the earring, wishing she'd grabbed a glove or something to pick it up, but she hadn't even thought that what she was seeing was evidence. Kicking herself wasn't going to help anything. She handed the bag to the chief.

"I'll have Carrie get this on its way." He paused. "Actually, I'll ask Missy to do it. It's something easy and I think she needs to do something right in Carrie's eyes."

"You think that's wise? It's possible someone inside this office stole the evidence."

He hesitated. "I'll call ahead and let them know she's bringing it—and I'll let Missy know that I've called ahead. Hold on a second." He disappeared into the lobby area. When he came back he nodded to the door at the end of the hall. "Let's go look at the footage."

Lee had been awfully quiet during everything, just watching and listening. She glanced at him with a raised brow. He just shook his head. They followed the chief into another small area that housed the security computers. He sat in front of the nearest one and clicked the mouse. "Newfangled stuff. Let's hope it's worth all the money the good citizens of Desert Valley put into it."

Surprisingly, he managed to bring the footage up without much trouble or backtracking. He muttered a lot, but Ellen could deal with that if she got to see the video.

"There." On the screen, a figure dressed in black approached the evidence room door, inserted the key and was inside faster than Ellen could blink.

"Well," she said. "There you go."

"Black hoodie, black pants, black gloves. Never looks up at the camera, never hesitates," Lee said.

"And now the door is opening," the chief said, "and the person is coming out. Again, never looks at the camera and the hoodie disguises any features. I can't even tell if it's a man or a woman." He slapped the desk in disgust.

Carly jumped and stood. Ellen placed a hand on the dog's ears and gave her a scratch of reassurance. Satisfied, Carly laid back on the floor and settled her head between her paws once more.

"What about the camera inside the room?" Ellen asked. "Could we see if maybe the person pushed the hoodie back or something while he or she was in there?" Chief Jones didn't answer. "Sir?"

His cheeks flushed and Ellen knew she wasn't going to like what he had to say. "It stopped working about a week ago and hasn't been repaired yet." Ellen stared at him. He sighed and rubbed his eyes. "I know. You don't need to say anything."

She bit her lip. So many cases could have been compromised. But that wasn't her problem. She had to focus on finding Veronica's killer. "All right. I won't say anything."

"It'll be fixed by tomorrow."

Unfortunately, that was too late for them. "Okay," she sighed. "At least this hasn't been a complete waste of time." She bit her lip and looked at the chief. "Chief, I know you think it's a long shot to find anything on the earring, but I say there's always hope." She paused and frowned. "What would make the person steal the evidence now? Why not months ago when the evidence was placed in the room?"

The chief shook his head. "I don't know. There wasn't any new evidence in there, but we've been pulling that box pretty regularly, going over and over the material in there. Maybe it was making someone nervous."

"Or it was the camera," Ellen said. "The person knew the camera was broken inside the evidence room. Getting in and out without being detected would be a breeze with that camera not working." She paused and tapped her chin, then leaned forward. "What if it was just simply a moment of opportunity for this person? He, or she—" she said with a nod to the chief, "—saw his, or her—" she held up the earring "—chance and grabbed it."

"Could be," the chief said.

Ellen nodded. "What if we start focusing on our suspect in a different light?"

"What kind of light?"

"What if we start thinking the killer is a woman?"

"A woman who was angry at Veronica?"

"Or even jealous?" Ellen asked. "She seemed to have

a history with just about every man in town." She cut her eyes to Lee. "Sorry."

He shrugged, but she saw the pain there. "It's true."

"Jealous of Veronica?" Chief Jones let out a low, humorless chuckle. "Honey, that's three-fourths of the Desert Valley female population."

Ellen resisted rolling her eyes and rubbed them instead. "I know, but maybe coming at this case from a different perspective will allow us to see things a little differently. Maybe it will shake something loose. The fact that the person obviously had a key sounds a huge alarm for me. It's possible this is an inside job."

"Or someone was able to steal a key from one of the DVPD personnel." Chief Jones shrugged. "All right. I'll notify the other rookies and tell them we might be looking for a woman. Sure can't hurt. It's not like we're overrun with male suspects. At least not ones we haven't already cleared."

"Great." Her phone buzzed. She glanced at the screen. "That's a text from Sophie."

"What'd she say?"

Ellen read the message. "She said she's not at the facility today, but she can check the puppies' chips first thing in the morning." She gave a nod. "That'll work. We'll do the stakeout tonight and then take the puppies in to Sophie in the morning."

She stood. Chief Jones did, as well. "You're a good cop, Ellen."

She raised a brow. "Thanks, Chief."

He cleared his throat. "I've...ah...let things go. Too many things. I'll make sure that camera's fixed ASAP."

She nodded. "Good." Carly joined her, and they headed for the exit.

As she and Lee passed through into the lobby, Ellen noticed Carrie at the reception desk. "Thanks for your help, Carrie."

The woman looked up. "You're welcome. Again, I apologize for Missy." She glanced at the glass door where Missy was just walking down the steps. Probably on her way to mail off the earring. "Honestly, she looked great on paper. I'm not sure what happened."

"It's not your fault, Carrie. Sometimes you just have to work with someone awhile before you can know their strengths and weaknesses."

"Well…" She pursed her lips. "Not to be ugly, but I don't think I'm going to have any trouble ascertaining her weaknesses." She sighed. "So I'll just have to look for her strengths and work with those, right?" She flashed a smile and adjusted her glasses.

"That's the spirit."

Carrie laughed. "Right." She cut her eyes to Lee. "Good to see you, Lee."

He nodded at her. "You too, Carrie."

"So sorry about Veronica. It's just unbelievable that someone in this town could do such a thing."

He gave her a tight smile. "I know. Thanks for the condolences."

Ellen felt Lee's hand on her back and figured he was ready to get out of the station. When they stepped outside, the dry heat hit her. As did the feeling of being watched. She sucked in a breath and glanced at her phone. "I've got an appointment with a client in ten minutes." She looked up and let her gaze roam. Was someone watching her and Lee right now?

"I'll walk over to the center with you."

As they walked, Ellen examined everyone she

passed. Their faces and their body language. No one stood out as particularly interested in her. Other than the usual attention she and Carly attracted.

"Will it be dangerous?" Lee asked.

Ellen glanced at him. "What?"

"The stakeout."

"Probably not. Stakeouts are usually pretty boring in spite of what you see on television."

"But if they show up?"

"We nab him. We'll far out number them."

"True. There will more of you than them."

She stopped at the door of the training center. "Are you worried?"

"Why would I be worried? This is what you're trained to do, remember?"

She heard the underlying thread of sarcasm and grimaced. "Yes, I am." They went inside and Ellen saw her client sitting in the waiting area. "We'll talk later."

"I'm going to check on my truck and work with Dash for a bit, but we'll definitely talk later."

She watched him walk away.

Now, what did that mean?

Lee held Dash in the crook of his arm and stopped on his way to the training yard to watch Ellen work with the client and the dog. She was amazing. And incredibly patient. Which was funny to him because he knew she had not been blessed with an abundance of that particular trait. But somehow she found an extra measure of it whenever she worked with the dogs and her clients.

Lee found a handful of treats and tucked them into his front pocket. He made his way to the nearest outdoor training yard. There were three indoor training areas, but he preferred to be outside. He chose the puppy-run area as there were fewer distractions there than the other with the obstacle course–like objects.

He set the puppy down, grabbed a tennis ball from the bucket near the door and threw it. Dash let out a happy bark and took off after it. He'd let the dog run off some energy before getting down to business.

It was hot, but it felt good to be outside in the sun. He'd spent too much time in a prison cell. Being outside no matter what kind of weather was always a healing balm to his wounded spirit.

With the woods to his left and around the back of the center, he also relished the privacy. Being around other inmates day in and day out with no time to just be alone had been one of the hardest things for him to adjust to. And truthfully, he never had. He'd just endured and drawn as little attention to himself as possible. That course of action had worked relatively well and he had to admit, he'd probably come out of prison as unscathed as was possible.

He took several treats from his pocket even as he tossed the ball again. It rolled against the fence at the far side of the run.

Dash bolted after it and clamped down on it. He started to bring it back to Lee, then spun back toward the fence, the ball dropping from his mouth. He raced to the fence and barked. Then rose up on his hind legs and continued his high-pitched yapping.

"Dash. Come!"

The dog ignored him, his full attention on the woods just beyond the fence.

Uneasiness slithered through Lee. "Dash! Come!" Was someone in the woods watching? He narrowed his eyes and let his gaze run the length of the woods. He saw nothing that alarmed him but decided to use common sense and be safe. “Come!”

Dash dropped to all fours and turned to look at him, then whirled back to the fence to voice his displeasure at whatever was out there.

“Lee?”

Lee turned to see Ellen come out the access door and into the yard. “Hey.”

“What’s going on?”

“He’s going nuts. I think someone may be in the woods out there past the fence.”

Her hand went to her weapon. “With all that’s been going on, we don’t want to take any chances. Let’s get him back inside. I’ll get Carly and we’ll go investigate.”

He frowned. “Be careful.”

“Always.”

She waited, standing guard while he gathered the wriggling puppy and carried him inside.

Once back in the protection of the facility, Ellen took off for the exit that would lead her toward the woods.

TEN

Ellen walked toward the woods, her weapon a comforting weight in her hand. She didn't like being so exposed as she crossed the expanse of yard to the tree line. Carly trotted beside her, her ears raised, nose quivering.

Ellen spoke into the radio on her shoulder. "Suspicious activity in the east woods of the Canyon County K-9 Training Center. Request backup."

Her radio crackled softly. "Ellen, this is Tristan. I'm on the way out there."

"What's your ETA?"

"I'm just up the street. Give me two minutes."

He was close. "Meet me at the edge of the woods." She looked down, studying the ground. It was dry and hot, but she thought she found a shoe imprint. Maybe. "Carly, track." She knelt and pointed. Carly sniffed. Her sides quivered.

"Don't do anything until I get there," Tristan said.

"I'm not, but Carly's going tracking."

She held the end of the leash in her left hand, her weapon in her right. Carly's ears swiveled and something just ahead in the woods caught her attention. She let Carly take the lead. The dog pulled her closer and

Ellen felt much better when she slipped into the protection of the tree line.

At least the trees covered her somewhat. But she knew that even though she wore a vest, it wouldn't offer any protection against a head shot.

Her radio crackled to life again and she plugged her earpiece in. "I'm here," Tristan said. "Coming through the woods from the side."

"I'm just inside the tree line near the fence. Work your way around toward me. I'm going to let Carly loose and see what she can find."

"Stay covered. Don't let him get a shot at you."

If there was a him. She was going on the assumption there was someone with a gun in the woods somewhere. "That's the idea." She fell silent and her gaze scanned the trees, between them, around them and beyond. She was looking for any kind of movement, something to indicate someone was hiding.

And got nothing. She unhooked Carly's leash. She didn't know if Carly had gotten anything from the shoe print, but maybe she'd find something anyway. "Seek."

Carly lifted her nose into the air, then took off through the woods. Ellen followed, watching the dog as she sniffed the ground. Every so often she'd raise her head. Finally she stopped and sat. Ellen walked over and squatted next to the dog. "You find something, girl?"

Carly jumped at the tree next to her then sat again.

Ellen looked up. A dark T-shirt had been tossed over a branch about a foot above her. "Good job, Carly." She slipped the dog a treat.

Ellen rose and turned in a circle. Stopped and listened. Watched. So there had been someone in the trees.

He'd tossed the shirt in order to throw Carly off the scent. Or at least slow her down a bit.

A snapping sound to her right. Her head swiveled. Her fingers tightened around the grip of her weapon. "Police! Show yourself!"

"It's just me, Ellen," Tristan called.

The breath whooshed from her and she lowered her weapon. Tristan stepped out from behind the tree followed by Jesse. "He's gone," Ellen said.

"Did you see him?"

"Nope." She sighed and tucked her gun into her holster. "He was probably gone before you even got here."

"Maybe. He had to have had a vehicle waiting."

"That seems to be his MO. He always has some kind of escape plan ready and waiting."

Tristan held up a gloved hand. He held something that looked like a piece of material.

"What's that?" she asked.

"Not sure. Part of his shirt or something."

"Could it have been there awhile?"

He sniffed it. "Has a hint of fabric softener on it so I'm going to say it's recent."

"Think it could match that?" She pointed up.

His gaze followed and he nodded. "It's the same color."

"Let's send it off to Flagstaff and have the lab analyze it. Maybe they'll find something."

"You don't sound too hopeful."

"And you are?"

He gave a low laugh, grabbed the shirt from the branch with his gloved hand and held it up. "There. It's ripped." He held up the small piece. "I'd say that's a perfect match."

Ellen sighed. "He knew we'd have the dogs if he got caught."

"Yeah. And knew exactly how to slow them down."

Together they walked back to the edge of the woods. When they stepped into the clearing, she looked toward the building and could see Lee coming toward her.

He met them halfway. "Nothing?"

"No. Someone was definitely out there, but we don't have a clue who it was."

"Well," Tristan said, "we have a little clue, but we're not sure it'll tell us much." He showed Lee the bit of fabric.

Lee sighed. "Great." Then his jaw tightened and he nodded to the building. "I'll use one of the indoor training yards. I've got work to do."

Tristan clapped Ellen on the shoulder. "See you tonight."

"Just after dark."

She prayed that the stakeout worked and they caught the person after the puppies. Because if they didn't, she wasn't sure what the next step would be. But the feeling in her gut said if they didn't catch this person soon, someone else was going to get hurt. Or killed.

Lee stepped back inside the assistance center and made his way to the indoor training yard. He could tell by the way Ellen and Tristan walked and talked, there was no longer any threat outside. He carried the puppy to the center of the area and pulled a treat from his pocket. "Sit."

Dash sat.

"Stay."

Lee held the treat in front of him and walked backward. The puppy squirmed, but stayed put.

"Come."

Dash bolted to sit in front of him and Lee gave him the treat, then pulled a rope toy from his pocket for a game of tug-of-war. He tossed the puppy the end and Dash clamped down on it with glee in his brown eyes. Lee pulled hard enough to challenge the little guy, but not so hard he pulled him off balance.

He heard footsteps behind him and turned to find Ellen watching. She gave him a small smile. "You're looking good."

He blinked. "Sorry?"

Her cheeks pinked. "You and Dash. You're looking good. Together. As in he's responding well to your training."

"Oh. Thanks." He relished the praise then forced himself to shove aside the feeling. She was his boss. And she was leaving town after this assignment was over. He cleared his throat. "Hope the stakeout goes well."

"Me, too." She looked away then back. "I don't like this tension between us, Lee."

"I don't, either."

"So what do we do about it?"

He shrugged. "I don't know, Ellen. I've got to keep myself at a distance. You're leaving and I don't need another broken heart."

His honesty seemed to leave her at a loss for words. Frankly, he was surprised he'd let the words pass through his lips. She simply stared at him, her throat working. "Right."

Once again Lee wished he'd kept his mouth shut.

Then again, part of him was glad it was out there. He stepped forward and touched her cheek. “Ellen, you’re amazing. The determination you’ve shown to branch out on your own and out from under your mother, the career path you’ve chosen, this.” He waved a hand to indicate the assistance center. “You’ve got an incredible future ahead of you. I’m not going to do anything to come between you and that.”

She nodded, and looked away from him. “And you still need to finish vet school.”

“One day.”

She met his eyes again. “One day soon, Lee.”

“Yes, that’s the plan.”

She nodded and Carly nudged her thigh. She reached down and scratched the dog’s ears while Lee processed the fact that Ellen might once again be walking out of his life and soon.

His intention had been to let her do so in order to spare himself a broken heart.

Unfortunately, he’d just discovered he was too late to avoid that.

Ellen leaned her head back against the headrest and glanced over at Tristan. “How’s the kid sister?”

He blew out a sigh, then took a sip of coffee from the thermos he’d brought. Ellen had one, too, but she hadn’t needed the caffeine. Thoughts of Lee were enough to keep her adrenaline racing. Tristan lifted a shoulder in a light shrug. “Mia. She’s…hanging out with the wrong crowd, secretive, argumentative. She’s…struggling.”

“And you are, too?”

“Yeah.”

“I’m sorry.”

Another shrug. "I keep hoping she'll come around and see that I'm not the bad guy in her life."

"She will. Just be patient."

"That's the plan."

She spoke into her radio to Shane and James, who were parked just a bit farther down the street with a different view of the house. They could see the backyard while she and Tristan covered the front. "Nothing here. How about you guys?"

"All's quiet."

"Think this is a waste of time?"

"Probably," Shane grumbled in her ear.

She sighed and shot a look back over at Tristan. He was a good-looking guy with his brown hair and blue eyes. If she had to be attracted to someone, why couldn't it be someone like him? Someone who understood her job? Someone she didn't have any baggage with?

"What is it? You're staring."

She blinked. "Oh. Sorry, just thinking."

"About?"

"A lot of things. Men. Life."

He gave a low chuckle but she noticed he kept his eyes on the house. "It's not any greener on the other side, Ellen. No matter what man you wind up with, he's going to have his issues."

She gaped. "Did I speak my thoughts out loud?"

"You didn't have to. I've watched you and Lee over the past couple of days. I know you guys have a history together." At her frown, he shrugged. "Word travels fast in a small town. I can see you struggling and wish I could help."

"But you can't."

"Nope. I'm not one to get involved in other people's love lives. This is between you and Lee."

"And my mother," she muttered.

He frowned. "What?"

"Nothing. Just…nothing. And I don't have a love life."

He gave a low chuckle. "Yes, you do."

"Do not."

"Okay, if you say so."

"I say so."

He fell silent, but she heard him whisper under his breath, "But you do."

The next three hours passed mostly in silence. Just like she told Lee it would be, the stakeout was quiet and boring.

Finally, they told the family to come home and they waited until they were safely inside.

Tristan pulled away from the curb. "Thanks," Ellen said.

"For what?"

She gave him a soft smile. "Just thanks."

Ellen knew she needed to figure out what to do about Lee, but Tristan was right. Everyone had issues, battles to fight in life. She just had to decide if she wanted to do that with Lee. In Desert Valley.

The sinking in her stomach at the thought of living near her mother was the answer to that question.

ELEVEN

The next morning Ellen swung by Lee's and picked him up. Things were quiet between them, but not uncomfortable. "Sophie texted me earlier to let me know she's at the center and we can come on in," Ellen told him.

"Great. Nothing happened last night? I haven't heard anything on the news," he said as he climbed into her SUV. "I figured if you caught the person responsible for all the break-ins, I would have heard about it." Carly greeted him with a swipe of her tongue. Lee scratched her ears and she settled back on the seat.

"No. It was a bust."

"Are you all going to try again?"

"Yes. Tristan and Shane are arranging to do it again tonight with the other home owner."

"Good."

She wasn't going to bring up anything personal. Not now. They were on the way to the assistance center, which was only a five-minute drive from Lee's house. When she pulled up in front, Lee opened his door. "I'll get the dogs if you want to wait here."

Ellen shook her head. "I'm going to come in for a

few minutes and check on things. I need to make a phone call, too." She'd been thinking about their visit with the chief ever since she'd walked out of the station yesterday.

He nodded and disappeared inside. She pulled her phone from her pocket and dialed Ryder Hayes's number. He answered. "Hayes."

"Ryder, this is Ellen. I need to know if you ever investigated Chief Jones during the time of Veronica's murder."

"No, I don't think we officially investigated him, but we didn't have to. He was at his birthday dinner when he got the call about Veronica's death."

"Ah. Okay, so an airtight alibi?"

"Definitely."

"Good to know, thanks."

"Want to tell me why?"

"It's not important now. If you truly want to know, I'll fill you in later."

"Okay. Anything else?"

"Nope. Talk to you soon."

She hung up and walked inside the assistance center. Just like every time, she felt a jolt of happiness flow through her. Here something good was happening. Here people found a reason to smile again. She walked into the training area and found two of her employees working. One had Frisbee, a recent rescue, on a leash and was teaching him to retrieve items dropped from a wheelchair. The other worker, with a blindfold on, had Samson, a beautiful Lab, guiding her through an obstacle course. Satisfaction filled Ellen. Soon these two dogs would be ready to help others.

"You ready?"

She turned to find Lee with the three puppies leashed and ready to go. Dash strained toward the door, ready for his next adventure. King and Lady sniffed Ellen's shoes. "Sure."

Together, they walked them over to the K-9 Unit Training Center. Once inside, Ellen went to find Sophie while Lee waited in the lobby.

"Sophie? You here?" She went to the office first and found it empty. She walked out into the nearest training yard and found Sophie with a German shepherd puppy on a leash. They would walk, then Sophie would stop and give a command. If the puppy obeyed, he got a treat.

"Hey, Sophie, we're here."

Sophie looked up. "Hey, Ellen, what's going on? You weren't real clear about what's happening other than you want me to read the chips on the dogs."

"Yesterday we were talking with Chief Jones and think we may have a lead on the attempted break-in at Lee's the other night."

"Hey, yeah, I heard about that. Everything okay?"

"For now. We brought the three puppies you donated to my training center. We just wanted to make sure the chips say what they're supposed to say."

"Of course. Give me a few minutes to finish up here and I'll get right on it. You can put the dogs in the kennel if you want to come back later."

"We'll just wait. Thanks."

Ellen returned to find Lee working with the puppies in his own special way. "Down," he said as he pointed to the floor. When Dash dropped his hind end to the floor, Lee smiled and slipped the puppy a treat.

"He makes those disappear fast," Ellen said.

Lee nodded. "He's a smart one."

"Sophie said she'd be right out. She's going to check the chips while we wait."

"Great."

"Lee, I know the others have asked you this, but—"

He looked up. "But?"

"But can you think of anyone else who would have it in for Veronica? Females, I mean?"

He sighed. "I've thought long and hard on that. I mean, she was only nice to people who could do something for her. I don't mean to talk ill of her, but we both know how she was."

"I know."

"Yesterday, I honestly thought Chief Jones was going to confess that he'd killed her in a fit of rage or something."

"I wondered about that myself, but I don't think he did it. He has an airtight alibi anyway."

"How do you know?"

"I checked."

"Right."

"And they've ruled out her ex-husband, William Pennington."

"Yes." Lee frowned and pursed his lips. "I can't believe everything he was into. A drug runner, of all things."

"I know, I think that came as quite a shock to a number of people."

Lee sighed. "And Lloyd Harglow had an airtight alibi." Veronica had been seeing Lloyd while still married to Pennington.

"Any other ex-boyfriends out there?"

He shrugged. "I'm not the one to ask. Veronica didn't come to visit very often while I was in prison."

"I'm sorry."

"I am, too. Now."

"So the women," Ellen said. "What woman might want to kill Veronica?"

"Well, I'm sure Lloyd Harglow's wife wasn't too fond of Veronica for cheating with him. What about her?"

"We checked her. And while she hated Veronica, she didn't kill her."

"Another airtight alibi?"

"Afraid so."

Sophie stepped into the area. "I can check the puppies now if you want to bring them into the room."

Lee stood and walked the puppies behind Sophie into a lab-like area. She picked up a device and held it over Dash's neck. Then King's, then Lady's. She wrote each of the numbers down and handed the paper to Ellen. "All the puppies are showing as belonging to the Canyon County Prison."

Lee closed his eyes and blew out a breath. Ellen felt her shoulders droop. "Well, that was a bust."

Ellen studied the paper. "Maybe not." She held it out so he could see it. "Look at these ID numbers. Two are pretty similar, but one is a bit different. It's Dash's number."

Lee looked. "You're right. It's very different. I wonder why."

Ellen studied Sophie's intense expression as she stared at the little golden puppy. Sophie tapped her lip. "What is it?" Ellen asked.

"Just thinking why that number would be so off."

Lee frowned. "Could it be some kind of code?"

"Maybe." Ellen looked at Sophie.

"I didn't chip these puppies. The vet next door and

her tech did. Veronica already had the puppies before she died. I just inherited them. When you told me your plans to start up your facility, I thought they'd make a good addition."

"And they do, thanks." She looked at Lee. "Why don't we see if we can talk to Tanya a bit about this?"

"All right." He rubbed the back of his head.

"What are you thinking?" she asked.

"Tanya Fowler's clinic at the prison is where Freddie and I would help out. I know Dr. Fowler. The thing is, I can't see her doing anything illegal, but if I've calculated the timing right, Freddie would have been out of the program before the puppies were chipped."

"Okay, so it wasn't Freddie who did it." She paused then said, "Could it possibly be the other inmate who's working in the Prison Pups program?"

Lee shrugged. "It's worth finding out."

"But if someone is putting inmates in this particular position with the intention of microchipping dogs with messages or something, that means someone at the prison is involved."

"Or Ken Bucks arranged for it."

"True." She pursed her lips then nodded. "Let's go talk to Tanya."

Lee and Ellen walked the dogs next door to the veterinarian's office. The air-conditioning was a welcome respite from the heat of the day. A man in uniform, identifying himself as a corrections officer, sat in the waiting area reading a magazine. Lee blinked. He knew him from the prison. Another younger man in a lab coat stood behind the desk. When he looked up, his eyes widened slightly before he glanced back down at the computer. "Help you?"

"Is Tanya around?" Lee asked. He noticed the tattoos on the man's fingers.

"Sure, I'll get her." He practically bolted from the room and into the back.

Lee looked at Ellen and she raised a brow. "What was that about?"

"I don't know. Good question."

Tanya appeared in the doorway. "Hey, Ellen, Lee, what can I do for you?"

Ellen nodded to the back. "I see you've gotten a new tech."

"Yes, Gerald Nees. He started working here about a month ago on a work-release program."

"I thought I recognized him," Lee said. "He's an inmate."

"Yes, but he's due to be released in just a few weeks and he met all the requirements for the program." She nodded her head to the man in the chair to their right. "That's Phillip Carr. He's a prison guard. He brings Gerald in for several hours a day for his shift to help with the dogs."

Officer Carr looked up at the mention of his name and gave them a short nod.

"Is Gerald the one who chipped these goldens?" Ellen asked Tanya.

"He could be. Are these the three Sophie donated to your program?"

"Yes."

"Then, he would have been the one." She looked at Lee. "As you know, I had to fire Freddie. That left me quite short staffed so I asked about a replacement. Gerald looked great on paper other than his incarceration issue." She gave them a wry smile.

"'Looking good on paper' seems to be a popular thing these days," Lee muttered.

Ellen shot him an exasperated look and he shrugged.

"Anyway," Tanya said, "Gerald had expressed an interest in working with animals, and since he'd kept his nose clean while in prison, we decided to give him a chance."

Lee pulled the paper with the ID numbers on them from his pocket. "Can you tell me why this number would be so different from the other two?"

Tanya looked at them and frowned. "No, that's weird. If the dogs were chipped at the same time then all three numbers should be sequential. See these two? This one ends in the number one. The next one ends in two and the last one should end in either zero or three. But it doesn't." She shook her head. "You've got all these letters and numbers mixed in. This really doesn't make sense."

A low thud sounded and Tanya's eyes went wide. Lee blinked as she gasped and slowly sank to the floor.

"Tanya!" Ellen rushed to the vet when another thunk echoed. This time the prison guard mimicked Tanya's actions and slid from his seat to the floor. "Lee! Get down!"

For a fraction of a second, he stared at the dart protruding from the guard's chest. And he realized someone was shooting at them. He released the dogs and spun to the door to see Gerald aiming for his next victim—Ellen.

TWELVE

Lee lunged toward the inmate, who backpedaled and turned the weapon on him. Gerald pulled the trigger and Lee hit the floor rolling. Lee heard the dart slam into the wall behind him. With a swipe of his left foot, he caught Gerald in the back of his right knee. The man hollered and went down.

"Police! Freeze! Drop the weapon now!"

Gerald ignored Ellen's orders and once again tried to get a bead on Lee. Then the weapon was flying through the air to land with a clatter on the floor behind Gerald.

Gerald screamed and grabbed his wrist. "You broke it!"

"Get on the floor!" Ellen gave him another shove, and he fell onto his stomach. She landed on his back with her knee and Lee heard the breath whoosh from the man's lungs. Before he could blink she had his hands cuffed behind his back. Gerald still hollered about his wrist. Lee hoped it was painful.

She rose to her feet and kept her weapon trained on the gasping man. "Lee, you okay?"

"Yes. You?"

"Yeah. Call 911."

Lee rolled to his feet in a smooth movement and jumped the counter to grab the phone and punch in the numbers. As close as the police department was, backup would be here quickly.

He gave the information requested and asked for an ambulance. He heard the dispatcher yell something, then come back on the line. "Chief Jones just ran out the door. He's on the way there, too."

"Thanks." He hung up and moved to the unconscious prison guard. Ellen was still bent over the vet. "How's Tanya?"

"Out cold, but her pulse is strong. She's breathing okay."

"What were they shot with?" He checked Phillip's pulse and found it strong, as well.

"Looks like a tranquilizer dart—the one weapon Gerald could get his hands on."

Sirens sounded. Gerald fought the cuffs. "Let me go, you have no right!"

Ellen ignored him. Lee wanted to knock the breath out of him again.

The door burst open and Chief Jones stepped inside. Sweat rolled down his red cheeks, his breath came in pants. "What happened here?"

"Gerald went a little crazy," Ellen said. "Where's the ambulance."

"On the way."

Ellen stood and swiped a hand down her face. "I think they'll be all right. It was a tranquilizer gun. I think they were mild darts, but they definitely need to be checked out."

Chief Jones knelt by Phillip, the prison guard, and laid his fingers on the man's neck. "Still strong."

Ellen did the same once more with Tanya. "Hers, too."

The chief sank into a chair and stared at Gerald. "So. What set him off?"

Lee's gaze bounced between Gerald and the three goldens who'd crawled under the chairs on the far side of the room and were busy chewing on their leashes.

"The dogs," Lee said.

"What?"

"He was shocked to see them come in. At first, I thought it might have been me, but it was the dogs. I'm going to guess he's working for the people who are after them."

Ellen nodded. "And I'll also hazard a guess that he made a phone call soon after we got here."

Chief Jones nodded. "I'll check the phone records." He looked at Gerald. "So what do you have to say for yourself?"

Gerald tightened his lips and glared. The chief stared at him. "I got nothing to say to any of you," Gerald finally snarled.

The ambulance pulled up to the door and Chief Jones stood and hitched his belt. "Fine. We'll hash it out at the station."

"We won't hash out nothing. I'm not talking. Talking gets you dead." His glare intensified. "And after today, I can promise you're all next."

Ellen glanced at Lee. He was barely holding his temper in check and she didn't blame him. Finally they had someone in custody who might know something about Veronica's murder. The chief hauled Gerald to his feet. Paramedics rushed in and Ellen directed them to the two who needed them. While they worked on them, she followed Chief Jones and Gerald outside. Red lights flashed on top of the emergency vehicles. "I want to question him, Chief."

"Get in line." He hauled the man into the back of the cruiser.

"I need to see a doctor," Gerald grumbled. "I think she broke a rib."

Gerald glared up at her. Ellen stared back without a blink. He finally looked away and she glanced up to see the chief watching. A small smile played around the corners of his lips and she lifted a brow. He cleared his throat. "Meet us at the station."

"I'm on the way."

"I'm coming, too," Lee said. "I'll drop the dogs with Sophie and fill her in. Then I can walk over."

Ellen frowned. "I don't know that's the safest thing to do."

He looked at Gerald. "I think the danger is past. He was the other one outside my window the other night."

"You're sure?"

"Yes, I recognize the voice. The other one was Freddie."

"And he's still on the loose."

He looked around. "I'll be fine."

She sighed. "I'll walk with you, then we can go over to the station together."

"Ellen—"

"Seriously. Until Freddie is caught, we have to watch each others' backs." She planned to watch his whether he liked it or not.

He gave a slow nod. "All right. Thanks."

Ellen explained to the chief that she'd be there

shortly. He drove off with a still-protesting Gerald in the backseat. Ellen sent a text to Sophie.

Had a situation at the vet's office. Need to leave the three goldens in your kennel right now. Is that all right?

Bring them on over, Sophie texted back.

The ambulance left with Tanya and the prison guard. Ellen turned the sign in the vet's window to Closed and drew in a deep breath. She set the clinic's door to lock behind her and pulled it shut. She and Lee walked the dogs to the training center and Sophie met them at the door. "What's going on? I saw all the chaos."

"Tanya's vet tech opened fire on her and his prison guard with a tranquilizer gun."

Sophie's eyes went wide. "What? Why?"

"We think it has to do with the puppies we're leaving with you, so make sure you set the alarm and don't open the door to anyone you don't know." She quickly explained what happened.

Sophie's eyes narrowed. "Do you need help with this?"

"No, we're on the way to the station to sit in on the interview with Chief Jones."

"All right, keep me posted."

"Will you update the others?"

"Of course."

Ellen and Lee left to walk the quarter of a mile to the police station. Ellen bounded up the steps and Lee followed close behind her. He reached around her to open the door for her and she raised a brow. "Thanks."

"Of course."

Once inside, Ellen found Carrie at the desk. Another desk had been added next to Carrie's, and Missy seemed to be engrossed in whatever was on her computer screen. "Hi, Carrie, Missy," Ellen said. "Where's the chief?"

"In the interrogation room," Carrie said.

"Thanks. Could you do me a favor?"

"Sure, what do you need?"

"Could you get me everything you can find on Gerald Nees and then bring me the iPad with his info?"

"Of course."

Ellen paused. "Did the chief already ask for the information?"

Carrie looked at her over the top of her glasses. "No."

Ellen pursed her lips and nodded, then motioned for Lee to follow and headed down the hall. "You'll probably have to wait outside, but I promise I'll fill you in on what I can."

"What you can?"

She sighed. "Go through that door right there. You'll be able to see and hear everything that goes on in this room. The chief will probably be in there in a few minutes. If he doesn't kick you out, then you can stay."

He nodded. "That works."

She shot him a tight smile and knocked on the door. "It's Ellen, Chief."

Footsteps sounded then the door swung open. Chief Jones had a scowl the size of the Grand Canyon on his face. "You can take over for a bit. I'm about to send this guy into next week."

Ellen slipped her weapon from the holster on her hip and handed it to her boss. "Hold on to this for me, will you?"

He took it and she entered the room. The chief left

and pulled the door shut behind him. She knew he'd be watching from the room next door. She figured Gerald knew it, too.

Gerald sat at a small rectangular table in a hard wooden chair. His hands were cuffed behind his back and his left foot shackled to the floor.

"You've got yourself into a bit of a mess, don't you?"

"Shut up." The sneer he'd left with still sat on his face.

"Well, that's certainly an option. I could shut up and just leave you here, but how is that going to help either of us?" He stared at her. She filtered her words. Considering and discarding at the speed of light. She had to say the right things. She walked over to the chair opposite him and sat. Then put her feet on the table. "You hungry?"

He blinked. "Yeah. Why?"

"Well, we're required to feed prisoners. What do you want?"

"What is this? Good cop, bad cop?"

Ellen made sure her facial expression didn't change. "Do you want something or not?"

"A hamburger all the way and fries."

She pulled her phone from the clip on her side and dialed the front desk. Carrie answered and Ellen placed the order. Carrie's silence echoed through the line. Then, "Ookay. Is it all right if I send Missy to pick it up?"

"Of course. I'll pay her back."

She hung up and Gerald stared at her. "Why'd you do that? I'm not talking to you."

She shrugged. "I know, but like I said, we're required to feed prisoners."

She sat there in silence, watching him. He shifted under her gaze and wouldn't meet her eyes. Her phone buzzed and she looked at it. From the chief. What are you doing, Ellen?

Just let me play this out, she texted back.

Fine.

For the next twenty-five minutes, Ellen sat quietly while Gerald picked at his fingernail. Or shifted in his chair. Or spoke one sentence. "I'm not talking to you." When the food arrived, the chief brought it in and dropped it on the table in front of Ellen. His eyes met hers and she winked. He gave a minuscule shrug and didn't say a word as he walked back out the door and shut it once more.

Ellen pushed the food across the table in front of Gerald. He looked at it and licked his lips. She figured it had been a while since he had a good juicy hamburger. "I guess you need your hands."

"I guess." He still hadn't taken his eyes from the bag with the food.

"I'll uncuff you, but if you so much as twitch wrong, my boss will be in here within seconds, understand?"

"I'm not going to do anything." He sighed. He shook his leg and the chain clanked. "It's not like I'd be able to get very far. And besides, I want that burger."

She walked behind him and uncuffed his hands. He attacked the bag, had the hamburger unwrapped and a bite in his mouth faster than she could blink.

He swallowed and took another bite. "Good?"

"Yeah."

"Can you tell me why you're after the dogs?"

"Nope."

"Why?"

"Because I like breathing," he said with his mouth full.

"Do you know who killed Veronica Earnshaw?"

"The dog lady? I heard about that."

"Right, the dog lady." Ellen leaned forward.

"Nope. I don't know who killed her. Wasn't me, obviously." He smirked around another bite of the burger.

"Obviously. But you might have heard something."

"Hmm… No, not really. Just that she'd been killed."

Ellen bit down on her frustration. "Look, Gerald, you and I know that seeing those dogs set something off in you today or we wouldn't be sitting here. We've already checked the chips and one of them reads funny. We've figured out that it's a code for something, and it's only a matter of time before we crack it. You keep insisting you're not going to talk, but you could make things go a little easier on yourself if you would help us."

He froze. Then pushed the remnants of the burger away from him. "I want a lawyer."

And that was that.

Ellen leaned back, frustrated and satisfied all at the same time. "So it's a code. Thanks for that. I'll put the word out you helped us."

He shot to his feet. Ellen didn't blink, just stared up at him. "You can't do that!"

"Of course I can. You did help."

"I did not!"

"Well, everyone knows it's only the snitches who get the good food. Once it gets out that we're feeding you from the Cactus Café, who's going to believe you didn't give us some information in exchange for the hamburger and fries?"

With a howl of rage, he swept the table of the remains of his food and lunged at her. Ellen had expected his reaction and remained out of reach. The chain shackling him to the floor stretched and yanked him back. He landed with an awkward thump back in the chair. His chest heaved as he seethed and glared at her. She smiled. "Thanks, Gerald. I'll let the chief take over now and he can call your lawyer for you."

The door opened. Chief Jones met her eyes and she saw the respect shining there. They exchanged a small smile and Ellen slipped out the door.

THIRTEEN

"You really enjoyed that, didn't you?" Lee asked when she stepped into the hall.

"Oh, yes, that was fun. I just wish I could have gotten more out of him."

Lee took her hand. "You're a good cop, Ellen."

She looked surprised. "Thanks."

He frowned. "You still need to watch your back, though."

She echoed his frown. "I can take care of myself."

"Hmm. Right."

She sighed and let out a rueful laugh. "Except when inmates get their hands on a tranquilizer gun." Her eyes softened. "Thanks for that, by the way."

"Of course." He sighed. "He didn't know anything about Veronica's death."

"No, I don't think so. I think whatever's going on with the veterinary techs and the three puppies is something completely separate from Veronica's murder."

"So you don't think whoever is after the golden retriever puppies killed Veronica?" he asked.

"No, I wouldn't think so. She was microchipping the German shepherd puppies at the time of her death, and

I do think the one that she let escape may have information related to her killer. But I don't think the golden puppies and the code on Dash's chip connect to that. I think her death is something else entirely."

"I think you're right." He rubbed his eyes. "So this has originated from the prison."

"That's what I'm thinking. Whoever is behind this—and it could be Tanya even as it galls me to say it—is using the inmates. Having two crooked vet techs isn't a coincidence. I'm going to see if the chief will talk with Ken Bucks to see if he can get anything out of him if he's involved in this."

Lee snorted. "Ken's already given up what he's going to give up, I'm guessing. I really think that if we figure out what the numbers and letters mean on Dash's chip, we'll have a good idea why someone is so intent on stealing the dogs."

"I agree, but I'm going to recommend the chief do it anyway."

Lee nodded. "All right. In the meantime, I'm going back to the training center. We have that group of summer camp kids coming for their field trip."

"Good," she said. "We start our camps next month, full-blown all-day camps. You think we're ready?"

Lee gave her a slight smile. "Of course. We have a few more staff we need to hire, but I'm going through the résumés and pulling some I think will be good matches."

"Great."

He frowned. "We still have one problem for the moment, though."

"What's that?"

"Where to keep the golden puppies. I don't want to

keep them at the center, not as long as Freddie is still on the loose and looking for them. I don't want to take a chance on putting the children in danger."

Ellen's eyes went wide. "You're absolutely right. We have to protect the people coming into the center." She bit her lip. "I don't have room at my house. Maybe Sophie—"

"I do."

"Your house?"

"I'm set up for it."

"But are you sure you want them there? Freddie's probably working for someone. The same someone who had him shoot at us and try to break in to your house, remember?"

"Yes. I mean, think about it. They've already come looking for the dogs once at my house. I'm guessing they might not come back."

"Maybe, but I sure wouldn't want to stake my life on it."

"I don't think it's a huge risk. I'm going to ask a friend to watch over the property and the dogs. If he sees anything suspicious, all he has to do is dial 911."

"Who are you thinking of?"

"I shared a cell with him for a year. He was released at the end of that year."

"And you trust him?"

"I do."

She shrugged. "All right, sounds good to me."

Lee nodded. "I'll call him from the training center and have him meet me there. He can take the dogs to the house and I can work with the kids. We've been rather absent from the center the past few days."

"Tell me about it," she muttered. "I'll find someone

to stay with you while you're at the center. Ryder or Tristan can probably do it."

He frowned. "I'll be fine."

"I know."

"But you're still going to ask someone to shadow me."

"Yep. I have a feeling the chief is going to ask me to ride with him to transport our prisoner to the prison. That's an hour's drive away. I don't want to leave you alone and unprotected while I'm out of town."

"I get that, but who's going to protect you?"

"Lee, I'm a trained police officer. Not only can I protect myself, I'll have the chief watching my back."

"And we've seen how efficient he is. You still bleed red just like anyone else," he snapped.

She stamped a foot. "Ooh, you are so frustrating sometimes. You still see me as that little high school girl who couldn't crawl out from beneath her mother's thumb. Well, I'm not that girl anymore and it's time you opened your eyes and saw that."

"Ellen, it's not that, I'm just—"

"You're just what, Lee? Concerned? Worried?"

"Yes," he snapped back. "Concerned and worried about a lot of things."

"Like what?"

"Like when your mother wakes up, she'll call the shots with you once again."

She blinked. "That was really random. Where did that come from?"

He swallowed. "I don't know."

"Well, you don't have to worry or be concerned about that, Lee. I'll be gone from Desert Valley so fast it'll make your head spin. I'll leave before I'll let that happen again."

Lee stepped forward and planted his lips on hers before he had a chance to think about what he was doing. It was a hard kiss—and maybe a bit desperate. When he lifted his head, he stared down into her shocked eyes. "Just something else for you to think about while you're thinking about leaving."

He spun on his heel, opened the door, stepped out of the room and let the door close with a quiet *snick*.

The perfect exit. A movie-scene-worthy exit.

And his heart was breaking with each step that took him farther and farther away from the woman he'd never stopped loving.

As she absently watched the chief make absolutely no headway with Gerald Nees, Ellen nursed her wounded heart and held her fingers over the lips Lee had just very thoroughly kissed. "You're not helping yourself here," the chief said.

"I'm not helping you, that's for sure," Nees shot back. "No matter what kind of food you give me."

Shortly after Lee's exit, Tristan had stuck his head in the observation room door and raised a brow. Ellen had shrugged and Tristan hadn't questioned the stormy atmosphere. He'd simply promised to keep an eye on Lee. She felt good about that. She and Lee had argued and said things she felt they both probably regretted. She didn't feel so good about that. Then he'd kissed her.

She was still feeling that. Good or bad didn't factor in. Just…wow.

While Carly snoozed in the corner, Chief Jones continued to wrangle with the stubborn prisoner. Ellen finally managed to shove Lee to the back of her mind. The more she watched the proceedings through the two-way mirror, the more she wanted to go through it, grab Gerald by his throat and give him a good shake in hopes something would jog loose and spill from his tongue.

The truth, a lie. She didn't care at this point. Just something. But he was tight-lipped and hard-eyed. "I have a good lawyer," he said. "I'm not saying anything until I talk to him. I can still beat this."

The chief laughed. An incredulous, "you're dumb as a rock" laugh. "You were caught red-handed. There are witnesses who saw what *you* did. Who are in the hospital recovering from the wounds *you* inflicted. What reality are you living in?"

Nees tightened his lips, locked his arms across his chest and fixed his stare on the table.

The chief finally stood and shook his head. "Fine. We'll get you transported to the prison, where you can wait to see the magistrate."

Gerald didn't look up.

Ellen met the chief in the hallway. He shut the door that locked from the outside and met her gaze. "Feel like taking a ride?"

"I thought you might ask."

He grimaced. "Sorry, but I'm not getting anything out of him."

She shrugged. "He's lawyered up anyway. It's fine."

"Let me just call the prison to let them know we're headed that way."

While the chief made the call, Ellen took Carly into the woods at the back of the station. She dug a ball out of her bag and gave it a toss. Carly took off like a shot to snag it and bring it back to her. For the next five minutes, she threw and Carly fetched.

When the chief waved to her from the back door, she whistled for the dog and they headed inside. "You get it all arranged?" she asked.

"Yep. Let's go."

She followed him to the room where Gerald Nees still sat. "Ready to ride?"

"Whatever."

"Your lawyer's meeting you there."

Gerald's glare never lessened. Chief Jones led him to the DVPD SUV he drove and opened the door. He helped Gerald get in and made sure his seat belt was fastened and his hands were secured so that he wouldn't be able to reach into the front seat at any time. Ellen opened the passenger's front door and motioned for Carly to get in. The dog did. "I wouldn't normally put her up front, Chief, but I don't want her in the back with this guy." She glared at the perp.

Ellen climbed into the backseat behind the dog and waited for Chief Jones to heft himself behind the wheel.

"Keep an eye out, Chief," she murmured. "My nerves are twitching."

He shot her a glance in the rearview mirror. "Okay. I'll be watching the mirrors."

She nodded, checked once more to make sure Gerald's hands were bound securely and unclipped the strap over her weapon. It would be an hour there plus time to process Gerald and then an hour back. She'd be home shortly after the training center closed. The argument with Lee played in her mind and she winced. She owed him an apology. Another one.

She pulled her phone from her pocket and sent Lee a

text. Meet me at the training center around six? I owe you an apology. I'll order delivery. We'll eat and discuss the plans for the camp. If you already have something and can't make it, we'll just get together tomorrow.

She slipped the phone back onto her belt and glanced in the rearview mirror. "You really think Freddie has the guts to try something?"

Chief Jones grunted. "I don't know about Freddie. Maybe whoever he's working with."

"Maybe. It bothers me that Gerald thinks this is going to go away. Like there's someone who can take care of it and *will*."

The chief shook his head and started the vehicle. He pulled out of the parking lot and Ellen sent up a prayer for everyone's safety. When the chief pulled past the training center, she noticed Tristan's, Shane's and Ryder's vehicles out front. "Did you call in reinforcements, too?" she asked.

"I did."

"Excellent."

"They'll follow Lee home and keep an eye on things there, as well."

With that much police coverage on the puppies and Lee, Ellen felt like she could relax a bit. The goldens were safe at Lee's home also with protection. All should be well.

Should be.

Except why did she still feel the pinch of apprehension? Like the other shoe was going to drop, and if she didn't duck fast enough, it was going to land on her head?

She sighed and watched the scenery pass by, all the while watching the mirrors. So far so good.

She prayed it stayed that way.

Because a killer that was still at large and possibly looking for the next victim.

FOURTEEN

Lee clapped the nine-year-old on the shoulder and high-fived him. “Great job, Henry. I think you have a future in dog training if you want it.” Lee picked up Dancer and held the animal in the crook of his arm.

Henry flushed his pleasure and stroked the silky dog’s ears. Lee looked up and caught the teacher’s eye. She’d explained that she’d set up this field trip specifically for Henry, a child who’d come from an abusive background and refused to speak. He was currently in foster care and was up for adoption. The family he was with had already filled out the paperwork, and gone through the extensive process to make him a part of their family. Everything would be final next week.

“I think a therapy dog would be great for Henry,” Mrs. Ivan had said on the phone the first day Lee had been on the job. She was a sharp woman in her early fifties who obviously loved her students and went above and beyond the call of duty by volunteering to teach summer school—referred to as summer camp by her and her students. “His parents have given the green light, so maybe you could see if you have a dog to pair with him?”

"I think I have the perfect dog. We'll need Henry's parents to come in and give the final seal of approval."

"Of course. I think the other children will benefit from seeing your program in action, so the field trip will be good for all."

Now it was time for the small class to leave. Henry slipped his small hand into Lee's and looked up at him. Though he didn't move his lips, his eyes spoke for him. Lee lightly squeezed the boy's small fingers. "You're welcome."

Henry smiled, looked longingly at Dancer, the black cocker spaniel he'd bonded with almost instantly. He reached out for one more scratch behind the ears and Dancer licked his fingers. A giggle escaped and Lee heard Mrs. Ivan smother a light gasp. He met her eyes and saw the joy there. Henry reluctantly moved to get in the line in front of his teacher.

"We have time for one more question," Mrs. Ivan said. Three hands shot up and Lee pointed to a cute girl with Down syndrome and blond pigtails.

"Yes, ma'am," he said.

She giggled. "I'm not a ma'am."

"What's your question, Tabitha?" Mrs. Ivan prompted.

"Where do these dogs come from? Were they all borned here? In America?"

The teacher cleared her throat. "Born."

"Yes." Tabitha nodded. "Born."

Lee, still holding Dancer, moved to the wall map and pointed to North America. "Okay, kids. What's this piece of paper here?"

Several children chuckled. "A map!" Several voices overlapped.

"Exactly. You guys are smart." More giggles. "Now even though this training center has only been open for a short time, we have several dogs that came from Texas. Can anyone find Texas?"

All hands went up. Lee picked the nearest gap-toothed boy. "Show us." The nine-year-old went to the map and pointed to the correct state. "Excellent," Lee said. "Now we also have several that came from New Mexico, Utah and Nevada. Can you show me those states?"

"I can."

And so it went until the teacher nodded to Lee. "And that's it kids," he said. "Thanks for coming by today. The animals loved it and I hope you did, too."

Cheers and claps erupted and he smiled. Henry held his gaze for another moment then walked out the door, last in line, in no hurry to leave.

Lee waved. Henry spun on his heel and ran back to Dancer. Lee bent down and Henry kissed the dog on her head. "She'll be waiting for you, Henry."

Another smile lifted the child's lips and he ran back just in time to slip through the door and join his class.

Lee glanced at his watch and wondered how Ellen was doing. Then he looked at his phone and read her text. Six o'clock at the training center. To discuss plans for the camp? He sighed and rubbed his face. He wanted to talk about more than plans for the camp but wasn't sure how receptive Ellen would be to the idea. He knew he was her employee; he respected her position and knew that if he pushed things romantically, it could muddy the waters.

But he'd been crazy about her in high school and he'd never forgotten her. Now a second chance with her might be staring him in the face. If he didn't grab hold of it with both hands, he could lose her forever. His heart shuddered at the thought yet indecision gripped him. She'd already broken his heart once. Did he want to put himself in the position that would allow her to do it again? He glanced at his watch then rubbed his eyes.

The door pinged and automatically opened. A young man in his early thirties, seated in a wheelchair, rolled himself through. Lee straightened. "Hi. Can I help you?"

Hard blue eyes met his. "I heard about this place. Heard I could get a service dog to help me out."

"I'm sure we could work something out. I'm Lee Earnshaw."

"I'm Travis Lyons."

Lee shook the man's hand and noticed the callouses. "What happened to put you in the chair?"

"Took a bullet to the spine, thanks to my best friend. He decided I wasn't good enough for his sister and—" he shrugged, but Lee could see the anger beneath the surface "—he took it upon himself to see that I wasn't. Doc says I'm going to be in this chair for the rest of my life and I need to come to terms with it. Suggested I check this place out."

"Well, we're about to close, but I don't mind giving you a quick tour."

The eyes thawed slightly. "That'd be great. Thanks." He jerked a thumb toward the door he'd just rolled through. "You have an awful lot of security around here."

"Yeah. There's a reason for it, but don't worry, those guys are good. As long as they're out there, we're fine in here."

Travis nodded and gave another shrug. “Good to know.”

Lee led the way through the facility, his mind only partially on the tour. He couldn’t push Ellen from his thoughts. She continued the invasion all the way through the tour. The last stop was the kennel. “This is where we keep the dogs while we’re training them.”

“Cool.” He rolled past one kennel, then the next and the next. Finally, he spun to face Lee, his expression hard. “I like dogs. I don’t like the reason I need one.”

“I understand.”

“Yeah.” He looked away a minute, then back at Lee. “All right. I’ll be in touch.”

“Want to schedule an appointment? We’ll do an interview, see what kind of dog would match best with your personality.”

“I’ll call you. I’ve got some thinking to do. You got a bathroom I can use before I go?”

“Of course.” He pointed. “Just down that hall and to the left. You…ah…need any help or anything?” As soon as the words left his lips, he flushed. “Sorry, I guess I need to brush up on my wheelchair etiquette.”

Travis flashed a grin, the first sign of something other than hard anger in his eyes. “Naw, man, I’m good.” He rolled down the hall and disappeared into the bathroom. While Lee waited for Travis, he finished doing some of the daily closing chores. When he took the trash out, he noticed the door-open sign on the alarm system panel. “Weird,” he muttered. He came back in to find Travis in the lobby heading for the door.

“Thanks again for your help.”

“Sure. See you soon.” He showed the man out and watched him roll toward the gray van parked in the handicapped spot near the front of the building. Lee shook his head. Okay, he had to admit, his own problems seemed minimal in light of Travis's.

"Have a good night, Lee."

He looked up to see one of the other workers headed for the door. "You too, Miranda."

"The dogs have all eaten. I also cleaned all the kennels and put fresh water in the bowls, so they should be good for the night."

"What would we do without you?"

"Scoop a lot more poop?"

He laughed, his weariness fading a bit with her teasing. "That's for sure. See you tomorrow."

Miranda left and Lee looked around to see if he needed to do anything else before locking up—or planting himself in the office to wait for Ellen.

The door. He walked to the back to check on the door indicated on the panel and found it shut. He checked the panel again and saw that it was fine. He frowned and made a mental note to mention it to Ellen. Could be a glitch in the system. He glanced in each room as he passed, checked the dogs one more time and pondered what his next move would be. Stay? Or go?

The people who'd broken in and attacked the guard were after the puppies. Now that the puppies were no longer at the facility, the problem should go away. Or at least be transferred to Lee's property.

And with all of the rookies, along with the rest of those on the force, taking turns watching his place in pairs, he didn't think the intruders wouldn't be back. But he felt sure they were watching for the next opportunity to grab the golden retriever puppies should it present itself. He didn't intend for that to happen.

His mind circled back to the problem at hand. Stay and eat with Ellen or go home and lick his wounds? He sighed. He'd enjoyed the field trip today. And seeing Henry's eyes light up had made his week. He thought about his plans to finish up school and become a veterinarian. It seemed as though something was always getting in the way and slowing him down.

Like his feelings for Ellen.

He walked over to the desk and grabbed his keys. His eyes fell on the map and he smiled. The kids had their geography down pat.

He froze.

Wait a minute.

Geography.

Something niggled at the back of his mind.

He frowned. What was it? He continued to ponder what was trying to come to the forefront of his brain, but he couldn't quite grasp it. But it had to do with the map. He sighed and shook his head. Maybe if he didn't think so hard, it would come to him.

He looked at his phone.

Dinner with Ellen or go home?

Heartbreak or play it safe?

He turned on the alarm and locked the door behind him.

Ellen was tired. Gerald and his lawyer had clammed up and Chief Jones had stalked out, muttering under his breath about retirement looking better and better every day.

Within minutes, they were on the road and on the way back to Desert Valley. Ellen's senses were alert but she was glad to have made it to the prison without incident. She'd been tight and tense the whole drive, sure someone would follow them to try to help Gerald escape. But all had gone well, and now it was time to get back and hash out a plan with Lee. If he was up to dinner. Her pulse picked up speed at the thought of spending time with him, being in the same space as him. "It's just business," she whispered. "Just business."

"You say something?"

She jumped. "Oh, talking to myself, Chief. Sorry."

He eyed her for a second then turned his attention back to the road. "Thanks for riding out here with me. I wouldn't have put it past the guy to have someone watching us."

"I know. But nothing happened. Which makes me nervous."

"How so?"

"Gerald is obviously a part of some ring. Those numbers on that chip mean something."

"I know, I agree."

She glanced at her phone. Still no reply from Lee.

"You expecting an important call?"

"No, I just left a message for Lee to call me, but he hasn't." She dialed his number and listened to it ring. Four times then voice mail. "Hey, Lee, can you give me a call? You haven't answered my text and you're not answering your phone. I'm getting a little worried. Please call me back." She hung up.

Chief Jones shook his head. "That was a raw deal Lee Earnshaw got with Ken framing him. I'm ashamed that man was even a part of my force—or my family." Ken Bucks was the chief's stepson.

"I agree. It was an incredibly raw deal, but Lee's handling it well." She considered calling Shane or Tristan but knew if something was really wrong, one or both of them would be in contact.

Which meant that Lee didn't have his phone on him and hadn't seen that she was trying to get in touch with him.

Or he was ignoring her, and that stung.

She bit her lip and checked the mirrors, then the time.

She'd arrive back at the training center about ten minutes before six. She texted, Do I pick up dinner or not?

Almost instantly her phone dinged a response.

Not tonight, thanks. We'll talk tomorrow.

FIFTEEN

Ellen stepped into the training center, and the chief took off for home. Eddie Harmon sat outside and waved as she shut the door behind her. She stood in the dark lobby for a few moments, taking in the smells and the fact that she had done something good. Something that helped others. That part felt amazing, but the fact that she had no one to share it with created an emptiness inside her. She fought the urge to shed a few tears and ignored the stinging in her heart while she checked on the dogs. They were all excited to see her, and she stopped by each kennel to scratch ears and offer words of praise and love. Carly padded at her side casting anxious glances her way as though she could sense the turmoil raging inside her master.

Ellen made her way into the office, dropped some bags of food on the desk and plopped into her chair. Lee wasn't here. He really wasn't. Why she was so surprised she couldn't put her finger on, but she was. Even though he'd said he wasn't coming by, she knew she'd subconsciously expected him to be there.

Just like when she'd graduated from high school, she'd looked out into the audience, looking for her father. He hadn't been there. She'd spotted her mother, smiling brightly, but her dad had been nowhere to be seen. She remembered the heartbreak and realized the emotion she felt now mirrored that on her graduation day. She'd let her defenses down and, in a matter of days, Lee had slipped right back into her heart. Who was she kidding? He'd done that years ago and had been there ever since. Now what was she going to do?

Carly laid her head on Ellen's thigh and sighed. Ellen couldn't help it. One tear escaped and then another until she had a river flowing. She rested her forehead on her arms and gave in to it. The stress of her mother's medical condition and the fact that her attacker still roamed free, the emotional roller coaster her relationship—or the lack thereof—with Lee had her on and the indecision of whether to make a life in Desert Valley or follow through with her plans to leave once her mother was awake and Veronica's killer was caught. A silly thing to cry over, maybe, but she knew she needed the release. Then again, calling her life decisions "silly" wasn't right, either. They weren't silly; they were things she needed to deal with. She definitely deserved the cry.

Finally she sniffed, grabbed a tissue and cleaned herself up. "Okay, Carly, pity party's over."

Carly cocked her head then stood on her hind legs to swipe Ellen's face with her pink tongue. Ellen let out a shaky laugh and scratched the dog's silky ears. "I just wish God would send me an email, you know? Subject line reading, 'What to do with your life.'" She sighed. "Then again, maybe He's already sent his emails in the form of His word, eh, girl?" Carly sat on the floor.

A low thud from the back of the building had Ellen's nerves shivering. Carly popped to her feet and spun toward the door. Her ears swiveled and a low growl rumbled in her chest. Ellen rose to her feet, listening. "What do you think it is, girl?" Had Lee come back after all? She walked to the door. But if it was Lee, why was Carly's fur standing on end?

Ellen pulled her weapon and moved to the door. "Lee? That you?"

She listened.

Silence.

A footfall in the hallway.

Her stomach clenched. Her heart thudded a faster beat. She gripped her weapon and stepped out of the office, Carly at her side attached to her leash. She didn't need Carly bolting into a situation that would get her killed.

Senses sharpened by her surging adrenaline, she headed down the narrow hall toward the kennels. "The puppies aren't here!"

Silence. A stillness invaded the building and yet the air felt electrified, raising the hair on her arms and at the back of her neck. She placed one foot in front of the other.

When she came to the storage room, she tested the knob with her left hand. Locked. She kept going. Carly stayed with her, her nose quivering, ears twitching. Should she send the dog ahead? But if the person had a weapon…

Ellen kept Carly near and continued her search. Call it in? Or not?

Better safe than sorry.

She reached for her phone when she heard the soft *snick* of a door closing.

* * *

It was six thirty. Maybe he wasn't too late. He dialed Ellen's number again and it rang twice before transferring to her voice mail. Weird. He texted her. *I'm on my way to the center. You're right, we need to talk. I think I know what the odd code on Dash's chip is.*

Lee rubbed his eyes and shoved his key into the ignition. He was a jerk. She'd said she owed him an apology. He could have at least had dinner with her. He called again, and again got her voice mail. Shane waved at him and Lee lowered his window. "I'm sorry, but I'm going in to the assistance center."

"Now?"

"Yes, I need to clear something up with Ellen and she's not answering her phone. She left me a message saying she'd be at the assistance center so I'm going to go check on her."

"All right. It's fine. I'll follow you. Tristan will stay here with the guy you've got watching the dogs."

"Thanks." Lee started back to the Jeep with the thought that he really needed to check on the progress of his truck's repairs when he turned around and walked back to Shane. "I think I know what the code is on Dash's chip."

Shane lifted a brow. "What?"

"We had kids in on a field trip today and we were looking at the map and—" He waved a hand as though to push aside the explanation. "I think it's longitude and latitude running together. Or vice versa. I think it's a spot, a location."

Shane nodded. "Can't hurt to check it out. I'll call Ryder and see if he can put the numbers in and see what pops out."

"Great." He climbed into the Jeep and tried Ellen again one more time. When she still didn't pick up, he frowned. Now he was worried. He sent her yet another text. I'm heading your way. Let me know if you're still at the center and want me to pick up some food.

He pulled out of his drive and headed toward the main street of the town. He and Ellen needed to have a heart-to-heart chat, and now was as good a time as any. Avoiding the situation was only going to make him lose sleep, and he was fed up with that.

Shane's truck stayed with him about two car lengths behind. He liked having someone watching his back. He liked the security. He would like it even more if Ellen would listen to what he had to say.

Being in prison had taught him a lot of things. One of those was that life was unpredictable, that God was faithful no matter the circumstances or if it looked as though all was lost. And that he didn't want to be alone the rest of his life.

But it wasn't just that he didn't want to be alone, he wanted to have that special someone by his side. A woman he loved, who loved him in return. A teammate. Someone who would just do life with him. Maybe have a few kids. He swallowed at the thought. What kind of father would he be? His knuckles turned white on the wheel as he made a left onto the road that would take him to the center. He wouldn't be anything like his own father, that was for sure. As long as he did the opposite of what his dad had done, Lee was sure to be a great dad.

Maybe.

He just had to make sure Ellen felt the same way. He had no doubt he'd hurt her feelings tonight. Maybe she was giving him a taste of his own medicine and ignoring his attempts to reach her. He grimaced. No, she wouldn't do that. So why wasn't she answering? She was probably working with a dog in order to take her mind off the fact that he'd been a jerk to her.

Well, he was done with his momentary lapse into immaturity.

So, ready or not, he was going to spill his heart out to her and see what she said. If she sent him packing, so be it. He'd find a way to live through it, but he wasn't going to go through life with regrets.

Now if she'd just answer the phone.

Ellen glanced into the break room to her right. The overhead lights were off, but the small night-light in the socket next to the counter allowed her to see into the room. All seemed well. Carly stayed silent, but pressed against Ellen's leg. The dog had definitely picked up on her tension and had been alerted to the fact that someone was in the building. Or if it wasn't a person, *something* had gotten her attention.

With one hand holding her weapon, she looped Carly's leash over her wrist and reached for her phone. It buzzed against her hand. She glanced at the screen. Lee.

A scuffing sound behind her brought her head up and around before she had a chance to respond. "Who's there?"

Had she armed the alarm when she'd entered? Of course she had. So who could possibly be inside? Only someone with the code. The new code she'd programmed the system with after the last break-in.

She frowned. Why would someone come back here? The dogs weren't here, so what would be the purpose in breaking back in to the center? Of course, the person wouldn't know the dogs weren't at the center, so maybe he'd come back to try again? Her adrenaline rushed.

Ellen pressed the button to answer Lee's call only to find he'd already hung up. Instead of calling him back, she pressed the number for Dispatch. It was time for backup. The dispatcher answered on the second ring. Ellen held the phone to her ear. "Need backup at the Desert Valley Assistance Center," she whispered. Carly growled and tried to lunge forward, pulling her hand with the phone. Ellen lifted her arm so the leash couldn't slip over her wrist. "Carly, no." The dog reluctantly settled. Back into the phone, Ellen whispered, "There's definitely an intruder in the building. Need assistance ASAP."

"I have a unit on the way."

"Thanks."

Carly's hackles were raised, her attention on something at the end of the hall. The kennel? Were the dogs in danger? She shoved the phone into her pocket, still connected to the dispatcher, but she needed both hands. She gripped her weapon in her right hand and Carly's leash in the other. She moved cautiously in the direction Carly's attention was so focused on and stopped just before the door that led to the kennel area. She hadn't locked it after she'd checked on the dogs earlier because she'd planned to go back in one last time before leaving for the night. Pushing a silent breath through barely parted lips, she glanced through the glass window.

The kennel's lights were muted, but she could see well enough. The dogs didn't seem disturbed. They were quiet except for the couple that barked just because they were dogs and that was what they did. The barks weren't frantic or upset or angry.

Nothing that said "intruder." From her position near the window, all looked clear inside the area. She pressed the handle that would open the door. Carly growled and lunged at the door behind her. Ellen spun to see the craft room door cracked. She let the dog go. Carly bolted into the other room. Ellen heard a hissing sound, then Carly's yelp.

"Carly!" What had happened? Where was her backup? She moved toward the door, weapon outstretched. She shoved her back up against the wall. "Come on out! That room's a dead end. No way out!"

And the door was flung open. Her finger tightened on the trigger, but she couldn't see who to shoot at. Then something misted in her face. She gasped. Smelled a sickeningly sweet odor and tried to turn away from it.

She felt dizzy.

Her muscles went slack. Weak.

She heard her gun hit the floor.

Then she felt someone catch her.

The darkness wanted to close in, but she fought it. She turned her head. Saw Carly on the floor, not moving.

Drugged. Someone had sprayed them with something.

Then she felt herself being dragged.

Heard the sirens approaching.

And then knew nothing more.

SIXTEEN

Lee arrived just as the swarm of officers pulled into the parking lot. He jumped out of the Jeep and hurried toward the building.

"Police! Freeze!"

Lee spun, his hands in the air.

Shane got out of his vehicle and waved the others down. "He's good! He's with me." His German shepherd, Bella, stayed at his side.

"What's going on?" Lee shouted.

"Ellen called for backup," Ryder said. "Get back in the Jeep and stay there," he said to Lee.

Lee's fingers curled into fists. What was going on? Why would Ellen need backup? "Where is she?"

"That's what we're going to find out. Stay put."

"Ryder, come on, tell me what you know."

"She reported an intruder and asked for backup. Get back in the Jeep now!" Ryder and his partner, Titus, headed into the building.

Lee did as ordered, his heart in his throat as he watched the officers stop at the glass door. Ryder tried it and it was locked. He came back to Lee. "You have the key?"

Lee handed him the card to swipe. Within seconds, Ryder was back at the door. He swiped the card and Lee watched them stream inside one behind the other, weapons ready.

An intruder? Lee's gut clenched and he slammed a fist against the wheel as he watched law enforcement once again take over Ellen's business. Officers on the outside kept watch on the trees and the wooded area behind the building. Guilt swamped him. He should have been here. If he hadn't been so prideful, so worried about getting his heart broken—had he stayed, maybe he could have helped her.

He closed his eyes. *Please, God, give me another chance. I know I've used up a lot of them, but I don't care what chance I'm on, don't let anything happen to her. No matter what she decides, whether to stay or go, I need her to be okay. Please.* He didn't know how long he prayed, but it felt as though an eternity passed before the tap on his window jerked his eyes open.

Ryder. The tension around the man's mouth didn't bode well. Lee opened the door and climbed out. "What is it? What'd you find?"

"The building's been cleared. Carly's down and Ellen's missing."

Lee swayed. Caught himself on the door. "Carly? Down? Ellen's missing?"

"Carly's alive, but unconscious. No visible trauma. We're getting her over to the vet now. Tanya's in the hospital, but we have another one coming from a nearby town. He said he'd be here in twenty minutes."

"Good. What about Ellen?"

He nodded to the back of the building. "Her SUV

is parked near the back entrance, but there's no sign of her."

"How did someone get in? The front door was locked. What about the back?"

"Locked and the alarm was turned off. Shane's pulling up video footage as we speak."

"Ellen would have had to turn the alarm off to enter the building, but she would have armed it once she was inside."

Ryder rubbed his jaw. "She could have forgotten. You sure?"

"Yes, I'm sure." And he was. "With all the crazy stuff going on around here lately, she wouldn't have taken any chances."

Ryder nodded. "I'm inclined to agree. So whoever was inside knows the code."

Chief Jones pulled up and climbed from his cruiser. "What's going on? I heard something about Ellen going missing."

Ryder filled him in while Lee continued to send up prayers and began to pace, thinking.

Chief Jones blew out a breath. "All right, who's searching for her?"

"James and Hawk are looking for her trail right now."

"Good. Let me know if they pick up her scent. In the meantime, we got a hit on the DNA on that glove used in the bank robbery."

Lee couldn't believe his ears. "Why are you worried about the bank robbery when Ellen's missing?"

"Because there's a connection."

"What kind of connection, Chief?"

"The DNA didn't match anyone in the system, but

the lab tech ran the markers. There was a ninety-nine percent match to someone who *is* in the system."

"To who?" Lee asked.

"To the brother of the man who used to be Freddie Parrish's cell mate in prison. A long-time career criminal."

"What's his name?"

"Trevor Little. Here's his picture." Chief Jones held up his phone.

Lee leaned in and gasped. "He was here this afternoon. At the center."

"What?" Ryder, Shane and the chief echoed the question.

"He came in a wheelchair and he said his name was Travis Lyons." He ran a hand through his hair, his nerves standing on end. "I gave him a tour of the facility. He said he took a bullet to the spine and he was paralyzed..." Anger boiled. "Is he even in a wheelchair?"

"No. I'm guessing you were played and he was just casing the place."

"But he left. He wheeled out and got into his van and left. He may have cased the place, but that still doesn't explain how he got in after-hours and with the alarm set."

"Did you leave him alone at any time?" Ryder asked.

"No, I gave him the tour and he—" Lee froze.

"He what, Lee?" the chief pressed.

"He went to the bathroom. Just before he left. He was alone then." He pressed the heels of his hands to his eyes. "And shortly after he left, I noticed the alarm system said there was a door ajar. When I checked, I didn't find anything wrong and the alarm system went back to normal. I just figured it was a glitch and made a notation for Ellen to have it checked."

"He propped it open," Shane said. "Circled around and slipped back inside. Probably had someone else in the van to drive off after he was back in the building. He was already inside when Ellen came back."

Sickness swept over Lee. "It's my fault," he said. "I didn't do a thorough check of the building. I should have been more concerned about the signal on the panel." He pinched the bridge of his nose. If anything happened to Ellen…

"It's not your fault, Lee."

"We have to find her."

James and Hawk, the bloodhound who could sniff out just about anything, returned from the trees bordering the property. "What did you find?" the chief asked.

James trotted over and, with a huff, Hawk flopped onto the ground next to him. "Hawk had the trail up through the woods and out the other side. It leads to the road. He had a car waiting."

"How did he get her there?"

"Had to carry her."

"Which means he's strong."

"The guy who came in," Lee said, "his upper arms were well muscled. Ripped. Like he worked out a lot. He wouldn't have any trouble carrying her."

"Or rolling her," Shane said.

"What do you mean?"

He held out an iPad. "Check out the video footage."

Lee leaned forward and watched the black-and-white film. The outside front cameras showed the man Lee knew as Travis leaving in his van. When Shane switched to the back cameras, it showed him coming though the woods toward the building pushing a wheelchair.

And then he was inside the building, leaving the wheelchair outside next to the door.

"What about the cameras inside?" Lee asked softly.

Shane tapped the screen and brought up another view forwarded by about an hour. "There. He was hiding in the back room across from the kennel area."

"That's the kids' craft room," Lee said.

Ellen came on-screen with Carly at her side. They watched her check the kennel door then saw Carly lunge at the craft room and Ellen let her go.

Then Ellen had her weapon held in front of her as she moved to the door. Then she jerked back, brought a hand to her face and stumbled.

"What did he hit her with?"

"He sprayed her with something."

"It knocked her out pretty fast. Chloroform?"

"Maybe."

Lee watched Ellen wobble, try to regain her footing. The craft room door opened, and the guy caught Ellen as she started to sink to the floor. He gathered her up and pushed out the back door.

Another quick tap on the screen took him back to the outdoor camera. "And here they come. He puts her in the wheelchair and off they go," Shane said. "Smart, not carrying her out. No one would give it a second thought if he was seen rolling her in a wheelchair."

Lee felt sick. "Yeah, if he was carrying her..."

"Yeah," Shane said.

"But why would they come after her? I thought it was the dog they wanted. Why Ellen?"

"She has something they want?"

"What?"

"Like you said, they want the dog," Shane said.

"But she doesn't have the dog, I do."

Shane blew out a slow breath. "Everyone, stay close to your phone."

Ellen opened her eyes and blinked. Then immediately shut them. Pain, nausea, dry mouth. Dizziness. Even in her prone position, her head was spinning. What was *wrong* with her? The flu? Had she passed out?

She kept her eyes closed and waited for the dizziness and nausea to pass. While she waited, she forced herself to think. Carly. Her eyes flew open and she stared at a white ceiling. A single bulb stared back at her. That was not her bedroom ceiling in her mother's home.

What had happened? How had she gotten here?

She moved her fingers. And gasped. Her hands were bound in front of her and the tape was tight. She felt a rough blanket beneath her. She was on a cot. A hard one. Her stomach rumbled. She was hungry in spite of the queasiness in her belly. Maybe hunger was part of the queasiness. *Think, Ellen.* She had a flash of being in the center, Carly at her side with her gun drawn.

Her gun.

She moved her hands to her right hip. Felt her holster. Empty.

Panic threatened. Why couldn't she remember?

Where was she?

And why were her hands bound?

She rolled to her side and groaned. The room shifted, her nausea intensified. She closed her eyes again and stayed as still as possible. And while her body remained motionless, her mind spun.

She'd been at the center. She'd had her gun drawn. She remembered Carly's growling and lunging at the door then…

…nothing.

Okay, she'd have to remember later. Right now she needed to get out of here.

Wherever *here* was.

She had to move. The nausea had subsided with her stillness and she was loath to do anything to bring it back.

But…

Ellen took a breath and slowly raised her upper body, letting her legs fall off the cot.

The room whirled; the sickness returned. She stayed still. Found a spot on the far cement wall and locked her gaze on it. She wasn't sure how long she sat, but finally everything seemed to settle. Her stomach, her head. She dared let her eyes move from the spot on the wall.

It was a large room. Cement walls, white ceiling. Metal rails on the ceiling. No windows. "Of course not. That would be too easy, wouldn't it?" Her muttered words echoed around her.

Slowly, oh, so slowly, she slid from the cot and stood on shaky legs, careful because if she fell, it would be next to impossible to break the fall. Okay, she was feeling better. Why was she here? What did the person who'd snatched her want?

She'd been at the center. She'd been sad that Lee wasn't going to be joining her for dinner. And then she'd heard a noise. Or rather Carly had. Right, she remembered all that.

And Lee…poor Lee. Did he know what had happened? She swallowed—or tried to. Her throat was so dry. “Lee, I’m sorry,” she whispered. “I’m sorry.”

When he found out she was missing, he would blame himself. She couldn’t let that happen. Fear shivered through her and a desperation to live, to find out what her future held. And make sure Lee was a part of that future. She knew that she wasn’t supposed to live though this. She was simply a pawn in these people’s deadly game. When they finished with her, got what they wanted, they’d toss her aside like yesterday’s trash. If she was going to survive, she was going to have to get away.

Time to explore her surroundings.

And figure out how to get out before whoever put her here came back.

SEVENTEEN

Lee thought his head might explode. No one had a lead on Ellen's whereabouts. The only thing that made him feel slightly better was that Carly was now fine and sitting in the back of Shane's vehicle along with Shane's dog, Bella. The consensus was that Carly and Ellen had both been sprayed with the same substance. Other than being very thirsty, the fact that Carly had bounced back so fast was reassuring.

That Ellen was still missing was not.

He walked over to Chief Jones, James and Hawk. "What's next?" His phone rang before anyone could answer him. He snatched it off his belt clip and slapped it to his ear without even looking at the screen. "Ellen?"

"You have the golden retriever puppies?"

Lee froze. "You're not Ellen."

"No. I'm not. But I know where she is. You have the puppies?"

"Yes." Lee motioned to the chief and the others and pointed to his phone.

"Put it on speaker," James hissed.

Chief Jones motioned for everyone to be quiet. The noise level died down.

Lee pressed the button. The man's voice floated into the night air. "…you want to see Ellen again, I want the puppy, the small one, in my possession within the hour."

"Where do I bring him?"

"I'll text you. And don't try tracing this phone. I'll save you the trouble. It's a burner. And I'm going to toss it as soon as we hang up. The text will come from a different number."

"How do I know Ellen's alive?"

"Because as long as you're bringing me the puppy, I have no reason to kill her."

"I'll bring it. But I want proof Ellen is alive."

"You'll just have to trust me. And leave the cops out of it."

Lee winced and met Chief Jones's eyes. Too late for that. "So you're going to trade me Ellen for the puppy?"

"Yes. As long as you follow my instructions, you'll get the cop back in one piece."

"Fine. What are your instructions?"

"In a few minutes, I'm going to text you an address. You come to that address with the puppy only, and you might get your girlfriend back."

"I need some proof she's alive."

Silence fell on the other end. Then his phone dinged. "There's your proof. Now, when you get the address, be there within the hour. If I see even a hint of the police, I'll kill her. You understand?"

Fear clenched Lee's throat. The man was serious. His tone was no-nonsense. "Yes, I understand."

"Good."

"What about—" But he was talking to dead air. Lee pressed the button to pull up the picture he'd been sent.

He gasped.

Ellen lay on a cot, her eyes closed, hands bound in front of her. She looked so pale and still. And small. Everything in him raged that someone would do this to her. He looked up into the chief's eyes. "Not getting her back is not an option." And he was going to do everything in his power to help, because the first thing he was going to tell her when he held her again was how much he loved her.

Ellen examined every square inch of the large room, desperate to find anything that she might be able to use to facilitate her escape. She had to get her hands loose. They were tingling and soon would be numb. She opened and closed her fingers. What could she use to cut through the tape? Her teeth hadn't done much good.

She looked around again, this time focusing on the walls. She needed something sharp. A nail. Anything. The room had been a garage once upon a time. No doubt about it. But it had been closed in and cleaned out. The door had two deadbolt locks. One that locked from the inside and one from the outside. She wasn't getting out the door.

Originally she'd thought there weren't any windows, but upon closer inspection, she saw they'd just been boarded up and painted over to match the walls. If she could get one of the pieces of plywood loose, she might have a chance to get out. The bottom of the window came to the top of her head. She'd broken three nails trying to pull the wood off and quickly figured out that wasn't going to work. Her hands simply weren't strong enough.

Thankfully her head had quit spinning and her muscles were starting to feel stronger again.

She stood at the center of the room flexing her fingers. A table leaned against the back wall. An old chair sat in the corner. No toolbox, of course.

A scrape just outside the door sent her running for the cot. She lay on her side, positioning herself so she could kick out in a smooth move. Assuming her kidnapper got that close.

The lock snicked and the door opened. She cracked her eyes and saw a man shut the door behind him. And lock it with the key. He slid the key into the front pocket of his jeans. Her heart thudded. Self-defense moves came to mind, but if she managed to knock him down and get to the door, she couldn't get out without the key. And with her hands still tightly taped, she was fairly helpless.

On a positive note, he didn't seem to have a weapon on him. Which might mean he was pretty confident that he didn't need one.

"I know you're awake."

His voice rumbled through the garage. She didn't try to keep her eyes shut any longer. She opened them fully and got her first good look at the man.

Tall, he was at least a couple of inches over six feet. He had on a muscle shirt that displayed arms as big as her waist with tattoos running from shoulder to wrist. She would not be going hand to hand with him in a fight even if her hands were free. Ellen stayed still and just watched him. Fear threatened to choke her, but she kept her face blank. She hoped. "What do you want?"

He didn't move to enter the room, just stood in the doorway. "All I want is the puppy. You give me the little golden puppy and you're free to go."

Right, like she believed that. She'd seen his face. She

knew what it meant. "You want the one with the code embedded in his chip."

His eyes narrowed and his nostrils flared. "Yeah."

"What does it mean?"

"Doesn't matter to you." He checked his phone. "Be ready to go for a ride."

"Where?"

"You'll find out. And if your friend can't follow directions, you're dead."

She swallowed. "What friend?" Surely he didn't mean Lee.

"Dude with the dogs."

He meant Lee. While fear had been right there with her ever since she'd awakened in the room, it hit her full force now. She stood. "What are the directions he's supposed to follow?"

"The ones I gave him. But all you need to worry about is that as long as I get the dog, they get you."

Ellen found no comfort in the words because, while the words sounded good, the look in his eyes said he had no intention of letting her go anywhere. He unlocked the door, stepped outside and then back in. He tossed her a bottle of water and she caught it with hands that were close to numb. "Be back shortly."

"Can you at least loosen the tape? I can't feel my hands."

He laughed. And then he was gone. The soft click of the lock told her the clock was ticking and she needed to figure something out fast. She flexed her fingers around the bottle. As much as she wanted to chug it, she couldn't take a chance it had been drugged. She flung the water bottle on the cot, moved to the wooden chair, picked it up and slammed it against the wall. It shattered into several large pieces. She picked up one of the bigger ones and hefted it. It could work. Maybe.

But first she examined each broken piece for something sharp. *A screw.* It would have to do. She sat on the floor and positioned the piece of wood with the screw sticking out of it between her feet. Then she leaned forward and started scraping the tape over the sharp end of the screw. Sweat ran down her face but she didn't stop, and finally she cut into the tape far enough that a hard yank pulled it apart.

Blood flowed. The pain was sharp enough to make her eyes tear. She took a deep breath, flexed her fingers and massaged her hands. First one, then the other.

Finally, when she felt she could, she grabbed the piece of wood with the screw and took it over to the window. She slid the end of the screw into the shallow crack left between the plywood and the wall. With a grunt, she shoved it hard and heard the squeak of nails as the wood started to separate. She pressed again and the bottom edge popped out. She tossed the piece of chair aside and wedged her fingers underneath.

She started to pull when she heard the lock turn once again.

"I have to go," Lee said. "You heard what he said. I'm to come alone and no cops."

"It's too dangerous," Tristan protested again.

Lee kept his temper under control. Barely. "It's too dangerous for Ellen if I don't show up. He called *me*. He told *me* no cops. If we mess this up, Ellen could die."

"He's planning on killing her anyway," Ryder said quietly. "But as long as he believes we're following his orders, we might be able to get to her before he does it."

Lee flinched at Ryder's words. "Then, someone better come up with a plan that gets her out in one piece because her death is not an option."

"No, it's not," Ryder said. "Lee's right. He needs to be there and he needs a wire. We'll cover him."

Lee nodded. "Fine, get me the wire."

"I've got one in my SUV," Tristan said. He went to get it. When he returned, Ryder went to work, getting Lee wired up and checking to make sure everything was working. He clapped Lee on the shoulder. "We're good to go."

Chief Jones leaned against his vehicle and watched the action. He had a sad, resigned look on his face. When he caught Lee watching, his features hardened and he cleared his throat.

"Could you get a location on her phone?" Tristan asked the chief.

Chief Jones hitched his belt. "No."

"So she could be anywhere," Lee said. "What if he doesn't have her with him?"

"If he wants the puppy," Ryder said, "he'll have her with him. You're going to hold the puppy and demand that he allow you to see her. Once you see she's alive, we'll take it from there. Is your earpiece working?"

"Yes."

"Then, you'll hear everything I say, and I'll be able to hear you. Don't take matters into your own hands, understand?"

"Yes."

"Send me the address."

Lee did.

Tristan looked up. "I've got it programmed in. According to my information, it's an abandoned house on the outskirts of town. Used to belong to the Colson family, longtime residents of Desert Valley, but it was foreclosed on when the senior Mr. Colson died a year and a half ago. His children never made a single payment on the house and the bank repossessed it."

"Let me guess, the same bank that got robbed," Lee said.

"Yes." Lee waited while the man studied the information in front of him. "But the house was never sold and has been sitting empty for the past few months. They must have found it and moved in while they planned how to get a hold of the dogs." He shook his head. "There's no way to sneak up on this guy. Not in vehicles. He'll see us coming a mile away. Literally."

Shane pointed to the lake that abutted the backyard. "We can come in this way. In a boat."

"Where are you going to get a boat at this short notice?" Lee asked.

"Someone who lives on the lake will have one somewhere," Ryder said. "We'll simply borrow one for this, then put it back when we're done."

"And if they don't?"

Ryder rubbed a hand over his jaw. "We'll figure something out. If worse comes to worse, we can swim across."

"But the front," Tristan said. "We've got to approach from the front and he's going to be watching."

Lee drew in a deep breath. "Then, I've got to go in alone."

"No way," Shane said. He motioned to Tristan to move closer. "Let me see the property layout."

Shane, Tristan and Ryder crowded around the tablet. Lee watched them mutter and listened to them plan. Never had he prayed harder in his life.

The chief blew out a sigh. “All right. We don’t have any more time to discuss this. We’ll get the puppy from Sophie and get this wrapped up.”

“Let’s move folks.”

Lee took the passenger seat of Ryder’s SUV while Ryder helped his dog, Titus, into the backseat, then slipped behind the wheel.

Ellen stared at the man who’d opened the door. The gun in his left hand was steady—and trained on her chest. She gripped the piece of wood, ready to use it as a weapon. “Freddie?”

He jerked. “You remember me?”

“Of course. How did you get mixed up in this mess?”

“You meet all kinds of interesting people in prison.” He licked his lips and glanced over his shoulder. She almost made a move, but he looked back to her too quickly. If she could distract him…

“Where’s your partner?” she asked. “The big guy?”

“Taking care of stuff.”

His shifty eyes and nervous shuffling had her on high alert. “What is it?”

He licked his lips again. “I want it all for myself and you’re going to help me get it.”

“Are you using, Freddie?”

“Doesn’t matter. Now tell me what was on that dog’s chip.”

“Why?”

“Because it will tell me where the money is.”

“What money?”

“From the bank,” he snarled. “I had a cell mate who

told me all about his big haul and how he was going to be living it up when he got out."

"And who is this cell mate? Where is he?"

"Dead." Freddie glanced over his shoulder and back again so quickly she had no chance to move. "He'll be back soon."

"Who is he?"

"My cell mate's brother, Trevor."

Ellen's mind was clearing fast. He was talking about the bank robbery in Flagstaff from six months ago. The big guy who'd kidnapped her was the brother of Freddie's cell mate. A cell mate who was now dead. And that cell mate had been involved in the bank robbery. "Where did he go?"

"To get everything set up." He shoved the gun at her and she flinched. Ducked. "So while he's occupied, tell me where the dog is now."

"And if I tell you, what do I get?"

"I don't shoot you."

She shivered. "You can't shoot me, Freddie. Trevor needs me. He's going to exchange me for the puppy. If you shoot me, he's going to be very unhappy with you."

"Won't matter if I'm not around for him to kill. Now—" he jabbed the gun at her again "—where is the dog?"

"Hidden away," she said softly. "We knew you were after him, so we hid him."

"I know that! Where?"

He took a step closer and she swung the piece of wood like a baseball bat, catching him across the arm. He screamed, and the gun fell from his fingers and skidded across the concrete floor. She brought her palm up and caught him in the jaw with the heel of her hand.

His head snapped back and he let out another cry. A final kick in the stomach had him doubling over. She had no time to retrieve the weapon.

She bolted from the room and slammed the door. Before she could turn the key that was still in the lock, he had it open. She turned to run. Felt his fingers twist in the back of her shirt. He slammed her against the wall and her head snapped back. Pain raced up her neck and into the base of her skull, but she couldn't stop now. She kicked out and caught him in the knee.

He cried out, and dropped to the ground.

A gunshot sent her diving beside him. Freddie screamed again and then again as another shot sounded. Ellen froze, waiting for the pain to kick in, but when nothing happened, she opened her eyes and found herself staring into Freddie's dead, vacant eyes. "No," she whispered.

She rolled to her feet and spun toward the exit.

Something hard pressed against the back her head. "Ah!" More pain raced through the lower part of her skull.

"Move and you'll die," the man behind her growled.

She froze.

"Good girl. Now walk."

EIGHTEEN

Tristan pulled to a stop just at the edge of the property out of sight of the house. The van behind them did the same. The land stretched out, and Lee knew it went all the way up to the front door of the house. A house that sat in a shallow valley on the edge of a lake that might be a point of entrance for them. Trees dotted the yard.

"A good place to hide someone you kidnapped," Lee muttered.

"Yes." Tristan left the van running. Dash yapped in the back in his carrier.

Lee slipped out of the vehicle and around to the driver's side. Tristan vacated the driver's seat and Lee took it over.

"Now remember," Tristan said, "keep him talking. I'm just going to get situated, then you can go."

"He's probably going to check the vehicle. You think he won't know about stow-'n'-go?"

"He might know about it, but hopefully he won't think about it. It's a chance we have to take. I can't let you go in there without protection. This van's been altered to fit an officer under the floorboard. I can get out and get a shot at him as long as you can keep him distracted."

Lee grunted. "I'll keep him distracted, all right." He glanced in the back at the dogs. "Are you going to let them out?"

"No, he'll just shoot at them. We'll keep them in here for the time being."

Lee waited until Tristan was hidden by the removable panel in the back then put the van in Drive and stepped on the gas pedal. His heart thudded as he rolled slowly toward the house. Finally it came into view. The house was a two-story Victorian and needed a good coat of paint. It had an attached two-car garage with another garage set apart from the main house.

Had he hurt her? Would she be all right? Of course she would. *Right, God? Please, God, let her be all right.*

Lee stopped about three-quarters of the way up the long drive. A gray van sat parked off to the side, backed up to the edge of the house.

The front door opened and Ellen stepped out onto the porch. A man followed right behind her. The same man who'd come to the center in a wheelchair. The same man who now had a gun pressed to the back of her head. "Ellen!"

She blanched when she saw him. "Lee! What are you doing here?"

"Trading a puppy for you."

Trevor pushed Ellen in front of him, his eyes never landing in one spot for very long. "You came alone?"

"That's what you said to do."

The man's gaze roamed again. Apparently he liked what he saw. "Bring the dog up here."

Tristan's voice came through the earpiece loud and

clear. "He's not going to check the van. I'm not sure I like that. Something happened but we don't have time to figure out what. Ask him where Freddie is."

"Where's Freddie?" Lee asked.

Trevor froze. "Freddie's got you covered, so if you try anything, he'll blow you away."

"There's no one out here, Lee," Tristan said. "We checked."

"Freddie's dead, Lee! He killed him!" Ellen's voice sounded breathless. Trevor gave her a violent shake and she cried out.

Lee started forward, his only thought to get Ellen away from the man hurting her.

"Come any closer and she dies, Mr. Hero."

Lee froze.

"Distract him. Tell him to let Ellen go first."

Lee shifted the puppy's crate to his other hand. "I have the puppy. Let her go."

"I want to see the dog! Now!" He jammed the gun tighter against Ellen's head.

She flinched but never took her eyes from Lee. He tried to reassure her with just a look. Her gaze darted to the van. He gave a slight nod. Her eyes narrowed and he could almost see her brain spinning as she tried to formulate a plan.

Lee set the crate on the ground and opened the cage. He pulled a leash from it and then snapped it to Dash's collar. The puppy walked out of his portable home and started sniffing the ground around him. Lee looked back at Ellen and the man who held her. "Now let her go."

"Walk him up here and give him to her. Hand her the leash."

Lee hesitated.

"Do it!"

"Go ahead, Lee," Tristan said. "I've got you covered. Shane and James are coming up the back now that we've got Little's attention focused on us out here. They came across the lake in a small boat and are now on land in the backyard."

Lee stepped forward and Dash trotted at his side like a good puppy. Like Lee had taught him to do. He kept his eyes on Ellen. She looked beyond him and he knew she was looking for backup.

Lee continued to approach. He passed the leash to Ellen, who took it without looking away from him. He could see her mind whirling, searching for escape, for the right move that would release her but wouldn't get her killed. It was all he could do not to grab the gun from the back of her head or try to land a punch that would allow her to run. But he couldn't take that chance.

"Now back up and get in your van."

Lee didn't budge. "I'm not going anywhere until you release her."

"You can get back in your van or I can put a bullet in her head then yours. Now move!"

Lee locked eyes with Ellen. Fury and fear smoldered there. He backed up as ordered.

"Keep going, Lee," Tristan said.

Lee continued his backward walk until his back was against the front fender of the van. "What now?" he called.

"Now we get in my van and drive away—I'll release her when I'm sure I'm not being followed."

Lee took a step forward only to stop when Little pushed Ellen ahead of him, down the steps and toward the gray van. He had to do something. “Not yet, Lee,” Tristan said. “Just hold on.”

Ellen wasn’t quite sure who was where, but she knew no one would have let Lee come out here alone. Assuming he told anyone where he was going. Yet she had a feeling there was someone in the van with him—she just wasn’t sure who. She’d flipped through escape scenario after escape scenario and hadn’t thought of one that wound up with her not being shot. And now Lee was part of the equation.

She let Trevor push her toward the gray van but had no intention of letting him get her inside. Because once she was in, she was dead. She held the leash and the puppy, who happily walked along beside her while the muzzle of the gun never left the back of her head.

They stopped at the van. “Pick him up and put him in,” Trevor ordered.

“I’m going to have to bend down to do that,” she said.

“Bend down. My bullet will reach that far.”

Her heart thudded as she bent. His gun followed her. One twitch of his finger and she would be dead. The fact didn’t do a whole lot for her nerves, but an idea hit her. She unclipped the leash from the dog’s collar and slapped his hind end with the metal end. He gave a startled yelp and darted under the van.

Trevor shouted a curse. “Get him!”

And for a brief second, the gun was gone from the back of her head. She dived to the ground and rolled, kicking out. She caught his wrist and the pistol flew from his hand. She scrambled to get away from him, but fingers clamped down around her left ankle. A shot rang out and Trevor gave a scream, but didn't release his hold. She kicked again, but had no leverage.

"Ellen!"

Another shot hit the dirt next to him. He jerked her toward him and she saw his fist coming toward her. Ellen threw her arm up to block it. The pain lanced through her and she knew she had to get away from him.

Then he was off her. She rolled to see Lee and Trevor exchanging blows. She launched herself to her feet and flinched when Trevor caught Lee with a harsh jab to his left cheek. The skin split and blood streamed, but Lee didn't stop. He came back around with a hard elbow to Trevor's chin. The man spun and went down, and Ellen threw herself onto his back, a knee to his spine. The air whooshed from his lungs and then they were surrounded by law enforcement. "Police! Don't move! Don't move!"

Ellen held a hand up. Tristan slapped his cuffs into her palm, and she snapped them around the still-breathless criminal. Then pushed off his back to land on the ground with a thud. She let out a breath then found herself enveloped in a crushing embrace.

She breathed in. Lee. "Ellen, are you okay?"

"Yeah. Yes, I'm fine. Major headache, but that means I'm alive if I can feel pain. I'm all right with that. Are you okay?"

"Yes, but I wasn't kidnapped and held prisoner for the past few hours." He pulled her out of the way while Tristan, Shane and the others hauled Trevor to his feet. Blood flowed from the wound in his shoulder. Lee followed her gaze. "Looks like he'll live."

"That's more than can be said for poor Freddie."

"You said Trevor shot him."

"He did," Ellen said.

Chief Jones had been listening in and moved toward the house. "He's not in there," Ellen said. "He's in that separate garage."

The chief nodded. "Are you sure you're all right? He didn't hurt you?"

"Like someone once told me, I've got a pretty hard head. I'll be fine."

He gave a relieved smile. "Good." He headed for the garage she indicated and motioned for Deputy Donaldson to follow him.

Louise touched Ellen on the arm as she passed. "I'm glad you're all right."

"Thanks.

"Sure."

She watched them go, then turned back to Lee. Everyone else was busy with the crime scene. They seemed to have forgotten she and Lee were there. He led her back to the van out of sight of the others and leaned down and kissed her. Ellen froze for only a second before she kissed him back, putting all of the emotion she'd had to hold in check over the past few hours into the kiss. In turn, she felt his fear come through, fear he'd never see her again, never hold her again. When he lifted his head, the sheen of tears in his eyes mirrored hers. "I love you, Ellen," he whispered.

And she couldn't hold back the tears any longer. "I love you, too, Lee. I always have. I never stopped. I'm so sorry about everything."

He swiped the tears from her cheeks with his thumb. "I don't know what it will take to make sure we live happily ever after, but I'm telling you right now, we're going to figure it out. Okay?"

She choked on a teary laugh and nodded. "Okay."

He pulled her back to his chest and kissed her head. "I know your mother doesn't like me, but maybe I can win her over."

"I think she just doesn't know you," Ellen said. "Once she hears how you helped save my life, she'll be forever grateful."

He dropped to one knee and held her hand. "I don't have a ring yet. I'm not very good with fancy words, but I almost lost you today and I'm not waiting another second."

Ellen's heart thudded, nearly popping from her chest. "Lee," she whispered. "What are you—?"

"Ellen, this isn't the time or the place or how I thought about doing this, but after what we just went through, I'm not waiting a second longer. I want to marry you. I love you. I've loved you since high school. Will you do me the honor of becoming my wife?"

She dropped to her knees in front of him and cupped his face. "You're sure?"

"Never more sure of anything in my life."

The look in his eyes convinced her. "Then, yes, I'll marry you. Tomorrow if you want."

He kissed her. Hard and swift and full of leashed passion. Then he trailed little kisses over her eyes and nose, cheeks and chin. The smile on his face was brilliant. She knew hers rivaled his.

"So are you guys getting married?"

Ellen jerked and turned to see Shane, Tristan, James, David and the chief watching them with silly grins on their faces. She looked back at Lee. "We sure are."

NINETEEN

Two days later

Lee held the door while Ellen stepped inside her mother's hospital room. She walked to the woman's side and reached for her hand. "Sure wish you would wake up, Mom," she said softly.

Lee took note of the machines and wires and the fact that Marian looked as though she'd aged twenty years. All the anger he'd harbored toward her over the past years fell away. He walked over to Ellen's side and put an arm around her shoulders. She leaned into him and sighed. "We won't stop praying for her," he said.

"I know. Thank you for forgiving her." She turned and slipped her arms around his waist. He'd never tire of her doing that. He held her, relishing the feel of her finally where he'd wanted her to be for so long. "And we won't give up on finding Veronica's killer."

He kissed the top of her head. "Yeah. I know." He sighed and just enjoyed having her in his arms. "How's your head?"

"Better."

"Nightmares?"

"A few. But mostly about losing you."

He squeezed her closer. "Never."

"And what about you? Do you have nightmares, too?"

He ran a hand through her hair and tilted her chin so he could look into her eyes. "Only about losing you."

Tears swam to the surface and she blinked. Her arms tightened around him. "Never," she whispered.

The door opened and the doctor entered. He nodded. "Hi there."

Ellen slipped from Lee's arms and acknowledged the man with a smile. "Hi."

"She's still being stubborn about waking up, isn't she?" he asked. He walked over to check the machines.

"Well, stubborn has her still alive, so..." Ellen shrugged. "She'll wake up when she's ready." Maybe if she kept repeating that, she'd believe it.

The doctor nodded. "Yes. I think she might actually be doing a bit better. She's not awake, but she's responding to some stimuli when we touch her feet."

"Really?" Hope shone in her eyes and she moved to her mother. She leaned down and kissed her cheek. "Wake up, Mom. I want to talk to you."

Lee stepped up beside her. "Wake up, Marian. We've got a lot to discuss. Like the fact that Ellen let me drive your Jeep."

Ellen choked on a laugh and lightly punched his arm. "Lee!"

"Well, you did."

"Yes, but you weren't supposed to tell her."

"If it gets her to wake up, then it's worth it."

Ellen's gaze softened. "Yes, yes it is. Wake up so you can yell at me about it, okay, Mom?"

There was no response, but Ellen couldn't help but let herself believe that her mom had heard her.

"Are you ready to go?" Lee asked softly.

"Sure."

The doctor lifted a hand in goodbye and Lee held the door for her. She slipped out of the room and into the hall. Lee stayed right by her side. "Want to get Carly and Dash and go for a hike?"

"Sure, that sounds great."

They left together and headed for the assistance center to pick up Dash. Once there, they found work going on. Gabby and her mother were working with Popcorn, who was responding beautifully to the little girl's commands. After a hug, Ellen exchanged a few words with the other employees while Lee went to get Dash.

The puppy spun in circles of excitement when he saw him, and Lee knew he'd have a hard time putting the animal in someone else's hands. But he would do it. Because that was the way it was supposed to be.

He snapped the leash on the dog's collar and walked back into the lobby to find Ellen speaking with Tristan.

"I think a puppy would be great for her."

"For who?" Lee asked.

"Tristan's sister."

"She's having a hard time right now," Tristan said.

"I'm sorry. That's tough."

"Yeah." He tapped his chin, a thoughtful look on his face. "So I think I'll go by the county shelter and take a look around."

"Take your sister with you," Lee said. "Let her pick the one she wants."

Tristan nodded. "Good idea. The only problem is, I may wind up with more than one if I do it that way."

Lee laughed and Ellen smiled. Tristan sighed. "All right. I guess I'll get out of here. I've still got work to do on Veronica's case."

Lee sobered and shook the man's hand. "Thanks for all you're doing." He glanced at Ellen. "I've had my eyes opened to the fact you're all doing more than I thought you were."

"Of course. I know it's hard. Sometimes it's a slow process."

"I've come to realize that."

"Ellen said you were heading back to finish vet school."

"Someday soon, I hope."

"You'll be a good one."

"So what was the code on the chip on Dash?" Ellen asked. "It's been so crazy, I haven't had a chance to even find out."

"Lee figured it out," Tristan said. "It was latitude and longitude for where the money from the bank robbery was buried."

"No way," Ellen said. "Someone actually buried the money?"

"Yeah. Lee told us to try the coordinates and there it was. Easy peasy."

She looked at Lee. "Impressive."

He felt the heat in his neck and gave a shrug. "I was working with some kids at the training center and the map on the wall gave me the idea. I didn't know for sure, but turns out it was a good guess."

"Exactly. So," Tristan said, "that's one case closed. Now to find out who stole the evidence from the police station, find Marco, the missing puppy, and get Veronica's case shut. See you guys later."

Tristan left. Ellen scratched Carly's ears. Dash jumped at her and Carly nudged him away. The puppy came back for more and soon it was a game between the two.

Ellen laughed at the two animals and looked around her. She was blessed. Her gaze landed on Lee. Super blessed. Why had she fought it so hard? Being kidnapped and almost killed had certainly put her into a different kind of mind-set.

Life was short and it was precious. It was time to spend it with those she loved. Including Lee. True, Veronica's murderer was still out there, but she had a feeling it wouldn't be too much longer until the person was found. Each day they seemed to get closer.

Lee pulled her close for a quick kiss and her heart tripped over itself in joy. She smiled up at him. "I could get used to that."

"Me, too. When do you want to get married?"

Her eyes widened. "Um. I don't know."

"You haven't even thought about it?" He looked slightly wounded.

Ellen slapped his shoulder with a light punch. He caught her hand and kissed her fingers. She sighed. "Of course I've thought about it. I've thought of little else. And I can't decide."

He sobered. "We can wait until your mother wakes up on one condition."

"What's that?"

"That you don't change your mind."

She kissed him long and hard. When she pulled back, she looked into his dark eyes. "I'm not changing my mind. Get that through your head."

"Okay."

"Okay?"

"Yep. You've convinced me. We can wait until she wakes up."

Ellen bit her lip. "I don't think that's necessary, but I love you for offering."

He kissed her again. "And I love you."

"You realize I might be assigned out of town once the murders are solved."

"I know. It's okay. Once you find out your assignment, if I have to change schools to go with you, I will. Or whatever. We'll figure it out." He tapped her nose. "So when?"

"Soon."

"That's good enough for me. Ready?"

"Ready."

His fingers closed around hers and, with the dogs at their heels, they walked out of the center together.

She'd come to love that word. *Together.*

Forever was her next favorite.

Forever together.

* * * * *

SPECIAL EXCERPT FROM

Love Inspired® SUSPENSE

A K-9 cop must keep his childhood friend alive when she finds herself in the crosshairs of a drug-smuggling operation.

Read on for a sneak preview of Act of Valor *by Dana Mentink, the next exciting installment in the True Blue K-9 Unit miniseries, available in May 2019 from Love Inspired Suspense.*

Officer Zach Jameson surveyed the throng of people congregated around the ticket counter at LaGuardia Airport. Most ignored Zach and K-9 partner, Eddie, and that suited him just fine. Two months earlier he would have greeted people with a smile, or at least a polite nod while he and Eddie did their work of scanning for potential drug smugglers. These days he struggled to keep his mind on his duty while the ever-present darkness nibbled at the edges of his soul.

Eddie plopped himself on Zach's boot. He stroked the dog's ears, trying to clear away the fog that had descended the moment he heard of his brother's death.

Zach hadn't had so much as a whiff of suspicion that his brother was in danger. His brain knew he should talk to somebody, somebody like Violet Griffin, his friend from childhood who'd reached out so many times, but his heart would not let him pass through the dark curtain.

LISEXP0419

"Just get to work," he muttered to himself as his phone rang. He checked the number.

Violet.

He considered ignoring it, but Violet didn't ever call unless she needed help, and she rarely needed anyone. Strong enough to run a ticket counter at LaGuardia and have enough energy left over to help out at Griffin's, her family's diner. She could handle belligerent customers in both arenas and bake the best apple pie he'd ever had the privilege to chow down.

It almost made him smile as he accepted the call.

"Someone's after me, Zach."

Panic rippled through their connection. Panic, from a woman who was tough as they came. "Who? Where are you?"

Her breath was shallow as if she was running.

"I'm trying to get to the break room. I can lock myself in, but I don't… I can't…" There was a clatter.

"Violet?" he shouted.

But there was no answer.

Don't miss
Act of Valor *by Dana Mentink,*
available May 2019 wherever
Love Inspired® Suspense books and ebooks are sold.

www.LoveInspired.com

LISEXP0419

WE HOPE YOU ENJOYED THIS

LOVE INSPIRED® SUSPENSE

BOOK.

Discover more **heart-pounding** romances of **danger** and **faith** from the Love Inspired Suspense series.

Be sure to look for all six Love Inspired Suspense books every month.

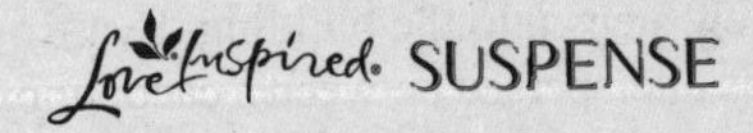

www.LoveInspired.com

LISHALO2018

SPECIAL EXCERPT FROM

When a guide-dog trainer becomes a target of a dangerous crime ring, a K-9 cop and his loyal partner will work together to keep her safe.

Read on for a sneak preview of Blind Trust *by Laura Scott, the next exciting installment in the True Blue K-9 Unit miniseries, available June 2019 from Love Inspired Suspense.*

Eva Kendall slowed her pace as she approached the training facility where she worked training guide dogs.

Using her key, she entered the training center, thinking about the male chocolate Lab named Cocoa that she would work with this morning. Cocoa was a ten-week-old puppy born to Stella, a gift from the Czech Republic to the NYC K-9 Command Unit located in Queens. Most of Stella's pups were being trained as police dogs, but not Cocoa. In less than a month after basic puppy training, Cocoa would be able to go home with Eva to be fostered during his initial first-year training to become a full-fledged guide dog. Once that year passed, guide dogs like Cocoa would return to the center to train with their new owners.

A few steps into the building, Eva frowned at the loud thumps interspersed between a cacophony of barking. The raucous noise from the various canines contained a level of panic and fear rather than excitement.

LISEXP0519

Concerned, she moved quickly through the dimly lit training center to the back hallway, where the kennels were located. Normally she was the first one in every morning, but maybe one of the other trainers had gotten an early start.

Rounding the corner, she paused in the doorway when she saw a tall, heavyset stranger scooping Cocoa out of his kennel. Panic squeezed her chest. "Hey! What are you doing?"

The ferocious barking increased in volume, echoing off the walls and ceiling. The stranger must have heard her. He turned to look at her, then roughly tucked Cocoa under his arm like a football.

"No! Stop!" Panicked, Eva charged toward the man, desperately wishing she had a weapon of some sort.

"Get out of my way," he said in a guttural voice.

"No. Put that puppy down right now!" Eva stopped and stood her ground.

"Last chance," he taunted, coming closer.

Don't miss
Blind Trust *by Laura Scott,*
available June 2019 wherever
Love Inspired® Suspense books and ebooks are sold.

www.LoveInspired.com

LISEXP0519

Love Inspired®